TOUCH THE SKY

TOUCH THE SKY

Harold Livingston

William Morrow and Company, Inc.
New York

It is the policy of William Morrow and Company, Inc., and its imprints and affiliates, recognizing the importance of preserving what has been written, to print the books we publish on acid-free paper, and we exert our best efforts to that end.

Library of Congress Cataloging-in-Publication Data

Livingston, Harold.
    Touch the sky / Harold Livingston.
      p.   cm.
    ISBN 0-688-07719-6
    I. Title.
    PS3562.I934T6   1991
    813'.54—dc20   90-25429
                                                   CIP

Printed in the United States of America

First Edition

1 2 3 4 5 6 7 8 9 10

BOOK DESIGN BY M. C. DEMAIO

*The high that proved too high, the heroic for
earth too hard,*

*The passion that left the ground to lose
itself in the sky,*

*Are music sent up to God by the lover
and the bard;*

*Enough that he heard it once; we shall
hear it by and by.*

—ROBERT BROWNING

PART ONE

THE SKY FIGHTERS

1

Below, at the zigzag patchwork of trenches, the front was quiet. No artillery flashes, no movement of men or vehicles, only an occasional shard of sunlight glinting off the tin cans strung along the staggered rows of barbed wire in the open areas separating the lines. From six thousand feet on this chilly March morning of 1918 it looked almost serene.

Serene, the pilot of the Nieuport thought, such a pleasant, comfortable word. He twisted around in his seat and gazed into the distance behind him. Beyond the black, blocked numerals 4 8 7 and the tricolor emblem on the airplane's rudder, he thought he could still see a thin trail of oily gray smoke rising up from the snow-mottled clearing some fifteen miles away to the east, behind German lines.

No, he was much too far away to see it now. But the scene remained vivid in his mind: the Fokker D-7 burning in the snow where he had machine-gunned it after it landed, the German pilot lying dead on the ground nearby. You weren't supposed to kill them on the ground. Bad form, as the limeys might say. Poor sportsmanship.

He faced forward again and scanned the sky for a glimpse of the other Nieuport. The pilot of that Nieuport had witnessed the entire incident and then, as though abhorring the presence of a man who had committed a cold-blooded murder, immediately sped away.

This man, the man flying Nieuport 487, the alleged perpetrator of the crime, was an American who held the rank of *sous-lieutenant* in L'Armée de l'Air. His name was Simon Conway, and that very day he had become an ace with his fifth victory, a Halberstadt observation machine, which was followed almost at once by his sixth kill, the Fokker.

Even before they had taken off on the two-man patrol that morning, Simon Conway knew that he would bag his fifth and become an ace. He knew it as surely as he knew that he was twenty-three years old and that seven years ago, five hundred feet above the seventeenth fairway of a brand-new Massachusetts golf course, he had fallen hopelessly and helplessly in love.

With an aeroplane.

An old Curtiss Pusher that resembled a flimsy man-carrying box kite more than a genuine aeroplane. But it was the most beautiful object Simon Conway had ever seen, especially after that first ride, strapped into a wicker chair beside the pilot, deafened by the ear-blasting noise of the propellers that sounded like a thousand pieces of cardboard flapping against the blades of an electric fan, inhaling the sickly-sweet odor of gasoline, feeling the wind slamming into his face.

He knew that from that day on nothing in his life would be more important than flying. Nothing, of course, except surviving. Surviving, another lovely word, he thought and now, ahead, saw the steeple of the church in the little village of Saint-Pol-sur-Mer and, four kilometers from the town square, the line of poplar trees bordering the airdrome. Beyond the trees the high morning sun glared down on the copper roof of the chateau.

For pilot safety the roof should have been blackened, but the army was reluctant to deface the building, which had been requisitioned from people of prominence. It was bad enough that the estate's once beautiful green lawns and lush flower beds were trampled and flattened under ramshackle tool huts and three huge canvas hangars.

Shielding his eyes against the sun, Si brought the Nieuport in low over the trees. He flared out, feeling for the grass, working the throttle to hold the little airplane steady. He flew her onto the surface, gauging the distance he could roll before cutting the power so she would coast all the way up to the line where eleven other Nieuports, 17s and 27s, were parked, and come to a dead stop no less than two feet from where Corporal Crespin, his *mécanicien*, stood waiting.

Some half-dozen pilots, including young Jimmy Forrest, the squadron *bébé*, also waited. Jimmy's eyes shone with adulation as he grasped a wing edge of Si's Nieuport to help turn the machine around. Si cut the switch and unstrapped. He opened his fur-lined coveralls, removed his helmet and goggles, and climbed down from the cockpit.

"Si, I heard!" Jimmy shouted. "You're an ace! A bloody ace!" He pumped Si's hand.

The others added their congratulations. It was more a ritual than any display of esteem. Clearly, Simon Conway would win no popularity contest here. If it disturbed him, he gave no indication, and he expected nothing more from them anyway. What concerned him was that they talked of his "fifth" victory, not the fifth *and* sixth.

The sixth: the Fokker.

But then he realized they could have heard of it only through Capitaine Ledoux, commanding officer of the squadron, N.124, a unit composed mainly of American volunteers and known, unofficially, as the Lafayette Flying Corps or Escadrille Lafayette. Ledoux had flown the other Nieuport, the one that accompanied Simon Conway on the patrol, and had apparently chosen not to confirm the kill. The *capitaine* was ashamed.

Si walked over to Crespin, who was inspecting the Nieuport, his eyes alert for buckled wires and bullet holes. The sun glistened off the squadron insignia emblazoned on the Nieuport's fuselage: the fierce profile of an American Indian in full-feathered Sioux warrior regalia. Directly behind this was an immaculately painted figure of an American eagle in flight, talons clutching a letter *C*, Simon Conway's personal crest.

"What did Ledoux tell you?" Si asked Crespin in French.

"He said you got a Halberstadt."

"That's all he said, a Halberstadt?"

Crespin did not immediately reply. Si thought that his French might have confused the corporal. Si spoke the language in a rolling Burgundian accent that, if not altogether fluent, was certainly functional. When Si first arrived in France he had served for a brief time as a volunteer ambulance driver and had learned the language fast, a crash course administered by the Burgundian medical corpsmen of those early ambulance days.

But Crespin had understood. "Yes, my friend, that was what the captain said: one Halberstadt."

Si brushed past the crowd and strode toward the chateau. Jimmy Forrest shouted after him, "Watch out for the old man, Si! He's really in an uproar. When I said we had to have a party to celebrate your fifth, he nearly bit my off my head. He even made the bar off limits until lunchtime! What the hell happened?"

Si did not answer. He hurried into the chateau. Ledoux's office was directly off the dining room, a cubicle formerly the butler's pantry. The door was closed. Si hesitated before knocking. He knew Ledoux would read him the riot act and he did not want to lose his temper, not with Georges Ledoux. He admired and respected the man too much.

Si knocked on the door and entered the office. Ledoux sat rigidly at his desk. A pair of ivory-handled walking canes hung neatly from the armrest of his chair. He did not rise or return Si's salute.

"Do you intend to claim that Fokker?" Ledoux spoke in English. He wanted Si to comprehend every word.

"Of course," Si said.

"Don't," said Ledoux.

"May I sit down?"

Ledoux nodded curtly. The tiny room's only other furniture was a sagging mohair divan and two wood folding chairs. The chateau's owners had prudently removed their own valuable furniture, leaving the rooms barren but for the bits and pieces randomly purchased by the men, or "requisitioned." Si slid one of the chairs over the tiled floor and placed it before the desk. He sat facing Ledoux. The *capitaine's* face, exposed directly to the sun streaming in through the skylight, was grim and expressionless.

Si said, "The Fokker landed intact after I shot it down. I went down to finish it off on the ground. I did not—I repeat, did not—deliberately kill the pilot. I thought he was out of the airplane, and a safe distance away."

"That is your explanation?"

Si dug in his shirt pocket for a cigarette. He had none. Ledoux nudged a hammered silver cigarette case and matching silver lighter across the desktop. Both lighter and case were embossed with the stork emblem of Escadrille S.103, Les Cigognes, the elite unit Ledoux had flown with before taking command of the Lafayette. The late legendary Capitaine Georges Guynemer had also served with S.103. Schoolchildren were taught that Guynemer was not dead, that he had flown too high ever to come down.

Ledoux, whose full name was Georges Albert Ledoux, was a *capitaine* of L'Armée de l'Air, a graduate of Saint-Cyr, and a regular officer in the French army since 1909, the same year the great Louis Blériot became the first man to cross the English Channel by air. Ledoux learned to fly a year later, his instructor none less than Blériot himself.

Although credited with twenty-two victories, Ledoux was no longer obliged to fly. Seeking his eighteenth, he had crashed on take-off, fracturing both legs so severely he required the use of two canes while walking. But he knew that with the United States now in the war, the Lafayette was soon to be disbanded and its American pilots absorbed into newly organized United States Air Service squadrons, and he would be transferred into another squadron in a nonflying status.

Si lit a cigarette and placed the lighter on the desk atop the case. "Yes sir," he said. "That's my explanation."

Ledoux said nothing a moment. He studied Si, whose face was streaked so black with oil that it resembled a Halloween mask and whose shock of unruly brown hair always made Ledoux wonder if the "enigma," as he often privately referred to Si, ever combed his hair. Indeed, if he owned a comb.

Enigma, Ledoux thought, his eyes still fixed on Si. More than an enigma, a heretic. A brash and sometimes arrogant young man not at all reticent about proclaiming himself N.124's best pilot, which certainly did little to endear him to his squadron mates, whom he treated like naive schoolboys, never hesitating to remind them that they were here to fight a war, not to enjoy a spirited adventure, and that there is no honor in dying, no matter how gloriously.

"Your explanation is unsatisfactory," Ledoux said.

"Is that why you're asking me not to claim the kill?"

"I am not asking you, lieutenant. I am ordering you."

"May I know why?"

"I'm sure you know why."

Si said dryly, "I've committed a crime. I broke the rules."

"The first statement is the correct one," Ledoux said. "You committed a crime."

Jesus H. Christ, Si thought, enough is enough. "Georges, aren't we carrying this a little too far? Killing your enemy is hardly a crime."

"The man was helpless," Ledoux said.

"Yes," Si said. "And now he's dead! And he'll never be able to kill any of us! Now what the hell's got into you? I did what I'm paid to do, the same thing you're paid to do: kill!" He mashed out the cigarette in the brass shell casing used for an ashtray. "Are you afraid, because it was Eisler's group, they'll come gunning for us? Is that what's bothering you?"

Si had never seen Ledoux so angry. The deep-blue eyes were cold and hard, the aristocratic, hawklike nose quivered. The *capitaine* gripped the ivory handle of one of his canes and strained for composure.

"What I am 'afraid' of, lieutenant, is that they will use this incident as an excuse to repay us in kind. Would you like that? Would you like one of our people to be murdered in so barbaric a manner?"

Ah, yes, of course, Si thought. There it was, all the chivalry and sportsmanship. Eighteenth century minds fighting a twentieth century war. He said, "I'm sorry, sir, I see this in an entirely different light. And may I remind you, please, that I spent more than a year in the trenches. Nobody gave a damn how they killed the enemy, only that they did it."

Si's last few words were almost mumbled. He had a sudden sensation of unreality. What the hell was he doing here, involved in such an inane conversation?

". . . you have a forty-eight-hour leave due you," Ledoux was saying. "I suggest you take it. Perhaps a day or two in Paris will clear your head." He nodded at the door, a gesture of dismissal.

Si rose. "I assume you will confirm my fifth kill, the Halberstadt?"

"Your fifth victory was legitimately attained."

Si fought an impulse to try reasoning with Ledoux. But that would be tantamount to pleading. To hell with him. To hell with the whole French army. Let them have their "chivalry" and their "gentleman's war."

"Sir, I request permission to apply for a transfer."

"To where?"

"To the United States Air Service, sir."

"Permission granted."

"Thank you, sir," Si said, and saluted smartly. Ledoux did not return the salute.

2.

Five months ago, on a cold October morning one week after Karl Eisler shot down four enemy aircraft in a single day, the entire squadron had assembled in dress uniform on Jasta 24's tarmac to watch the Crown Prince himself present Karl with the Pour le Mérite, the Blue Max. Behind the men, lined wing to wing, were the blue-yellow-and-green-striped D-7s. In the exact center of this formation, parked a few feet ahead of the other airplanes, was a lone Fokker Triplane. In contrast to the gaudy D-7s, the Triplane was totally black but for a gleaming white engine cowling.

The black Tripe was Karl Eisler's machine, as unusual as Karl himself, as the Crown Prince had amusingly remarked when later, at the reception, he asked Karl why he chose to call attention to himself in this manner.

"I would think it makes you an inviting target," the Crown Prince said.

At the time, Karl had knocked down twenty-six Allied airplanes. He had not accomplished this, or attained the rank of captain and command of Jasta 24—or lived to be twenty-seven years old—by taking unnecessary risks. Or being a fool.

"That, your majesty, is the idea of it," he had replied. "I want them to single me out. They consider me so arrogant, it becomes a personal issue. They allow their emotions to guide them and they lose their tempers. A fatal error in battle."

So now, five months and eleven more victories later, in the same all-black, white-cowlinged Tripe, just crossing over into Allied territory at five thousand feet, he was thinking about the irony of that remark. For he, Captain Karl Eisler, had lost his temper.

With an American murderer.

Ahead, white puffs of antiaircraft fire dotted the fast-darkening western sky. Karl eased the stick forward. The little Tripe's white nose dipped downward. She picked up speed. The 110-horsepower Oberursel rotary, although full-out, sounded exceptionally smooth. The airplane began sliding to the right with the engine's torque. Karl tapped the left rudder bar. The white nose straightened.

In the distance, wispy clouds extended down to the serpentine waters of the Somme. Far beyond the river, miles to the west, a wall of thick gray cloud obscured the setting sun. It must be raining like hell in Paris, Karl thought, continuing to descend. He would fly very low to avoid antiaircraft fire.

He reached down to the cockpit floor and fingered the brass 20mm shell casing. Inside the casing, which was affixed to a tiny parachute, was a message he had spent the better part of an hour composing, and another hour reviewing with the squadron medical officer, who happened to be a University of London graduate. Although Karl's own command of English was as fluent, if not more so than the doctor's, he wanted the grammar and syntax absolutely correct.

He rapped his knuckles on the shell casing. The message filled him with rage, as it had from the moment he put the first word on paper:

To the pilot of Nieuport 487,
Escadrille N.124:

Lieutenant Max Braun, the man you brutally executed at 0945 yesterday, 12 March 1918, was an officer under my command.

I offer you an opportunity to repair this dishonorable act by meeting me alone, in combat, tomorrow morning, 14 March, at 0630, at nine thousand feet over the village of Monmedy. Should this prove inconvenient, I will await you at the same time and place for the following three days.

Eisler
Captain, Imperial Air Service

Childish, yes, and emotional, and certainly foolish. But Karl had been fond of Braun, twenty-two years old, a fine pilot, a veteran with fifteen kills, deserving of a better death, particularly at the hands of another veteran. Shiller, the Jasta 24 pilot accompanying Braun, himself seriously wounded, had managed to return from the patrol to report that Nieuport 487's pilot was skilled and experienced.

No, Karl needed to do this. Not as a matter of honor; it transcended honor and became a question of decency. He laughed aloud in the slipstream. Four years of war, of killing and maiming, of seeing your friends die, and he was worried about "decency."

Of course, some of those so-called "friends" were men who indulged him more than befriended him. These heirs of nobility and wealthy families, the officer class, did not exactly take to their bosoms the son of a Bavarian shopkeeper who made no secret of his desire to be accepted as a social equal.

In the beginning, behind his back, they called him "the little engineer," not a pejorative comment on his height—he was nearly six feet tall—but a snide reference to his three years at the gymnasium at Stuttgart studying for an engineering degree. The war interrupted Karl's education, to his advantage as it turned out. He had learned more about aircraft and aeronautical engineering in a half-dozen casual after-dinner chats with Tony Fokker than in all the three years of schooling. A Dutchman, Anthony Fokker was a genius of an aircraft engineer and designer whose airplanes, from the E-1 to the Triplane to the D-7, constantly outflew and outfought the finest Allied machines.

Fokker, on his part, considered Karl one of those rare pilots for whom the airplane was an extension of himself, his personality, his ego, his very body. Karl had tested nearly every Fokker model before it became operational. The Dutchman relied heavily on Karl's suggestions and advice.

Fokker and Karl not only liked each other, they respected each other. Fokker's respect surpassed mere professional admiration. He knew how hard Karl had worked for the rank and status he now enjoyed, to transfer from the Engineering Corps into the Air Service, first as a technical officer and then flying duty as a gunner-observer, and finally flight training. In those early days only the most privileged attended *Jastaschule*, let alone won assignment to the Air Service.

Yes, he had come a long way, perhaps too far to culminate it with the foolishness of a man-to-man duel. An act of revenge. Act of idiocy, more accurately, and most assuredly forbidden by any and all regulations. If one of his pilots suggested such an endeavor, that man would face immediate and harsh discipline.

Very well, he told himself, upon my return I will order myself confined to quarters for forty-eight hours. The idea amused him; if only it were possible. He could use a forty-eight-hour break. He stamped his feet on the cockpit floor to warm them. Even at this low altitude, three thousand feet, it was so cold the extra pair of wool stockings under the fleece-lined leather boots were of little help.

Ahead, in the near distance, was N.124's airdrome. Karl recognized it from reconnaissance photographs at group HQ. The tall poplar trees bordering the field, the three tent hangars billowing in the breeze, the handsome chateau. Like directional signals, thin wisps of white smoke trailed up from the chateau's twin chimneys.

From the kitchen, Karl thought. Dinner on the stove. He was hungry himself. At the Jasta 24 mess tonight there would be roast beef, the first in weeks. The chef, Sergeant Stolz, knew Karl liked his beef blood-rare and took great care to satisfy the *Jastaführer*.

The field was dead ahead. Karl dropped down another thousand feet and steered slightly left to come in over the trees on the south side. And canned peaches for dessert, swimming in heavy cream, he thought, if the one cow that remained in the farm near the field cooperated.

Karl went down to treetop level and swooped in over the poplars. Blue and khaki-clad figures scurried about, some leaping into the circular sandbagged machine-gun positions. The guns, heavy water-cooled Brownings, were fixed to wagon wheels for fast, easy swiveling. Their muzzle flashes twinkled brightly in the dusk.

Karl flew past the chateau so low he could clearly see the startled expressions on the faces of men standing on the outer terrace. He heaved the casing out and at the same time yanked back the control stick. The Tripe roared upward in an almost vertical climb. Below, at the field, the little parachute had opened. The brass casing floated down in front of the line of parked Nieuports and, he noted interestedly, two Spads. The bastards were being reequipped with new Spads. From all directions men converged on the parachute. Karl wondered if one of them was the pilot of Nieuport 487 and thought it would be marvelously ironic if that man was the first to read the message.

Karl had no way of knowing that it was impossible for Simon Conway to be the first man to read the message. At the moment of delivery, which was 4:32 P.M. on the second day of his two-day Parisian holiday, Simon Conway was in a bar, getting very drunk.

3.

The incident that had precipitated Karl Eisler's challenge to the American pilot of Nieuport 487 had taken place some thirty hours earlier, four hours before Simon Conway embarked upon his Paris leave.

Si and Ledoux had first encountered a formation of three Halberstadts. The Nieuports were at nine thousand feet, three thousand feet above the enemy observation machines. Ledoux spotted them and blipped his engine to attract Si's attention. The two Nieuports surged forward. They would fly straight and level until well to the rear of the Halberstadts. Then, turning, they would dive with the sun at their backs to fall upon the unsuspecting enemy like hawks attacking sparrows.

The pilot of the lead Halberstadt saw the attacking Nieuports and alerted the others. Ledoux flat-skidded toward the leader, while Si tracked the second Halberstadt in his ring gunsight. The Halberstadts, which had been flying in a loose V formation, swung out to give their rear gunners a clean field of fire. The whine of the Halberstadts' engines under the sudden full power momentarily drowned out the raspy roar of the Nieuports' rotaries. The staccato crack of Ledoux's front-firing Vickers gun was echoed by the slower, hollow boom-boom-boom-boom of the Halberstadts' rear gunners' twin-barreled Parabellums.

Both Nieuports flashed past the two-seaters and banked tightly around to come back in for another pass. From a hundred yards, flying straight and level, Si came in behind and below the second Halberstadt. The Nieuport's top-mounted Lewis, angled to fire over the propeller arc, was lined perfectly on the bottom of the Halberstadt's rear cockpit. Right up the poor bastard's ass, Si thought, as he grasped the metal ring attached to the wire trigger cord dangling from the gun breech.

He pulled the cord. The Lewis's recoil vibrated along his arm and into his body. Eight good rounds, each cartridge emitting a tiny puff of acrid nostril-crinkling cordite smoke. The steel-jacketed slugs stitched a vertical line on the Halberstadt's underside. Si turned slightly right and pulled up alongside the Halberstadt. The rear gunner's head lolled inertly against the circular gun mounting, his fingers still curled around the Parabellum's trigger. His eyes, open, stared lifelessly through his goggles. He looked almost relaxed, although mildly surprised, and perhaps slightly offended.

The Halberstadt's pilot, whirling around to look at his rear gunner, promptly put the airplane into a steep, full-power dive. Si dove after him. The Halberstadt's front cockpit and the top of the pilot's helmeted head loomed huge in Si's ring sight. He fired the Vickers, a long, steady burst. The tracers sped like an unerring yellow line into the very center of the cockpit. The pilot's whole body jerked upright, then pitched forward into the windscreen. The Halberstadt rolled over on its right wing, spiraled once, then again, and then spun toward the ground. A thin streamer of white smoke poured from its engine.

Simon followed, but at a distance, allowing the German to fall away. He was taking no chances. Both sides used the old trick of pumping castor oil onto the hot cylinders to produce smoke. My fifth kill, he thought, with neither elation nor remorse, thinking he should feel something, but thinking only of what Kiffin Rockwell had told the then *Sergent* Conway on the first day Si reported for duty with N.124: "Believe me, you'll earn your dollar-and-a-half-a-day pay. . . ." That was the same day four D-1s ambushed Kiffin. He burned all the way down. He earned his dollar and a half that day.

Ahead, to his right, Si saw the lead Halberstadt trying to outrun Ledoux, who was on his tail, firing. Ledoux's bullets hit the pilot and gunner with the same burst. The Halberstadt rolled over and, inverted, plummeted downward. Ledoux broke off and raced after the third Halberstadt, which had immediately turned east when the Nieuports attacked.

The Halberstadt Si had hit was far below, spinning aimlessly like a discarded piece of debris. Down, down, down, and then it plunged nose-first into an open field glazed over with ice from the night's frost.

The Fokkers came out of nowhere. Two of them, D-7s, their fuselages and wings an eye-dazzling collage of bright yellow, green, and blue stripes, their white-tipped propellers creating an illusion of a solid white ring revolving about their blunt noses.

And they had momentarily boxed Si in, one firing from behind, the other angling in on the Nieuport's starboard side. Si pushed right rudder and right stick, rolled into a tight turn, and flared out behind the Fokker that had been on his tail. All this was pure reflex, as was his finger tensing on the Vickers's trigger and his brain computing the distance and angle between him and the Fokker. His brain also registered the Fokkers' multicolored insigne and black-and-white iron cross emblems. Si knew they were Jasta 24 machines, part of Jagdgeschwader 2, Richthofen's old group, and that Jasta 24 had recently replaced its Triplanes with the newer and incredibly advanced D-7s. Up to this moment at least, they had operated much farther south.

Si also knew Jasta 24 was commanded by Captain Karl Eisler, thirty-seven victories, formerly Von Richthofen's deputy, and that

Eisler was not one of the D-7 pilots. Eisler preferred his old, arrogantly conspicuous Triplane, an all-black Tripe with a gleaming white engine cowling.

Si fired the Vickers, two bursts of eight rounds, and then broke left to evade the second Fokker that had chandelled up and around and was maneuvering to slip in behind him. Si barrel-rolled to the left and came out inside the second D-7, slightly aft of the iron cross emblem on the Fokker's rudder. He eased the stick right. The Fokker's cockpit lay squarely in the cross hair of the Nieuport's gunsight. Si squeezed the trigger. The Vickers reverberated with the discharge. The white, cordite-stinking smoke from the spent cartridges wafted back into Si's face.

The Fokker pilot's head slumped forward. The D-7's nose dipped downward. But now the other D-7 had turned into Si and was racing at him head-on. The muzzle flashes of the Fokker's twin Spandaus glared like dozens of tiny suns.

Si lowered the Nieuport's nose and yanked the Lewis gun cord. He fired a short burst of five rounds as the Fokker roared past overhead, so close that Si could clearly see the spokes of the Fokker's wire wheels revolving slowly in the wind.

Ledoux's Nieuport raced past on the left and zoomed up and around in a climbing turn that put him above and behind the Fokker. The German seemed unwilling to fight, or could not. He dove away from Ledoux, who set out after him.

Si directed his attention now to the Fokker he had hit. It was far below, at least five thousand feet. The German, miles behind his own lines, was attempting to land in a small clearing, a field covered with light snow and ringed on three sides by tall bare-branched trees.

The Fokker fluttered down toward the trees. It skimmed the tallest branches and began settling. The wheels touched, bounced, and touched down again. The airplane rolled bumpily through the snow. It continued rolling, slower and slower. Finally, propeller still spinning, it stopped.

The pilot sat motionless a moment. Then, with great effort, he pulled off his helmet and goggles. He was very young, with curly blond hair so light it was almost white, and almost the color of his skin, which was deathly white. One gloved hand, rocking back and forth like a pendulum, dangled from the cockpit. From the black-leather-jacketed arm a stream of blood dripped down onto the snow.

Some German infantrymen arrived. Two clambered up on the Fokker's lower wing and helped the pilot out of the airplane. Just as they began dragging him away, Simon Conway's Nieuport swooped in over the trees, both machine guns firing.

The bullets plowed along the ground and into the downed Fokker. The airplane exploded in a ball of yellow flame and black smoke that enveloped the pilot and the two infantrymen and hurled their bodies high into the air.

A single horrifying image was drawn across Si's line of vision: the bodies of the pilot and the two soldiers tumbling over and over like discarded rag dolls. He had not seen them until too late. He had come in so low, angling in on the Fokker's starboard side, that only the empty cockpit was visible. The men were on the port side, obscured from his view by the airplane itself.

The intent was to destroy the airplane, not strafe a wounded, helpless pilot. He would have never knowingly done that. Yes, he would have attacked the infantrymen, but never the pilot. This was what he told himself, and in truth believed, at the same time knowing there was not the slightest difference between killing a man in the air or on the ground. If there was a difference, no one had ever bothered to acquaint him with it.

From the east, Ledoux's Nieuport unexpectedly appeared. He had seen Si's bullets tear into the Fokker. He flew alongside Si and, for a long, hard moment, stared blandly at him. Then, gesturing Si to return home, he banked his Nieuport over and headed west. In his faster Nieuport, a 27, Ledoux would arrive well ahead of Si's older model, a 17.

Climbing away, Si glanced down at the clearing. The Fokker was a mass of flames, its fuselage fabric entirely consumed and the skeleton afire. The force of the fire had pushed the wings upward and then down, until they collapsed inward on themselves like those of a giant insect burning to death. The bodies of the soldiers and the pilot lay on the snow near the destroyed enemy airplane. The pilot's blond hair fluttered gently in the hot wind from the fire.

2

It was true that from the day of Simon Conway's first flight, flying became the most important thing in his life. Nothing took precedence. Not school, not baseball, not even girls. And certainly not family, which consisted of his father, Frank, a physician, and Madeline, Frank Conway's second wife.

Madeline was responsible for shattering young Si's dream of attending the Massachusetts Institute of Technology, the only school in the country offering a course in aeronautics. It happened on a Saturday afternoon in 1912, two weeks before Si graduated from high school and exactly three days after the Dustin High School baseball team had advanced to the semifinals of the Massachusetts Schoolboy championship.

Si and Henry Fulton, Si's oldest and closest friend, were cocaptains of the Dustin High baseball squad. Si, then seventeen, had nearly attained his full height and weight, six feet two, 170 pounds. He was the team's center fielder and cleanup batter. In the quarterfinals against Lowell, he had driven in all Dustin's three runs with two homers and a triple. Dustin's pitcher, Hank Fulton, shut out Lowell on two hits. For both boys, a day of glory.

Glory, that three days later was smashed into a thousand irretrievable pieces. Si worked after school and Saturdays at the downtown A&P grocery store. They had let him go early this Saturday, and he planned to use the free time for an extra flying lesson at Barnes Field. Nearly every cent of his $11 monthly salary went into those lessons.

He had to stop by his house for his goggles. He entered the house through his father's office at the front, plucked the goggles from the coat tree in the doctor's waiting room where he always left them, and started out. From upstairs, from the big bedroom, he heard Madeline laugh.

The bedroom door was ajar. Si heard Madeline laugh again, this time more of a long, giggling moan. He went up to the landing and peeked into the room. Madeline and Si's father lay naked on the bed, she underneath him, her legs wrapped around his buttocks. Si felt his face flush and his heart race in the heat of shame for having witnessed his father and Madeline making love.

It was not his father.

It was Hank Fulton.

Si ran from the house and spent that whole day and part of the night out at Barnes Field. He sat up in the loft of the barn that served as a hangar for the Curtiss Pusher, gazing at the aeroplane but seeing Hank and Madeline. He hated Hank now, but hated Madeline more. For days afterward he fantasized confronting her, accusing her, and demanding she pack her possessions and leave at once. He would keep the terrible truth from his father. He pitied the man, and then hated him for being so weak. Only a weakling would have married such a woman.

A few days later, after baseball practice, Hank caught up with Si and asked why Si was avoiding him. Si was too embarrassed to tell him, and never did. What could he say? "You've been screwing my father's wife!" But Hank insisted on an answer, and the more he persisted the more Si's fury increased. In the end he lost control.

He beat Hank up. Pummeled him mercilessly and damn well might have killed him had not the assistant coach and the school janitor stopped it. The incident filled Si with guilt and shame, not only because Hank was four inches shorter and thirty pounds lighter, but because Si remembered his own excitement in the few seconds he had stood in the doorway watching. He had never done it with a girl, not even the ones who worked in the tanneries on Mill Street and who everyone said were sure things.

If living at home never had been a bed of roses anyway, after that it was plain hell. Bad enough Si's teammates blamed him for Dustin's loss in the final game—the beating Si administered to Hank Fulton prevented Hank from pitching—Si could not stay in the same house with Madeline, and with a father he pitied and who was drinking more than ever. And Si knew that his temper, which had always gotten him into trouble, might sooner or later explode and end up with him telling his father what had happened. It would kill the old man.

A week after high school graduation, on a night Madeline and his father were too drunk to notice, Si packed a few things into a battered leather valise that had once belonged to his mother. He caught the last trolley into Boston, walked to the South Station railroad yards, and crawled into an empty freight car.

He learned to survive. He learned how to ride the rails, and to hobo, and fight skillfully, which was another word for dirty. He traveled the width of the country, all the way, to the state of Washington. In Seattle, his luck turned. He met a grizzled old machinist named Connie Wilcher who was building a flying boat.

Si talked Connie Wilcher into hiring him as part-time mechanic and test pilot, in the process learning everything Connie knew about airplanes, aeronautics, and aircraft construction. And salesmanship. Si helped sell the flying boat—hydroplane, as it was called—to a wealthy furniture manufacturer named William Boeing.

Boeing took a shine to the kid from Massachusetts, teasing him endlessly about his New England twang but agreeing with him that airplanes were not necessarily rich men's toys and that you could make money with airplanes by flying mail and passengers.

By then it was 1915, and with the war on in Europe, Si had a far more immediate market in mind: warplanes. For the Allies, not the Germans. He hated the Germans for what they'd done to the Belgians. Bayoneting babies, for Christ's sake!

Give the Allies airplanes that did more than merely "observe," airplanes that attacked ships and dropped bombs on key installations. Si spent weeks drawing up plans for such a machine, a massive twin-engined hydroplane, bigger than anything that had ever flown. He brought the plans to Mr. Boeing with the proposal that they become equal partners in the venture, Boeing to finance the project, Si to build the airplane.

The furniture manufacturer tried to let Si down gently. For all Si's brash cocksureness, he liked the boy. But the last thing he needed was a twenty-year-old business partner with grandiose ideas. My God, he'd even designed his own trademark: an eagle holding a letter C in its talons.

"It's a good concept, Si, but impractical. There isn't an engine yet built with enough power to move a plane as big as this."

"But the Allies need our help," Si had said.

He's like a bulldog, Boeing had thought. Once he gets his teeth into something, he won't let go. "Look, if you're so darned eager to fight, why don't you take yourself a ferry ride over to Vancouver and enlist in the Canadian Air Service?"

Which is precisely what Si did, expecting them to welcome him enthusiastically for his vast experience. By now he had accumulated nearly 150 flying hours. The Canadians welcomed him, and with enthusiasm, but Si refused to swear an oath of allegiance to the King.

On the ferry back to Seattle he met another young American, a fellow New Englander, Cecil Taylor, returning from a visit with his grandparents before sailing for France. A Harvard graduate, Chip Taylor had signed on as a driver with a Quaker-sponsored volunteer ambulance group.

If Si was so determined to enlist in an Allied air service, Chip suggested he try the French. They required no oath of allegiance. And the fastest way to reach France was through the ambulance unit. Once there, said Chip, Si could sign up with L'Armée de l'Air.

The letter from Madeline arrived three weeks after he arrived in France.

Frank Conway was dead. A seizure.

Si felt an aloneness he had never known, and at one point his eyes moistened and his chest tightened. He did not cry, although he wanted to and knew it would make him feel better. He also wished he had tried harder to understand his father, to accept him for what he was. But he had not, and now it was too late.

Si served four months with the Quaker ambulance group before enlisting in the Foreign Legion. Transferring out of the Legion into the air service was not so easy. The transfer did not come through for nearly a year. A year in the trenches of Verdun and Neuve-Chapelle. A year of pure hell.

He had to learn to fly all over again at Issoudun. But after Verdun and Neuve-Chapelle anything was tolerable, from the daily 5:30-A.M. parade-ground drilling (to remind the student pilots they were military personnel!) to the instructors who resented the young American's combat stripes and almost patronizing attitude. They were as glad to see him leave Issoudun as he was to go, an achievement which now, so many months later, seemed not so great.

The great achievement, of course, was being alive and sitting at the bar of a small Montparnasse café, watching the rain beat against the café window. It was a light, steady rain that formed hazy rainbow-colored halos around the opaque tops of the gas streetlamps outside on the boulevard and glistened dully off the wet sidewalk. A marvelously Parisian rain, warm and pleasant, not like the rain that fell at the front, always accompanied by artillery flashes and the sound of the guns, and soaked through your clothes and chilled you to the bone.

He had been sitting for hours here at the bar of Chez Denise, listening to voices and laughter and clinking glasses, and the soft sultry voice of the girl singing at the piano in the center of the room. She sang, of course, in French; a language, he thought, invented specifically for song.

Turning from the window, he glanced down the brief length of the four-stooled zinc bar at the *patronesse*, Denise. She was perched formidably at her high-chaired *caisse*, idly fingering the pince-nez glasses dangling from the end of a black cord attached to a diamond brooch above her heart.

Si called out to her in French, "You get prettier every day."

"Yes," she replied wryly. "And you are drunk."

He was drunk, all right, but not incorrect: Denise still bore vestiges of great beauty. White-haired and wrinkled, at least sixty and probably older, she had been a successful Comédie Française actress and, it was said, the longtime mistress of a cabinet minister whose money had financed the purchase of the café and who, it was also said, had died in her bed.

Not a bad way to die, Simon Conway thought, looking away from Denise and fixing his eyes on the girl seated at the piano. The piano, surrounded by a number of small circular checkerboard-clothed tables, was located directly under the room's only overhead light, a low-hanging Tiffany chandelier. Tobacco smoke swirled around the roseate lampshade like wisps of blue fog.

Every table was occupied. In addition to some dozen French officers, there were three Yanks—two captains and a major—an Italian colonel, and two Polish captains. Many were accompanied by young, attractive women, although here, unlike other, similar Montparnasse *boîtes*, the women received no commissions for drinks purchased by their escorts. Denise prided herself on not encouraging such commerce. You came here to drink, to relax, and to enjoy the songs of the young woman at the piano.

That young woman, wearing a silvery-sequined V-necked gown, looked at Simon Conway. Their eyes met, and held, and she continued singing. To him. To him alone.

He raised his glass to her and drank. A little frown of admonishment turned the corners of her mouth down ever so slightly and narrowed her eyes. They were deep, large, clear brown eyes that blended perfectly with her bobbed chestnut hair and coppery, silky-smooth skin. Her face was delicate and angular, with high cheekbones passed down from generations of Slavic forebears. She was not particularly tall—the top of her head barely reached Si's chin—but certainly not petite. Not with that firm body, those fine breasts, flat stomach, and wide hips that Simon Conway claimed could conquer the world.

Her name was Andrée Chabral, not the name she had been born to, which was Chabralovich, a very old and venerable Serbian name. In point of fact, Andrée was a bona fide Baroness, her father having inherited the title from his father, who was the seventh generation of the family to carry it. He had been dead some twenty years, by his own hand, an impoverished exile in Paris, stripped of property, title, and all assets for having foolishly become involved in a muddled, amateurish plot to establish an independent Serbian state.

Now, again, she frowned disapprovingly at Si. He had just asked the barmaid, Michelle, for another cognac. He reminded Andrée of a spoiled child. But then he was a child, five years younger than she, although sometimes when he talked about what it was like in the air, killing other men whose faces you often saw, he was a hundred years older.

From the moment they had met, two years ago, she knew he was different from the others. It was in the Métro, at the Etoile station, and had been like an Alphonse et Gaston stage routine. She leaving, he entering; she walking up the stairs, he walking down; she stepping to her left, he to his right. And how insulted he was when she teased him about his French, that *accent atroce*! He spoke the language better than most Americans, didn't he? Later, she realized that no matter what he did—from drinking to flying to lovemaking—he was determined to do it better than the next man.

She knew, from that very first moment, she would sleep with him. There was no special magic or chemistry, just a desperate need she sensed in him. Fulfilling his need of course fulfilled needs of her own. Up to now it had been most gratifying. Where it would all end she dared not allow herself to wonder. But the end was inevitable. It always was.

She concluded "La Perme," and turned away from Simon. She started a new song, "Je Connais une Blonde," thinking it an apt number for the two French artillery captains seated in the first row of tables with two blond women dressed too tastefully to be *poules*, although a shade too garishly for wives. But what difference did it make who or what they were? Simon Conway's friends probably considered her, Andrée, a *poule*. Who cared what anyone thought? But, my God, he was getting drunk!

Si, having drunk half his cognac in a single swallow, was thinking that exact thought and had motioned Michelle for a fresh drink. Michelle glanced questioningly at Denise, who shrugged: Si was so far gone that another drink hardly mattered.

Michelle served the drink and hurried to the other end of the bar to serve two Tommies, Royal Marine sergeants who had just entered. Immediately following the marines was a tall young man in a French uniform without unit markings. Si was just sober enough to recognize him.

Si said, "Jesus Christ. . . !"

"Dammit!" the young man said. "I thought without my crown of thorns and the beard nobody would know me!" He pronounced beard as "beeahd," in a New England twang even broader than Si's.

It was Chip Taylor, from Boston, the man responsible for Si's joining the volunteer ambulance group. Although they had seen each other only once in the past two years, they had exchanged many letters. In the last one Chip wrote that he had a week's leave coming and would phone Si at Saint-Pol-sur-Mer.

". . . somebody at your squadron said you were in Paris, and told me to look for you here," Chip was saying. He jabbed a finger into Si's tunic, the ribbonless area above the left breast pocket. "No medals? I'd have thought you'd have a chestful by now."

"I'm up for the Médaille Bordel," Si said. "They give you that for five visits to a whorehouse." In French, Si called to Michelle, "Two more, *chérie*. A double for my friend here."

Denise climbed down from her stool and walked over to them. In French, she said to Si, "Why don't you eat something? I know you haven't had dinner."

"I'm not hungry," Si said.

"But thirsty, eh?" Denise tapped her pince-nez on Si's glass, which was still half full. Then, aiming the pince-nez at Si, she addressed Chip. "Why don't you see that this boy eats? You seem older—you should look after him."

"*Pardon?*" said Chip, whose command of French was limited to certain brief words and phrases related to ambulances and wounded men, and the mandatory bedroom vernacular.

Si said to Chip in English, "She says we both need a drink. Michelle!" Si wagged two fingers at the barmaid.

"No, Michelle, no more," Denise said. "First, he eats."

"No," said Si. "First I drink. Michelle!"

Michelle, bottle in hand, stood uncertainly. Denise said, "*Si tu bois encore, tu vas vomir!*"

"She says if I drink anymore, I'll puke all over the place," Si translated for Chip. He spoke loudly. At the piano, Andrée had just completed her song. The room was noisy with applause. Si reached for the bottle. Denise slid it away from him.

"If you insist on drinking more, I shall have to ask you to leave," she said.

"I insist," Si said.

"Then please leave," Denise said.

"With pleasure," Si said.

He got off the stool, put on his cap, folded his raincoat over his arm, and walked to the door. Chip followed. At the door, Si turned. He saluted Andrée, who regarded him coldly and continued playing.

2.

"Where the hell are we?" Chip asked.

"Somewhere in France," Si said. He pulled a bottle of cognac from his tunic pocket and held it up to the light. It was nearly empty. "Where the hell *were* we?"

"Somewhere in France," said Chip. "I think."

They were sitting on the damp curb of a narrow street, in front of a butcher shop. Above the shuttered entrance Si could make out the silhouette of a horse's head.

"Looks like the boulevard down there," he said. "Montparnasse, I guess, from the traffic. I can see a lot of hooded headlights."

They looked at each other now. Even in the dark the welt that had risen just under Si's right eye was visible. His uniform tunic was torn and dirty. Chip's nose was blood-caked, his uniform also torn.

"Good thing it stopped raining," Si said. "I lost my raincoat."

"You left it in the third joint we hit," Chip said. "The place with all the Moroccans. You started the fight, they finished it."

"Oh, yeah." Si fuzzily recalled it. He had fondled some woman's behind. She turned out to be the girlfriend of a huge Legionnaire sergeant. The sergeant hit him in the stomach with a chair.

"What were we celebrating?" Chip asked. "You never did tell me."

"My fifth kill. I'm an ace."

"Congratulations," said Chip. "Open the bottle, we'll drink to the sixth."

"I already have the sixth."

"Then we'll drink to the seventh."

Si uncorked the bottle. He handed it to Chip, who took a long drink and then returned it. Si did not want to drink anymore; he knew it would make him sick. He said, "I must have left my cap in that place, too."

"I wouldn't go back for it if I were you," Chip said, and offered Si a cigarette from a thin silver case. Si lit his cigarette and Chip's from the same match. He allowed the match to burn just long enough to see an ugly bruise on Chip's cheek.

"They did a good job on you," Si said.

"I think my nose is broken. Let me have the bottle."

Chip took another long pull from the bottle. Si said, "It's a wonder we didn't get arrested."

"Thank God for that," Chip said. "I'm going home at the end of the month."

"Home? The States?"

"All the way."

"I thought you were going into the army," Si said. "The U.S. Army."

"They won't take me," Chip said. "Asthma. There's one for the books: two years at the front, three ambulances shot out from under me, and my own army says I'm medically unfit."

"Count your blessings," Si said.

"Yeah," said Chip, and then both fell silent a few moments. A man and a woman walked past on the opposite side of the street. They were discussing their visit to a hospital, the woman saying she would not return to that place for a million francs, the man reminding her that it was her own brother they had visited. He's a vegetable, the woman said. A vegetable! she repeated, and their voices faded.

Chip said, "My father's going to Washington for the War Industries Board. 'Dollar-a-year man,' they call it. He wants me to work in the bank. He wants somebody there he can trust."

Si shifted around. The seat of his trousers was soaked through from sitting on the wet pavement. "How's your sister, by the way?"

"Still with the YMCA," Chip said. "Still giving the doughboys at South Station doughnuts and coffee. Haven't you heard from her?"

"Not for a while," Si said. He had never met Chip's younger sister, Margaret, but corresponded with her for a brief time in 1915. Chip had thought it would be good for Si to have a pen pal. In one letter Margaret—she preferred to be called Meg—included a photograph. A nice-looking, well-bred, typically upper-class girl. The correspondence had tapered off through mutual disinterest.

Chip drank again from the bottle and offered it to Si. Si shook his head, no. Chip said, "Yeah, my dad says there's more money around than he's ever seen. Everybody's working, making good pay. All the war contracts."

Si was not listening. Fifty feet away at the top of the street, a taxi appeared. It was one of the high-bodied, blunt-hooded Renaults, the famous *taxis de la Marne* that in 1914 had transported thousands of French soldiers from Paris to the Marne front, thereby thwarting the German offensive and saving the city.

Si momentarily considered getting up and hailing the cab. It seemed too much trouble. He struck a match and looked at his wrist-watch. The glass was shattered, the hands frozen at 9:22.

"What time is it?" he asked.

"Light another match," Chip said. He brought out a large Waltham pocket watch and guided the match in Si's hand over to it. It was after one. Chip drained the last few drops in the bottle and placed the empty bottle carefully and almost lovingly upright on the curb. He rose. "I'm going home."

"To take over your old man's bank. You told me."

" 'Home,' my hotel, you idiot. I want some sleep. They're sending us back into the line tomorrow. Five days of it, my final tour before I go—" in the dark he nodded, pleased—"home."

Si rose and faced him. "I guess that's where I'll see you then. Back in the States."

"Keep in touch," Chip said.

"I will," said Si. They started down the alley toward the boulevard. All at once Si stopped. "You want an investment that's surefire? After the war, the biggest thing will be aviation. People will want to fly places. Boston to New York, Detroit to Chicago. Flying will get you there twice as fast as on a train. And that means mail, too, and freight. Think of it! The whole bloody world will open up!"

"Sure thing, Si," Chip said. "Whatever you say."

"Goddammit, Chip, you don't understand a word of what I'm saying."

"Aeroplanes, Si, are military tools. Period."

"*Air*plane," Si corrected. "Nobody calls them aeroplanes anymore, not even the limeys."

"Okay, airplanes," Chip said. "They're good for war, sure, and maybe for sport for people that can afford it. But how can you compare a plane with a train or a ship? You're the one that's not thinking."

Si did not reply. He was pondering that very problem, size, both of airframes and power plants. The British flew gigantic machines, Handley-Page bombers. The German Gothas were even larger. Those huge airplanes could stay in the air for hours and fly hundreds of miles. To convert them for civilian use you needed only to remove their armament and replace the bomb bays with seats or cargo space. True, passenger and cargo capacity might be limited, but speed would compensate. And more powerful engines were being developed. Rolls-Royce, Si had heard, was working on an engine half the size of existing models with twice the horsepower.

". . . we'll talk about it," Chip was saying. "When we're both back home."

At the boulevard, they parted. Si had planned to return to the café and get Andrée away early. But he was so tired now he wanted only to sleep. Andrée lived in a small *pension* on Rue d'Odessa, which was nearby. The concierge, a grizzled one-armed Franco-Prussian War veteran, liked Si. At Si's last visit, Christmas Eve, the old man had brought a bottle of Tavel to the room.

Si walked along the darkened sidewalk, vaguely aware of the bustle of people and vehicles. His head was beginning to throb. But he knew it was not a hangover. It was the picture in his mind of the burning Fokker and the dead pilot. He forced that picture away and replaced it with one of himself awakening in the morning, Andrée's body next to his, her breasts and stomach molded into his back, the light scent of her perfume blending excitingly with her own fragrance.

Her leg would be wrapped around his so that he had only to turn slightly and place his hand on her belly and then slowly slide it down into the hollow below, and onto the silky moistness between her thighs. In her sleep she would moan and spread her legs wider. He would move his fingers slowly, gently, up and down against the moistness, and then, all at once, she would awaken. "Simon?" she would whisper, and throw her arms around him and kiss him, at the same time opening her legs fully and rolling underneath him. "*Chéri,*" she would whisper. "*Tu est mon chéri! Mon amour, mon amour!*"

"Oh, Jesus!" he would say. "Jesus to Jesus!" Which, now, thinking about it, he did say, aloud, and laughed self-consciously. No one paid him the slightest attention. He was so absorbed in the delightful reverie he almost walked past Rue d'Odessa. Halfway up the street a sliver of light splashed out onto the sidewalk. The light, from a slightly torn blackout curtain in the window of the little bistro adjoining Andrée's hotel, had always been his guide. A beacon in the night.

He stepped back to the corner and nearly collided with three *poilus*. The soldiers' tin mess gear, dangling from heavy knapsacks, clanked metallically against their bayonet sheaths. He moved closer to the wall of a building, grateful for the blackout. No one could see his wet, torn uniform and bruised face. He waited until the *poilus* passed, then started up Rue d'Odessa. He walked briskly toward the light.

3.

She was awake, watching him as he slept. He had asked her to wake him no later than noon so he could arrange for transportation

"I love you."

She studied him a long, silent, pensive moment. Then, "You do love me. I know you do."

"I just said I did."

"Say it again."

"I love you."

"I'm the first one, aren't I?"

"No, you're the one-hundredth," he said. "No, the ninety-seventh."

"Not the 'hundreds' you've been to bed with. I don't care about that. I mean the first one you truly loved."

"Yes, you're the first one," he said, which was true.

"Simon, don't go back."

He said nothing. He did not know what to say. He knew she was serious and knew exactly what she was going to say.

"If you leave now, I'll never see you again." Her voice, flat and toneless, matched her expression. She sat up in bed and slipped into a white silk kimono. The sleeve edges were frayed. He promised himself to buy her a new robe. Yes, on his next leave.

"Don't go back," she said again. "Stay here with me."

"That's called 'desertion.' They shoot you for it."

"They'll never find you," she said. "You've done your part. You owe them nothing anymore. They owe you everything."

He said nothing. He wondered what they owed him. My life, he thought, that is what they owe me. They owe me the next fifty years. The chance to be somebody, to make something of myself.

The chance to build the airplanes that would fly the passengers and cargo across the oceans. That was what they owed him, and it all could be lost in the single firing of a single gun.

"I'm a soldier," he said, feeling foolish. "I have a job—"

"—'job!' A job to do what? To kill men you have never seen, who have never harmed you? Or yourself, to allow yourself to be herded like a sheep to the slaughter? That's your 'job'?"

What disturbed him—no, terrified him—was that the idea of not returning held a strange appeal. Because of that premonition, of course, but he knew that everyone had such premonitions, the normal fear experienced by any soldier in a war.

"Yes," he said. "That's my job."

He sat up and swung his legs over the bed, his back to her, staring at the worn carpet. He did not want to look at her. He was ashamed of himself for even thinking of not returning to duty, and resented her for having sensed his weakness.

He felt her fingers stroking his hair, and the warm firmness of her breasts against his back. He wanted to take her into his arms and lower his head onto those breasts. He wanted to kiss her and make love to her again, and hold her. He told himself that if he did that, if he held her in his arms, he would live. If he did not hold her and make love to her, he would report back to duty and be killed.

Killed.

The word seemed to burn itself into the carpet in flaming letters. You are tired, he told himself, tired and afraid, and think you have run the string out, and used up all your luck. He remembered once when Guynemer described that precise feeling.

Georges Guynemer, the standard to which all French pursuit pilots aspired. Fifty-four victories. A man with no weaknesses. A man who lived, made love, drank, and fought with an almost mystical *élan*. An immortal.

"Yes, Simon, I think I have used it all up," Guynemer had said. A few weeks later on a routine patrol he simply flew into a cloud and was never seen again.

"I'll come back," Si said to Andrée. "Nothing will happen to me, I promise you." He got up, dressed, kissed her, and left. He wanted to say "I love you," but did not. He wanted to say he would always love her, but did not. He did not even say goodbye.

3

The previous day, when Karl Eisler had delivered his message to N.124's airdrome, the first man to reach the parachuted shell casing was Jimmy Forrest. He read it aloud to the others. Karl's challenge to the pilot of Nieuport 487.

". . . signed, 'Eisler, Captain, Imperial Air Service,' " Jimmy said. "Jesus!"

A short, wiry American, Tom Atcheson, tapped his finger on the paper still clutched in Jimmy's hand. " 'Brutal execution'? What the hell does that mean? What happened?"

"A mistake, it was a mistake!" Ledoux said. "The Boche is mistaken!" He turned and strode back to his office.

Jimmy said, "Four-eight-seven, that's Conway's plane," and all eyes turned to the tarmac where the Nieuport was parked. "Mistake or no mistake, when Si sees this, he'll go charging off after that Kraut like Grant after Lee!"

Mike Gordon said, "I hate to disillusion you, kid. When your hero Mr. Lieutenant Conway sees the note, he'll tear it into a thousand pieces and toss it into the W.C.!"

"You're crazy," Jimmy said. "You don't know what you're talking about!"

But Mike Gordon did know what he was talking about. When Si returned from Paris he publicly announced his intention to disregard the challenge. Ledoux followed with a statement approving Si's decision, which terminated any further discussion. Ledoux then informed the group he was leaving for Nancy that evening to attend a meeting at 2nd Army HQ. In his absence Lieutenant Arnaux, the squadron adjutant, was in command.

After dinner Si went immediately to his room to compose a letter to his friend Captain Mark O'Meara, CO of the 103rd Aero Squadron of the U.S. Air Service. This was the unit Si wished to be transferred to, not some rah-rah squadron composed of eager college-boy pilots just out of cadet training.

Si's room had once been the chateau's main guest quarters, but its lovely Louis XVI furniture had long since been replaced by three canvas cots and a few mismatched bureaus and chairs. He sat at the dressing table, arranged a pad of yellow legal paper before him, and started to write. He had got as far as "Dear Mark" when Jimmy Forrest burst into the room.

"Si, you *have* to meet Eisler!"

Si did not look up at him. "I don't 'have' to do anything," he said. "I don't 'have' to do a goddam thing."

"I can't believe you're saying that!"

A tall, dark-haired, lanky boy, Jimmy was the only child of a millionaire Rhode Island machine-tool manufacturer. He had dropped out of his sophomore year at Brown to sign up as a YMCA volunteer and sailed for France shortly before the United States entered the war. He was fresh from Issoudun, with no combat experience and, like N.124's other Americans, would soon be transferred to the U.S. Air Service.

". . . and dammit, Si, your honor's at stake," Jimmy was saying. "Your honor! Doesn't that mean anything to you?"

Si laughed. "Honor?" he said. "It's a word, kid. A dirty one at that. Now get the hell out of here and let me write this letter."

He tried to concentrate on the letter but could feel Jimmy's disillusioned eyes boring into him. Now he turned and looked at Jimmy. "You should have been at Verdun," he said. "You'd have learned about 'honor.' "

"A man doesn't need Verdun to know about honor," Jimmy said. "It's like 'class.' You either have it or you don't."

Si glanced at the two vacant cots, both unoccupied for nearly a month. The second roommate, young Bill Sturdevant, had been shot down over Monmedy. The same Monmedy Karl Eisler had chosen for the duel.

"I think you're afraid, Si," Jimmy said.

"Will that satisfy you?" Si said. "If I admit I'm afraid? All right, I'm afraid. Now you said your piece, now get out."

"Then you're not meeting Eisler?"

"No, I am not meeting Eisler."

"You really are afraid of him."

Si wanted to laugh again. This kid was too much. "All right, I'll meet him," he said, and paused. Jimmy's crestfallen expression had abruptly changed to an expectant smile. Si continued, "If you and four others will wait over Monmedy at ten thousand feet, I'll sucker Eisler in, and then you guys jump him."

Jimmy's smile vanished. "You'd do a thing like that?"

"I certainly would," said Si, who had suggested the ambush facetiously but now could not resist baiting Jimmy. "But I know none of you heroes would."

"Neither would Captain Eisler," Jimmy said. "Eisler would never do anything like that."

"Don't bet on it," Si said, but he knew Jimmy spoke the truth. Eisler had given his word. German officers lived by their idiotic codes of honor. And died by them, too.

Jimmy nodded tightly. "I think you did gun that man down on the ground. I honest to God believe you did!"

Si did not reply. He looked down at the writing pad again. After a moment he heard the metal cleats of Jimmy's cavalry boots on the hardwood floor of the corridor outside and then on the stairs. Kid, Si thought, now you know the meaning of clay feet. He resumed writing the letter.

The sound of the engine woke him. A Nieuport's rotary, spitting and coughing in the chill air. Outside, through the partially closed window louvers, the sky was black. Too early for the dawn patrol. He groped on the floor for his wristwatch. He found it inside one shoe and brought it to eye level. The radium-tipped hands read 6:05.

Outside, the engine roared louder, smoother, full-out. Si rolled off the cot and threw open the window shutters. The massive tent hangars loomed up out of the dark, their canvas walls billowing gently in the early-morning breeze. On the tarmac the silhouettes of parked airplanes were outlined against the gray-black sky. Beyond this, the field extended into darkness. And then, as though someone had hurled a torch spurting red-and-orange fire over the tops of the trees at the far edge of the field, he saw an airplane's exhaust flames. The flames and the engine sound quickly faded in the distance and were gone.

Si slipped into his uniform and shoes, wrapped his trench coat around his shoulders, and rushed downstairs. On the stairway he nearly collided with Arnaux. The adjutant was buttoning his jacket with one hand and lighting a cigarette with the other. He was an almost anemically thin man, several inches taller than Si, with a heavy black mustache perennially speckled with food and tobacco crumbs.

"Who was that just taking off?" he asked.

Si shook his head; he did not know. But he did know. He was afraid to say the name, as though that itself might somehow make it true. Both men hurried into the dining room. Arnaux continued to the door and out to the tarmac, as Mike Gordon and two other pilots also entered the dining room. All wore flying clothes. They were scheduled for dawn patrol.

Behind the bar the walrus-mustached mess orderly, Dubois, was pouring coffee into large porcelain mugs. Gordon and the others chatted loudly, but Si was not listening. He was studying the chalked names on the blackboard duty roster. The only names listed were those on dawn patrol.

"Who was in that airplane?" Si asked in English. He had addressed Gordon, but Arnaux returned just then. With him was Si's *mécanicien*, Crespin.

"It was Sergeant Forrest," Arnaux said in French. He looked at Si. "He used your machine."

"He said he had your permission, lieutenant," Crespin said to Si. "A special sortie, he said."

Si's legs suddenly began trembling. He sank down into one of the lounge chairs. "The fool," he said softly. "The damn fool!"

That day he hardly remembered flying two patrols—and flying one of the new Spads, since his own Nieuport had been "borrowed." On both sorties no enemy aircraft were encountered, and each time he returned to the field he rushed into Arnaux's office for any news of Jimmy Forrest. They waited all morning, and into the afternoon. A dozen calls to HQ for word of a downed N.124 Nieuport brought the same negative response.

At dusk, the black Triplane came in low over the trees. It raced across the field, dropped a package on the tarmac, and was gone. Arnaux, who had ordered the antiaircraft gunners to hold their fire, sprinted to the tarmac with half a dozen others. Si remained on the chateau terrace. He knew what the package contained.

Arnaux walked slowly, wearily, to the terrace. He held up a helmet and goggles, a wallet, and an oval brass dog tag.

Mike Gordon said to Si, "Nice work, Simon."

Arnaux handed Si a folded piece of paper. The same stiff linen stationery that Karl Eisler's challenge had been written on. Si did not unfold the paper.

"I know what it says," he said.

"Read it anyway," Arnaux said.

Si slipped the paper into his shirt pocket. "Later," he said. When I'm drunk, he thought, but did not say it.

"As you wish," Arnaux said. He and the others turned and entered the chateau, filing past Si one by one. No one looked directly at him. He wanted to shout out, I didn't tell the kid to go! I can't be responsible for fools! But the words remained deep in his throat, for he knew they were empty and meaningless.

He stood on the terrace, alone, shivering in the cold night air, gazing at the tarmac, the parked airplanes, the trees at the far end of the field. He was only vaguely aware of lights on in the chateau dining room and the loud, familiar buzz of dinnertime chatter. And Victrola music. They were singing in English, "Mademoiselle from Armentières." Jimmy Forrest's favorite song. The kid enjoyed inventing clean lyrics for it; he claimed the original, British version was an affront to the people of France. Si strained to listen for the toast to the dead man, which would be followed by another toast, "Hurrah for the next man who dies."

But he heard only the scratching of the record when it finished, and then another tune he did not recognize. He wanted a drink but did not want to face the men inside. My comrades-in-arms, he thought wryly. He wanted to explain to them why he had not flown to meet Eisler, but he also knew that what he truly wanted was their forgiveness.

He stepped into the chateau foyer. Under the dim light of the two low-wattage bulbs protruding from the cracked glass ceiling fixture, he read the note:

Regretfully enclosed you will find the possessions of Sergeant James C. Forrest.

He was severely wounded in an encounter three miles east of the village of Monmedy at 0635 today, 15 March 1918.

Despite his injuries, and the damage to his machine, he was able to maintain enough control to crash-land behind our lines.

Sergeant Forrest was buried with full military honors at 1300, this same day.

Eisler
Captain, Imperial Air Service

Si read the note twice. Then he folded it carefully and replaced it in his shirt pocket. Aloud, quietly, he said, "Hurrah for the next man who dies."

2.

Even before they engaged, Karl knew the Nieuport pilot was no novice. This was no Sergeant James C. Forrest, so amateurish he had approached Monmedy at seven thousand feet, two thousand feet below the rendezvous point, and such an invitingly conspicous target that Karl's first, most obvious reaction was that the Nieuport was a decoy. If so, it was the clumsiest ambush ever devised, for any aircraft attempting to position themselves in the sun above and behind Karl would have been spotted long before their arrival.

Karl had even waited for Nieuport 487 to reach altitude and allowed him the first pass. The Niueport had skidded sloppily, presenting Karl an unmissable, textbook deflection shot. His very first burst hit the pilot.

He had followed the Nieuport down, certain this was not the pilot who killed Braun, and so disappointed he had decided that if the man was alive he would disengage, let him go.

But now it was different, as he knew it would be, as he had known only a few hours ago when the American flew so brazenly over Jasta 24's field and dropped the message. They were at lunch. Everyone rushed from the tables to the dining-room windows. The window-panes rattled as the Nieuport roared past. Brunfeld, C Flight leader, said, "A regular postal service, for Christ's sake! Us to them, them to us."

The note was brief. The Nieuport pilot shot down yesterday by Karl Eisler was not the man he sought. That man, Lieutenant Simon Conway, would be flying Nieuport 832 and would await the captain's pleasure this very day at 1600 hours, nine thousand feet over Monmedy.

Karl sensed rather than saw Simon Conway's airplane angling in behind him on the starboard side. In the split instant before Si fired, Karl racked the Tripe around in a tight left turn. The bullets buzzed harmlessly under his right lower wing. The Nieuport hurtled past, turning left, climbing to get above.

Karl pulled the stick back into his stomach. The little Tripe's nose was nearly vertical. She hung on her propeller, then responded. She climbed straight toward the Nieuport, which had executed a perfect, almost graceful *renversement* and was diving head-on toward the Tripe. The muzzle flashes of the Nieuport's front-firing gun were blindingly bright in Karl's eyes as he pumped the cocking handles of his own guns and fired. The Tripe reverberated nose to tail with the recoil of the twin Spandaus.

The Nieuport banked right, then barrel-rolled over and down, obviously planning to come out under the Tripe. Karl, anticipating the maneuver, had rolled out of his climb into an immediate dive. When both airplanes recovered they were some five hundred yards apart, straight and level. They jockeyed for position like boxers dancing about each other, feinting, testing, probing for weak spots.

Karl had to admire Simon Conway's skill. The man could fly and understood his machine, its capabilities and limitations. A worthy adversary. It would make the victory that much more gratifying.

In all directions, as far as the eye could see, the sky was empty. It was as though this was all that existed, this was the sum and substance of the whole world. In the twilight the ruins of the village two miles below resembled a murky reconnaissance photograph, ghostly and unreal. Roofless shells of buildings, a half-demolished church steeple, rubbled, deserted streets. All that was real was himself, Karl Eisler, and the man he intended to kill. The man trying to kill him.

Simon Conway aimed the Nieuport straight at the Tripe again. Karl watched it race toward him. Tracers from the Nieuport's Lewis gun arced over the Tripe's top wing like a bright dotted yellow line. Karl banked sharply right, knowing the Nieuport would try to turn inside him. He rolled over, then pulled up in a shallow chandelle. The Nieuport climbed to follow the Tripe. But Karl turned left so that once more the two came head-on at each other.

Si dove away. The Tripe followed, but Si's Nieuport was faster. Down, down, down; the scream of the wide-open engine blended with the musical pitch of the wind whistling through the airplane's guy wires. The altimeter unwound like a clock spinning backward. The ground loomed up. Closer, closer. At a thousand feet, Si pulled out. He climbed up, and around, and leveled out three hundred yards behind the Tripe.

Si fired the Vickers. Three short bursts. Too far away for accuracy. The Tripe swung left, then right, left again, all the while climbing. Si followed. They climbed to five thousand feet, then seven thousand. Karl continued upward and then, at seventy-five hundred, turned and came out straight and level. He expected the Nieuport to roll with him and come out on his port side.

But Si had continued climbing. Now he was two thousand feet above. He banked over and down, and dove on the Tripe. Karl yanked the stick back and aimed the Tripe's nose at the oncoming Nieuport, a maneuver Si never anticipated. He thought the German would dive away from him, not pull up and come straight on in. Now neither could turn without conceding to the other an advantage.

And neither man intended giving way. The Nieuport dove toward the climbing Tripe. Unless one swung away they would crash head-on. Karl envisioned the two airplanes locked together, spinning downward, burning, and a single thought quickly blotted out the million others that were surging through his brain. The Nieuport pilot, the American named Simon Conway, was insane.

This same thought, in the same context, filled Simon Conway's mind. He was convinced of Karl Eisler's madness and, to be sure, his own. Especially his own, for only a crazy man would have flown over the German airdrome at high noon with a reply challenge. Only a crazy man, or an angry one. And Si was angry. Karl Eisler had to have known that the pilot in Nieuport 487, Jimmy Forrest, was inexperienced and impulsive. Under the unique circumstances—the so-called "duel"—the German should have, and easily could have, avoided the meeting. Shooting Jimmy Forrest down under those circumstances was more of a "murder" than Si's alleged crime.

Si had felt compelled, then, to issue the return challenge. For his own self-respect if for no other reason. In truth, he had no choice. With Ledoux absent and Arnaux little more than an administrative officer, Si was the actual operational commander. This time, the loss of squadron "honor" could not be scoffed away.

And, strangely, for all his misgivings he did not want to scoff it away. By refusing the initial challenge he had forced Jimmy into taking his place, thereby incurring an obligation he could not ignore. Perhaps he was after all responsible for fools.

The Pariah would be the Redeemer.

A dead Redeemer, for at that instant he was convinced this was his last instant on earth. He knew the two airplanes would collide. He was as determined to ram the Tripe as, apparently, Eisler was to ram the Nieuport. He saw himself lying dead in the snowy field of his premonition.

A voice screamed in his head: Break off! Break off! But no, that would give the German an almost insurmountable advantage. Wait, the voice screamed. Suppose Eisler veers away? Then the advantage is *yours*. You simply tap your rudder bar in the same direction and raise the Nieuport's nose. The whole bottom of the Tripe's fuselage will be under your gun.

The Tripe's white cowling grew huge in the Vickers's ringed gunsight. Si was hardly aware of his finger holding the trigger and the gun hammering. He could see the tracers smashing into the Tripe's white cowling. But each bullet into the Tripe echoed with the Spandau's bullets tearing into the Nieuport.

The two airplanes hurtled toward each other. The white cowling was so close Si could see the individual propeller blades spinning. He jerked the stick to the right and kicked the right rudder bar. The

Nieuport turned right, right wing angling down almost vertically. The Triplane also swung away, to its right, right wing down. Both airplanes veered past each other, so close their left wingtips brushed.

For both men it was a reflex, a signal transmitted from adrenals to brain to muscles. A survival reflex, an uncontrollable, primordial memory, passed down from ten million centuries of similar reflexes.

The centrifugal force of the dive prevented Si from turning his head to look behind him. But he knew that the Tripe, climbing, had already rolled over and fallen away in a controlled descent and was following him down.

The Nieuport could outdive and, at this speed, outrun the Tripe. But Si did not want to outrun Eisler. He wanted to kill him, no simple task with a damaged airplane. It was a miracle the Tripe's guns had not blown the Nieuport to pieces. Si only hoped he could pull the airplane out of the dive without buckling its wings. He was afraid to pull up too sharply; already fabric was shredding from the lower wing.

He eased back on the stick. The little airplane responded instantly. The pressure pinned Si's body against the back of the seat. The sky became gray, then almost black. He gasped for breath. A steamroller was crushing his chest. Slowly, the sky was gray again, and then blue. The weight on his chest lessened.

The moment he leveled out he heard the hollow, steady chug-chug-chug of the Tripe's guns. A neat line of holes punctured the Nieuport's lower right wing. And then he felt the pain in his right leg, just below the knee. It was like an electric shock. He screamed and clamped his hand on the boot. The slug had torn a jagged hole in the leather. The boot's fleece lining came away wet and sticky in his hand. Bits and pieces of fleece clung like bright viscous red cotton candy to his fingertips. The whole bottom of the wool sock inside his boot felt damp. As he twisted around in his seat to look behind him, at the Tripe bearing in again, the Nieuport's engine stopped.

Karl could hardly believe his luck. After absorbing the head-on fire his Triplane still functioned and the Nieuport was lined squarely in his gunsight, helpless. Not only were the wires of its upper and lower right wing shot away, its engine was out, its propeller turning over and over slowly in the wind.

It was not mercy that froze Karl Eisler's finger on the trigger. Or chivalry. Or even shame at killing a helpless enemy. Not even professional pride. He had decided that death was too honorable for this animal who took pleasure in gunning down a wounded enemy. Karl wanted to humiliate him. He wanted to put the son of a bitch on display, the way the Romans had paraded their prisoners.

Karl lowered the Tripe's nose and swung right and flew alongside the Nieuport. He could see the pilot clearly, the broad shoulders and erect carriage of a tall man whose oil-streaked face, even behind the goggles, revealed heavy-boned symmetrical features, an angular nose, firm lips, square jaw. He appeared young, not youthful but young. Probably early or middle twenties.

It was then, peering into Simon Conway's eyes, Karl Eisler realized the American was wounded. Now, for all his hate and promise of revenge, Karl was glad he had not finished him off. He would not stoop to the other man's level.

They had drifted northeast in the battle, inland over Belgium, behind German lines. The snow-covered marshlands stretched below. Karl blipped his engine and gestured downward and ahead, a signal for Si to land. Si nodded in acknowledgment and lowered the powerless Nieuport's nose slightly to maintain speed.

Although the marsh looked smooth enough to Si, unless it was frozen sufficiently hard to support the landing airplane, the wheels would catch and flip the machine over. But he might get lucky. The first weeks of March had been unseasonably cold, with snow and frost that delayed the spring thaw, leaving the ground in some places winter-hard.

In Si's windscreen, through the windmilling propeller, the marsh loomed huge and white. The wind whistling through the wires sounded almost as loud as the drone of the Tripe's engine close behind him. He felt no resentment toward Karl Eisler. The German had outfought him, and won. He was the better man. There is always someone better, always.

The snow rushed up at him. He eased the stick back and flared out. The airplane floated along the surface, then touched. The wheels rolled. The ground was frozen. It was a perfect landing. The Tripe, less than a hundred yards behind and almost at ground level, flew past, climbing. At a thousand feet Karl made a *renverse* and started back in from the opposite end of the field.

The Nieuport had already slowed to a stop. Si hoisted himself from the cockpit and gingerly dropped to the ground. He reached into the cockpit and removed a Very pistol and flare from the side map pocket. He loaded the flare into the pistol, cocked the hammer, and aimed the muzzle into the cockpit at the oil reservoir. He pulled the trigger. The shell plunged into the cockpit with a dull thud. He tossed the empty pistol into the cockpit and began hobbling away.

Behind him, the Nieuport exploded in an almost quiet *whoosh*. The force of the blast knocked him down. He lay facedown a moment, arms outstretched, fingers clawing the cold, wet snow. Then, mustering his strength, he rolled over and sat up. He stared at the orange flame and black smoke rising from the burning Nieuport.

And at the Triplane coming in low, to attack.

He is going to gun me down, Si thought. The Kraut bastard is going to do it. Every nerve in Si's body seemed paralyzed. He could not move a muscle. He sat there waiting for the bullets to tear into his body.

Karl aimed the Tripe at the figure on the ground and fired both guns. Si saw the bullets churn toward him in twin rows of erupting white puffs of snow. He closed his eyes. Ten yards from Si, Karl stopped firing. He had no intention of hitting him. It was only a gesture, a graphic reminder. Si opened his eyes as the Tripe sped past overhead, climbing.

Karl never saw the N.124 Spad diving in behind him. It was Georges Ledoux. The *capitaine* had returned to Saint-Pol-sur-Mer less than ten minutes after Si took off and immediately set out in pursuit, using the faster Spad instead of his own Nieuport. He had hoped to overtake Si and order him to return. He arrived too late to have witnessed the duel but spotted Si's burning airplane. He reached the scene just in time to see the German strafing the helpless figure on the ground.

Karl never had a chance. Ledoux's first and only burst ripped into the Tripe's engine and shattered the propeller. The Tripe plunged nose-down into the marsh, cartwheeled to the right, and flipped over. The wrecked airplane slid across the snow on its back and came to a stop not fifty feet from Si.

Ledoux had planned to come back in for a closer look and perhaps land on the frozen marsh. But directly ahead, five thousand feet above and three miles away, were four Albatross D-IIIs. Ledoux knew they had seen him. He had no choice but to immediately reverse course and speed away.

Ledoux twisted around in his seat to glance back, down at the ground at the two crashed airplanes, and at Si, now only an inert brown-clad figure in the snow. The Nieuport was a mass of flames and skeletal wing and fuselage spars. The Triplane resembled a large black bug that had fallen upside down into the snow.

Si watched the Spad vanish into the distance. Far behind the Spad the four D-IIIs raced after it. Si laughed weakly; they would never catch him. "Thanks . . . whoever you are," he said, and then again became aware of the pain in his leg. No, not so much pain now, more of a dull, constant throbbing. The snow under his right boot was stained red.

He looked away, at the Triplane. The pilot's helmeted head dangled upside down from the seat. A thin wisp of gray smoke trailed from the Tripe's engine, and a flicker of yellow flame. A ruptured oil line, Si thought, as the trace of flame became a series of small, narrow, burning rivulets of oil that merged into a single stream of fire flowing back toward the fuselage.

The flames were consuming every inch of fabric in their path as the fire crept relentlessly toward the fuel tank and cockpit. The pilot's head twitched, as though avoiding the heat. The poor bastard was alive. Si closed his eyes. He did not want to watch the man burn.

3.

Later, when they told him he had crawled across the snowy marsh to pull Karl Eisler to safety only seconds before the blazing Tripe's fuel tank exploded, he told himself he must have been out of his mind. No sane person would attempt such an act. The entire incident, start to finish, was a complete blank. Not until three days later, in the German army hospital at Antwerp, did the memory begin coming back to him, and then only in bits and pieces.

The leg wound itself was not serious—a 7.92mm Spandau shell embedded in the calf—but he had lost considerable blood. If not for the doctors and nursing sisters speaking German, he might have been in an Allied hospital, the care and treatment was that first-rate. With a private room and excellent food, which surprised him, for he had heard the Germans were literally starving. An English-speaking army chaplain explained that the hospital was under specific orders to provide the best for this particular POW.

"Seems you saved the life of one of our pilots," the chaplain said.

That was on the fourth day. The following day he had another visitor. Despite the bandages covering the man's forehead, Si recognized him immediately. The same cold eyes, whose color was a deep blue, the same aquiline nose and tight-pursed firm lips, and strong chin.

The eyes softened with a sudden warmth. A hint of a smile played over Karl's mouth. In his lightly accented English, he said, "Yes, lieutenant, it's me. Eisler."

Si brought his hand to his forehead in a limp mock salute.

"I hope you're feeling better," Karl said. "I certainly am." He offered Si a cigarette, lit it and one for himself, then sat in a wicker armchair beside the bed.

Si waved his hand around the room. "I understand I have you to thank for all this attention?"

"It won't last much longer," Karl said. "You'll soon be transferred to a POW camp."

"*C'est la guerre,*" Si said, and drew on the cigarette. It was unexpectedly strong. He coughed, and then again.

"It's German," Karl said apologetically. "All we can get these days. I ran out of my last Turkish a week ago."

"Some Caporals were in my jacket pocket," Si said. He pointed to the closet.

Karl stepped to the closet. He rummaged through the neatly hung clothes and brought the package to Si. Nearly half the pack remained. Si replaced their German cigarettes with the Caporals. Both inhaled luxuriously.

"Genuine Virginia," Karl said. "It's a miracle the soldiers who found us didn't steal them."

Si tossed him the pack. "Keep it."

"I will," said Karl. "Thank you."

They fell into a brief silence, smoking, regarding each other. Then Si said, "I didn't gun that man down. I didn't think he was anywhere near the plane."

Karl thought about that a moment. "I believe you," he said. "Why did you risk your life to rescue me?"

Si did not want to admit he remembered little of the rescue. Let them believe him a hero. He took another drag on the cigarette and carefully snuffed it out. He would keep the butt for a later smoke. He answered Karl's question with one of his own.

"Why didn't you finish me off when you had the chance?"

"Let's just say I'm glad I didn't."

They studied each other another moment, then Karl rose. He opened the Caporal wrapper and counted out five cigarettes. He placed the cigarettes and a box of matches on the enameled white service tray beside the bed.

"We'll share them," he said. "I'll probably not see you again. Is there anything you need?"

Si said, "A blonde, maybe. And a bottle of good Armagnac."

"The blonde might be somewhat difficult under these conditions," Karl said. "The Armagnac is easier, although you may have to settle for *schnapps*. I'll see to it." He flipped Si a crisp salute and left.

Si lay back and gazed at the ceiling. He was a POW, yes, but things could be worse. In fact, it might not be so bad a war after all. He picked up the snuffed-out cigarette and lit it. He smoked, forming a chain of rings as Raoul Lufbury had taught him before Luf transferred into the U.S. 94th Pursuit Squadron. Si thought he should have written Lufbury about his own transfer rather than to Mark O'Meara. Of course, it made little difference now.

His mind wandered to Paris, to Andrée. He assumed the Germans had reported his capture. Eventually Andrée would know. He wondered how she would take the news. He tried to concentrate on this, but his thoughts continually returned to Karl Eisler.

Eisler was smart, all right. He realized that neither he nor Si could offer a rational explanation for their behavior, Eisler's for sparing Si's life, and Si's for rescuing Eisler. And yet there had to be an explanation. He thought about it a long time, through dinner and for hours afterward. Just before he fell asleep he found the answer.

Discounting insanity—which in his case, he told himself, could not so easily be discounted—the explanation was that there was no explanation.

4

Under ordinary circumstances, Unteroffizier Erhard Unger might have enjoyed his duties as chief clerk to Stalag 12-A's commandant, Major Bruno Haase. The camp was a short bicycle ride from Magdeburg and an equidistant two-hour automobile drive from Berlin and from Unger's own hometown of Leipzig, with ample time off to visit either place. And Magdeburg was pleasant enough, a cosmopolitan city with excellent cafés, hospitable people, and friendly, lonely women.

And what job could be softer than senior noncommissioned officer at a POW camp for high-ranking Allied officer-prisoners? With better food than the German army provided its own officers and, since 12-A's inmates were all field-grade officers or higher, little or no worry about discipline. Their advanced years and limited physical powers also minimized any serious escape attempts.

Unteroffizier Unger had devoted twenty years of his life—more than half his lifetime, including three years in the trenches—to Kaiser and country. Twice wounded, he was holder of the Iron Cross 2nd Class and had an assignment that was the envy of every senior sergeant in the Imperial Army, especially serving under such an easygoing commandant as old "Lefty" Haase.

It was precisely this casual, almost friendly manner of Bruno Haase's that Unger found so disquieting. Little wonder they called Stalag 12-A the Saxony Rest Home. Haase ran the camp like a resort, not a POW stockade. One hundred and twenty-two Allied prisoners —two of whom held general's rank—were treated more like honored guests than enemies. Only in the past few months, with food so scarce, had Haase even begun to shorten the rations.

A-12, located on the site of a former sugar-beet-processing plant five miles outside Magdeburg, was a small, compact installation enclosed by a barbed-wire-topped chain-link fence. The camp consisted of a single watchtower at the main gate and two ramshackle factory buildings. One building had been converted into a prisoners' barracks, the other housed camp personnel. The commandant's office was on the lower floor of a two-story, six-room wood-frame structure just outside the gate. The upper-floor rooms served as the commandant's living quarters.

At night, depending upon the electricity available or the condition of the generator, a searchlight in the tower occasionally swept the compound. This, however, also depended upon the availability of sentry personnel, for the tower was seldom manned, and then only by Home Guard volunteers, too old to respect a superior, too stubborn to take orders, too stupid to learn. The young soldiers were either dead or at the Western Front.

Unteroffizier Unger was thinking all this sitting at his desk, legs propped up on a chair, gazing across the orderly room to the open window. It was a lovely July morning, the air scented with the sweetness of the nearby beet fields and the aroma of newly cut grass.

Through the window, he had an unobstructed view of the gate and its two sloppily uniformed Home Guard sentries, so casual and unmilitary you might think they were posted outside a Magdeburg butcher shop to maintain order among a queue of impatient *Hausfrauen*. It was enough to break a regular army man's heart and, in Unger's case, did. Rejects, all of them. But then Unger was himself a reject, compliments of British mustard gas at the Somme.

And, appropriately, the chief reject was the commandant, Major Haase. A tall, handsome man of thirty-two whose brush-cut hair had turned totally white, and who had only one arm, his left, Haase was a genuine Air Service hero. He had lost the right arm in a duel with four British Sopwith Camels. He had shot down three of them before the fourth got him.

A Mercedes staff car was approaching the gate, with a single passenger in the rear. Unger recognized the passenger, Major Haase's good friend and former squadron mate Captain Karl Eisler. This was Eisler's third visit to Stalag A-12 in as many months. The purpose of these visits, he claimed, was to interrogate an American flyer he had shot down. Unger knew it was through Eisler's influence that the American, Simon Conway, had been sent here to "Lefty's Social Club," for he held the rank of *sous-lieutenant*, the only officer of such minor rank in the camp.

From his office, Haase shouted, "Unger! Show Captain Eisler in!"

The *Unteroffizier* leaped to his feet. He buttoned his collar and strode to the door, thinking that Haase must have seen Eisler from the office. With Unger handling all the paperwork and administrative thinking, the commandant had little to do but look out his window at the twin spires of Magdeburg's famous medieval cathedral. Those needlelike parapets outlined against the sky were a constant, resentful reminder to Unger that not fifty yards from the cathedral, at Koenigstrasse 38, was one of the finest whorehouses in the state of Saxony—for officers only.

Karl Eisler entered the orderly room, Unger clicked his heels smartly. "Herr Hauptmann . . ."

"Good morning, Unger."

"The major is waiting for you, sir."

"Get my driver something to eat, will you?" Karl stepped past Unger and went into the office. A moment later, Karl's chauffeur, an army corporal, charged into the orderly room with a shoe box wrapped in brown paper.

"The captain left this in the car," the chauffeur said.

Unger took the box from the chauffeur. He knocked on the office door and opened it. Karl and Haase were shaking hands, left-handed. "I believe this is yours, sir," Unger said to Karl.

"Thank you," Karl said. He tucked the box under his arm and resumed his conversation with Haase.

Unger closed the door again and said to the corporal, "The whole fucking country's starving, but that son of a bitch sees to it that the enemy prisoners have a feast!" He knew, from past experience, the box contained a gift for Eisler's Yankee friend, Lieutenant Conway. Caviar, probably, and a bottle of Armagnac.

The office door, which Unger had not completely closed, was flung open. Unger found himself facing Haase. Quietly, almost conversationally, Haase said, "You have a big mouth, sergeant. One of these days it will land you in the shithouse."

Unger stared straight ahead, his eyes riveted on the blue-enameled Maltese cross fixed to the center button of Haase's choker collar. They wore their Blue Max medals to bed, these Prussian bastards. "No offense was intended, sir," he said.

"That's good to know," Haase said in the same pleasant tone. "It means I won't have to worry about your being offended when I send the regimental quartermaster a report on some of your little business dealings with the town merchants."

"Sir . . . ?" Unger felt his stomach sinking.

"The butter and coffee you steal from camp supplies and sell on the blackmarket." Haase smiled pleasantly. "I hope you're keeping an accurate account of the profits." He smiled again and closed the door in Unger's face.

Haase walked to his desk and sat, motioning Karl into an arm-chair. "Did you see the look on that insufferable pig's face?" Haase said. "It made my day."

Karl placed the shoe box on the edge of Haase's desk, and his cap and gloves atop the shoe box. "If you dislike him so much, why keep him around?"

"It's too much trouble to get rid of him."

"Plus the fact that he gets things done, eh? Listen, I hope you're free for dinner?"

"Of course," said Haase. He pointed at the shoe box. "But that is another gift for Lieutenant Conway?"

"It's the least I can do for him."

"You haven't brought him a woman yet," Haase said. They had jocularly discussed this at Karl's last visit, after spending several interesting hours at "38," as the Koenigstrasse brothel was popularly known. Karl said it would be a humanitarian gesture.

"I've been thinking about that," Karl said. "Do you recall our argument, our exchange of drunken philosophy? Debating the futility of war: men slaughtering each other, men supposedly civilized, well educated, who without their respective uniforms couldn't be told apart."

"I recall it vividly. And I still maintain I'm correct: our species is endowed with some genetic flaw that makes war a necessity. An evolutionary necessity, if you will."

"I was getting at something else," Karl said. "That morning, as I was leaving, you claimed that no matter what uniform a man wore, a knowledgeable person could discern the man's nationality from various facial characteristics and mannerisms. You claimed it was possible to go into a steam room and know who was German, who was a Slav, an Italian. Do you stand by the statement?"

"I do."

Karl said, "Suppose I tell you that most people are so stupid and unobserving that an enemy soldier could walk in front of them in his own uniform, and no one would pay him the slightest attention. No one would give a damn!"

"That's absurd, Karl, and you know it."

Karl lit a cigarette. He did not offer Haase one; the major did not use tobacco. He exhaled slowly and watched the smoke curl toward the window. "I'll bet you two hundred marks and dinner that I'm right."

"How would you prove it?" Haase asked, and continued immediately, "Oh, no! I see where you're going. No, Karl. I'm stone sober and so are you. Forget it."

"We'll let Lieutenant Conway stroll the streets of Magdeburg in his own blue French army uniform," Karl said. "I say no one will pay him the slightest attention, not even the police. Two hundred marks." Karl slid four crisp fifty-mark notes from his billfold and slapped them on the desk. "We'll even give him a night on the town. Is it a bet?"

"And how does he explain it to the first policeman or MP who arrests him?" Haase asked lightly. He could not believe Karl was serious.

Karl said calmly, "We—you and I, Bruno—we'll walk a few feet behind Conway. If he's stopped, which won't happen—and I'm willing to back up my conviction with two hundred marks—then we'll come forward and simply say that we're escorting the prisoner into the city for medical care."

"You're crazy," Haase said, but he spoke quietly and almost contemplatively. The "crazy" idea was not unappealing. Nor was two hundred marks. Plus a dinner. "You're trying to trick me," he said. "You'll insist we do it at night when a strange uniform is less likely to be noticed."

"We'll do it at twelve noon, if you like."

"Early evening, when people are strolling the streets," Haase said. "The sun will still be high."

"Agreed," said Karl.

Haase hesitated. It had just occurred to him that Stalag A-12's prisoners were all well fed, unlike the half-starved POWS in other camps. The American's unfamiliar uniform might not attract that much attention. On the other hand, the odds were overwhelming that someone, an alert policeman or a soldier on leave from the front, would take notice and act appropriately. No, this was too good a bet to pass up.

"What makes you think Lieutenant Conway will agree?" he asked after a moment.

2.

Si saw Karl Eisler's car arrive. He had been walking the camp perimeter with a British Royal Engineer colonel. The colonel, a short, stout, red-faced man of forty, also saw the car.

"Your benefactor," said the colonel, whose name was Wallace Rowland and who walked with Si every day at this time, eleven in the morning.

"My 'benefactor' uses me as an excuse to visit his old friend, the major," Si said. "They like to get drunk and then go out and get laid."

"Quite," said Rowland, and increased his pace.

Si struggled to keep stride with Rowland as they passed the administration building and continued on around the perimeter. The little man was a fanatic on exercise and had literally ordered Si to accompany him on the brisk four-mile daily walks. He claimed it would strengthen Si's wounded leg.

"Sir, could you slow down just a little?" Si asked.

"Certainly not," Rowland said. "One of these days you and I will leave this camp. And we'll go all the way to Bremen, on foot. This is how you'll build up your endurance. Now stay with me."

When Rowland described Karl as Si's "benefactor," it was not said in derision, but in admiration and respect, and with good reason: Si shared Karl's gifts of liquor and food with the colonel. For his part, Si was pleased to share. He owed Colonel Rowland. From the moment Si arrived, the colonel had taken him under his wing. Si's total wardrobe had consisted of his flying clothes, including the mangled leather boot. Colonel Rowland ordered from his own Savile Row tailor (through the Red Cross) two French L'Armée de l'Air uniforms for Si, and from his Bond Street bootmaker, two pairs of black cordovan shoes. All items were delivered within twelve weeks (through the Red Cross).

But Si liked Rowland for himself. He considered Rowland, captured at Passchendaele while leading a night sapper mission, one of the few brass hats who really understood war and the soldiers he commanded. He was also one of the few prisoners who had flatly refused to give his word as an officer and gentleman not to attempt to escape. He accused the others of having lost their guts. Nearer the truth, as all realized, was that life in Stalag 12-A was too good. Why exchange it for the dirt and death of the trenches?

As they walked, Rowland chatted away, reminding Si of a scheduled German-language class that afternoon. But Si was not really listening. He was thinking about Paris, and Andrée. He had written her three letters, and all three had been returned, stamped *Destinataire Inconnu*. Addressee unknown, no forwarding address.

Si did receive some mail from Paris, however. One letter was from the American Ambulance Field Service in reply to a note he had written to Chip Taylor. The letter regretfully informed Mr. Conway of Cecil Taylor's death on March 25, 1918. Details on request. Painfully simple details, as Si discovered sometime later. Chip's ambulance, stalled at a crossroads, had taken a direct hit from a German 210.

Another letter was from Ledoux, who had learned of Si's capture through the Red Cross. Ledoux identified himself as the Spad pilot who had knocked down Eisler's Triplane. Si smiled when he read that. Georges Ledoux, he of the war of "chivalry." Believing Eisler about to gun Si down, Ledoux took the German out. Si wondered what the *capitaine* would think of Si's own "chivalry," risking his life to save Karl Eisler. Si himself found that one hard to believe.

After Karl's hospital visit, Si did not see him again until Stalag 12-A. On each of the previous two visits they had spent several hours together talking flying, and airplanes. They also shared a mutual interest in two other pleasures: food and women.

It was this that had inspired Karl to make the bet with Major Haase. With the winnings, Haase's money, Karl intended to treat Simon Conway and himself to a fine black-market meal and a night at "38."

As Karl anticipated, Si readily agreed to the "experiment," but with a condition: Colonel Rowland also must be invited. For all Karl Eisler's kindnesses and apparent good-fellowship, Si did not entirely trust him. Colonel Rowland's participation in the operation was a kind of insurance policy.

Rowland was only too delighted. If nothing else it would relieve the boredom. Major Haase was equally pleased. It doubled not only the stakes, but also the chances of winning: one officer in an unusual uniform might be overlooked, but two were almost certain to attract attention.

At Haase's instruction, Unteroffizier Unger issued the necessary papers for the prisoners' "medical examination," and that very same evening the four drove into Magdeburg in Karl's open touring car. The chauffeur pulled up at the porticoed entrance of the city's finest hotel, the Brandenhof. Although it was after seven, the sun was still high, the day as bright as at midafternoon.

The hotel doorman, a white-haired army veteran, saluted the car's occupants, four officers. Two of the officers were immaculately uniformed in conventional field gray; the other two wore strange but remotely familiar uniforms. One, the youngest of the four, wore a parade-ground-fresh blue uniform and pillbox cap that resembled those sometimes worn by Frenchmen.

The doorman nodded his thanks for the coin placed into his gloved hand by the one-armed officer, whom he vaguely recognized as an occasional hotel visitor. He ushered each officer through the revolving doors with a crisp salute.

Karl nudged Haase and whispered in his ear, "Round one for me, Bruno."

The spacious atriumlike marble-floored hotel lobby was bustling. Bellboys, none older than twelve, rushed back and forth among guests and their visitors, who sat chatting and drinking. Many of the men were in uniform, all officers. Many of the women were young and attractive. Here and there, among the potted rubber plants and ficus trees, small children darted about.

Si felt as though he had just been rescued from a desert island. He inhaled deeply. The sharp smell of tobacco blended with the musky odor of perfume and powder into an intoxicating aroma all its own. He wanted to gather it in his arms, immerse his entire body in it, wallow in it, die in it.

Karl led the group across the lobby to a quieter corner. He addressed Si and Colonel Rowland. "Now, gentlemen, for exactly one hour you may stroll about freely. You may visit the bar if you like. You each have been given twenty marks for that purpose. The time is now seven-ten. If, at any time during the ensuing hour, you are recognized as Allied officers . . . the contest is immediately over." He nodded at Haase. "With Major Haase the winner. At eight-ten, should you remain unrecognized, I am the winner. At all times, Major Haase and I will be in sight."

Haase said, "Questions?"

There were none.

"All right, lads," Rowland said impatiently. "Let the games begin!"

"One moment," Karl said. "I must ask both of you to give me your parole not to attempt to escape or behave in any other manner that might prove embarrassing to Major Haase and me."

Instantly, Si said, "You have my word."

Karl looked at Rowland. The colonel hesitated. Si knew exactly what he was thinking: a more promising escape opportunity might never again arise. For one terrible moment Si feared that Rowland's code of ethics would prevent him from giving his word and he would simply tell the Germans to go to hell. The delightful prospect of roaming about the hotel, drinking at the bar, being treated like a human being—plus the grand prize: an evening at "38"—all began disintegrating in front of Si's eyes.

But Rowland said, "Yes!" It sounded more like a groan. "Yes, dammit, you have my word!"

3.

Unteroffizier Unger loved driving the staff car, a twelve-cylinder Daimler, sturdy as a battleship yet as responsive as an airplane, or as responsive as he imagined an airplane to be. He rolled the big car through the predawn empty Magdeburg cobblestoned streets, turned into Koenigstrasse, and pulled up in front of number 38.

Major Haase had ordered him to be outside the building at 5:30 A.M. From past experience Unger knew this meant a wait of at least an hour. By the time old Lefty untangled himself from his companion of the evening and staggered out to the waiting car, the sun would be high in the eastern sky and the shops and cafés would be open. The *Hausfrauen* would be queued up at the bakery or at the butcher, hoping against hope a pound of bread or scrap of meat might be available. The civil populace of Germany was starving.

Unger did not like to think about that. He felt guilty enough about his black-marketeering, which reminded him of Haase's snide remark yesterday. The arrogant bastard was probably helping himself right now to a fast farewell fuck. In a house as swanky as "38" the women were so attractive that even in the morning you wanted a shot at them.

Thinking of the women at "38" infuriated Unger. Nearly a year ago those bastard officers had declared "38" off-limits to other ranks. Unger lit a cigarette, inhaled, and angrily shook out the match. One of these days he would simply walk into the place and demand service. He took another deep drag and settled back to wait.

In "38" a few hours before—to be precise, at 2:45 A.M.—Simon Conway had been listening to a love song about a woman waiting for a soldier she knew was never coming back but for whom she had promised to wait. The German lyrics spewed tinnily from a black cellulite Victrola speaker horn across the room. Si understood the words easily, which was not surprising. When you are drunk, foreign languages come easily because you do not bother to concentrate on translating the words.

And he was drunk—was he ever—but not half as drunk as Colonel Rowland. The two, Si and Rowland, each wearing only their underwear—silk, no less, courtesy of Rowland's Savile Row haberdasher—were in the opulent sitting room of the brothel's Shanghai Suite. The decor was appropriately Chinese, even to the dragon-emblazoned wallpaper. A door at each end of the sitting room opened on separate bedrooms. Two floor lamps encased in imitation Ming vases dimly illuminated the room.

Si sat on the floor, his back against the wall, an open champagne bottle propped between his knees. Twenty feet away, Rowland lay on a divan, his head nestled in the lap of a huge Valkyrian blonde. The girl, whose name was Monika, was dressed as a maid. Her "uniform" was a black lace frilly cap perched atop her flowing yellow hair, a black silk band supporting two of the biggest but firmest breasts Si had ever seen, and a matching black apron. Below the apron, which covered only the curve of her belly, she was naked.

The voice from the Victrola stopped, replaced by the clicking and staticky hissing of the revolving turntable. Rowland waved a limp hand at Si and said, "One of us should get up and turn it off, don't you think?"

"To hell with it," Si said.

"I agree," said Rowland. "Nice way to fight a war, eh, laddie?"

Si raised the champagne bottle in reply. It was a Moët & Chandon '11, rich with sparkly flavor and dry as powder. Four other bottles, empty, were strewn about the room.

"Where's your lady?" Rowland asked.

"Off giving aid and comfort to the enemy," Si said. His lady, a slender brunette named Trudi, had excused herself some time ago to visit the adjoining suite, the Adlon, occupied by Karl Eisler and Bruno Haase and their two escorts. He had not discouraged her from leaving; she had all but exhausted him. But he thought he was ready to go again; he might be inspired to rise to the occasion.

Si and the others had arrived at the brothel immediately after finishing dinner at the Brandenhof, compliments of Major Haase, who had lost the bet. Haase had never had a chance. For one hour Si and Colonel Rowland had roamed the hotel, strolled about the lobby, and drunk beer and schnapps in the bar. The only person who gave them even a second glance was an elegantly dressed, elderly, white-mustachioed gentleman; he believed the two Allied officers were members of a theatrical troupe. The old man had looked Rowland up and down, sourly noting the well-tailored khaki uniform, shaken his head sadly, then prodded Si with the tip of his cane and said, "For shame! Instead of play-acting, why aren't you in the trenches with the rest of your countrymen?"

If that was pleasant, the dinner that followed was positively ecstatic, the Brandenhof dining room echoing with talk and laughter and the music of a string orchestra, and enveloped in that dizzying odor of perfume and powder and femininity. And the food had been a two-star meal, courtesy of the local black market. A salmon mousse for appetizer. An entree of *Kalbsreisfleisch*, braised veal and rice. For

Rowland lowered Monika to the floor. "If you're going, Simon, you'd best move!"

On the floor, Monika stirred. Si said to Rowland, "What'll you do when she wakes up?"

Rowland said, "Whack her again, I suppose."

Si opened the door and looked up and down the corridor. No sign of life. "Thanks, colonel," he said.

"Good luck, laddie," Rowland said.

Si stole quietly along the plush-carpeted corridor to the landing. Halfway there, he realized he had forgotten Eisler's pistol and holster. To hell with it, he thought, and continued on to the stairs to the parlor.

A sliver of morning sun seeped through the drawn window drapes of the dark and empty parlor. The place resembled a disaster area. Bottles and half-filled glasses were strewn everywhere, the ashtrays overflowing with cigarette and cigar butts. The room reeked of rank tobacco and stale whiskey.

Si strode to the foyer and started opening the heavy mahogany front door, then stopped. It had just occurred to him that once he stepped outside in this German officer's uniform he was an escaped POW who could well be shot on sight. But he had come too far to stop. There was no turning back.

The street, lined with huge linden trees, appeared empty. He hurried down the flagstoned walk to the wrought-iron gate. Only after he had swung open the gate did he see the staff car parked at the curb and, at the wheel smoking a cigarette, Unteroffizier Erhard Unger.

Unger heard the gate hinges squeak. He tossed the cigarette away and scrambled from the car to open the door for the officer who had just emerged from the house. A captain, Eisler. Unger wondered where Haase was. He clicked his heels and saluted.

"Good morning, Herr Hauptmann—" Unger's voice trailed off as he faced Eisler. It was not Eisler. It was Eisler's Yankee friend, the POW.

Erhard Unger's first reaction was regret at not carrying a sidearm. Major Haase disapproved of Stalag enlisted personnel wearing weapons outside the compound. The second thought was gratification that this spoiled-child plan of Haase and Eisler's to "entertain" the POW had obviously turned into a fiasco.

All this occurred to Unger within the millisecond of recognizing the American POW in Eisler's uniform. Another instant passed as the two studied each other. In the American's eyes Unger saw his own expression reflected, an expression of total comprehension and therefore acquiescence. Intuitively, Unger knew no harm had befallen Eisler. But where was the other POW, the English colonel?

Unger suddenly wanted to laugh. He wanted to ask the American about the colonel, and at the same time he saw himself, in his mind, turning around and walking back to the car. He saw himself sitting in the front seat, smoking a cigarette, waiting for his commanding officer, the same commanding officer who only the previous day had accused this loyal subordinate of having a big mouth that someday would land him in the shithouse. Well, when the details of a certain POW's escape became known, it would not be Erhard Unger in the shithouse.

By the time Unger's brain had digested all this and transmitted orders to the appropriate muscles to turn and walk back to the car, to ignore what he was seeing, Simon Conway had himself turned and was walking away.

Unger stood quietly and watched.

Si walked fast but with no panic. He turned the corner and vanished. Unger returned to the car. He got in, lit a fresh cigarette, and stared at the deserted street. He, Unteroffizier Erhard Unger, had never seen an American POW in a German uniform. He had seen nothing.

5

Emma Guedhuis's late husband, the deputy postmaster of Arnhem, Holland, had adored the way his wife braided her long black hair into chignons over each ear. He especially enjoyed helping her take it down in the evening, she seated at the dressing table mirror, he standing behind her, slowly and fastidiously unfastening each braid, then joining the two sections into one. He loved burying his face in that satiny smoothness; he said it was like immersing himself in strands of black gold.

She was forty-three, childless, a big woman in every sense of the word, taller than the postmaster, who was not a short man, and outweighing him by some thirty pounds. When they made love she preferred the top position, which a doctor once said might have been the cause of her infertility.

At forty-three, widowed, she had no intention of disproving the doctor's theory. Which was why, at seven o'clock on this morning of November 8, 1918, she sat atop Simon Conway, straddling him, her thighs spread wide, her knees bent, her buttocks resting against his knees. It felt as though his whole body was inside her.

"Don't move!" she whispered in Dutch. "Stay still!" It was a command for him to remain completely motionless while she slid up and down against the huge pole inserted into her. It provided her the control she needed to time her approaching climax to his. She could feel him pulsing inside her. Beads of perspiration formed on her upper lip and in the cleft of her chin. She closed her eyes and thrust faster. Long, smooth, steady strokes. Up and down, up and down. Her breath came in ever shorter gasps that became a series of staccato grunts that quickly changed to screams and moans that almost mimicked similar sounds from him.

"Now!" she cried, opening her eyes and staring down at him. "Now!" She heard him groan louder and felt his whole body stiffen and explode inside her and her own muscles contracting in a succession of spasms that electrified every nerve in her body.

She screamed, and then closed her eyes again and arched her back and leaned away from him, the whole upper part of her body bent nearly backward. For Emma—"Big Emma," as Simon Conway liked to call her in English—it seemed only an instant and it seemed forever, an interval in which she was at once grateful and ashamed. Grateful for the convenient presence of a man able to fulfill her need for a man, ashamed at the weakness of flesh and spirit creating such a need.

It had started one week after the day in August, three months before, when she agreed to take as a boarder into her home a young American soldier who had escaped from a German prisoner-of-war camp. With neutral Holland having limited facilities for interned Allied military personnel, escaped POW—at their respective government's expense—were occasionally billeted in private homes. The Dutch hosts also received a share of the meager salaries the internees might earn working in local farms or factories.

Not only could Emma use the money, $10 weekly, but her heart went out to the tall good-looking boy who reminded her of the son she never would bear. Besides, she was lonely and longed for the sound of a man's heels on the tiled kitchen floor or, as it soon was to turn out, the bleached hardwood floor of her own bedroom.

And when she heard his story, she knew that by taking him in she had done what any decent God-fearing Dutchwoman would do. The poor, brave lad's story sent shivers up and down her spine: escaping from that horrible camp and, in a German uniform, fearlessly boarding a train to Bremen and making his way to Bremerhaven and stowing away on a Dutch freighter.

Yes, Emma had done the only decent thing.

On Simon Conway's part, as the young American embassy official who periodically came down from The Hague to check on internees said, it was like falling into the proverbial tub of grease and coming out smelling like a tulip.

True enough, but Si had come out smelling like a tulip more than anyone realized. He had met Anthony Fokker. Daily, bicycling to his job at a small cheese-processing plant in the village of Zeenvenaar, five miles from Emma Guedhuis's house outside Arnhem, he passed a chocolate factory, a long low building in the center of a large field whose grass always looked fresh-cut and as smooth as a golf links fairway.

No chocolates were made at this factory. None ever had been or would be. For months now, as the German military position deteriorated, Fokker had quietly moved tools and material from his German factories to factories and warehouses in Holland. Rumor had it that he was here in Zeenvenaar, at the "chocolate factory," manufacturing a new airplane.

Each day, pedaling past the factory, Si always slowed up, hoping for a glimpse of Fokker, a chance to speak with him. One morning near the main entrance, hearing airplane engines high overhead, too high to be visible, Si stopped to peer up into the sky. A trim, well-dressed, sandy-haired man, also attracted by the sound of the engines, emerged from the factory.

He was young, not much older than Si, but Si knew immediately that it was Tony Fokker. He walked the bike over to him, not quite sure how to start the conversation. Fokker saved him the trouble.

Fokker pointed into the sky and, in Dutch, said, "A dogfight, obviously drifted over the lines. Three of them. Two Allied, one German."

"I'm sorry, I don't speak Dutch," Si said in English.

Fokker's eyebrows arched upward with surprise, but he repeated the statement in fluent English.

"No sir," Si said. "It's one Allied machine, two Germans."

Fokker listened carefully to the engine sounds. "You're right, one Allied plane, two Germans. You've had some experience, I see."

"Some," Si said, and introduced himself. "And you're Tony Fokker. We have a lot in common."

They chatted a few moments. Fokker, as Si anticipated, was impressed with his background and invited him into the "chocolate factory." Here, unseen by German eyes, Anthony Fokker was constructing the F-8, a giant twin-engined biplane designed to fly the Atlantic nonstop and win the £10,000 prize offered by the London *Daily Mail* for the first successful Atlantic flight. Although contest rules barred the entry of any enemy airplane, obviously no contest could be held until after the war, when, as Fokker said, there would be no enemies.

Si saw the F-8 that very first day in the factory, a low-ceilinged room half the size of a football field in length and some fifty feet wide. Illumination was provided by rows of naked electric bulbs hanging from the ceiling, which was a maze of belts and pulleys. Lathes, presses, and other machine tools anchored to the concrete floor occupied one entire side of the room. In the center, supported by a series of stout wood sawhorses, were the F-8's nearly completed fabric-covered wings and huge skeletal fuselage.

". . . as you see, there is no wood in the fuselage construction," Fokker had proudly explained. "The entire frame consists of metal tubing."

"I know the 'F' stands for Fokker," Si said. "What's the 'eight'?"

"For the eight passengers she'll carry."

"It looks big enough to carry eighty," Si said.

Fokker had replied, "For the time being, I'm satisfied with eight. All traveling in comfort, with parlor chairs and room to stretch their feet. But I have to put the plane into the air as soon as possible. The moment an armistice is signed, and that can be any day now, you'll see a dozen different people rushing to fly the Atlantic."

"Two thousand miles won't be easy."

"Eighteen hundred and eighty miles," said Fokker. "That's the distance from Newfoundland to Ireland. The prevailing winds are west to east, so it can be done. The British already have the machines for it. Not only does the Vickers Vimy have the range, but they've flown a Handley-Page bomber two thousand miles without stopping."

"And now there's the F-8," Si said.

"Yes," said Fokker. "Now there's the F-8."

Again, for Si, it was love at first sight. He decided then and there that if he did nothing else in his life, he would fly this airplane, the F-8.

Tony Fokker responded to Si's enthusiasm. He arranged for Si's work assignment to be changed from the thrice-weekly chores at the cheese-processing plant to four afternoons a week at the "chocolate factory," a task comprised mainly of engaging in endless discussions about aviation with Fokker and observing the F-8's progress. Si listened, observed, and learned.

He had also learned to use the F-8 to his advantage in a more earthly fashion. Unbeknownst to Emma Guedhuis, much of the credit for her sexual gratification belonged to the F-8. Si had trained himself to instantly think of the F-8, whenever Emma uttered the command "Don't move!"—to concentrate on it as Big Emma, riding him, soared toward her climax. And when at last she cried "Now!" Si closed his eyes and saw the F-8 flying into the air, her two engines pounding with a thunder that vibrated through the entire house and shook the very ground outside.

So now, months after that first meeting with Tony Fokker, as Big Emma rolled off him, the image of the F-8 remained vivid in Si's mind. They lay silently a few moments. Emma's fingers played over Si's stomach and down onto his crotch. She closed her fist around him.

"So small," she said in Dutch, and then in German. "*Der kleine!*" She leaned up and kissed his cheek. "Can you do it once more, darling?"

"I have to get up and go to work," he said.

"So you'll be a few minutes late," she whispered, and he felt her beautiful hair trailing silkily over his chest and belly, and then she had engulfed him with her mouth. The F-8 flew off into the clouds.

An hour later, wearing a peacoat and denim trousers—trousers courtesy of the International Red Cross, peacoat courtesy of the late deputy postmaster—Si rode into Zeenvenaar on his bicycle. A Daimler touring sedan was parked near the main entrance of the chocolate factory, the only car in sight. The front license plate—black numbers, 4386, on a white background—was unfamiliar to Si. In the town of Zeenvenaar there were not a dozen automobiles, including Tony Fokker's white Mercedes roadster. The Daimler did not belong here.

Si could make out the figure of a derby-hatted man behind the wheel, but the frost-streaked windshield obscured the man's features. Two workmen on bicycles pedaled past the parked sedan. They paid no attention to the car or its occupant.

Inside the car the man, whose derby hat was a pearl-gray color that did not match his dark-brown suit and brown silk tie, watched the two bicycles turn the corner. The moment they were out of sight, he removed a Luger from his suitcoat pocket. He drew back the pistol's breechblock and slammed a cartridge into the chamber. Then he slid over to the passenger's side and opened the door. He stepped onto the sidewalk and confronted Si.

"Good morning, Lieutenant Conway," Karl Eisler said quietly. He jabbed the Luger muzzle into Si's stomach. "Get into the car, please."

2.

On the Dutch side of the border, an immaculately uniformed customs officer stepped out of the kiosk and flipped a cigarette into the dirt-encrusted snowbank piled along the road. He gazed blandly over the candy-striped barrier to the barrier on the Aachen side of the frontier. It was the sanguine gaze of man content to be where he was and not on the German side where, at the customs shed, some half-dozen men milled aimlessly about.

These men wore civilian clothes or various combinations of civilian clothes and field-gray army uniforms or blue naval uniforms. All had rifles slung over their shoulders and red armbands wrapped around their left sleeves.

A quarter mile away, from the rear seat of the Daimler touring sedan, Karl Eisler observed the same scene. Karl sat directly behind Si, the muzzle of the Luger pressed into the back of Si's neck. Si had driven the Daimler all the way from Zeenvenaar, and the car, engine idling almost silently, was now parked on a narrow side road.

"All right, so what do we do now?" Si asked. His breath formed a little cloud that fused onto the windshield like a rainbow-colored smear.

"We wait," said Karl.

"It's cold," Si said. "We'll freeze to death, for Christ's sake!"

"I said we wait."

"Jawohl, mein Hauptmann!"

"You won't find this so amusing when you're in a disciplinary barracks, believe me."

"You're kidding yourself, Eisler," Si said. "You'll never get across that border."

"I'm taking you back," Karl said. "Dead, or alive, and which way makes little difference to me."

During their three-hour drive from Zeenvenaar, Karl had made it quite clear that he would not hesitate to shoot his prisoner rather than allow him to escape again. Karl had suffered considerable embarrassment and reproach because of Simon Conway.

Karl had entered Holland from Aachen two days before, and planned to reenter Germany at the same border crossing. But the regular customs officials had now been displaced by the rifle-carrying civilians with the red armbands.

They were Revolutionary Guards, deserters and mutineers from the German army and navy who roamed the countryside, looting and killing. In some parts of the country Revolutionary Guards were shooting officers on sight. Civilian clothes were no disguise. Two days ago, at great personal risk, accompanied by an Imperial General Staff colonel and another officer, Karl had left Berlin and driven to Aachen. The streets were deserted except for occasional small groups gathered on corners or in front of shops whose empty display windows contained only crudely printed signs proclaiming "No meat," or "No bread," "No vegetables," "No coal," "No firewood."

Germany was starving, and freezing. Not even the army was adequately fed, an army that each day seemed to disintegrate further. Wholesale desertions, entire units mutinying. The country verged on revolution and anarchy. The nation's rulers no longer ruled. The very nature of the mission that brought Karl Eisler to Holland—to select a suitable residence in Holland for Kaiser Wilhelm should his majesty decide to abdicate—was evidence of that.

Diplomacy was hardly Karl Eisler's forte, but he had enthusiastically volunteered for this particular mission, and not out of any concern for the Kaiser's welfare. Karl had his own good reasons. Or, more accurately, reason singular.

Simon Conway.

Karl was determined to apprehend and return to Germany the escaped POW. The man of no honor, who had broken his word of honor and set off a chain of events that had resulted in Karl's being relieved of command of Jasta 24 and very nearly court-martialed. Karl was spared that disgrace only through the efforts of the officer who replaced him as Jasta 24 commander. That officer, Hermann Göring, a captain with twenty-seven aerial victories, managed to quash the whole nasty business, readily admitting that he had done this not from any altruism or camaraderie, but simply because he needed Karl in the squadron.

In any event, Karl was determined to take Simon Conway back to Germany and personally hand him over to Bruno Haase, who would then personally deliver the recaptured POW to the disciplinary barracks at Torgau. Completing the circle.

If he lived to be a thousand, Karl would never forget that morning at "38" when he had awakened to find that the American, his erstwhile "friend," had broken his word and escaped. And, adding insult to injury, in Karl's own uniform.

Karl had unhesitatingly assumed full responsibility. His written report stated that he alone escorted the prisoners into Magdeburg. A slight distortion of the facts rather than an outright lie. It served to absolve Haase. After all, it made little sense for them both to face a court-martial.

Ironically, it was through Anthony Fokker that Karl discovered Si was in Holland. In a letter to Karl regarding modifications on the D-8, Fokker's new monoplane fighter, Fokker mentioned meeting an interned American, an escaped POW and a Lafayette Escadrille pilot. Quite a remarkable young fellow, Fokker wrote. Clearly, the "remarkable young fellow" had not revealed to Fokker the details of the escape or the identity of those involved. So Simon Conway had demonstrated at least that much decency. Karl suspected Simon was himself ashamed of the incident.

Then, a week ago, Karl learned that the Dutch government had offered the Kaiser refuge, and that Colonel Erich Westenfeld had been ordered to travel to Amerongen, Holland, to negotiate the matter. Amerongen was a few miles from Arnhem. If Colonel Westenfeld needed a guide, Karl was his man. Karl said he knew the countryside like the back of his hand, which was a gross lie, but a careful study of a map made it almost true.

On the pretext that Anthony Fokker might be of assistance, Karl obtained Colonel Westenfeld's permission to visit his old friend in nearby Zeenvenaar. Karl's intention, of course, was to apprehend Simon Conway and return him to Germany. But now, with Revolutionary Guards patrolling the border, that would not be so easy.

Si read Karl's thoughts. He laughed. "Why don't you give yourself up to the Dutch?" he said. "Maybe they'll put you in with me. We can share a room. Fokker's a friend of yours. He can arrange it."

"You would do well, Conway, to stop talking."

"Listen, you damn fool, I'm serious. Stay here with Fokker and me, and help with the F-8. You've never seen the F-8. You won't believe your eyes. She's the most beautiful thing in the air!"

"Save your breath. I'm taking you back. All right, let's go."

"Go where?"

"To the border."

"You're crazy!" Si said. "First of all, I don't have any papers."

"We won't have to stop on this side," Karl said quietly. "The Dutch will wave us right through. They don't give a damn who leaves the country. Between the two barriers you'll start accelerating. When you reach the German side you'll break through the gate and keep moving. Now do it!"

"Go and fuck yourself, captain," Si said. "You understand what that means? Fuck yourself!"

"I have nothing to lose, Conway. If those guards stop us, they'll probably shoot me—and you, too. If you don't do as I say, *I'll* shoot you!" Karl tapped Si's jaw with the Luger. "Drive."

The Dutch customs officer raised the barrier and saluted the car's occupants as they raced past. He lowered the barrier and started back to the kiosk. The car had not slowed up to enter the German side, where two Revolutionary Guards stood at the barrier waving it down.

In the car, Karl shouted at Si, "Faster!"

Si aimed the Daimler's silver-plated winged "D" radiator ornament at the red-and-white striped barrier, hoping the barrier was wood, not steel. He jammed the accelerator to the floor. The men at the gate stared at the car hurtling toward them and then, simultaneously, dove to safety.

The Daimler struck the barrier at radiator level. The barrier was metal, but hollow and only the thickness of a flagpole. The big car snapped it neatly in half and raced on into Germany. A bullet from a guard's rifle shattered the rear window. Shards of glass showered Karl's head and shoulders.

Si swerved wildly to follow the road around a sharp bend. The wheels straightened but then slid sideways over a patch of ice. Si swung the wheel hard in the direction of the skid. The car continued sliding another instant, but then rolled onto dry asphalt and straightened.

"Where are we going, for Christ's sake?" Si yelled.

Karl did not answer. He glanced through the smashed rear window at the empty road behind, then faced forward again. Ahead, a farmer's horse-drawn cart plodded along the left shoulder. They roared past the cart so fast that the elderly driver had to grasp his cap to prevent it from flying off. Beyond the trees and hedgerows lining both sides of the road the terrain became large open farmland.

"Where are we going?" Si asked again.

"We'll be in the city in few minutes," Karl said. "We'll be safe."

"Safe from what?"

"Those socialist pigs—"

Karl never completed the sentence. Si had just steered the car around another sharp curve and onto ice again. The angled front tires caught on the ice and lost their traction. The car flew across the road. It caromed off the shoulder, teetering on two wheels as it skidded along the snowbanked roadside, and smashed head-on into a large tree. The impact burst the car doors open and pitched both men out into a row of hedges.

Abruptly, all was silent but for the hissing of steam from the cracked radiator. Far in the distance a dog barked impatiently. It sounded very loud and insistent to Si, who lay on his back staring up at the darkening sky. He felt no pain, which at first he believed was a sure sign of serious injury. But then he wiggled his toes, flexed his fingers, and felt the cold wetness of the snow under his hands.

After a moment he grasped the brambled hedge and raised himself to a sitting position. At the base of a nearby tree he saw Karl's Luger, and Karl groping for it. Si reached for it but Karl was faster. He snatched up the pistol and leveled it at Si.

"Get up."

Si rose unsteadily. He took a deep breath, then another. No ribs broken. "You really are crazy," he said. "All right, so now what?"

Karl got to his feet, keeping the gun trained on Si as he backed toward the car and retrieved his overcoat and derby hat. "Now we walk into the city and find an army garrison."

"That might not be as easy as you think," Si said. He pointed at the road, at a motorcycle approaching from the east, from the city.

It carried two men, one in a sidecar, both wearing red armbands. A machine gun was mounted on the prow of the sidecar.

"They're coming from Aachen," Karl said. "They won't know what happened at the border."

Si laughed harshly. "They'll still shoot us."

"They'll see the car and stop. We'll be behind the shrubs." Karl nodded toward the hedgerows and patted the Luger's muzzle. "They'll never know what hit them."

"Neither will we," Si said, indicating the road. A truck was following directly behind the motorcycle. At least a dozen men with rifles slung over their shoulders stood in the open truck bed.

"Those scum!" Karl said in German. "All right, we'll just have to take our chances. Maybe I can bluff them." He realized Si had not understood and repeated it in English.

Si looked at him, and then at the motorcycle and the truck, which were almost at the road bend where the wrecked car would come into full view.

Si said, "They don't know where we came from. I can say I'm an escaped POW trying to get *into* Holland." He reached into his shirt for the string that held his oblong French dog tags. He jingled the disks. "It'll work!"

"And I?" Karl said. "Who will I tell them *I* am?"

"You don't tell them anything!" Si said. "You won't be here!" He pointed at the hedgerow. "Get down behind the hedges!"

Karl did not hesitate. He plunged through the hedgerow and fell to his stomach on the other side. Si walked back to the Daimler. He leaned against the fender and waited for the motorcycle and truck to arrive. Just as the vehicles swung over to the roadside Si noticed a huge gap in the section of hedgerow that concealed Karl. The shrubbery had not sprung back into place after Karl went through it.

There was nothing Si could do. The motorcyclists got out and confronted him, while two of the men from the truck began poking about the staff car. One motorcyclist, a thin, cadaverous man of middle years, spoke enough English to comprehend Si's story. Si talked fast and convincingly. He identified himself as an escaped POW, his civilian clothes "borrowed" from a farmhouse outside Aachen. He said he had seen the car parked at an Aachen restaurant, keys conveniently in the ignition. So, hoping to reach Holland, he simply got in and drove off.

One of the guards who had been examining the Daimler said in German, "It's a staff car."

The other laughed. "I wish I could see the pricks' faces when they come out to find it!"

The English-speaking guard was staring curiously at the gap in the hedgerow. Si called over to him, "If you're going to the border, I'd like to go with you."

The guard looked away from the hedgerow long enough for Si to further distract him by repeating the request. The guard translated Si's words for the others. All agreed to allow Si to accompany them. What the hell did they care? As far as they were concerned the war was over. Si was no longer their enemy. Not only would they escort him to the border, they would show him a place he might cross unobserved by Dutch frontier guards. Once inside the country, the Dutch would be forced to intern him.

"Yes, I heard they did that," Si said. "I heard they interned escaped prisoners of war."

He climbed into the truck with the others. The convoy started off. Si, knowing Karl had seen and heard everything, flipped a casual salute to the hedgerow. The men thought he was saluting the abandoned Daimler. They all laughed.

3.

Holland was so small that from nine thousand feet Si thought it seemed possible to see the whole country. The green of the fields, blending with the whites and reds of the tulip beds and the crisscrossing blue lines of the canals, all resembled a vast multicolored quilt, not unlike the quilt on Emma Guedhuis's bed, hand-sewn and of the finest eiderdown.

Si had promised to have supper with her this evening. He had seen her only three times since New Year's Day 1919, five months ago, when he moved into his own flat at Zeenvenaar.

Seven months had passed since the war ended and Tony Fokker had obtained special permission from the Dutch government for Si to remain in Holland. Seven months of grueling but eminently gratifying work, seeing the F-8 become a reality and himself an integral part of that reality. Under Anthony Fokker's tutelage, Si had received an education he considered worth more than ten Massachusetts Institutes of Technology. He learned about engines, and aerodynamics, aircraft design, and aircraft construction.

Every waking minute was spent either planning the Atlantic flight, flying the F-8, or modifying the airplane after each test. And Fokker had begun relying more and more upon Si to supervise the project. Fokker was beset with other, equally important business in the form of Allied inspection teams intent on confiscating and destroying the hundreds of airplanes and engines he had smuggled out of Germany before the Armistice.

Well, everyone had his problems, Si thought, which brought to mind Karl Eisler. The man was a fool. If he had listened to Si and remained in Holland, today he would probably be working with Si on the F-8. Neither Si nor Fokker had heard a word of Karl since that afternoon at Aachen.

Andrée, too, had vanished. Si had finally stopped writing her. All his letters had been returned, stamped as before, *Destinataire Inconnu.*

Now, at ten thousand feet, he locked the throttles and listened carefully to the engines, first the left one, then the right. Both sounded smooth and steady. He raised his goggles to read the glass-enclosed instrument gauges fixed on the inboard nacelle of each engine, the fuel and oil-pressure gauges and rpm indicators. All were in the green. The needle of the airspeed indicator on the cockpit instrument panel held steadily at 200 kilometers per hour, 120 mph.

At this altitude in the open cockpit, exposed to the icy wind and cold air, with two heavy wool sweaters under his leather coat and two pair of wool socks inside the lined flying boots, he should have been uncomfortable, yet was not. How could you be uncomfortable in so perfect a machine as the F-8? And someday, in the enclosed cabin below his open cockpit, eight passengers would be seated in their wicker chairs, snug and secure.

He removed his hands from the wheel. The big airplane flew serenely on through the clear May sky. He put her into a gentle left bank, then again released the wheel. Immediately, the F-8's wings straightened and she flew straight and level. Si flew another few minutes, hands off, then banked around to the original course.

"Beautiful!" he shouted aloud into the wind. "You are beautiful! The most beautiful lady in the world!"

This was Si's fourth test flight in the F-8 and, at three hours, the longest. If the fifth and final flight went well, the F-8 would be crated, loaded aboard a fast steamer, and shipped to St. John's, Newfoundland. Then, the second or third week of June, thousands of feet above the same ocean, the airplane would return to Europe with Simon Conway at the controls.

And win the *Daily Mail* contest.

£10,000, winner take all.

He flew another thirty minutes before heading back to the field at Zeenvenaar. Now, painted on the roof of the "chocolate factory" were huge black letters: FOKKER VLIEGTUIGENFABRIEK, and an arrow tipped with N for north. Plans were to eventually illuminate the sign.

Si nudged the wheel gently forward. He throttled back and lined the F-8's nose with the wind sock at the edge of the field. He came in over the grass, working the throttles to maintain constant stability, although he knew that big and strong as she was, this airplane was so stable she could virtually glide in.

He flared out, allowed her to continue floating an instant, then felt the wheels skim the ground. He raised the nose ever so slightly and closed the throttles. The airplane touched down and began rolling. Si eased back farther on the wheel to lower the tail. The tail skid had just thumped onto the grass when he felt the right wheel sink. It happened so fast that he was unable to apply power to pull up. The right wheel's oleo struts snapped with the sound of a matchstick breaking. The entire wheel assembly collapsed.

Si slammed the master ignition switch to off and spun the control wheel left to raise the right lower wing. It was too late. The wingtip caught on the grass. The right engine plowed into the ground. Chunks of grass and dirt chewed up by the propeller ricocheted off the fuselage's drum-tight fabric. The airplane careened wildly, whipsawing Si back and forth against the canvas safety belt strapped around his hips. He saw people running across the field toward him and wondered how severely he would be injured and if someone knew how to administer first aid and who would break the news to Tony Fokker. The airplane swung around in a violent, almost 360-degree turn and came to an abrupt, shuddering, stop.

Si sat slumped forward against his safety belt. His whole body ached. But he was conscious, and only stunned, and knew he was not seriously injured. What concerned him most was how to explain the accident to Fokker.

"Explanation?" Fokker said. "The explanation is a flawed section of wood in the main undercarriage spar. I don't hold you responsible, Simon. And it will delay us only a week. Perhaps not that long. The damage wasn't extensive, thank God."

They were in the sitting room of Si's apartment. It was the evening of the crash. Si was resting uncomfortably on the divan, nursing his bruised ribs with a bottle of good Dutch gin. The flat, on the second floor of a bakery on Zeenvenaar's main street, was quite pleasant. It had a tiny kitchen, a bedroom, and a sitting room overlooking the little canal that ran through the center of town. Fokker paid the $6 weekly rent, which he deducted from Si's $80 monthly wage.

"And thank God you weren't injured," Fokker said.

"Believe me, Tony, God had nothing to do with it. It's called 'luck.' "

"Yes, I would say so," Fokker said. He wrinkled his nose and sniffed curiously. "Something smells good."

"*Erwtensoep*," Si said. "A gift from my former landlady." *Erwtensoep*, a national Dutch dish, was a porridge-thick pea soup that Si had become quite fond of.

Not two hours before, Emma, hearing of the crash, had dashed to Si's flat with a huge serving of her own special *erwtensoep*. Si had once enthusiastically described Emma's version of the dish to Albert Mansveldt, Fokker's chief machinist, who knew the lady. Mansveldt had remarked that Emma's "special recipe" sounded a little too spicy for conventional *erwtensoep*. Knowing Emma, he said, she probably peed in the soup to give it flavor.

Fokker had stepped into the kitchen and sampled a ladleful. "Very good," he said, and tasted another portion. "Exceptionally delicious."

"Tony, listen to me, please," Si said. "You know that Alcock and Brown are ready to make the Atlantic flight. They're in Newfoundland, and the newspapers say they're only waiting for the weather to clear. You say we might be delayed a week. We may not have a week."

"Simon, a half-dozen others are also ready, or almost ready, including those four U.S. Navy flying boats. Even if the F-8 was repaired today, we need at least two weeks to pack it on a ship and get it to St. John's. Stop worrying. Whether we win the prize or not, we'll still fly the Atlantic."

Si said nothing. It was not the British team of Alcock and Brown that worried him. It was the Americans in their four new Curtiss flying boats, the NC-1, NC-2, NC-3, and NC-4, the "Nancies." He, Simon Conway, wanted to be the first American to make the flight.

". . . so take a few days off until the plane is repaired," Fokker was saying. "You've earned a vacation. Go to Paris and have a good time."

Early the following morning Si was on the Amsterdam-Brussels express. At Brussels he boarded the Paris train and arrived at the Gare du Nord shortly before two in the afternoon. Nothing had changed. The glass-domed railway station echoed with the same impatient clamor of people coming and going and the ear-piercing shrillness of locomotive whistles. The porters were still as rude. The air reeked of strong tobacco and garlic. It was Paris. It was wonderful.

After exchanging $40 worth of guilders into francs at the railway station's Crédit Lyonnaise kiosk, Si took a taxi straight to Andrée's hotel on Rue d'Odessa. The one-armed concierge still sat dozing in the battered mohair armchair in the tiny *bureau*. His memory was fading. He did not recall Si, but certainly remembered Andrée. A man she was in love with had been killed, an American, a flier. The poor girl had packed all her belongings into a small valise and gone away. Two years ago—or was it three?—and no one had seen or heard from her since.

Si tucked a ten-franc note into the old soldier's vest pocket and left. In the mirrored column of a restaurant facade on Boulevard Montparnasse he caught a glimpse of himself. A tall, well-built young man wearing a brown wool suit whose coat was too tight and sleeves too short. The suit, purchased ready-made several months before from an Arnhem tailor, had seemed to fit nicely when he first tried it on, although certainly not as well as the handsome uniforms made for him by Colonel Rowland's Savile Row tailor. Si often wondered what had become of the colonel. Home in England, hopefully.

When he reached the corner of Rue du Lambre, Chez Denise was exactly as he had last seen it two years before, the scripted white letters CHEZ DENISE in a wide semicircle at the top of the plate-glass window, the paint of the D slightly faded, the window curtained at the bottom half with the same neat but fraying velvet curtain of an indeterminate dark color, and the same tarnished brass curtain rod. He half expected to hear the piano, and Andrée's voice.

But no sounds came from inside the café. The room was dark and empty. Si did not have to try the door to know it was locked. Through the dust-grimed window he saw the four barstools stacked upside down on the bar. Tables were lined against the wall in rows of two, each table placed top down atop the other, chairs piled haphazardly in the center of the room in the space once occupied by the piano.

He walked away. He walked aimlessly for blocks. Every café and bistro he passed was loud with American voices. With the Peace Conference underway, the city was filled with American tourists. He was hungry and thirsty, but he did not want to stop anywhere. He did not know what he wanted; he knew only that Paris was suddenly a very lonely place, and that he had left nothing here, only memories. You cannot drink with memories, you cannot talk to them, and you certainly cannot make love to them.

The instant Si saw Tony Fokker he realized something was wrong. He had sensed it when he phoned Fokker from Paris to tell him he was cutting short his Paris vacation. Fokker had asked, "What's wrong? Aren't the girls in Paris wet and willing anymore?" But the humor was forced. Si knew Fokker's mind was elsewhere.

Fokker met Si in Amsterdam and drove him back to Zeenvenaar

in the Mercedes roadster. The summer day was perfect for the three-hour drive with the tonneau down. But, again, as on the telephone, Si sensed something ominous. Not until they stopped for lunch on the Utrecht road at an inn Fokker said served the best *rijsttafel* outside Djakarta did Si even begin to learn what was wrong.

". . . the bloody Allied commission," Fokker said. "The bastards caught up with me!" And Fokker went on to explain that, as Si knew, Article IV of the Armistice terms called for all Fokker D-7 fighter planes to be destroyed.

All the careful and clever scheming that had brought six train-loads of airplanes and engines from Germany was undone. One hundred and twenty D-7s and four hundred engines had been seized last week by the Allies.

"The whole kit and kaboodle," said Fokker. He paused, as though unsure of his use of the phrase. "Everything."

"You expected it," Si said.

"When you say you 'expect' something," Fokker said, "you really are saying you hope it won't happen."

Si knew all about expectations. He had left his in a vacant café in Paris. He forced his thoughts away from Paris. He wanted to discuss the possibility of redesigning the F-8's oleo struts with a new metal alloy of incredible strength and lightness called Duralumin.

". . . so, Simon, I felt I had no choice. I had to destroy her. It killed me; it was like murdering one of my own children. But if it had to be done, I wanted to be the one to do it."

Si leaned across the table. "Are you trying to tell me you destroyed the F-8? You *destroyed* it?"

Fokker nodded. "Last night. I ordered it doused with gasoline. I soaked a rag with more gasoline, lit it, and tossed it into the cockpit—"

"—but why?" Si asked, almost shouting. A woman at an adjoining table glared at him.

"I told you why," said Fokker. "The Allied inspection team ordered me to turn the airplane over to them no later than noon today."

"So you torched it instead?" Si wanted to seize Fokker by the shoulders and shake him. At the same time he wanted to believe it was a joke, and that Fokker would grin and confess the truth.

"I'm sorry to have to tell you this way," Fokker said. "But you had to know."

"Why didn't you ask me?"

"Why didn't I ask you? Am I supposed to consult with you before I make a decision, Simon?"

"I could have flown it somewhere. They wouldn't be able to find it."

"Simon," Fokker said patiently. "The airplane had no undercarriage. Remember?"

No, Si thought, but did not say it. No, I did not remember. I forgot that small item. Instead, he said, "It's too late to start all over again. By the time we built a new one somebody'll have flown the Atlantic."

"There won't be any new one," Fokker said. "Not for a while at least. The Allies have informed the Dutch government that any attempt by me to manufacture airplanes or airplane engines will be considered an unfriendly act. So I'll retool the Amsterdam factory for . . ." he smiled sourly, trying to think of something witty. "For lawn mowers," he said. "And the Zeenvenaar plant for eggbeaters. Fokker Eggbeaters. What are you planning to do?"

Now it was Si's turn to smile sourly. "Is that a nice way of saying I'm fired?"

"I have nothing for you."

"In that case, I resign."

But Si had already decided his next move. He had heard of hundreds, thousands, of surplus airplanes in the States that could be picked up for a song, DH-4s. The Liberty-engined bombers were big enough to convert into freight carriers. He would start with one, make enough money with it to buy and convert another, and then another. In no time the airplanes of Conway Air Transport Service would cover the continent.

On June 10, 1919, he sailed from Le Havre on a French Line ship named, appropriately, *Lafayette*. Thanks to Tony Fokker's generous $1,000 severance gift, Si treated himself to a $212 first-class cabin, although for the amount of time he spent enjoying the deluxe service he might as well have gone steerage. He remained in his cabin most of the voyage, working at a makeshift drafting board, planning various design features for the DH-4 conversion. The whole concept excited him even more than flying the Atlantic with the F-8.

On the 15th of June, two days out of New York, he saw a typewritten notice posted on the *Lafayette* radio officer's door:

WORD JUST RECEIVED THAT BRITISH FLIERS CAPT. J. W. ALCOCK & LT. A. W. BROWN IN VICKERS VIMY MACHINE SUCCESSFULLY CROSS ATLANTIC FROM ST. JOHN'S, NEWFOUNDLAND, TO CLIFDEN, IRELAND, IN TIME OF 18 HRS, 12 MINS.

A great achievement for them, he thought, a failure for Simon Conway. But if Simon Conway was not the first to fly the Atlantic, he would be the first to fly freight and passengers across the American continent.

Conway Air Transport Service. He spoke the words aloud, to the wind, and to the water. Conway Air Transport Service.

It sounded good.

6

Morris Tannen liked Los Angeles. The weather was never too warm or cold, and the air was crisp and clean with the scent of oranges and lemons. Nearly every day was bright and sunny, and even into late afternoon and early evening the sun continued to cast a golden glow over the sky. At night the city lights sparkled like diamonds in a jeweler's showcase.

Morris liked the small-town feel of Los Angeles, which was hardly a small town, although not nearly as big as his hometown, Detroit, and with none of that city's hustle and bustle or what they called its "dog-eat-dog" attitude. Nor, to be sure, Detroit's dirt and grime. Here in Los Angeles, from the palm trees that lined the streets of Beverly Hills to the moving-picture palaces on Hollywood Boulevard, everything was fresh and immaculate.

What constantly amazed Morris Tannen, however, was the extraordinary number of peculiar characters the city attracted. The customer to whom Morris was trying to sell a new pearl-gray fedora on this October afternoon in 1920 was a perfect example.

The man, who claimed to be a pilot, had come in initially for a pair of trousers. His old ones, he said, were simply worn out from sitting day after day in his plane, flying it across the country.

"So what do you think?" the customer, who was Simon Conway, asked. He slanted the fedora's brim low over his eyes.

"The way you had it before is better," Morris said. He adjusted the hat to rest half-perched on the back of Si's head. "It gives you a nice Angeleno look."

"Yeah, not bad," Si said. "What the hell is an Angeleno look?"

So Morris explained that Angeleno was the way Los Angeles

residents referred to themselves, and meant a kind of easygoing style of living, although this tall lantern-jawed young man seemed anything but easygoing. He reminded Morris of the lumberjacks up in Oregon in the days before the war when he traveled around the lumber camps selling clothes from a wagon.

". . . Angeleno?" Si was saying. "Okay, from now on call me an Angeleno."

"You're in good company, believe me," Morris said. "Listen, how about a nice work jacket to go with the pants? I can give you a terrific buy on a corduroy. This leather one of yours is too good to be wearing in the plane all the time. You want to take care of it." He fingered the sleeve of Si's leather jacket. "Genuine cowhide. I bet it cost a pretty penny."

"Three plane rides," Si said. "I picked it up off a farmer in Des Moines. He swapped it for rides for himself and his two grandsons. Don't worry, this is the only jacket I'll need for a long time. It'll last forever."

"Hey, my friend, nothing lasts forever."

"Can I write that piece of advice down?"

"Sure, and remember where you got it, and that it was free. All right, so what about the hat?"

"How much?"

"Take the hat, I'll throw in a shirt. Seven bucks for the lot."

"With the pants?"

"Sure, with the pants. Believe me, I'm not making a dime on it. But it looks so good on you, maybe you'll tell your friends."

Si laughed. "If I had any friends. Okay, I'll buy it." He pulled some loose dollar bills and a handful of change from his pocket. Four dollars and seventy-five cents. He fished in the other pocket. It was empty. He smiled ruefully and removed the hat. "I guess we'll have to forget the hat."

"That's all the money you have?"

"For right now." Si handed Morris two one-dollar bills and a fifty-cent piece. "I'll just take the pants."

Morris returned the hat to the display case. He felt bad for the man, but business was business. He folded the trousers onto some thin brown wrapping paper on the counter, folded the paper once, then again, tied the package with string, and presented it to Si.

"There you are, my friend."

"Thanks," Si said. He tucked the package under his arm and started out.

"Hey!" Morris shouted. "Where'd you say your plane is?"

Si, almost at the door, stopped. "I think they call it Gilbert Field," he said. "No, Gilmore, that's it. Gilmore Field. Not far from here."

"I know it," said Morris, who did indeed know it and considered the area a most valuable parcel of land, a large grassy field on the corner of Wilshire Boulevard and Fairfax Avenue. "I almost bought half of it instead of this store."

"You sound sorry you didn't."

"I am," Morris said. He plucked the hat from the display case and brought it over to Si. "Make you a deal," he said. As he spoke he was thinking, You schmuck, what the hell are you doing? Ruth will kill you! But the words kept coming. "You give me a ride in this plane of yours, we'll call it even." He placed the hat on Si's head, tilting it back at the angle he knew Si liked. "Okay?"

"Okay," Si said.

Later, whenever he thought about that airplane ride, Morris Tannen always had to laugh at his own lack of foresight, at his failure to realize how the sudden impulse to fly was to change his life. At the time, he explained it to himself as "tempting fate," although he was careful not to use that phrase in explaining it to Ruth. A woman five months pregnant with their first child could hardly be expected to understand a husband's "tempting fate."

Morris's father, a tailor, had settled in Detroit after fleeing the Russian pogroms of 1891, and within three years owned his own small but increasingly prosperous tailoring business. Morris, who served as his father's apprentice, continually exhorted him to open a retail outlet, but the old man refused. He was satisfied and grateful to God for what he already had.

Morris was also grateful to God, but wholly unsatisfied. At twenty-one, with $500 and his father's best wishes, Morris traveled west to Northern California, then up into the lumber country, where on Saturday nights the men who worked all week in the camps poured into town and spent their entire wages on liquor and whores. It was obvious to Morris that if someone went from camp to camp selling the men items they needed, from playing cards to dry goods, a modest but steady profit might be realized.

Indeed, in three years Morris had saved nearly $4,000 and might have amassed twice that sum had he not been drafted into the army during the war. Not an especially cruel twist of fate, for in the army, serving as a Signal Corps telephone switchboard operator at Fort MacArthur, he discovered Los Angeles and, at a Young Men's Hebrew Association dance, Ruth Progelman.

One week after the Armistice they were married and three months later, for a cash price of $3,500, he purchased the small two-story building at 224 West 6th Street. Two one-bedroom flats were on the second floor. Morris and Ruth occupied the larger apartment, which had a dining room. The other apartment was rented to a young lawyer, Philip Granger. On the ground floor, formerly an apothecary—the chemical odor of medicines and pharmaceuticals were ingrained in the walls—Morris opened the Manhattan Shop, a men's haberdashery.

Men's clothing was not what Morris wanted to devote his life to, and after that first airplane ride with Simon Conway he confided to Ruth that in aviation he saw his real future. She, in turn, suggested it was not aviation that intrigued him so much as Simon Conway himself.

"He's what you'd like to be," she said. "A dashing American gentile, a genuine war hero."

Ruth had discerned all this on that very first day the two men met. Morris had brought Si home for supper after the airplane ride. One look at the *goy*, and Ruth knew what he was and why Morris was so enchanted.

She had made *kasha varniskes*, one of Morris's favorite dishes: buckwheat groats and onions fried in chicken fat, then mixed with bowtie noodles.

"You know, this isn't bad," Si said, after his first taste. "What'd you say it was? Kosher varnish?"

"*Kasha varniskes,*" Morris said. "Famous old Jewish dish."

"Jewish food, eh?" Si said. "Not bad at all for Jewish food."

Ruth glowered at Morris. She said to Si, "Have you had much Jewish food, Mr. Conway?"

"Call me Si, won't you, please?" Si said. "No, no I can't say as I have had much of it. I like it, though."

"I'm so glad," said Ruth. She decided she truly loathed this man and regretted setting out the good china and the genuine Towle silverware and her only linen tablecloth on the bridge table in the tiny dining room.

". . . matter of fact," Si was saying, and paused to swallow down a mouthful of groats. "As a matter of fact, I think Morris is the first Jew I've seen since I left my hometown as a kid. I knew a lot of them there, though."

"With or without horns?" Ruth asked.

"Excuse me?" Si said.

"Ruth likes to make jokes," Morris said with an admonishing

frown at Ruth. "You were telling me about this air-service idea of yours. What'd you call it, an 'airline'?"

Instantly, Si's whole demeanor changed. He pushed his plate aside and sat forward to face Morris. " 'Airline,' that's right. Like 'steamship line' or 'rail line.' "

Morris said to Ruth, "Si wants to start an air service between here and Frisco. Carry mail and passengers."

"And freight," Si added.

"Si says an outfit in the Midwest is flying on a regular schedule between Cleveland and Detroit," Morris said.

"They call themselves Aeromarine Airways," Si said. "They're using flying boats."

"Flying boats, Ruth," said Morris. "What do you think of that?"

"It sounds fascinating."

If Si caught the sarcasm in Ruth's voice, he never showed it as he went on to describe in detail how he had spent the past year barnstorming his way across the country.

What truly disturbed Ruth was the way Morris hung on every word. She held the bowl of *kasha varniskes* out to Si. "Si, would you like any more of this Jewish food?"

"No thank you," Si said and, without missing a beat, continued talking to Morris. "I think a Los Angeles–San Francisco market, the business potential, is even better than a Boston–New York service would be."

Ruth said, "I'll fix some dessert and coffee." She got up and started to collect the dishes. "You do drink coffee, Si?"

Si rose to his feet. "Oh, sure."

She smiled tightly. "It's Jewish coffee."

Si returned the smile. "Then I'll love it."

Ruth felt herself redden. The bastard was trying to make a fool of her. She strained to think of a clever retort, and almost said, Yes, I thought you might like Jewish coffee. Simon is a Jewish name, isn't it? Instead, she forced another smile and said, "Why don't the two of you make yourselves comfortable in the living room. I'll bring in the coffee."

She gathered the dishes and went into the kitchen. She stacked the dishes in the sink and turned on the faucet. The tepid water flowing over her hands calmed her. For God's sake, she told herself, be rational! You are jealous of someone who is able to attract your husband's intellectual interest. So far, in fourteen months of marriage, their main topics of conversation had been—in order of importance—the baby, finances, and food. Once, just once, they had discussed next month's Presidential election. More accurately, she had tried to provoke a discussion. She told Morris she thought Woodrow Wilson's illness had seriously damaged the Democrat's chances. The Republicans, with Harding and Coolidge, would win in a landslide. He told her not to be silly, the country needed to continue its postwar recovery under the same administration, and then asked what was for supper.

From the living room she heard Morris's almost obsequious voice; and Si's, brisk and confident, but in that damn New England accent that sounded like chalk grating on a blackboard. Now, Ruth, she told herself, try to be pleased that Morris has found a friend. A man needs another man for a friend.

Her self-advice lasted all of ten seconds. From the living room she heard Morris say, ". . . all right, so how much will it cost me?"

"Five thousand will get us started," she heard Si say.

Morris's response was as loud as though shouted from the roof-top. "Sounds good to me, by God!"

Ruth slammed the dishes into the dishpan and rushed into the living room. Morris and Si were on their feet, shaking hands. Ruth wiped her hands on her apron and said, "Morris, what's going on here?"

For a moment Morris appeared flustered. But then his face tightened defiantly. "I've just made a business deal with Si," he said.

"Business?" Ruth said. "What business?"

"The aviation business. Tell her," he said to Si.

Si also seemed momentarily flustered. Ruth said, "Well, so tell me."

"Just what Morris said." Si pulled a cigarette from the package of ready-mades in his shirt pocket. "Do you care if I smoke?"

"Smoke, who cares?" said Ruth. "What's this about five thousand dollars?"

Morris said, "That's how much we're investing in—" He paused and plucked a cigarette from Si's pack. "In 'Conway Aviation Industries.' That's what we're calling the company."

"What about the five thousand?" Ruth asked.

"I told you," said Morris. "That's how much we're putting into it."

Ruth sank into an upholstered wing chair. " 'We'?" she said. She patted down the lace antimacassar on the arm of the chair. It did not match the divan, but Ruth planned to make slipcovers for all the furniture from a book of patterns she had sent away for. " 'We'?" she repeated. "Well, maybe you'll be good enough to tell me where 'we' are getting five thousand dollars?"

"From the store," Morris said.

"Have you looked at the account ledgers lately? 'We' have a balance of two hundred dollars and sixty-four cents."

"I can mortgage the building," Morris said.

Ruth's stomach tightened. For a frightening instant she thought it might be the baby. No, not at five months. It was fear. And anger.

". . . opportunity I've always wanted," Morris was saying. He continued talking, but Ruth could not concentrate on his words. Morris, you fool, she kept thinking. You dreamer! Then she became aware of a different voice addressing her, Simon Conway's.

". . . we'll manufacture our own airplanes for our own airline. And then we'll build them for other airlines. The aircraft business today is like the automobile business was twenty years ago. Morris is from Detroit, he knows."

Morris knows, she repeated to herself wryly. My God, they only met a few hours ago and this person acts as though he and Morris are lifelong friends. She wanted to stand up and tell Simon Conway to get out of her house and out of her life.

". . . people that made fortunes in automobiles were the ones that got there first," Si was saying. "Mrs. Tannen, I know what I'm doing. I know how to make this thing go. It's all I've thought about since I was a kid. I'm telling you, we'll end up owning the whole goddam world!"

Ruth heard her own voice. ". . . don't want to own the whole goddam world, Mr. Conway. I only want to be happy, and my child to be happy." And my husband, she thought, although she did not say this aloud. She adored Morris, and knew of his secret frustrations and ambitions. As clever and shrewd as he was, he wanted whatever it was that this man offered, and he would not be content until he had it.

Looking at Morris, at the expression on his face as Simon Conway talked—probably the same expression that was on the Apostles' faces when Christ talked—she knew she had no chance of bringing him to his senses. She had never seen him so enthused, and she did not have the heart to discourage him. A good wife went along with her husband, no matter what. But my God, mortgage the store? It was all they had in the world.

". . . don't want to spend the rest of my life selling clothes," Morris was saying to her. "I like selling, you know that, and that's why Si and I make the perfect team. He'll build the planes and fly them while I go out and get the business." In the same breath he said to Si, "I have an idea how to advertise cheap. We print up some ads on paper the size of regular stationery, and we give them away at the railroad station." Morris outlined an eight-by-eleven rectangle with his hands.

" 'Tired of the long, uncomfortable train ride to San Francisco?' it'll say. 'Then, next time, fly!' And on the bottom it'll say, 'C-A-T-S, Conway Air Transport Service.' " He turned to Ruth again. "How does that sound?"

She said, "C-A-T-S spells 'cats,' Morris."

"That's right," he said. "Makes it easy to remember."

"All this because he gave you a ride in a plane?" she asked. "One plane ride and you're an expert?"

"One plane ride, Ruth, and I'm a believer!"

"I see," she said. "You had a vision. Mr. Conway, I don't mean to be rude but I'd like to talk privately to my husband."

"Oh, sure," Si said. "I'll just take a walk around the block, how's that?"

"Frankly, I thought that you might come back tomorrow to continue your . . . business . . . with Morris."

Si looked at Morris. Morris said quickly to Ruth, "Honey, the fact is that I . . . well, I invited Si to bunk downstairs in the storeroom on that old army cot. He just got into town. He doesn't have a place to stay."

"Aren't the hotels in business anymore?"

Si said, "Listen, I'll be fine . . ." He moved to leave.

"He was going to sleep in the plane," Morris said.

"Under it," Si said. "Under the wing. I've done it plenty of times. Look, thanks for the supper, Mrs. Tannen. Morris, I'll talk to you tomorrow." And before Morris could say a word, Si swept his leather jacket and hat from the coat tree, clamped the hat on his head, and was out the door.

Morris and Ruth studied each other silently. "You don't know anything about aviation," she said finally.

"I know how to sell," he said.

"You meet a man, a total stranger, and you're ready to give him every dime we own?"

"I'm telling you, Ruth, I know what I'm doing!"

"If you're serious about putting money into this 'airline company,' and going out to get business for it, that means you're planning to make it a full-time job?"

"I think so, yes."

"What about the store? What about our bread and butter?"

"I was hoping maybe you'd take over."

"A woman in a men's haberdashery?" Ruth said. "How many times have you told me men won't buy from a woman, any more than women in a milliner's shop will buy from a man?"

"That doesn't mean it can't happen," Morris said.

Ruth patted her stomach. "And when the baby comes, I'll nurse him and sell a man a suit with two pair of pants at the same time?"

"We'll hire somebody."

Ruth nodded knowingly. "I'm tired, Morris. I'm going to bed." At the bedroom door she stopped and looked back at him. "The name of the company is Conway Aviation Company, you said?"

"Industries," Morris said. "Conway Aviation Industries."

"What happened to 'Tannen'?" Ruth asked. "Why isn't it Conway-Tannen Industries?"

"I never thought about it," he said.

"Well, think about it," she said, and went into the bedroom and slammed the door behind her.

2.

Simon Conway's journey across America to Los Angeles had begun sixteen months earlier on the rainy June Sunday in 1919 when the *Lafayette* docked in New York. He had barely stepped onto the pier when he discovered that his dream of Conway Air Transport Service was, temporarily at least, a pipe dream. A U.S. Army major greeted Si with the announcement that unbeknownst to him, just prior to his capture in 1918, he had been transferred into the U.S. Air Service and was still on active duty, with orders to report to Arcadia, Florida, for assignment as a flight instructor.

Ten months later—with the aid of a Congressional decision to reduce the size of the nation's armed forces and Brigadier General Billy Mitchell's personal intervention—First Lieutenant Simon Conway was allowed to resign his commission.

The time was not entirely wasted. Even on the meager army pay he managed to save almost $400. With the $600 remaining from the money Tony Fokker had given him, he had enough to purchase Conway Air Transport Service's first DH-4, although not nearly enough to convert the airplane into a two-passenger, freight-carrying machine. To tear the airplane down, rebuild it entirely, and install a new engine, he needed an additional $1,500.

The possible solution to that problem came on an impulsive visit to his hometown, Dustin, Massachusetts. Strolling along Merrimack Street, he passed a branch office of a Boston bank, the Massachusetts Bay Trust Company. He recognized the name immediately, and the name of its president, Burton Taylor, whose son was Si's late friend Chip Taylor, who had promised to speak to his banker father about Si's idea for a postwar aviation service.

Talk about omens.

Within two hours, after learning that Mr. Taylor was at the family's summer residence in Ogunquit, Maine, Si was on a Boston & Maine express to Portsmouth, New Hampshire. Shortly after five that same day he arrived in Perkins Cove, just outside Ogunquit, and a few minutes later he rang the front doorbell of the Taylors' three-story mansion.

The door was opened by a tall, willowy, fair-haired young woman. Before Si could introduce himself, she screamed, "Simon Conway!"

It was Chip's sister, Margaret, who pulled Si into the house and shouted for her mother and father to come meet Chip's best friend. They insisted he remain for the weekend, and that evening at dinner he entertained them with stories of the Lafayette Escadrille and his capture and subsequent escape.

"And now?" Burton Taylor had asked.

"Now, I start my own business, Conway Air Transport Service," Si had said, and described his plans for a New York–Boston mail and passenger service.

As he spoke, something in his voice changed. Something about him changed. Where before he had been easygoing and almost casual, suddenly he was grim and determined. He reminded Meg of William Jennings Bryan, the commencement speaker at her Vassar graduation last year. The former Secretary of State had delivered one of his famous hellfire-and-brimstone speeches. Simon Conway talked about airplanes with the same intensity Mr. Bryan spoke of God.

Meg found this new Simon Conway a little frightening, yet at the same time challenging. She knew a diamond in the rough when she saw one, and knew how to polish such a gem. Not change him. She wouldn't change him for the world, except to smooth out some of his bluntness and teach him to dress properly. Yes, if anybody could bring out the best in this man it was she, Meg Taylor.

On Si's part, in Meg Taylor he saw an attractive young woman, college-educated, self-assured and self-satisfied. He had encountered this "well-scrubbed" type of American girl before, in Paris as Red Cross or YMCA volunteers during the war and later, in Arcadia, as the wives of some of his brother officers.

In Paris he was of course involved with Andrée. In Arcadia, the few women who made their availability known were married. Fooling with a married woman did not seem worth the time and trouble. When you wanted to get laid you simply drove over to Tampa, to the Riverway section, and paid a visit to Mrs. Dodge's, the swankiest whorehouse in town and, at $10 a pop, the most expensive. But worth it.

But sex, at that moment at least, had been the farthest thing from

Si's mind, for he felt as though he had just found the key to the universe. It sat opposite him in the person of Burton Taylor, a heavy-framed, bushy-haired man who was every bit the typical Boston banker but, to Si, was a man of exceptional vision.

"You were Chip's friend," Burton Taylor said. "I'd like to help you if you need any help, and if I can."

The offer caught Si slightly off balance. He hadn't expected it to happen so fast, or so easily. A fragment of Burton Taylor's earlier conversation drifted into Si's mind. They had been discussing the Prohibition Amendment, which Burton Taylor considered an act of abject foolishness. Morality, he said, could not be legislated.

Morality.

The word disturbed Si. He knew he was exploiting his relationship with Burton Taylor's dead son, and that taking advantage of it was wrong. Or was it wrong to seize an opportunity? He was committing no crime, perpetrating no fraud. Besides, Burton Taylor was a businessman. Conway Air Transport Service would stand or fall on its own merits.

Si said, "As a matter of fact, sir, there is something I might need some help with."

"Name it."

"I told you about my idea for a Boston–New York air service," Si said, and quickly detailed his plan for purchasing and converting war-surplus DH-4s into mail and passenger carriers.

When Si finished, Burton Taylor had asked only two questions. The first question was "How much will it cost?"

The figure Si had decided on was $7,500. Enough for the airplanes, new engines, and even ticket offices and clerical help. Now he revised the amount. Why not go all the way?

"Ten thousand dollars," he said.

Burton Taylor's second question was "What do you have for collateral?"

Si was prepared for that question. "Myself," he said. "My own ability and confidence. What else do I need?"

"Give me a few days to think it over," Burton Taylor said, which Si knew meant yes. Burton Taylor simply did not want to make it too easy for Si.

That night Meg invited him for an after-dinner walk on the beach. They talked, first about Chip and then about her. Although she did not yet know what she wanted to do with her life, she knew what she did *not* want to do, which was marry the first boy who came along. In fact, she wasn't so sure she wanted to get married at all. She thought she might like to enter the banking business.

They talked for hours. Something about him—probably that he reminded her of Chip—drew her out. She told him things about herself known to no other human being, not even Chip. Her fears, her hopes, her fantasies. She told him these things, she said, because she wanted him to know her as she truly was, and because she knew she could trust him. He was Chip's friend.

For him, a whole new world began unfolding, a world of wealth and security, and a storybook romance: the budding industrialist marrying the beautiful young society woman. The prospect excited him, and so, suddenly, did Meg. She had tucked her arm tightly into his as they walked back to the house. He inhaled the fragrance of her hair and the vague scent of cologne from her body. He began fantasizing. He would steal into her bedroom and, not uttering a word, take her into his arms. The only conversation between them would be her whispered confession, "I'm a virgin . . . please be gentle."

By the time they reached the veranda he was hard as a rock. They started up the veranda stairs. Perhaps she wasn't a virgin after all, Si was thinking. These days college girls were pretty free and easy. The idea of being first in was really not appealing.

"Damn . . . !" Meg said, and at the same time Si heard a sound of fabric ripping. She had caught the hem of her long skirt on the metal edge of the mud scraper on the bottom veranda stair. The skirt was torn from the knee down.

"My fault," Si said. "I should have watched where we were walking."

"It's nothing. I'll have Irene fix it."

They faced each other in the dark a moment, and then Meg leaned up and kissed him, a gentle, affectionate kiss on the lips. She turned and hurried up the stairs to her room.

The kiss had sobered him and brought him back to reality. Certain as he was of her eagerness to have him—and he seldom misread this, he almost always knew—he also realized that out of respect for her, if for no other reason, this was neither the time nor the place.

You have performed a good deed, an act of nobility, he told himself, although it failed to ease the throbbing in his groin. Well, everything has its price, he thought, even nobility.

The house was very quiet, everyone was asleep, but Si felt wide awake. He was standing outside Burton Taylor's study, where, before dinner, Burton had invited him for a cocktail. Si opened the study door and entered the darkened room. Enough light came from the foyer to guide him to the cellarette. He found a decanter of brandy and a snifter. He poured himself a small drink, then another, and left.

And, in the foyer, nearly collided with the Canadian maid, Irene, almost knocking the kerosene lamp from her hand. "I came down to check the lights," she said.

Si had first seen her at dinner when she helped the cook serve. She was eighteen, from Montreal, employed only for the summer and, if not for the French accent, he might hardly have noticed her. She was not an especially pretty girl, narrow-hipped and small-breasted. Her eyes, though, were very interesting: big, blue, and expressive, with a message that could not have been any clearer had she delivered it in a telegram: "I'm yours. All you have to do is ask!"

He towered over her. She had to arch her head far back to face him. She wore a flannel bathrobe, tightly belted over a long white nightdress. Her black hair, down now, shone glossily in the flickering lantern light. The lantern flame also reflected those big blue eyes with the message.

Si said, "Where's your room?"

Five minutes later, in her third-floor room, his clothes strewn on the scatter rug at the foot of her bed, they lay naked under the brocaded quilt. She wiggled her body so that her hips were under his and spread her legs wider. She enclosed his erection in her fist and began guiding him into her.

"Oh!" she cried. "Oh, my God!" Her ecstatic moans completely muffled the sound of the door opening.

"I saw the light, so I knew you weren't asleep," said a woman who had entered the room. It was Meg. She walked toward the bed, the damaged skirt folded neatly in her hands. "I tore this and I want to wear it tomorrow—"

Si, on top of Irene, had twisted his head around so that he was looking straight at Meg. Even in the dim lamplight, Meg's face had turned a deep crimson.

Si recalled little after that, only Irene pushing him off her, and Meg muttering ". . . excuse me!" and the skirt tumbling to the floor as she rushed out. His only clear thought was the vision of a huge wind, a hurricane, devastating the countryside, sweeping into Boston airport, toppling a big sign atop a hangar, a sign that read CONWAY AIR TRANSPORT SERVICE. Each letter flew into the air and disintegrated.

It turned out to be a quite accurate vision. In the morning Meg Taylor told him not to bother waiting for her father's answer to his business proposition. The answer, said Meg, was a resounding No! She had seen to that. From spite, Si accused her. No, from common sense, she replied. Their words led to a terrible shouting match which reduced Meg to tears and achieved nothing for Si because, as he well knew, it was too late to salvage the wreckage.

It was like a curse after that, a jinx that followed him across the country. Instead of a DH-4, he bought a Jenny and barnstormed. A few dollars here, a few there. Airplane rides to farmers, recklessly foolish daredevil stunts, wing walkers, parachute jumpers, mock air battles with other former war aces. He had all but decided to fly up to Seattle and ask Bill Boeing for a job when, purely by accident, he landed at Los Angeles and met Morris Tannen.

Now, three months after the two had met, the Conway Air Transport Service sign that Si had envisioned actually existed, except that it now read CONWAY AVIATION INDUSTRIES and was stanchioned over the entrance of a small building on the southeast corner of an airport known as Mines Field, located in the Los Angeles suburb of Inglewood.

"Conair," Morris said.

The word meant nothing to Si. They were standing on the sidewalk across the street from the building with the sign. They had just had lunch at Skip's, the diner on Inglewood Boulevard. The so-called chili Si had bolted down lay in his stomach like a lump of lead.

"Conair," Morris said again.

"Morris, what the hell are you mumbling about?"

"Conair," Morris said. "That's what we call the company for short." He pointed at the sign. It was a large sign, if "sign" was a proper word for a brush-streaked plywood board ten feet long and three feet wide, positioned slightly off-center above the building entrance. On the board, which was painted white, large blue letters formed the company's name.

Paint ran down from the first two letters like blue tear drops, with the S in the last word slightly split. However, superimposed over this sloppy presentation was a flawless reproduction of the Conway crest: the American eagle in flight, talons clutching the letter C.

The crest was the work of a seventeen-year old Chicano street artist whose murals Morris Tannen had seen on the walls of several Olvera Street buildings. Morris, who himself had painted the sign's basic letters, negotiated a price of $5 with the artist for the crest. For another $3 the artist had offered to repaint the entire sign, but Morris demurred: the $5 already had strained the company budget.

Conway Aviation Industries, Inc., an enterprise duly incorporated in the state of California, capitalized at $5,000, had issued forty thousand shares of stock. Ten thousand shares were held by its president and general manager, Simon Conway, and nine thousand shares by the company's vice president and sales manager, Morris Tannen. Five thousand shares had been awarded to Charles Jensen, and five thousand more to Philip Granger. The remaining eleven thousand shares were held in reserve.

Charles Jensen was a thirty-five-year-old Delco Laboratories engineer whom Si had met in Dayton, Ohio, on a barnstorming stop. They had engaged in a long, spirited debate on the merits of water-cooled inline engines versus air-cooled radials. The size and payload of an airplane is limited only by the weight and power of its engine. Charlie claimed he could build an air-cooled Duralumin radial pulling more than 330 horsepower and weighing less than five hundred pounds. When Morris Tannen provided the money to form Conway Aviation Industries, Si offered Charlie Jensen a partnership.

Philip Granger, the corporation's secretary, was the attorney who rented the other apartment in the West 6th Street building owned by Morris and his wife. To be sure, Si was not pleased about giving Phil Granger so generous a share. But then again, no one had any money for legal fees. One hand washed the other. Moreover, Si and Granger were roommates. As part of the deal, Si bunked on Granger's couch.

They had purchased two DH-4s for $649 each from a Gilmore Field dealer, and now, in the company's third month of existence, the first DH-4—or 110, as the conversion model had been redesignated—was nearly ready. The airplane's forward cockpit had been widened and enclosed, both wings recovered and rerigged, landing gear strengthened, complete new instrumentation installed. All that was missing was Charlie Jensen's new engine, a nine-cylinder radial which Morris had christened the J-1.

"110" was also Morris's idea. One-one-oh, the number-one model of the first series. Si said it made no sense but sounded good. He, Si, couldn't care less what you called the airplane. Call it A or B, Tom, Dick, or Harry, just as long as it flew, and on or before January 28, five days from now, the promised date of delivery to its new owner, the U.S. Post Office Department, for a purchase price of $6,750. The narrowest of profit margins, and not a moment too soon. The company was flat broke.

All this was rolling around in Si's head as he and Morris approached the factory's narrow front door and Morris once more uttered the word "Conair."

"Conair," Si repeated. That's what you want to call us, Conair?" He spelled it aloud. "C-O-N-A-I-R?"

"C-O-N-A-I-R," Morris spelled back.

"You sure come up with these names."

"To be honest, Si, Conair was Ruth's idea."

Si stifled an impulse to say, How is she, that bitch on wheels? Instead, he asked, "How is she?"

Morris grinned. "Big as a house."

"That means it's a boy. All right, Conair it is," Si said, and walked into the factory.

The "factory," a long, low structure that had once been a roadhouse and dance hall, was owned by a Santa Monica dentist with whom Morris had negotiated a twelve-month lease at $75 a month. Inside, it stank of gasoline and oil, and engine exhaust fumes, and the bananalike odor of acetic acid from the layers of dope applied to the fabric of the wings and fuselages. One side of the room was crowded with bits and pieces of fuselages, propellers, wings, wheels, instrument panels, engine parts. In the midst of this was the partially assembled 110, lacking only its engine, lower wing, and tires for the wheels.

Conair's five full-time employees, two carpenters, two tinsmiths, and a seamstress, were busily at work. Si enjoyed watching them, the carpenters fashioning new wood wing spars, the tinsmiths molding aluminum tubing for the fuselages, the seamstress stitching the sheets of fabric together.

Near the windows, at the engine test stand, Charlie Jensen was tinkering with a J-1's carburetor. As Si approached, Charlie started the engine, and the whole room vibrated with the engine's roar.

Charlie Jensen was a slim, laconic Texan whose thick curly hair was totally white. Morris said that if Charlie grew a mustache he would bear a suspicious resemblance to the late Mark Twain.

"Sounds good, huh?" Charlie shouted happily.

Si listened a moment, then signaled Charlie to shut off the engine. "How many horses?"

"I'd say close to three-thirty."

"That's good enough," Si said. "Let's mount it and put this machine together and get her into the air."

"Only if it takes off without wheels!" said Morris, who had just joined them after checking the morning's mail. He waved a letter at Si. "A little love note from Thompson Rubber Company. Not only won't they deliver the four new tires we ordered, but they're suing us for a back bill of four hundred and sixty-eight dollars and twelve cents."

"Four hundred and sixty-eight dollars?" Charlie asked. "What the hell for?"

"All the custom work they did for us in designing the tires to our specifications," Morris said.

Si said, "Goddammit, Morris, you're supposed to take care of all that."

"The letter was addressed to you," Morris said. "It's been sitting on your desk for more than a week. I never knew a thing about it."

"Well, you should have known," said Si. "What the hell did I make you sales manager for?"

"You didn't 'make' me anything, Si," Morris replied. "I'm a partner, remember?"

"Then do your goddam job!"

"I can't read your mind. You get letters like this"—he crumpled the letter and tossed it at Si's feet—"tell me about them!"

"Hey, for the love of Pete!" Charlie Jensen shouted. He stepped between Si and Morris. "We're all 'partners'! We're all breaking our backs to make this thing go. So relax, huh?" He was addressing Si, who glared a moment at Morris and then relaxed.

"How serious is it?" Si asked.

"They've obtained a writ of attachment," Morris said. "Unless the bill is paid by seven A.M. on the twenty-sixth—that's the day after tomorrow—they'll serve it. On you personally, Si. That means they come in and take the planes and everything else in here."

Si turned to Charlie. "How long will it take to mount the engine?"

"A day," said Charlie.

"Then we're okay," Si said. "I'll fly the airplane up to San Francisco first thing in the morning and turn her over to the Post Office."

"The tires, Si," Charlie said. "We don't have tires!"

"We'll get them. Stop worrying," Si said.

Charlie said, "Si, even if we found the four hundred and sixty-eight bucks somewhere, they'd still want cash for the new tires."

Si looked at Morris. It was a reflex. He expected Morris to have the answer. Morris said, "I've got an idea."

The Thompson Rubber Company factory and warehouse was an ornate three-story building occupying an entire block on the northeast corner of Washington Boulevard and Pacific Avenue in East Los Angeles. The night watchman, a fifty-four-year-old retired policeman from Milwaukee named John Mueller, had come west in hope that the warm weather would relieve his arthritis. It did not, a fact of which he was uncomfortably reminded this chilly evening after completing the first of his nightly rounds.

He sat in the little office adjacent to the main entrance on Washington Boulevard, his legs propped up on the rolltop desk. He held his hands out toward the wood-burning potbellied stove in the center of the room and began reading the *Los Angeles Record* which was unfolded on his lap. A front-page story caught his eye: John D. Rockefeller's pledge of a million dollars in aid for destitute Europeans. The whole idea of it infuriated John Mueller. Destitute Europeans? What about destitute Americans, for pity's sake?

Someone tapped on the glass windowpane of the office door. It was a woman, a very pregnant woman. Under the light of the single electric bulb fixed above the doorway, her face was tight with anxiety.

". . . wonder if I might trouble you for a glass of water," she was saying.

The woman looked as though she might pop any minute, a possibility John Mueller did not relish. But then, as the father of six children, he certainly appreciated the poor woman's situation. He opened the door.

"Come in," he said. "Sit down. I'll get you a glass."

"Thank you," said Ruth Tannen, and promptly fell to the floor in a dead faint.

Outside, as John Mueller directed his attention to the stricken woman, two men emerged from the shadows and stole into the warehouse. Immediately, the abrasive smell of rubber clogged their nostrils and burned their throats. The taller of the two trained a flashlight on the floor-to-ceiling storage shelves where thousands of tires of all sizes were lined neatly, but Si had been here before and knew exactly where to find what he wanted.

"Down here!" he whispered, shining the light on a shelf at the far wall. They started toward it. Si walked so fast that Morris nearly had to trot to keep up.

Si said something else, but Morris was not listening. He had clamped a handkerchief over his nose to keep from choking. His heart pounded with excitement. His whole body felt flushed. His mouth was bone-dry. He was committing a crime, the first of his life, and instead of remorse or concern he felt exhilaration and satisfaction. He only hoped Ruth could successfully carry out her part. When he had first proposed the idea of breaking into the factory she called him crazy. But he knew how to reach her. He told her that tomorrow, unless the 110 flew, they would lose their total investment. Everything. He knew his customers. Ruth agreed to do it.

"Yeah!" Si said. "I was right. These are ours!"

The flashlight was trained on four tires stacked separately. The tires were slightly smaller than automobile tires but with much heavier treads. Si and Morris each took two tires and, like schoolboys rolling hoops, maneuvered them across the floor.

In the night watchman's office, Ruth lay on the floor near the five-gallon water dispenser. Through half-closed eyes she watched John Mueller scurry about in search of a cup.

"Goddammit, there was all kinds of cups and glasses here the other day!" he muttered to himself. "Jesus Christ!"

Ruth was too angry to be frightened, angry at Morris and Simon Conway, who had put her into this ridiculous position, but more angry at herself for agreeing to be put into it.

". . . here, lady," John Mueller was saying. He had cradled her head in his arms, offering her water from the cup of his own lunchbox thermos bottle. "Here, please, drink this."

Ruth really needed water. The all-pervading odor of rubber from John Mueller's whipcord jacket was nauseating her. She opened her eyes. "Where am I?"

"Drink some water," John said.

"Oh, thank you," Ruth whispered. She drank some water. Her anger and nausea vanished, replaced with an almost irresistible urge to giggle. She had just remembered her girlhood ambition to become an actress.

Ruth Barrymore, she thought, and said to John Mueller, "I feel much better, thank you. You're very kind."

John said, "You're going to be fine, honest." He helped Ruth to her feet. From the window, Ruth saw Morris and Si rush past outside. She gasped. She clutched John's arm and swung him around away from the window. "My God, what is it?" John asked, alarmed.

Ruth clung to John another moment, then relaxed. "For a minute I thought my time had come." She patted John Mueller's hand. "I'll be on my way now. Thank you once again."

John opened the door for her. "You want me to call somebody for you, lady? Your husband?"

"Oh, I'm not married." Ruth patted John's hand again. "But if it's a boy, I'll name him after you."

"I wouldn't want you to do anything like that," John said. "Not on my account. Honest."

"God bless you," Ruth said, and left.

Thinking about it, though, John Mueller rather liked the idea of a child named after him. Only after he recapped the thermos bottle did it occur to him that the woman did not know his name and had never asked.

The same thought, at the same time, occurred to Ruth. Squeezed between Si and Morris in the front seat of Morris's Nash brougham as it raced along Pacific Avenue, she started to laugh. The four stolen tires were stacked in the backseat like enormous black doughnuts.

"I'm an actress!" Ruth cried. "Mary Pickford! I'm a regular Mary Pickford!"

"Mary Pickford, my foot!" Morris said. "Theda Bara, that's who you are! And Si and me, we're Doug Fairbanks and Jack Barrymore!"

Si slapped Ruth's knee. "You're all right, Ruth. In my book, you're all right!"

Ordinarily, this remark would have increased Ruth's dislike of Si. But she felt a certain unfamiliar warmth toward him. After all, they were co-conspirators in an exciting adventure. And an even more exciting adventure awaited her. She could feel the baby kicking.

"I can't wait to see that plane fly away tomorrow," she said.

"You'll see it," Si said elatedly, but he was not so sure. The night sky was heavy with thick, low-hanging clouds. "If the goddam weather clears," he added.

The weather did not clear. At dawn, when the 110 was rolled out onto the grass in front of the factory, the sky remained gray and ominous. Si knew it would not clear until early afternoon. It made little difference. He did not intend to take off until he was satisfied the new engine performed satisfactorily. He decided to wait a few hours before commencing a series of taxi tests.

Morris, Ruth, Charlie Jensen, and Phil Granger gathered around the 110. Morris said, "My God, but she's beautiful!"

And she was beautiful, a huge biplane, the mail and cargo area and the two side-by-side seats of the enclosed, isinglass-windowed passenger compartment just forward of the pilot's open cockpit. She was painted a sandstone brown, with the blue Conway eagle on the rudder, and even on this dull day her newly varnished wings and fuselage shone glossily. She exuded strength and power.

Ruth proposed a toast. "I christen thee . . ." She paused and looked at Morris. He shrugged. Ruth looked at Si. Si had no suggestion. Ruth gazed across the expanse of vacant land to the huge corrugated-metal dirigible hangars on the west side of Mines Field that had been erected during the war for the U.S. Air Service. No dirigibles occupied the structures, for none were ever built. On the domed roofs of the hangars gigantic black letters spelled out L O S A N G E L E S, C A L.

"*Pride of Los Angeles!*" Ruth said. She swallowed down the coffee in the paper cup she had been carrying and tapped the empty cup against the 110's fuselage. "I christen thee *The Pride of Los Angeles!*"

"The Pride of Los Angeles!" the others seconded.

"Okay, let's roll her back in and wait till—" Si started to say.

"Si!" Morris shouted in alarm. He pointed across the field. An automobile was lumbering toward them. Two men were in the car. One, leaning out of the passenger's side, waved a piece of paper. On the car's door white-painted letters spelled out U.S. MARSHAL.

"You said we had until tomorrow!" Si said to Morris.

Morris closed his eyes in dismay. "Maybe I got the dates mixed up."

"No, you had the dates right," Phil Granger said. "They're serving the writ now to make sure we don't skip!"

Si called to Charlie Jensen, "Let's get her the hell out of here, Charlie!"

As Charlie raced around to the front of the airplane, Si tossed his fedora into the open rear cockpit, vaulted up on the lower wing, and lowered himself into the seat. He put on his helmet and goggles, buckled his safety belt, and signaled Charlie to swing the propeller.

Charlie grasped the propeller blade. "Contact?"

"Contact!"

Charlie swung the propeller. It caught instantly. Charlie cocked an ear and listened, at the same time peering anxiously at the oncoming marshals' car. But Charlie could not repress an elated grin. The engine sounded beautiful.

Si pushed the throttle forward. The airplane began bouncing along the grass. Si lined up with the wind sock atop the factory roof and applied more throttle. The airplane rolled faster. Morris and Charlie, clutching their hats against the 110's propeller blast, ran alongside. Charlie pointed a thumb in the air. Si, who had reached the head of the oiled-dirt runway, gave Charlie a return thumbs-up, gunned the engine to wheel around into the wind, and began his takeoff roll.

The marshals' car was now only a few feet away and gaining. Si slammed the throttle to the wall. The 110 moved ahead sluggishly for a moment before picking up speed. She accelerated down the runway, faster and faster. Si eased the stick forward. The airplane's tail rose. Si nudged the stick toward him. The 110 flew into the air.

The marshal's car shot past underneath the airplane's still-spinning wheels. Si waved at the men in the car and continued climbing. He flew over a small grove of orange trees at the end of the field, banked around, and came back in from the opposite direction. The marshals' car had stopped in the middle of the runway. Two men scrambled out and stood shaking their fists at the airplane.

Si could not resist the temptation. He flew over the field once, turned, lowered the 110's nose and dove straight at the two marshals. The men gaped at the oncoming airplane, then flattened themselves on the grass. Si chandelled up and around, flipped the marshals a crisp salute, then eased the stick back and began climbing.

On the ground, Charlie Jensen said to Morris, "Well, Morris, it flies! It goddam good and well flies!"

Morris said nothing. He was gazing at the 110, now only a speck in the distant sky. He did not recall ever feeling so triumphant. He was not even fazed by the prospect of facing the two marshals. He could deal with them. He could deal with anything now.

He could even deal with fatherhood, an event which occurred two weeks later. On the same afternoon that the second 110 was to be delivered to San Francisco, an hour before Si took off from Mines Field, Ruth Tannen gave birth to a seven-pound-five-ounce boy.

The baby was not, of course, named after the hapless Thompson Rubber Company night watchman, but after Ruth's late father, Paul. Strangely, the infant interested Si almost as much as it did his father, Morris. Si never admitted this to anyone, nor did he ever admit that on the day of Paul's birth, landing at Bakersfield for refueling, he nearly flew the 110 straight into the ground. He was in a reverie, envisioning his own as yet unborn son. The boy would grow up tall and strong, with his father's love of the air and airplanes, and a natural talent for business as well. Together, father and son would build an empire.

Conair.

A dream, yes, but a dream Simon Conway knew would come true.

7

T he rain woke him, an early winter storm that sent the surf crashing up on the beach and rattled the hotel's windows. Si's room on the fifth floor of the brand-new Hotel Monica faced the beach. He had moved there nearly a year before, in late 1921, shortly after Morris Tannen persuaded a San Francisco investment banker, Ross Leonard, to loan Conair $45,000.

The money had enabled the company to expand into larger quarters and install a real production line. Shortly thereafter, with three new 110s, Conway Air Transport Service, CATS, initiated daily passenger and freight flights throughout California and as far east as Albuquerque, New Mexico, and as far north as Billings, Montana.

Although CATS continued to lose money, the U.S. Post Office Department had purchased six more 110s at $7,500 each, allowing Conair's manufacturing division in this 1922 third quarter to show a profit. Not much of a profit, $1,050.27, and certainly not enough to meet Ross Leonard's $45,000 note, which was soon to come due. But with the success of the 110, no one anticipated any difficulty renewing the note. In any case the "profit," such as it was, included all expenses, plus stock dividends for the executives in lieu of salaries—if you considered $120 a month an adequate salary. It paid the rent.

Si lay quietly in bed, listening to the rain and staring across the darkened room at the shaft of light zigzagging into the window from the electrically lighted hotel marquee. A lousy night to be flying, he thought, certain that the same thought occupied Freddie Silcox's mind. Freddie was flying a passenger to Salt Lake City tonight.

Frederick Silcox was tall and so lean it made you wonder when he had had his last decent meal. His black hair, always neatly pomaded, was parted in the middle, and his thin little mustache adorned a face that Morris Tannen said reminded you of a weatherbeaten fence. A former U.S. Post Office Department airmail pilot, Freddie certainly looked the part: helmet and goggles stuffed into the pocket of a long leather coat, whipcord riding breeches tucked into army puttees. He was the first pilot Si had hired and now, with five others on the payroll, functioned as CATS chief pilot under Si.

Si switched on the night table lamp and looked at his wristwatch. Five past one. He had been asleep at least two and a half hours. Freddie would already have landed at Las Vegas, refueled, and be halfway to Salt Lake City on the "errand-of-mercy" flight for which the passenger, California State Senator Kenneth O'Neil, was paying the premium price of $200.

Ken O'Neil was a big, bluff, disarmingly honest Irishman whom Si had first met seven months before at a ribbon-cutting ceremony celebrating the commencement of CATS Albuquerque service. He had phoned earlier that day asking Si to fly him to Salt Lake City. His twenty-one-year-old daughter, his only child, had smashed her car into a telephone pole and was not expected to live. Si, who had returned from San Francisco only an hour before and slept a total of two hours in the last twenty-four, had asked Freddie to take the flight.

Si turned off the lamp, lay back, and pulled the blankets up over himself. The naked warmth of the woman beside him felt good in the cold room. As though she shared the feeling, Ceil Bjornsted murmured in her sleep and nestled her head into the hollow of his shoulder. He loved sleeping with Ceil, with whom anything went, head to toe, with all the important stops along the way.

Thinking of Ceil brought Freddie Silcox to mind again. Freddie was crazy about Ceil. Ceil said she liked Freddie as a person, period. Si slipped one arm around her and, with his free hand, groped on the night table for cigarettes and matches. The movement wakened Ceil.

"What's the matter? What's happening?"

"Nothing," Si said. "Go back to sleep." He cupped his hand around one of her breasts and fingered the nipple, which immediately hardened. Ceil moaned contentedly.

"Oh, that feels so good!" she whispered. She kissed him. "What time is it?"

"Go back to sleep," he said.

"Are you kidding?" She kissed him again, her breath heavy with sleep but not at all unpleasant. Her tongue flitted into his mouth and then over his lips, and her hand slipped down to his stomach and onto his groin. In an instant he was hard, and in another instant she had slid over on top of him and inserted him into her.

"God, how I love to fuck in the rain!" she said, as she sat atop him and began pumping.

The phone rang.

At first Si thought the bell sound came from Ceil. She made so many strange noises when they made love. He felt her muscles tighten and himself locked inside her. The phone rang again.

"Don't stop!" Ceil screamed. "For Christ's sake, don't stop!"

He did not stop, nor did the ringing telephone. It kept ringing even as Ceil came and, an instant later, Si. For a long moment she sat motionless atop him. Then, with a loud sigh, she collapsed and rolled off.

Si picked up the phone. It was Freddie Silcox. He sounded angry. The thought crossed Si's mind that Freddie was calling to accuse Si of double-timing him with Ceil. Si had made Ceil swear never to reveal their relationship to Freddie. It would break Freddie's heart, and good pilots were hard to find.

". . . just too damn bad to fly!" Freddie was saying on the telephone.

"Where the hell are you?" Si asked.

"At the field."

"What field?"

"L.A.!" Freddie shouted over the phone. "I'm still here in L.A.!"

Ceil said to Si, "Who is it, honey?"

Si clamped his hand over the telephone mouthpiece and said to Ceil, "Go wash up, will you?"

"What for?" she asked.

"So you won't get pregnant, goddammit!"

Naked, Ceil tottered into the bathroom. She turned on the light and closed the door. Si said into the phone, "How long have you been there?"

"Since ten o'clock," Freddie said. "It's raining so hard we can't even light the runway flares."

"So park a couple of cars on each side of the runway and put on their headlights!" The runway was lighted at night by pouring gasoline into a series of trenches dug along each side of the runway and igniting it.

"You're not listening to me, Si," Freddie said. "The weather's bad all the way to Salt Lake. I just spoke to them again on the phone."

"So what am I supposed to do?"

"Senator O'Neil wanted me to call," Freddie said. "He wants to talk to you."

"Fred—" Si began. He did not want to talk to Ken O'Neil. The man's pleading voice made him uncomfortable.

But O'Neil was on the phone. "Si?"

"Ken, it's just too dangerous to fly," Si said. "You'll have to wait for the weather to clear."

"Si, please, I've got to get there to see her before . . . before . . ." O'Neil drew in his breath. "While there's still time."

Even as Ken O'Neil spoke, Si was envisioning an airplane flying in that weather, in a sky so black you could not make out the horizon, buffeted by the wind, the rain pouring into the open cockpit, the engine misfiring with damp points and condensers. But at the same time he saw Ken O'Neil seated in the forward compartment, grateful to be rushing to his daughter, his one and only child, now dying.

Si said into the phone, "Ken, let me talk to Silcox." A moment later Freddie was back on the phone. "What's the Las Vegas weather like?" Si asked.

"The last time I talked to them, a half hour ago, they had rain and thirty-mile-an-hour gusts. Si . . ." Freddie paused. "Si, I am not going to take off in this weather. That's all there is to it."

Si heard O'Neil asking to speak to Si again. Si said into the phone, "I'm coming out there, Freddie. I want to see for myself."

Si got out of bed and went into the bathroom. Ceil was at the mirror, combing her hair. Si ran some cold water over his face and told her he was going to the field but would be glad to drive her home. Ceil, Conair's bookkeeper and office receptionist, lived in an Inglewood rooming house not far from the field.

"You sound as though you want to get rid of me."

"You have to be at work in the morning, don't you?"

"Why can't I stay here and wait for you?"

"I don't know when I'll be back," he said.

"I'll wait," she said. "If you're not back in time, I'll still get to work. Don't worry."

"Suit yourself," he said. He returned to the bedroom, dressed, and hurried out to the hotel's Pico Boulevard entrance. His car, a brand-new Essex coupe, was parked on the street nearby. A small, square canvas placard was fixed to the driver's door:

**CONWAY AVIATION INDUSTRIES IN ASSOCIATION
WITH WILSHIRE MOTORS, YOUR EXCLUSIVE ESSEX DEALER.**

Morris Tannen had persuaded the Santa Monica Essex dealer to lease Conair three new cars for a dollar a year in return for the "priceless advertising."

The motor caught with the first push of the starter pedal. Si let it idle a moment, while he considered going back into the hotel and insisting that Ceil allow him to take her home. It made him uneasy knowing she was in his room, waiting for him. She had been getting on his nerves lately, hinting of marriage. Thinking of this, he smiled wryly. Not fifteen minutes before, when she straddled him, he had wanted the moment to last forever.

He smiled again, recalling Harry Fleet's definition of Eternity. Harry, a former Lafayette Escadrille squadron mate, said that Eternity was after you come and have dismounted, and can't wait for her to get dressed, put on lip rouge and powder, and get the hell out.

Eternity also described the ten seconds of Freddie Silcox's absolute, aghast silence at the airport after Si suggested that instead of worrying so much about the weather Freddie should simply get into the airplane and fly.

Freddie said, "If you're so darned cocksure the weather'll clear, Si, why the hell don't you fly it yourself?"

Later, Si was glad he did not follow his immediate inclination and fire Freddie on the spot. But he realized he could not expect a subordinate to undertake a task that he himself was not prepared to perform.

So Si packed Senator Kenneth O'Neil into the 110's enclosed passenger seat, climbed into the cockpit and covered his head with a mechanic's poncho against the rain, and took off for Salt Lake City.

The flight, which normally took five hours, required nearly twelve, but it nevertheless brought the senator to Salt Lake City in time to see his daughter before she died.

Ken O'Neil's gratitude knew no bounds. "Si, I won't forget this," he said. "I'll make it up to you someday. You have my word."

"Someday" proved sooner than either of them expected. Not ten days later the senator telephoned Si and asked to meet him privately. Si suggested a Santa Monica Boulevard speakeasy, Wally's, which he had patronized long before moving to Santa Monica. He enjoyed the food, which was basic old-fashioned American fare: steaks, chops, broiled fish and chicken, good coffee, and genuine, pre-Prohibition whiskey.

Ken O'Neil was admitted through the two-inch-thick steel-lined door and shown to Si's booth at the rear. After they shook hands and lit cigars, and O'Neil declined Si's offer of a drink but accepted coffee instead, the senator came immediately to the point.

"I'm probably risking my whole political career doing this, maybe even a jail sentence," he said. He glanced furtively around. It was ten in the morning, and all the booths and tables were empty. Three customers stood at the bar, workmen on a nearby construction project.

"I doubt they'll put you in jail for drinking coffee in a speak, Ken."

"The other night in Las Vegas while we were waiting for the rain to stop, you told me about the new plane you have on the drawing board," O'Neil said. "The two something?"

"The 220," Si said.

"You said you were having trouble raising money for the original model. The prototype, you called it?"

"It's not only money," Si said. "I need a top-notch design engineer to supervise the project. I'm no engineer, and Christ knows I'm not a designer." Which, he thought, was the understatement of the century. The 220 was planned as a twin-engined biplane capable of carrying twelve passengers in an enclosed cabin. Si's design was a variation on Tony Fokker's ill-fated F-8 but much bigger and, with Charlie Jensen's new 350-horsepower radial engines, far more powerful.

Si had been inspired by magazine pictures of Fokker's newest airplane, a twin-engined high-winged monoplane. When he wrote Fokker for more information, Fokker replied with detailed specifications and the news that Karl Eisler was responsible for the basic design.

Yes, Karl was alive, very much so and, according to Fokker, now in Russia teaching the Soviets how to build airplanes. Karl would have been the perfect man for the 220.

". . . so if you bid low enough, you'll get the contract," O'Neil was saying.

It jarred Si out of his reverie. "Say that again?"

O'Neil nervously fingered the knot of his tie. "I said, you could win the contract." He removed a handkerchief from his jacket lapel pocket and dabbed his brow; he was sweating. "Douglas already came in with the lowest bid. I happen to know their figures."

Si said nothing.

"Do you understand what I'm saying, Si?"

Si understood all too well. The U.S. Navy had requested bids on a modern pursuit plane of the navy's own design, a combination of the best features of the Sopwith Camel and the Spad. The navy's new airplane would carry two .30 caliber machine guns and attain a top speed of 130 mph.

Si said carefully, "How much did Douglas bid?"

"Nine thousand, two hundred and eighty dollars each," O'Neil said. "With engines. If the design is accepted, the navy will order twenty-five more."

$9,280, Si thought. $9,280 times twenty-five came to more than $200,000. You had to figure the cost of the prototype at three times the cost per unit, roughly $28,000, but a volume order of twenty-five units guaranteed a handsome net profit.

". . . suggest, therefore, your bid be no more than eighty-five hundred," O'Neil was saying.

All right, but that didn't change the price of building the prototype. It was still $28,000. Where the hell would they get that kind of money? The answer occurred to Si simultaneously with the question.

Ross Leonard, the San Francisco banker to whom Conair owed $45,000, would certainly want to protect his original investment and now, for a paltry $28,000, certainly could.

Si had a lot to learn.

2.

Not until 1912, his senior year, did Ross Leonard make Stanford's varsity football squad, and then as second-string left halfback. Late in the third quarter of the California game, the Big Game, Ross was sent in with a new, razzle-dazzle play. He fumbled. Cal recovered, but the coach allowed Ross to stay in. On Cal's very first play their quarterback crisscrossed into Stanford's secondary and broke into the clear. The one Stanford player between him and the goal line was Ross Leonard. Ross missed the tackle. The Cal runner scored the game's only touchdown.

Next morning's *San Francisco Herald* headline read, CAL 6, LEONARD 0. When Ross saw it, he smashed his fist into the heavy oak front door of his frat house and broke three knuckles on his left hand. The injury, which never healed properly, exempted him from wartime military service. He wanted very much to serve and envied those who did, an envy that over time turned to resentment.

During the war, on a tip from the lumberman father of a college classmate, Ross purchased large amounts of newly milled spruce and oak, which he then resold at great profit to aircraft manufacturers. By 1922, at age thirty, through clever speculation and considerable luck, he was a millionaire.

His wartime contacts with airplanes and airplane people had developed into an infatuation with both the machines and the industry itself. He took flying lessons and became a competent pilot. He purchased his own airplane, a war-surplus Curtiss N-9 Seaplane, which he hangared in a rented boatyard on the beach at Alameda, and which gave him a certain daredevil reputation. Although his main source of income was investment banking, he continually sought opportunities in the aviation field.

These opportunities existed by the dozens, but most were too risky. Ross had turned down Morris Tannen's first loan request. Morris's description of the company and its all but nonexistent capitalization was a sure formula for disaster. As Ross said, enjoying the play on words, it sounded much too fly-by-night.

But Morris's persistence impressed Ross, and he finally agreed to come to Los Angeles to inspect the operation and meet Simon Conway, the war hero.

The men took an instant dislike to each other. Ross considered Si brash, arrogant, and wholly unrealistic—if not downright ignorant—regarding sound business practices. Moreover, the man possessed not an iota of discretion or diplomacy. When Ross casually mentioned having a pilot's license, Si asked if he had learned to fly in the army. Ross, embarrassed, felt obliged to explain his college football injury. Si's response was, "Don't complain—it was probably the luckiest thing that ever happened to you."

Ross hated him for that, and in a perverse way it probably motivated his decision to loan Conair $45,000. Ross was convinced that Si would bring the firm down, thereby handing Ross Leonard Enterprises, Inc., a going company for next to nothing.

And now, nearly a year later in San Francisco, as Simon Conway entered Ross Leonard's mahogany-paneled, bookcase-lined office on the fifth floor of the Saunders Building at 250 Bush Street, Ross congratulated himself on his correct evaluation of Si's business acumen. He knew Si's visit was to request a renewal of the $45,000 note. He also knew it was a request he, Ross, would refuse.

They shook hands and Ross invited Si to sit. "How was the weather?" Ross asked. "I heard there was a big storm around Monterey. I mean, you flew up the coast, didn't you?"

"I took the train," Si said. "I heard about the storm, too. Nice place, Ross. Very nice." He wrinkled his nose. "Goddam smells of money."

"A pleasant smell, that's for sure," said Ross. "Listen, can I take your hat?"

"No, don't bother." Si tilted the brim of the hat down over his eyes and slouched comfortably in the leather club chair.

Ross almost laughed in Si's face; he knew that by keeping the hat on, Si believed he was getting Ross's goat. The hat, which Morris Tannen said he had sold Si years ago and which Si considered a lucky charm, resembled a greasy felt rag.

Ross said, "Still warm out?"

"Beautiful," said Si. "I think it's even warmer than down south when I left yesterday."

"And a hell of a lot warmer than the Polo Grounds in New York," Ross said. "I read where it was forty-one degrees at game time. No wonder the Giants won the series."

"They won because the Yankees' fifty-thousand-dollar-a-year star, Ruth, couldn't bat his way out of a paper bag," Si said. "Three hits in seventeen at bats, what do you expect?"

"For fifty grand, a lot more," said Ross. "All right, I know you didn't come here to talk baseball. What's on your mind?"

Si sat up. He perched the hat on the back of his head and said, "I want you to renew the note and lend us another twenty-eight thousand."

Ross thought Si was joking. "Would you mind repeating that?"

Si repeated it, then added, "The twenty-eight thousand will guarantee our being able to pay back the whole thing, the whole seventy-three thousand."

"Really? How's that?"

"You loan me the twenty-eight, I think I can get a contract to build navy fighter planes," Si said. "I happen to know the figures to submit for a winning bid. With the profits from the navy contract, I'll be able to start work on my new passenger airplane, the 220—"

"—hold it," Ross said. "You're already into me for forty-five thousand, which you can't repay, and you want me to toss in another twenty-eight so you can bid on a contract you think you can get?"

"I know I can get it."

"You 'know.' How do you 'know'?"

"I told you. I have the figures."

"Where did you get these figures?"

"I can't tell you. I have them, that's all that matters."

"I like the way you say 'I,' first person, all the time," Ross said. "I always thought a few other people were associated with you. Why 'I,' and no one else?"

"Because it is me," Si said. "It's my company. I make the decisions."

"What about your partners, the other stockholders?"

"Come on, Ross, cut the bullshit," Si said. "We both know the only reason you lent Conair the money in the first place was me. You didn't invest in Morris Tannen or Phil Granger or even Charlie Jensen. You invested in me."

"I invested in a company I thought might be successful."

"That's right," said Si. "And I'm telling you how you can secure that investment."

Ross said nothing a moment. He was thinking it shouldn't be too difficult to find out if the navy actually had asked for fighter-plane bids. "All right, let's say I do . . . 'secure my investment.' What do I get for it?"

"Your money back, plus two percent interest."

Now Ross did laugh. "I can't believe I'm having this conversation," he said. "All I have to do is demand payment on my note. I pull the plug on you and end up with the company, *and* your marvelous navy bid!"

"I think that time you got hurt playing football, it wasn't your hand you banged up, it was your head. The whole idea of the navy contract is to raise enough money to build the 220. It's the 220 that'll give Conair an important name, and a healthy profit. So you might end up with the company, but without me there'll be no 220!"

"I'll chance it," Ross said. He opened a leather-bound portfolio on the desktop and withdrew a single sheet of paper. "This is the note, due and payable on the twenty-fifth of September. Today is October nineteenth. You're three weeks late. Unless I receive payment in full no later than five P.M., October twenty-fourth, I will obtain a court order ordering your premises closed and all assets and inventory seized according to the terms of this note." He rose and said pleasantly, "Nice seeing you again, Si. Have a pleasant trip back to Los Angeles."

Si did not rise. "How much do you want, Ross? Three percent interest?"

"Five percent," Ross said, and sat down. He felt an inner glow of satisfaction. He had predicted, almost to the exact words, Si's response.

"All right, five percent," said Si. "That's more than a loan shark charges, but in this case it's worth it to me. Write up the papers."

"I don't think you understand, Si. I'm not talking about five percent interest on a note, I'm talking about a five percent interest in the company. Five percent of the existing stock." He smiled. "I'm your new partner."

Si's face tightened. He rose and walked over to the desk. He looked down at Ross. "I already have partners, three of 'em. I don't want any more."

"Suit yourself," Ross said. He stood again. "Have a good trip back." He stepped around the desk and walked across the Persian rug to the door. He opened the door and called out to the secretary in the outer office. "Betty, get my wife on the phone, would you please?" He stepped back to the desk and faced Si. "Today's the little woman's birthday. I promised to take her to Tadich's for lunch. Ever been there? They claim to be the oldest restaurant in San Francisco. For my money, best food in town."

"I'll give you the five percent," Si said.

Ross feigned surprise. "A minute ago you said you didn't want any partners."

"I know what I said."

"My God, Si, you're easy!" Ross could not keep a note of amusement from his voice. "Or desperate."

"Yes or no, Ross?"

"All right, I'll take a shot with you," Ross said. He extended his hand. "Congratulations."

"Thanks," Si said. He did not shake Ross Leonard's hand. He drew back his fist and hit Ross flush in the mouth. The blow sent Ross reeling backward into the desk, upsetting the goose-necked desk lamp, which overturned a marble pen stand and ink well and sent the candlestick telephone crashing to the floor. Ink spread blackly over the desktop and dripped onto the carpet. Any intention Ross might have had of striking back was swept away by the salty warm taste of blood on his lips. He pulled a handkerchief from his breast pocket and clamped it to his mouth.

"That's your first dividend," Si said. As he started for the door, Ross's telephone rang. Si picked up both sections of the phone, placed the handstand on the desk, and held the earpiece out to Ross. "Must be your wife," Si said. "Wish her a happy birthday." He smiled. "From your new partner."

Three days later Ross Leonard's $28,000 check arrived in the mail, along with documents assigning Ross the appropriate shares of Conair stock. The other stockholders, Morris Tannen, Charlie Jensen, and Phil Granger, agreed to allocate the shares from the reserve holdings. Si never told them what had happened that day in Ross's office; he felt foolish enough about it without subjecting himself to their lectures concerning his trigger temper.

The infusion of fresh capital enabled Conair to submit the winning bid of $8,500 per unit to the U.S. Navy for the new fighter plane. Within ninety days the prototype was flying. It was called the Conair Eagle, and was an instant success. The War Department not only commissioned Conair to manufacture fifteen Eagles, but six months later awarded the company a contract for twenty-five army and navy training airplanes. The trainer, the CT-1, was equally successful and became the forerunner of a long line of Conair trainers.

All this new business obviously required larger production facilities. Once again, Senator Kenneth O'Neil exerted his influence, this time quite legitimately: he arranged for Conair to lease—and eventually purchase—the two unused U.S. Air Service dirigible hangars on the west side of Mines Field. Conair moved into its new quarters on August 31, 1923.

Now Si directed his full attention to the twin-engined twelve-passenger cabin-enclosed airplane, the 220. Shortly after winning the CT-1 contract, Si had received a chatty letter from Tony Fokker, with a postscript saying that Karl Eisler had returned from Russia.

Si made up his mind then and there that Karl was the man for the 220. He sent Karl a letter, which Tony Fokker personally delivered. Karl's response, relayed through Fokker, was simple and succinct: if Simon Conway was the last man on earth, Karl would not work for the son of a bitch!

Sure, Si thought, the same son of a bitch who saved the dumb Kraut's life and was now offering him the chance to start a whole new life. And the fool turns him down. All right, let the stupid, stubborn Kraut ingrate starve with the rest of the Germans.

Si hired a designer for the 220, a bright young man he hired away from Donald Douglas. It was a mistake, as were the next two bright young men. Si needed Karl. Hiring Karl became an obsession. Morris Tannen put it another way: ego. Si's ego, which demanded that Karl give in.

Ego or not, Si was determined that Karl Eisler would design the 220, and if the mountain would not come to Si, then Si would go to the mountain. He would go to Germany and bang some sense into Karl's head. Once Si reached this decision it no longer was a matter of ego, principle, or even pride. It was, purely and simply, good business.

Si's partners were not enthusiastic about granting him a six-week leave of absence, and even less so about providing $2,000 of company funds for his expenses. But they grudgingly approved. It made life easier for all concerned.

Si booked passage on the *Mauretania* for an October 11, 1923, sailing from New York to Cherbourg. He arrived at Penn Station in New York on October 9, bought a *New York Times* at a Union News Company kiosk, and started walking to his hotel, the Maryland, a short distance from the station. He stopped in at a Seventh Avenue lunchroom for coffee and a sandwich. He had hardly stirred the sugar into his coffee when, on the newspaper's bottom front page, he saw the item. He read it once, then again, and then once more.

"... ham on rye," the counterman was saying as he served Si's sandwich. "Mustard's over there, you want it . . ."

The counterman was talking to himself. Si was gone. A fifty-cent piece lay on the counter beside his uneaten sandwich and untouched coffee. The newspaper was exactly as Si had left it, folded down on the bottom half of the front page on a half-column dispatch from Rome about Benito Mussolini threatening to march on the city. Directly below this was the item that had caught Si's attention. It meant absolutely nothing to the counterman.

From Our Special Correspondent

BOSTON, OCT. 8—The Coast Guard announced today that they have located the burned wreckage of a yacht containing the bodies of Boston financier Burton Taylor and his wife, the former Barbara Euston of Newton, Mass.

A Coast Guard spokesman said the vessel had apparently exploded at sea in the vicinity of Ogunquit, Maine, where the Taylors have a summer residence.

A daughter, Miss Margaret Taylor, is reportedly in seclusion at the Taylors' Ogunguit residence, and unavailable for comment.

3.

All the way to Ogunquit, from the time they left the railway depot in Portsmouth, the taxi driver never stopped talking. He rhapsodized on the beauties of a New England autumn. Then he praised the engineers who had designed this newly paved road that paralleled the coast as far north as Portland, Maine. Then he cursed the old fogies in the slower cars who never should be allowed to drive on the road, Route 1, as they called it.

Si, seated beside the driver in the brand-new Model T touring car, listened but hardly heard. Huddled against the cold, gazing at the roadside through the isinglass window, he wondered, as he had been wondering almost since the minute the train pulled out of New York nearly seven hours ago, why he had embarked on this—as he termed it—"odyssey." The answer evaded him, if an answer existed. By the time the Boston & Maine express to Portsmouth left North Station, he had begun thinking of it not as any odyssey, but as a fool's errand. Now, entering Ogunquit, he was again asking himself what he was trying to accomplish.

"Not a goddam thing," he said aloud.

"How's that?" the driver asked.

"Watch the road, for Christ's sake!"

"Oh, yeah, sure," the driver said good-naturedly. He was a young man, Si's age. Under his corduroy jacket he wore an olive-drab flannel shirt, army issue. Si wondered what outfit he had served with but did not want to ask. It would start the man talking again, and what the hell difference did it make anyway?

Ogunguit looked the same, the narrow main street lined with antique shops, the little bookstore on the corner, the A&P grocery market. Although Si had been here only once, and then for less than twenty-four hours, Perkins Cove was engraved in his memory.

"At the end of the main drag, there's a little bridge. You go over it and then maybe another mile past a dozen or so cottages until you come to a long dirt road. You'll see the house. It's the only one on that road."

The taxi rattled over the bridge, continued past cottages vacant and boarded-up for the winter, and turned onto the dirt road that quickly became a gravel drive leading to the house. A Mercer Runabout Si recognized as Meg's was parked near the veranda.

". . . guess this is it, huh?" the taxi driver was saying. "Damn nice spread, all right."

"To hell with it," Si said. "Turn around."

"Huh?"

"I said turn around, goddammit!"

"You're the doctor." The driver wheeled the car around, and they headed back over the dirt road toward the bridge, the driver commencing a long rambling dissertation about why anybody would come all this way and then all of a sudden turn around and go back.

Si had no answer for him. Si knew only that the moment he saw the house he realized why he had made the trip. It was no condolence call. He wanted Meg Taylor to see him as the success he had become, and that he had achieved this without her father's help. He wanted her recognition.

So you'll send her a card, he told himself.

On Conair stationery, of course.

". . . sure! I read about it!" the driver was saying as he guided the Model T onto the bridge again. "That banker they found drowned. That's who lives up there! Right?"

Si nodded absently. "Yeah, that's right."

"There's talk he did it on purpose," said the driver. "You're a cop, I bet. Or an insurance guy. That's why you come up here. Because they think he did it on purpose. But how come you changed your mind about going in the house?"

Si was about to order the driver to stop right there in the middle of Ogunquit. He would find another taxi. Then he realized what the driver had been saying.

" 'He did it on purpose?' " Si asked. "Who did what on purpose?"

"That guy Taylor, the banker. He was in big trouble with the bank examiners. They say he was embezzling all the customers' money. So he went out on that boat of his and blew himself and the wife to kingdom come!"

Si looked at the driver, but heard Burton Taylor's voice: ". . . you were Chip's friend. I'd like to help you if you need any help, and if I can."

"Turn around," Si said to the driver.

"Huh?"

"Turn around and go back to the house. And do me one favor."

"What's that?"

"Shut your mouth. Don't say a word. Not one fucking word!"

Meg answered the door on the first ring. "Yes . . .?" The word died on her lips. She stared at him in disbelief.

Except for her red-rimmed eyes and drawn appearance she looked the same, her hair still in the pompadour, the same strong face, the same tall, full-breasted figure. And with almost the same expression of shock and embarrassment as that night she had walked in on him and the little Canadian maid, whose name he had long since forgotten.

"How are you?" he asked, and after a moment when it seemed Meg could not find her voice, he went on, "Look, I have to get back to Boston tonight. Can I come in for a few minutes? I've been traveling close to seven hours to get here."

"Of course. I'm sorry. What about the taxi, though? Will he wait?" As Si turned to speak to the driver, Meg hurriedly continued, "Send him away. I'll drive you to the depot. There's a Boston train that stops here a little after ten. I have a timetable somewhere."

Later, she admitted that although he was the last person she thought she would ever want to see, she was really glad he had come. She was so lonely, so hungry for companionship. All her so-called friends seemed suddenly to have vanished. Earlier, as though she felt obliged to deal with the issue and get it over with, almost her first remark had been "I suppose you've heard the rumors about my father's alleged embezzling?"

"No," Si lied, "I haven't heard a thing."

The words poured out of her. Burton Taylor was not guilty of embezzling, only poor investment judgment. He had lost an enormous amount of the bank's money on ill-advised stock purchases. The classic story. Borrowing from one account to cover losses in another. It was, said Meg, like a silent avalanche, creeping up behind her father and engulfing him. But Burton Taylor was no coward. He would never have done away with himself, and never brought harm to anyone else.

It was an accident, Meg knew that. In any event, the bank's creditors had lost nothing. Every last dollar would be repaid. Life insurance and various personal assets, including both the Ogunquit house and the Taylor Boston residence, would satisfy all claims.

". . . so I'll be without a roof over my head, but I'll manage," she said. "I'm thinking of going into teaching." She drew in her breath to continue, then stopped. She wore a Wedgwood pendant containing a small watch. She cupped the pendant in her palm. "My God, is that the time? Five after six? We've been talking for almost two hours. Excuse me, *I've* been talking. Why did you let me ramble on like that?"

"I guess you needed to."

"But you haven't said a thing about yourself. Please, tell me what you've been doing."

They were in Burton Taylor's study, a fire roaring in the fireplace. Meg had fixed sandwiches and coffee, and they were sipping brandy. He told her about Conair, and the 110, and his plans for the new transport, the 220, and the purpose of the European trip, which was to bring Karl Eisler to America to design the 220. He apologized for having left the artist's depiction of the airplane in his suitcase back at the hotel in New York. The 220, he said, would fly nonstop from Los Angeles to San Francisco. He described the Conway crest emblazoned on the 220's fuselage: the American eagle with the letter C.

"I wish you could see your face," Meg said. "You had that same look—that same fire in your eyes, I suppose—the other time you were here, when you talked about your Boston–New York air service."

Ah, yes, he thought, my Boston–New York air service. The enterprise that, thankfully, never came into being, thanks to you, Miss Margaret Taylor. If you had not walked into the little Canadian maid's room that night, I probably would never have ended up in California and therefore probably never been president of Conway Aviation Industries, Inc.

"Listen, there's something we should clear the air about," he said. He paused. She blushed. She knew what air he wanted cleared. "That other time I was here," he said. "I behaved like a damn fool. I'm sorry."

"No, *I* behaved like a damned fool," she said. "I behaved very badly. Do you want the truth?" She blushed again. "I was jealous. All right," she went on in the same breath, "now we've put her to bed—" She clamped her hand over her mouth, abashed.

For a moment they stared at each other and then, simultaneously, both laughed. "And she's in bed alone," he said, and they laughed again.

"Honestly, I'm so glad you've done well," she said.

Which makes two of us, he thought, studying her as she talked. Seated in an armchair opposite him, her face shadowed in the glow of the flames from the fireplace, she bore a slight resemblance to Ceil Bjornsted. But what a world of difference between her and Ceil. Background, education, social status. Another picture of Meg came to him. Meg, as the mother of his children, strong, handsome, intelligent children who themselves would bear other similarly endowed children.

The Conway dynasty.

Si always remembered that moment as a moment of pure, absolute prescience. It was like turning the pages of a book, reading the story of your own future. He sensed Meg's loneliness and her need for someone with the strength and ability to return to her all that she had lost. Money, status, pride. He and Meg, each had something the other needed.

"Listen," he said, and paused, and then blurted out the words in a series of rapid, breathless, sentences. "I want to ask you something. I don't want you to answer until you think about it carefully. Very carefully." He paused again. She waited. "What I want you to think about is marriage. To me, I mean. Marry me."

And he also knew—again, as though turning the pages of that book—precisely how she would respond, her cheeks suddenly redder than the glow of the flames, her forehead wrinkled with perplexity.

"You can't be serious . . ."

"Do you think I'd joke about something like that?"

"What I think is that you're crazy!"

"Maybe. But then maybe you are, too."

"When did this crazy idea strike you?"

"About ten seconds ago," he said.

She looked at him, and then away, at the fire. She said, "Well, it is crazy. You're crazy."

He got up and walked over to her. He grasped her shoulders and gently turned her toward him. "So I'm crazy," he said. "What's wrong with being crazy?"

Meg shook her head, bewildered.

He cupped her chin. "Come with me to Europe," he said. "It'll be our honeymoon."

Meg laughed, a brittle little laugh. "There's no dowry. Every cent I have goes to pay off the bank."

"Jesus Christ in hell!" he shouted. The unexpected anger in his voice startled him more than her. "Is that why you think I'm proposing? I just got through telling you how well I'm doing! I don't need money! Not your money, anyway."

"You don't need a wife, either."

"Don't tell me what I need. I know what I need."

"No, I don't think so," she said. "I don't think you do know what you need."

"Yeah, well, I happen to know what *you* need—" He paused abruptly. Her face had flushed even a deeper crimson. "That's not what I meant," he said.

"What did you mean, then?"

"I don't know what I meant. All I know is that this is something that would be good for both of us. And if you're talking about 'need,' then this is something we both need."

They looked at each other. Meg's eyes glistened with tears. "I don't have a passport," she said. "You can't travel abroad without a passport, can you?"

"I'll get you one in Boston," he said. "And we'll find a justice of the peace to marry us. There's no time for a real church wedding."

"A justice of the peace will be fine," she said, after a moment.

It was, he knew, as unromantic a proposal as any woman ever received, and as unromantic an acceptance. On the other hand, both of them were realists: marriage was mutually beneficial. Each had something to gain. If nothing else, their relationship would be based on honesty.

Not until three days later, on the *Mauretania*, on their honeymoon, did he realize that not once had either of them ever mentioned the word "love."

4.

Ruth Tannen would never forget the morning Morris rushed home from the factory with the cable from Si. It happened to be their second full day in the new house, an imposing two-story English Tudor, which Morris claimed was a residence befitting a vice president and general sales manager of Conway Aircraft Industries, Inc. The property, with its spacious yard and dozens of fruit trees, had not come cheap—$5,250. But with Morris's salary now $75 weekly they could afford it, and it really was a steal for the area. On Lincoln Boulevard in Santa Monica, a three-minute walk to the beach, a ten-minute ride to the field.

That day she had just fed Paul his lunch, bundled him up, and put him out in the yard in the playpen. She was standing at the window near the sink where she could keep an eye on the baby while she washed the breakfast dishes, when she heard the front door slam. Morris rushed into the kitchen waving a small piece of white paper, shouting that she'd never believe *this*!

He flattened it out on the kitchen table for her to read.

MARCONI RADIO

22 OCT 1923 AT SEA CONAIR LOSANG STOP MARRIED STOP WRITING DETAILS LATER STOP SICONWAY

Ruth's wet hands dampened the paper. She dried her hands on her apron and tried to visualize Si's new wife. Was she tall? Short? Fat, thin, old, young? Or blond and brassy like Ceil Bjornsted, that tramp bookkeeper everybody knew he was sleeping with? No, for a wife he'd probably chosen the exact opposite, but no doubt also a tramp.

". . . knew you'd get a kick out of it," Morris was saying. "You're always talking about how he treats women like dirt and the one that married him would have to be crazy."

"She must be, is all I can say."

"What a surprise, though. He never said a word about it. I wonder how it all happened?"

"He probably picked her up on the street."

"Come on, Ruth, stop being so hard on the guy." Morris nodded pensively. "But that's so much like him. Goes off to find this designer friend of his and ends up getting married."

"Yes, at the company's expense," Ruth said.

"Call it a bonus," Morris said. He folded the cable neatly and slipped it into his inside suitcoat pocket. "I have to be getting back. Phil Granger's setting up a meeting with some hotel people he knows from San Diego. That ritzy Coronado Island place. I think I can talk them into a deal to fly hotel guests from here to Coronado on a regular basis."

"Morris, it's only two hours to San Diego by train. Why would anybody want to fly?"

"By train, you have to take a taxi from the depot to the ferry, and then wait for the goddam thing to go to the island. We'll land practically in the hotel's backyard. Ross thinks it's a good idea. He's in town, too. He says he'll help me sell the hotel people."

"Ross Leonard?" Ruth said. "He's your new hero?"

"Listen, he put up the money that saved the company. And he thinks I know what I'm doing, even if Granger doesn't. See you for supper." Morris kissed Ruth's cheek, ran out the kitchen door to the playpen, swept Paul up in his arms for a hug, and then dashed around the driveway to his car.

Watching through the window and annoyed with herself for forgetting to ask Morris to order a twice-weekly ice delivery, Ruth was thinking, Sure, no wonder Phil Granger knows the Coronado hotel people. They were anti-Semites like him, Granger, with his Abie-and-Hymie jokes.

What really galled Ruth was how Morris defended Granger, claiming the man meant no harm, it was just his way. Besides, he was a damn good lawyer. So Phil Granger had a lousy sense of humor, so what?

Coronado, my God! she thought. Didn't Morris care that the Coronado Hotel was restricted, no Jews? Why on earth would he want anything to do with them? But even as the question came to her, she knew the answer: business, with a capital B.

And as for Simon Conway, upon whom Morris was now more than ever convinced that the sun rose and fell, Ruth had heard with her own ears Si's responsive laughter at some of Phil Granger's jokes.

Again, she wondered what kind of woman Si had married. Whoever and whatever she was, Ruth pitied her. The poor soul would live a life of hell. What the conceited bastard needed was somebody who could put him in his place, teach him a lesson or two.

She began trembling so violently that the dish she was drying nearly fell from her hand. She ran out of the kitchen and into the bedroom, where she gripped the top of the dresser to steady her hands. Slowly, she raised her eyes to the mirror.

You are not beautiful, she told herself in the mirror, but neither are you unattractive. *Ivanhoe's* Rebecca, as her father had called her. Rebecca. If she and Morris ever had a daughter she would name her Rebecca. She closed her eyes to blot out the image of herself and Simon Conway, embracing, kissing, making love.

Morris drove up to the old factory, enjoying, as always, the sight across the field of the huge black letters C O N A I R on the corrugated metal sides of the refurbished dirigible hangars of the "new" factory. The Navy Eagles and CT-1 military trainers were manufactured there and, soon, the 220. The 110's continued to be assembled here in the old factory, where the company's executive offices were also located.

The original Conway Aviation Industries sign, painted three years ago for five dollars by the young Chicano street artist, still hung over the main entrance. Daily, Morris reminded himself to either replace the sign, which was now weatherworn and faded, or at least have it repainted. For some reason he could not do it. It would be like destroying a priceless relic.

Ross Leonard and Phil Granger were waiting for Morris in Si's office. The tiny room, hardly more than a cubicle, was thick with swirling blue tobacco smoke from their cigars. The walls reverberated with the noise of pounding hammers, lathes, voices. Morris pulled Si's cablegram from his pocket and slapped it into Ross's hand.

"I told Ross about it," Granger said.

Ross shook his head skeptically. "Maybe it'll mellow the son of a bitch," he said.

"That I doubt," Morris said to Ross, and then to Granger, "All right, so what time do we meet the hotel people?"

"I'm having lunch with them," Granger said. He consulted a large railroad watch that he had removed from his lower vest pocket. "Twelve-thirty, at the Ambassador."

Morris said, "What do you mean, 'you're' having lunch with them?" He looked around for a chair. Ross Leonard sat on a stool at Si's combination desk and drafting table. Granger occupied the only other chair, a collapsible metal camp chair.

"Ross wants you to meet someone else," Granger said.

"Who?" Morris asked.

"A Post Office bigwig," Ross said. "He might be in a position to help us."

"How, by selling us postage stamps wholesale?" Morris said to Ross. He turned to Granger. "I think this Hotel Coronado promotion is a little more important than Ross's Post Office bigwig."

"Morris, let me handle the hotel people," Granger said. "I know how to deal with them."

The message was clear: Granger did not want the hotel people to meet Morris, and Morris suddenly realized why. The Coronado Hotel was restricted and would hardly favor doing business with an airline whose sales manager was Jewish. Morris looked at Granger. Granger looked away and puffed carefully on his cigar.

"All right," Morris said after a moment. It was not worth making an issue over. Besides, all that mattered was getting the business, obtaining a contract for Conway Air Transport Service. Morris would sell CATS tickets door-to-door if he thought it would help erase the airline division's red ink. "All right, I'll see what Ross's Post Office man has for us."

"I'm sure it's about all the problems with the airmail service," Granger said, obviously relieved to change the subject. "And believe me, they're having plenty. Why do you think the newspapers call the Post Office's Airmail Service the Pony Express?"

Pony Express was certainly an apt term. Airmail Service pilots flew the mail via a series of stops. From Boston to Albany, for example, where mail and pilot transferred to another airplane that was waiting and warmed up for the next flight, to Buffalo. Then Buffalo to Cleveland, and another fresh airplane, and so on across the country.

The system worked if no weather or mechanical difficulties were encountered and if the pilot did not become lost. It would have been faster if the mail were flown at night as well, and the Post Office Department was already experimenting with powerful, flashing light beacons positioned at fifty-mile intervals along the established flight route. In clear weather, a pilot would always have a beacon in sight. The plan was to eventually install the beacons across the entire country, coast to coast.

"One of these days, the Post Office will smarten up and turn the mail over to private operators," Morris said. "That, gentlemen, is when CATS starts showing a profit."

"I have a feeling that's what this fellow wants to talk about," Granger said. He looked at his watch again. "I'd better get going." He shook hands with Ross, nodded at Morris, and left.

Ross said to Morris, "I don't think you like him too much."

Morris said, "Tell me, how do you like that new Chrysler of yours? I hear it's got four-wheel hydraulic brakes."

Ross laughed. "I can take a hint. I know when I'm being told to mind my own business." He got up. "Okay, let's go see the Post Office man."

The Post Office man, Walter Driscoll, awaited them in a Jefferson Avenue restaurant, the Chanticleer. Driscoll, a solemn, lean, middle-aged, silver-haired man, introduced himself as the Postmaster General's troubleshooter. He was on an inspection tour of the airmail system in the Western states.

While Walter Driscoll had hoped to speak personally with Simon Conway, he was more than delighted to meet Morris and Ross. After all, the Conair 110 had solved many of the Airmail Service's problems. Thanks to Simon Conway, no longer was the countryside strewn with the charred wreckage of Post Office DH-4s. Si had discovered that in a crash a DH-4's fuel tank invariably ruptured, spewing gasoline on the blazing-hot exhaust pipes of the water-cooled Liberty engine. Si recommended locating the exhaust pipes as far from the fuel tank as possible. Replacing the Liberty with a Jensen radial engine in the Conair 110 accomplished precisely that.

Jensen radials solved a myriad of other problems, not the least of which was the chronic leaking of water-cooled engines. More than one airmail pilot, engine temperature gauge high in the red, had been fortunate enough to spot a steam-driven threshing rig in a farm below. Landing on a level area near the farm—or even a road—the pilot borrowed water from the threshing rig's boiler and took off again.

Clearly then, with its 110, Conway Aviation Industries had made a most favorable impression upon the Post Office Department. Which brought Walter Driscoll to the point. For a big man he spoke softly, sometimes almost in a monotone, but his words were perfectly audible. Too much so.

". . . we plan, within the year or certainly no more than two years, to open airmail contracts to private operators. It should change the whole nature of the aviation business."

"It should also get the mail to where it's going on time," said Morris.

"Indeed," Walter said good-naturedly.

"Believe me, Mr. Driscoll, we appreciate the advance notice," Morris said.

"You understand, of course, that this information is strictly confidential," Driscoll said.

Morris wanted to laugh. It was such a silly little game. That the Post Office would eventually turn the Airmail Service over to private airlines was no great revelation. Everyone had been talking about it for the past year. Why the hell couldn't the crooked son of a bitch come right out and tell you how much of a bribe he expected to guarantee Post Office Department acceptance of a Conair bid for an airmail contract?

Ross said, "I'm sure we'll find an appropriate manner of expressing our appreciation, Mr. Driscoll. And I know I speak for Simon Conway when I say that."

"That's good to hear," said Driscoll. "Be sure and extend my heartiest best wishes to him on his marriage. He's honeymooning in Europe, you said?"

"Unless he changes his plans," Morris said. "He's supposed to be in Berlin on the twenty-ninth. He wanted to fly there from Paris on this new plane Junkers just came out with."

"Berlin, eh?" Driscoll said. "Not such a pleasant place these days, from what I hear." He signaled a waiter. "So now why don't we have a bite to eat? I'm famished."

Morris had no way of knowing, of course, but other than a minor change of itinerary, Si's schedule remained the same. He had flown to Berlin in Luft Hansa's new all-metal Junkers four-passenger transport. Not from Paris but from Amsterdam and, upon Tony Fokker's advice, alone. Fokker considered the political situation in Germany too volatile for Meg to accompany Si. She remained in Holland as a guest of Fokker and his wife, Elizabeth.

From Berlin Si sent Morris another cable.

MCKAY RADIO

CONAIR LOSANG 3 NOV 1923 ARRIVED BERLIN STOP WILL SNARE QUARRY AND HOMECOME FAST STOP SICONWAY

Morris was amused at Si's choice of words, "snare quarry," which was somewhat eloquent for Simon Conway, and Morris doubted that Karl Eisler would take kindly to being labeled "quarry." But Morris was more concerned about the turmoil in Germany. The newspapers were filled with accounts of that country's economic collapse, food riots, threatened coups d'état. For all that, Morris did not really fear for Si's safety. Si knew how to take care of himself.

Morris could never have anticipated that within two days of his arrival in Germany, Simon Conway would once again find himself fleeing the country.

Certainly, Si never envisioned it, or that his very life would be in jeopardy.

8

It pleased the taxi driver to see former officers down on their luck. This one, whom he had picked up outside a seedy Berlin West hotel-pension on Knesebeckstrasse, had flagged the cab by snapping the fingers of one hand and waving his cane in the other. The driver, a veteran of three years in the trenches, took his sweet time opening the door for him. He knew the man was an officer. You could smell the bastards.

And down on his luck, all right. His clothes gave him away. The black homburg fit well enough, but the black-velvet-collared overcoat looked like a tent and his shirt was sizes too large. True, the clothes were well cut and expensive—even the pearl-gray spats and the gloss-shined black low-cut shoes—but these clothes belonged on a body at least thirty pounds heavier.

The driver only hoped the son of a bitch didn't try to pay the fare in marks. The passenger was going to Tempelhof. Not so great a distance, and in the old days only a five-mark ride, but now, with the inflation, the same five marks were worth a cool fifty *billion*. Today, that was. Tomorrow, or even by the time they reached the airport, the fifty billion could well be a hundred billion. The government printing presses were running day and night. The bookpage-sized billion-mark notes made cheap toilet paper. Only yesterday a woman —a Joachimsthaler Strasse streetwalker, for sure—gave him a wris-twatch for a trip to Potsdam. Last week a man had paid with four cans of American peaches.

The passenger tapped the tip of his cane on the back of the front seat. "Would you please drive a little faster?"

"It's the petrol, sir," said the driver. "I'm trying to use as little as I can. It's hard to get, you know."

The sidewalks were crowded with the usual queue of housewives waiting resignedly outside the empty-shelved bakeries and butcher shops. Traffic was light, a few trucks and private automobiles, but scores of bicycles were darting in and out between the electric trams. Small groups of brown-shirted, swastika-brassarded SA troopers swaggered about amid the clusters of green-uniformed policemen in their peaked leather caps.

The passenger studied a young girl who had just wheeled her bike away from the curb and, mounting it, provided an intriguing flash of inner thigh. The girl resembled Selma, the little Silesian nurse at the hospital in Potsdam. Selma, she of the marvelous thrice-weekly back rubs, with those soft and dexterous hands so warmly moist with baby oil, working their way down the small of his back and settling in between his legs. The very recollection was exciting.

The taxi driver had correctly identified Karl Eisler as a former officer. As for Karl's being down on his luck, it only seemed that way from his place of residence and gaunt appearance. While Karl was not rolling in wealth, he enjoyed an adequate income. His father had died the previous year, leaving him an annual three thousand—in English pounds, thankfully—and then there was a "consulting" stipend from Tony Fokker. Karl had moved into the Knesebeckstrasse hotel-pension only until the Charlottenburg flat he wanted became available. His gaunt appearance came from a seven-week hospital stay. What the hell could you expect after seven weeks in a hospital bed?

A year in Russia, freezing his balls off, and never even so much as a runny nose, so two weeks after returning to Germany, in steamy August weather, he catches double pneumonia and nearly dies from it for lack of proper medicine in the so-called hospital. They were using paper bandages, for Christ's sake! It was as though the war never ended.

After living in Russia, trying to teach ignorant Bolsheviks how to manufacture airplanes, he thought anything in Germany would have been a pleasure. But in the three months since his return the whole country had gone to hell: inflation, food shortages, bands of Communists roaming the city, strikes, new political parties popping up every other day to demonstrate or threaten some kind of *Putsch*. In Munich there were riots in the streets, with three people killed.

Karl had gone to Russia at the request of the man who had replaced him as commander of Jasta 24, Captain Hermann Göring. Although Göring was officially no longer in the army—the "token army" allowed under the Armistice terms—he served as an unofficial adviser to its commander, General von Seeckt. Under a secret agreement between von Seeckt and the Russians, in return for permitting a limited number of young Germans to receive pilot training in Russia, skilled German technicians had opened an aircraft-manufacturing facility at a remote airfield near Moscow.

During Karl's stay in Moscow the Russians produced twenty Junkers all-metal J-13s, small single-engined low-winged monoplanes whose skins were composed entirely of corrugated metal. The J-13's cabin, with four wicker chairs, was completely enclosed. The cockpit, although an extension of the cabin, was open, and the reason for that, as the story went, was Otto Junkers's belief that pilots were hardly more than glorified lorry drivers. Of the twenty Russian-manufactured J-13s, seven had been sold back to Luft Hansa at a handsome profit. Talk about capitalism! In point of fact, it was one of those Luft Hansa J-13s that Karl was rushing out to Tempelhof to meet.

As though the driver had read Karl's thoughts, he looked at him in the rearview mirror and asked, "Where does the plane you're meeting come from?"

"Who told you I was meeting anything?"

"You carry no baggage, sir."

"Please don't concern yourself with what or whom I'm meeting."

The driver was unperturbed. "Traveling by air is getting to be fashionable, isn't it, sir?"

Karl said nothing but was thinking, Yes, and it will become more and more fashionable. Not long ago two American army pilots had flown nonstop from New York to California in twenty-seven hours. Twenty-seven hours! Damn the Americans! He envied them.

"Excuse me, sir, I was talking to you," the driver said.

Karl did not reply. The driver's cheeky attitude reminded him of Bruno Haase's top sergeant at Stalag 12-A, that insufferable fat pig who might have thwarted Simon Conway's escape that morning at the whorehouse in Magdeburg. Poor old Haase, dead from the flu in '19. He survives the war, even with an arm gone, and then dies from a bad cold.

". . . should be there in a few minutes, sir," the driver was saying.

"Thank you for the information," Karl said acidly. Reaching into his coat pocket for his cigarette case, his fingers brushed the folded telegram from Fokker. He knew it by heart: CONWAY ARRIVING 3 NOVEMBER TEMPELHOF LUFT HANSA 1330.

Karl fidgeted uneasily. Tony Fokker believed Karl had agreed to see Simon Conway as a personal favor to him. In truth, this errand to Tempelhof was being undertaken at the specific behest of someone else entirely.

Karl knew that the purpose of Si's visit was to persuade him to come to America to design airplanes. As though Karl were a war trophy. Well, the war was not over, not Germany's war. The nation had to be saved and, within the next month, would be.

Hermann Göring, along with his cohort Adolf Hitler, and the army's wartime "iron man," General Ludendorff, supported by 100,000 war veterans, intended to restore the monarchy under Crown Prince Rupprecht. Ludendorff and Hitler were at this very moment in Munich preparing to move. After declaring a new Bavarian government, the Monarchists were to march on Berlin.

Göring had summoned Karl Eisler back from Russia to assume an important role in a resurrected Imperial Air Force. Karl had up to now managed to evade Göring's urging to join their so-called National Socialist German Workers' Party, and he especially did not want to become involved with the SA, the Sturmabteilung, Göring and Hitler's private army. Some "army." Fifteen thousand unemployed war veterans who enjoyed beating up Jews and smashing their store windows.

Politics did not interest Karl. He cared only for Germany's future. If restoration of the monarchy solved the nation's problems, then Karl was for the monarchy. If Hitler could do it, then Karl was for Hitler.

". . . we're here, sir," the driver was saying.

Karl paid the driver with five ten-billion-mark notes. "Keep the change," he said, and got out of the taxi and walked away without closing the door. He stood on the sidewalk, all at once in his own world. He loved the clamor of an airfield, the music of engines and propellers, and the astringent smell of gasoline, the warm fragrance of oil.

During the war Tempelhof had been hardly more than two wood hangars and a grass field. Now, in addition to three more hangars, there was an administration building and a small terminal. On the asphalt hardstand an enormous Vickers Vimy of Instone Airways— London-Berlin twice weekly—was parked wing to wing with another huge twin-engined biplane, an Air Union Farman F-60 just in from Paris. There were four J-13s, two belonging to KLM and two with Luft Hansa markings, and some half-dozen other Luft Hansa machines.

Overhead, Karl heard the raspy buzz of a BMW engine. It was the Luft Hansa J-13 with its important American passenger. The little airplane's washboardlike metallic wings glinted in the sun. It banked smoothly and, descending, approached the field. Karl was glad the airdrome was crowded with so many airplanes. Simon Conway would be impressed.

Karl was right. Si was impressed. But then Si had been impressed with European air service from the moment at Le Bourget when he and Meg boarded an Air Union Farman Goliath for Amsterdam. It was like riding in a railroad parlor car, with its comfortable leather club chairs and a uniformed steward serving tea. There was no such service or equipment in America, where air travel resembled a frontier stagecoach line, especially Si's own Conway Air Transport Service.

But what most impressed Si was the all-metal J-13. The moment he saw it in Amsterdam, parked on the Schipol tarmac, he knew he was seeing the future. Metal-framed aircraft represented the ultimate in safety and durability, although Tony Fokker said that he personally considered them far too experimental to commit to production.

The J-13's 185-horsepower BMW engine, the largest engine that airplane could accommodate, still left it underpowered. For proper performance an engine twice the size was required, but the weight of such an engine would not permit the airplane to get off the ground. A Jensen engine, however, in an all-metal Conway airplane, was an entirely different story. No, Si thought, not one engine, two, perhaps three. Then you had sufficient power.

Other than the Luft Hansa clerk, Karl was the only person awaiting the flight. Fokker had told Si of Karl's illness. Well, Karl would recover, Si thought, searching for a clever opening remark. Maybe, "Tell me, Karl, have you run into any Revolutionary Guards lately?"

Their meeting was not as awkward as either had feared. They shook hands, exchanged a few comments on each other's appearance, and then got into a taxi. Karl told the driver to take them to the Bristol Hotel.

"I reserved a room for you there," he said to Si. "It's the best hotel in Berlin."

"Is it anything like that place in Magdeburg?" Si asked. "What was the name of it?"

" '38,' " Karl said blandly. He'd be damned if he'd allow Simon Conway to nettle him. "Perhaps we can manage an encore. I know a few interesting places here in Berlin. But you're a newlywed. I shouldn't be enticing you."

"Sure, Karl," Si said absently. He had just realized why the road looked so strange. There were only a few automobiles or trucks, but dozens of horse-drawn vehicles, farmers delivering their crops to market in half-empty carts whose contents—pumpkins, corn, apples, potatoes—appeared withered and old. So did many of the people.

Not a happy country, Si thought, but then what was happy about losing a war?

". . . had hoped to meet your bride," Karl was saying.

Si said, "Tony said it was too dangerous to bring her."

"I'm afraid he was right," Karl said. "Tell me about her. She must be very attractive."

She's attractive, all right, Si thought, but not much in the bedroom. Bedroom, he thought, wondering why that refined term occurred to him rather than "fucking," or "screwing." He was reminded once more of old Harry Fleet, his Lafayette squadron mate of the matchless maxims. Harry always said, "You never fuck wives, you go to bed with them."

Si said, "Yes, she is. Very nice-looking. What about you? Are you married?"

Karl had anticipated the question and had prepared a glib, cynical reply. But it would have been disrespectful to Erika. Beautiful, dark-haired Erika von Kurzfeld, daughter of a general who had made abundantly clear his disapproval of Karl Eisler as a son-in-law. A question of background and breeding, for all the good the background and breeding did now. The old general's monthly army pension wasn't enough to buy him a loaf of bread. He was dependent upon Erika's teaching salary, and had indignantly refused Karl's offer of help. Well, general, Karl thought, up yours.

He said to Si, "No, no marriage plans as yet. All right, so tell me about this wonderful business of yours. Tony Fokker says you're doing quite well."

So Si told him. About Conair and CATS, the 110s, and the navy Eagles, and the CT-1. The 220, though, was what would really put Conair on the map.

"Simon, listen to me," Karl said quietly. "I know your reason for coming here, and I am not interested. I have no intention of going to work for you."

"You know something?" Si said after a moment. "You really are an ingrate. I saved your life back there in Aachen."

"You did it to save yourself, Simon. You had no choice. If they found me, they would have shot us both."

"You're still an ingrate."

"As you wish. Shall I ask the driver to take you back to Tempelhof, or now that you're here would you like to enjoy the pleasures of Berlin for a few days?"

"When you see the plans and specs for the 220, you'll change your mind," Si said.

For a $5 bill the Bristol Hotel concierge gave Si a bright, sunny fourth-floor corner room overlooking the Kurfürstendamm. Si opened the terrace doors and stepped out on the balcony.

"Beautiful street, isn't it?" Karl said.

"What the hell is so dangerous?" Si asked. "Tony told me all kinds of stories. Riots in the streets, people gunned down. I don't see it."

"This country is again on the brink of revolution," Karl said. "And it is dangerous, believe me."

"Then come to work for me."

"Drop the subject, Simon, please. Look, why don't we go downstairs and get a drink?"

"When do we eat?" Si asked. "I'm starved."

"It's only ten after five. We're having dinner at seven with a colleague of mine, a pilot I flew with. He had twenty-seven kills."

"Twenty-seven," Si repeated, properly impressed, but still thinking of food. He hadn't had a thing since breakfast with Meg in the sumptuous dining room of Elizabeth and Tony Fokker's home outside Amsterdam. The sun, flooding into the room through the open doors, shone on Meg's hair like a gold halo. She looked the picture of a happy young bride, which Si thought was not at all the case, at least not when they made love. Submit, that was the word for what she did in bed. Submit.

". . . Göring," Karl was saying. "Hermann Göring. He's anxious to meet you. You know of him, of course?"

"The name rings a bell," Si said. "Twenty-seven kills?"

"Yes, and he was awarded a Blue Max," Karl said. "He took over Richthofen's squadron after I left."

"By that time," said Si, "I was in Holland. Remember?"

Karl looked at him sourly. "How could I forget?"

The Bristol bar, at 5:10 on a Saturday afternoon, was crowded, heavy with tobacco smoke and noisy with chatter and laughter. The dark, mahogany-paneled room had a bar running half its length, and a number of tables and banquettes. A four-piece string orchestra played tango music.

Si and Karl found stools at the end of the bar. Karl ordered two martinis, but Si said, "None of those fancy drinks for me. Scotch, neat."

"You really are a barbarian," Karl said.

"That's no way to talk to your future boss."

"That's probably a better reason than any for not accepting your offer of employment," Karl said. "The thought of you as my boss turns my stomach."

"Then I'll make you my partner."

"You already have several of them, you said."

"So I'll have one more. Listen, Karl . . ." Si paused as the barman brought their drinks. "Goddammit, Karl, I need you!"

"The answer is no."

"Do I have to get down on my hands and knees and beg?"

"It won't help," said Karl. He clicked his glass against Si's. "Cheers."

"Try 'Down the hatch,' " Si said. "That's what you'll be using in America."

"You just never give up, do you?"

"Never," said Si, and now raised his glass. "*Prosit.*"

"The answer is still no."

2.

Hermann Göring was a husky, self-assured, nice-looking man of thirty, quite dashing in his brown tweed *Lodenjacke* and twill cavalry jodhpurs. Si liked him, and the feeling was mutual. As former combat pilots they had much in common but, clearly, their common interests transcended flying.

". . . yes, I too had my eye on that one," Göring said. He spoke English haltingly but well enough. He had just noticed Si admiring a particularly attractive woman at the bar. "I think we share the same tastes."

"Simon has just been married," Karl said.

Göring said to Si, "It's obvious that your wife is not with you."

Karl explained that Si had been advised not to bring Meg to Germany because of the unsettled political situation. Göring's face wrinkled skeptically. "I really don't believe things here are that 'dangerous.' Karl does have a way of exaggerating." He spoke quietly in German to Karl. Si's German was good enough to grasp the gist of Göring's words. Göring had said, "On the other hand, you may be right. Things might well become difficult. I'm expecting word from Munich any moment now."

"Now?" Karl asked, surprised. "Today?"

"It could be at this very moment," Göring said. He smiled apologetically at Si and, in English, said, "Forgive us. A little private business."

They were at Die Grunewald, a small family-type establishment near the Tiergarten. Göring was consuming the second of two huge helpings of *Gekochtes Rindfleisch* with *Krensauce*, boiled beef with horseradish sauce.

"My 'firing-squad' meal," he said to Si.

Si said, "You keep eating like that, you won't need a firing squad."

Göring laughed good-naturedly and reached for the half-empty bottle of Moselle that lay in a wine basket on the table. Pouring glasses for Karl and Si, then refilling his own, he proposed a toast.

"From former enemies to future friends."

"*Prosit*," Si said, winking at Karl, and they drank.

From that point on, Göring never stopped talking. After relating some amusing wartime anecdotes, he began questioning Si intently on the state of American military air power. What new tactics had been adopted, what new equipment? Si told him what he knew, little really, for he was familiar only with his own products, the CT-1 trainer and the Eagle, which he described in detail. Göring jokingly said the Eagle sounded like an overdeveloped Spad. Si said the Eagle was in fact a Spad descendant, along with some of the Sopwith Camel's better qualities.

They finished dinner with cognac and cigars, Cubans, Romeo y Juliets, which Göring said cost twelve billion marks each. Göring then suggested they take a brief walk over to party headquarters so Si might see the offices. What he really wanted, as Karl well knew, was to present Simon Conway with a business proposition.

The National Socialist German Workers' Party headquarters was on the second floor of an antique shop just off Unter den Linden on a short, narrow street lined on both sides with small shops. An outside staircase at the rear of the building led to the offices, three rooms cramped with desks and chairs, filing cabinets, and other office equipment. The walls of all three rooms, obviously once an apartment, were plastered with political posters. One wall was covered with a large red-white-and-black swastika banner. In the kitchen the sink was piled high with papers, magazines, and pamphlets.

The only other person present was a blond, delicate-featured young man in a crisp brown uniform with a swastika brassard, Sam Browne belt, and high-laced boots. He had been sitting at the kitchen table reading a magazine but jumped to attention when the men entered. The ivory handle of the ceremonial dagger in his belt gleamed under the light of the single bulb fixed into the ceiling.

"I am Obersturmführer Anton Moerzer, Captain Göring's aide," he said in German, shaking Si's hand. The young man's hand was surprisingly soft and smooth. He helped Si and Karl off with their overcoats and draped them over an empty chair. "May I offer you some refreshment? Coffee, perhaps?"

"Later, Anton, thank you," Göring said. He waved Si into a chair, sat opposite him knee to knee, and said, "Simon, I want to discuss something with you. With your permission, I will speak in German. Karl, you'll translate."

Göring went on, "I am sure it will come as no surprise to you, Simon, to learn that many of us are dissatisfied with conditions in Germany today, and we believe the only solution to the intolerable situation that now exists is . . . well, in a word, a change of government. We believe—and by 'we,' I include some of the most prominent names, General Ludendorff, for one—we believe that only the National Socialist German Workers' Party can save our country. But we need help, Simon. Financial help."

Si required no translation for that. He said to Karl, "Is he asking me for money?"

Göring replied for himself. "Not you, personally. Your company," he said. "Conway Aviation Industries."

"You want my company to help you with money?" Si said. "You want Conair to give you money?"

"Believe me, your contribution will not go unrewarded," Göring said. "It could result in aircraft orders, technical assistance, a host of other benefits. We shall be building a new air force. Your company will be in on the beginning."

"I don't think the German companies will appreciate that," Si said.

Karl said, "The Armistice terms prohibit us from manufacturing military aircraft. It has to be done secretly, and for the time being out of this country."

The idea of orders for dozens of airplanes excited Si. He envisioned himself walking into Morris Tannen's office and tossing a $250,000 contract onto his desk. Now, he would crow, now who's the salesman?

". . . Ford, the American automobile manufacturer, has made a generous donation," Göring was saying. "A personal contribution of a substantial sum. But we need more. At least fifty thousand dollars."

Henry Ford might have fifty thousand to donate to foreign governments, Si thought, but Conair certainly doesn't. Conair needs every dime to pay its own bills. But he knew that between Phil Granger and Ross Leonard the money could be raised.

"Exactly how much of an order are we talking about? And what kind of aircraft?" Even as he heard his own voice asking the question, he was thinking, I am willing to bet a thousand dollars—or that many trillion German marks—to a dime, that if I took them up on this I would be breaking at least two dozen laws.

"Pursuit planes," said Goring. "And perhaps bombers. A squadron of each to start with."

The phone rang. Anton Moerzer answered it and said to Göring, "Reitzler, from Munich!"

Göring snatched the phone from the table and pulled the earpiece away from Moerzer. He spoke, listened grimly, spoke again, listened. Si gathered bits and pieces of the conversation about "the prince," and "Ludendorff," and "Hitler." From time to time Göring shook his head angrily. Finally, after shouting into the phone for nearly a full minute without once pausing for breath, he slammed the earpiece back onto the cradle.

"Stupid!" he said in German. "The goddam stupid son of a bitch!" He glowered at Anton Moerzer and then at Karl. "The Crown Prince, our 'savior,' is reneging. He says he might not join us after all."

Karl said in English, "I don't think we should bore Simon with any of that."

"We've already told him more than we should have," Göring said. "He might as well know the rest of it. We'll make him a conspirator. Simon, I am going to confide in you. That telephone call I just received concerned a plan for taking over the government of this pathetic, bedeviled, bewildered nation. In a word, the man who had promised to act in our behalf, the former Crown Prince, has apparently changed his mind."

Anton Moerzer said, "That shouldn't come as any news."

Göring frowned disapprovingly at the young SA trooper, then addressed Karl. "Well, I have just been told that with or without the Crown Prince, Hitler says that we are following through on our plans."

"Hitler is crazy," Karl said. "He doesn't know what he's talking about!"

"Really?" Göring said calmly. He slid the telephone across the table toward Karl. "Why don't you call him and tell him so?"

"Without the Crown Prince, we'll look like a bunch of rabble," Karl replied in an equally calm voice. "The army won't be with us. Our *Putsch* will end up in a slaughter. Of us!"

Moerzer said to Karl, "We swore allegiance to Hitler. Now you disobey him and say he doesn't know what he's talking about?"

"*You* swore allegiance to him, not I." Karl turned to Göring. "A corporal, for God's sake! How can you even pay attention to him? Half the time he's raving."

"He's a genius, Karl," Göring said seriously. "A corporal he may have been, but I tell you he is a genius." Göring rose and said to Si, "I am needed in Munich. I leave Karl in charge of making satisfactory arrangements with you." He clasped Si's hand. "You won't regret helping us, Mr. Conway, I promise you."

Göring started away. Karl called after him, "Hermann, I tell you that without the Crown Prince the army won't support us! We'll all end up behind bars!"

Göring, who had already opened the door, stopped. "We have no need of the Prince, or any of the monarchy for that matter, none whatever," he said quietly. "As a matter of fact, Karl, we were seriously considering dropping them."

"Then I'm sorry," said Karl, "I can't go along with you."

Göring stepped back into the room. "By this time tomorrow, Adolf Hitler will have been declared Chancellor of Bavaria, and a few days later, Chancellor of all Germany."

"I doubt it," said Karl. "Not unless you think these brown-shirted thugs of yours can take on the German army!"

"You're a coward, not to mention a fool and, I think, a traitor," Göring said. He pulled open the kitchen-table drawer and withdrew a Luger. He handed the gun to Anton Moerzer. "You'll keep our friend Karl here until I get back from Munich. We can't risk his betraying us."

Moerzer slid back the Luger's breech and cranked a shell into the chamber. He leveled the gun at Karl. The prospect of pulling the trigger seemed to please him.

"And you, Mr. Conway . . ." Göring sighed unhappily. "I must ask you to remain here with Karl. Just for the next day or so. Anton will see that you're comfortable."

Karl laughed, genuinely amused. "Hermann, you're out of your mind if you think I'll spend the next two days locked up with this little fag!"

"Behave yourself, Karl," Göring said, and to Moerzer, "I'll phone you from Munich."

Karl moved past Moerzer and called after Göring, "Just a minute, Hermann—"

Karl never completed the sentence. Moerzer raised the Luger and lunged forward, clearly intending to smash the gun barrel into the back of Karl's head.

"Karl—!" Si cried, and hurled himself at Moerzer. The momentum of his body sent both Moerzer and Karl crashing into the table. The table collapsed under them. The gun flew from Moerzer's hand. Si scooped it up.

Göring had rushed back into the room. "What kind of nonsense is this?" His eyes darted past Karl to Moerzer. "Anton, no!"

Moerzer, still on the floor in a half-sitting position, had pulled his dagger from its scabbard and thrust it upward at Si's stomach. Si sidestepped, then brought the Luger butt down onto the bridge of Moerzer's nose. The force of the blow cracked the cartilage. Moerzer screamed and fell backward. He dropped the dagger and clamped both hands over his face. Blood gushed from between his fingers and streamed down his arms onto his shirt. Karl picked up the dagger and threw it across the room.

"All right, that's enough!" Göring said. "Give me the gun, please, Mr. Conway."

Si swung the gun around on Göring. "Stay right where you are, captain." He looked at Karl, who was kneeling over Moerzer, examining Moerzer's face. Behind the blood, the loose skin of Moerzer's nose appeared flattened against his cheek.

Si said, "I think we'd better get the hell out of here, Karl."

"Mr. Conway, you are making a terrible mistake," Göring said in English. He pointed a trembling finger at Karl. "This man is a traitor!"

"To whom, Hermann?" Karl asked. "To you? To your idol, Hitler? I want to save this country, not hand it over to maniacs!"

Göring ignored Karl. He walked toward Si, saying, "Simon, give me the gun."

Si lowered the muzzle slightly. Göring stopped; his eyes widened. The Luger was aimed straight at his crotch. Si wanted to laugh; he felt a crazy sense of power. For a tantalizing instant he wondered if the bullet would sever Göring's penis cleanly from his body.

"The gun, Mr. Conway," Göring said. He started toward Si again, hand extended palm up. "Please."

Si angled the muzzle down and fired. The sound of the gunshot reverberated deafeningly through the room. Göring stood frozen. The bullet had whistled between his legs and thudded into the linoleum floor.

Göring stared at the small, neat hole in the floor at his feet, then looked at Si. Si slapped the gun into Karl's hand and said, "Come on, let's move!"

Karl needed no urging. He swept his coat from the chair and hurried from the room. Si followed. Leaving, Si caught a last, vivid glimpse of Hermann Göring and Anton Moerzer, Göring standing motionless, one hand outstretched, mouth agape, his face twisted in an expression more of disbelief than anger. The anger was in Anton Moerzer's eyes. Anger, and hate. Si had never seen such hate. It was frightening, and all the more so etched on the once-beautiful face, now so grotesquely smashed.

Karl and Si raced down the stairs to the street, past the shuttered antique shops, and out to Unter den Linden, where they slowed to a normal pace and mingled with the crowd.

"Well, I saved you again, *mein Hauptmann*," Si said. "That little fairy was about to take a chunk out of your skull."

"Simon, all you've saved me from—" Karl paused abruptly. Two policemen were walking a few feet in front of them. Karl pulled Si into the doorway of a darkened government building until the policemen were out of sight. "All you've saved me from," he continued, "is not being able to go home to my own apartment. I've made a fool of Hermann Göring. He'll never forget or forgive. Luckily, he'll be in Munich for the next few days and too busy to bother about me. But I guarantee you that as soon as their *Putsch* is over, those SA hooligans will be tearing up this whole city looking for me. And you," he added, not displeased, "are in it as deeply as I am."

"Then this country is no place for either of us," Si said.

"Where is a better place for us?" Karl asked dryly. "America?"

"For me, absolutely," said Si. "And since you're in so much trouble here, I'm happy to lend a helping hand."

"If I didn't know better, I would swear you arranged this whole episode."

Si grinned. "I couldn't have done such a good job."

"No," said Karl. "I doubt you could have."

Not until a week later when they were safe in Amsterdam did Karl learn that, as he predicted, the *Putsch* had failed. Hitler had been arrested and imprisoned. Göring had fled into exile in Sweden. But they had come so close to succeeding that Karl was convinced of the inevitability of their eventually assuming power. And as much as he would have desired a role in the new government, Karl Eisler knew that in Hermann Göring he had made an implacable enemy.

Exactly three weeks after that night in Berlin, Karl was on his way to New York with Si and Meg, aboard the *Berengaria*. For Karl to enter the country on such short notice required considerable diplomatic maneuvering, but a flurry of cables between California State Senator Kenneth O'Neil, the U.S. State Department, and the U.S. embassy at The Hague achieved the desired result.

Si's success in bringing Karl Eisler to Conair was not the only important event of that December week of 1923. On the *Sante Fe Special*, en route to Los Angeles, somewhere between St. Louis and Albuquerque, Meg became pregnant.

PART TWO

NEW YORK TO PARIS

9

"You're a million miles away," Ruth Tannen whispered into Meg's ear.

Meg, momentarily startled, smiled politely. "Not a million miles," she said. "A few thousand maybe. What were you saying?"

"I said I love this table." Ruth rubbed the flat of her hand over the polished pine surface. "You certainly didn't find it in any furniture store."

"It belonged to my parents," Meg said. The table was one of the few treasured items she had reclaimed from the Taylor's Ogunquit home. A large, graceful, trestled piece, solid pine, seating ten, it might well have been custom-made for the dining room here in Si and Meg's new house on Corona del Mar in Pacific Palisades.

They had moved into the new house eight months before, in August of 1926, the day after Richard's second birthday. The first words out of the child's mouth were "It's a castle, Mama! A castle!"

"And fit for a king," Si had said, hoisting his older son on his shoulders and carrying him across the threshold. Meg, with eleven-month-old Frank in her arms, had followed behind.

"Castle" was not so inaccurate a description. A 5,000-square-foot Monterey Colonial, the house was perched on a knoll behind a rolling, immaculately landscaped front lawn that extended far back from the street. There were four big bedrooms, a large dining room, an even larger living room, a paneled library, and, in the basement, what the realtor called a "rumpus room." The kitchen, with the most up-to-date appliances, had an eight-burner gas range, twin sinks, and a gigantic icebox. Servants' quarters were above the four-car garage. An enormous backyard overlooked the ocean.

The house had been built only two years before and the asking price was exorbitant, $27,500, but the moment Meg saw it she knew it was for her. And the timing was right. Business was booming. True, the 220 project had nearly bankrupted Conair—of the six airplanes manufactured, five were lost in accidents—but with Karl Eisler's next design, the 330, the company quickly recovered. The War Department, at newly elected United States Senator Kenneth O'Neil's urging, requested Conair to submit plans for a U.S. Army Air Corps bomber based upon the 330. Within ninety days of the Conair Conqueror's first flight the army ordered twenty five production models. This was followed by yet another War Department contract for an entirely new U.S. Navy pursuit airplane for shipboard operation on the two aircraft carriers then under construction, *Saratoga* and *Lexington*.

The airline division, Conway Air Transport Service, was also prospering. After being awarded the lucrative San Francisco–Los Angeles and Los Angeles–Salt Lake City airmail routes, CATS had hired fifteen new pilots and ordered a dozen 110s from its parent company, Conair.

As a result, the Conways were living quite comfortably. When their $13-a-week live-in Negro maid and cook went shopping, the greengrocers and butchers were only too pleased to offer unlimited credit. Meg bought her dresses at Bullocks and J. W. Robinson's, her hats at I. Magnin's new boutique in Hollywood. With the exception of the battered old gray fedora he refused to part with, Meg had managed to convince Si to wear better clothes. He now bought his suits from Harris & Frank Co.—no Brooks Brothers, of course, but it served the purpose. Next week, in New York on their way to Europe, she would somehow get him into Brooks for a whole new wardrobe.

"Meg, this roast beef is so incredibly tender," Jessica Leonard, Ross's wife, said. She sliced a sliver of meat from the small piece remaining on her plate. "Where did you buy it?"

"There's a new market called Jurgensen's," Meg said. "Down in the Larchmont area, near where they're putting up the Paramount studios. They deliver. All you do is phone in your order."

"Expensive?"

"No more than any other good market," Meg said. "Oh, I suppose a few cents more because of the delivery." She glanced down the length of the table at Si's empty chair. The chair to the left of Si's was also vacant. Ross Leonard had been sitting there. Ten minutes ago the two men had excused themselves to go into the library for a private conversation.

Their guest of honor appeared hardly aware of his host's absence.

Walter Driscoll, whom President Coolidge had recently appointed Assistant Postmaster General, sat with Morris Tannen on one side and Phil Granger on the other. It reminded Meg of a fox trapped by two hounds.

Seated opposite Morris and Granger, being very charming to Jessica Leonard, was motion-picture director Herbert Fallon. A handsomely graying man who affected an Oxford accent, Fallon came from New York's Lower East Side, the son of Irish immigrant parents. He had met Si and Karl nearly four years before on the *Berengaria*.

In Herbert Fallon the two wartime fliers discovered an instant admirer and drinking companion, and Karl had served as technical director and aerial-scene coordinator on Fallon's first big movie, a war story. At Morris Tannen's insistence, the phrase "Technical Assistance Provided by Conway Aviation Industries, Inc." appeared in the film's opening credits. Not only was the picture an artistic success, it grossed more than $1 million. For Herbert Fallon's new picture, *The Flying Circus*, budgeted at $450,000, Karl would once again coordinate the aerial scenes and personally fly an "enemy" airplane.

Tonight's dinner party was a "business dinner." Si disliked these functions. He much preferred the company of his pilots, drinking and carousing with them at Wally's, the Santa Monica speakeasy where he spent his spare time. When he had any spare time, which was seldom.

Karl Eisler, on the other hand, enjoyed the evenings at the Conways. Meg found him charming, intelligent, and considerate. Tonight, however, Karl was busy at his drafting table, working on the 445, the most important project Conair had yet undertaken.

New York to Paris, nonstop.

The 445 was Conair's entry for the Orteig Prize, $25,000, offered by wealthy New York realtor Raymond Orteig to the first man or men to complete the flight. So far, in this first week of April 1927, seventeen pilots—American and European alike—had entered the contest. Obviously, it was not the money that attracted them—$25,000 hardly covered the expenses incurred—but the achievement itself.

Si, with Freddie Silcox as his copilot, was determined to win, and in a Conway product, the 445. The airplane, christened the Viking by Morris Tannen, was a modification of Conair's first all-metal airplane, the 440, a trimotored high-winged monoplane. Nine 440s were already in regular CATS service. The version that would fly the Atlantic had three special souped-up Jensen engines and two extra fuel tanks in the cabin.

The very thought of flying terrified Meg, but whenever she mentioned her fear to Si he looked at her as though she were joking. So she no longer spoke of her terror, not even when Si took little Frank up in a plane.

Conair was growing so fast she could hardly tell the players without a program. Players without a program, a nice turn of phrase. She had seen it in a recent *Liberty Magazine* at the doctor's office, in an article by Grantland Rice, claiming Bobby Jones to be the world's finest golfer. How she missed the game! She could not remember when she had last played. But then who had time for golf when you were continually pregnant? Yes, again, which she had found out only that week. She hoped it would be a girl because, for sure, it was the last one.

". . . when will you and Si be leaving?" Ruth was asking.

"I'm sorry, Ruth. I was daydreaming again. What did you say?"

"I asked when you and Si are leaving for Europe."

"Meg and Si to Europe?" Jessica Leonard said. She rolled her eyes. "A second honeymoon, eh?"

Meg wanted to say, Second honeymoon? My God, I hope not! I don't think I've ever recovered from the first one. Instead, she replied, "I doubt there'll be time for any honeymoons. The whole purpose of the trip is for Si to prepare for the Atlantic flight. We're going first to Ireland, then England, and then France. He wants to practically walk over every inch of the flight path."

"That's our Si," Jessica said. "All business."

"In this case, it's necessary," Phil Granger said. "He wants to know the railroads, the highways, the rivers. Everything and anything that will get them to Paris."

Meg loathed Philip Granger. After Karl, Granger was the first of Si's associates she had met, and she would never forget his offhand remark about Morris and Ruth Tannen: "Yes, I'm sure you'll like them. They're Jews, but very nice."

Outside of a few girls at Vassar, Meg had never known any Jews. All she knew was that they were somehow "different," with a different religion and background, and somewhat odd customs. To Meg's surprise, Ruth Tannen was like any other American girl, and she had befriended Meg when Meg first arrived in Los Angeles and needed a friend. Taken her under her wing, as Ruth liked to say.

". . . but at least you'll see Paris," Herbert Fallon was saying.

"I certainly hope so," Meg said.

Just then the library door burst open and Si strode into the dining room. "Morris! Phil!" he shouted. "Come in here!" He returned to the library, slamming the door.

" 'His Master's Voice,' " Granger said dryly, but promptly excused himself and hurried into the library with Morris.

Walter Driscoll laughed uneasily. "I hope they're not going to kill each other."

"Don't be silly," Ruth Tannen said. "They're talking business."

In the library, Si resumed his place at the kidney-shaped desk and pointed an empty brandy snifter angrily at Ross. But Phil Granger spoke first. "Si, don't you think you should pay some attention to Walter Driscoll?"

"I call ten thousand dollars in his pocket for an airmail contract paying attention to him," Si said. "Now I want you to hear what this man is trying to pull." He pointed the glass at Ross again. "Tell them, Ross."

Ross sat sprawled in a leather club chair. The paneled wall behind him was lined with framed photographs. Except for an aerial shot of the entire Mines Field Conair complex and one enlarged photo of Si and young Frank in a 110 cockpit, most of the photos were of Si posing in front of various Conair airplanes, and one with Si and John Gilbert, who had played the lead in Herbert Fallon's first war picture.

Ross said, "I've been in Seattle all week, talking to Bill Boeing. They're offering to merge with us. They'll pay a half million cash for all our outstanding stock plus options for Boeing stock on a one-for-one basis. Do you realize what an opportunity this is?"

"Yeah, for you," Si said. "To make you richer, that's the opportunity!"

Ross, ignoring Si, addressed Morris and Phil Granger. "We not only put all that cash in our pockets, we become the biggest aircraft manufacturers in the country. Boeing says if we come in with them they'll drop their own plans for a new transport and gear up their whole production line for the 440."

"We don't need Bill Boeing," Si said. "We don't need anybody!"

"Simmer down, Si," Phil Granger said. "Ross, it's no secret that Boeing's so-called new transport isn't even a gleam in Bill Boeing's eye yet. He knows the 440 is the hottest thing that's ever come out of an American factory."

"He also knows how much we spent on development costs for that plane, and what it did to our cash situation, and how our esteemed leader refuses to improve that cash situation by selling the 440 to other airlines," Ross said.

Ross continued speaking, but all his talk of "costs," and "cash," and "sales," and "markets" bored Si. He was only interested in making the airplanes and flying them. Moreover, since Morris invariably and unquestioningly sided with Si, if Si opposed an action, that was the end of it. Although Conair had been reorganized when Karl Eisler joined the company, Si and Morris controlled it. Of the 500,000 shares of stock that had been issued, Si held 160,000, and Morris 120,000. Philip Granger and Charlie Jensen held 75,000 each. Karl Eisler had received 30,000 shares and a seat on the board of directors. Ross Leonard's original 5 percent interest now equaled 40,000 shares of stock. Ross's vote was meaningless.

Si poured himself a fresh brandy and lit a cigarette. The top of Ross's head obscured Si's view of the photo of himself and Frank. The Crown Prince, Si liked to call him. One and a half years old, and already he knew the difference between a biplane and a monoplane. And he loved to fly. Si had taken him up a dozen times. And he'd take Richard up, too, as soon as the older boy outgrew some infantile fear of engine noise. Whenever Richard heard an engine he clasped his hands over his ears in terror.

The conversation went on. Snippets of it penetrated Si's consciousness. ". . . if it's worth a half million to Boeing, it has to be worth ten times that much to us," Granger said. Then, from Morris, ". . . I'm sorry, Ross. I agree with Si. Forget it."

Ross's cool voice alerted Si.

"Say that again," Si demanded.

"I said, Si, that I'll sell my stock to Boeing."

"You're required to offer it to the company first," Granger said.

"All right, I'm offering it," Ross said. "Forty thousand shares at par value. Five bucks a share."

Morris gasped. "That's two hundred thousand!"

"A fair price," said Ross. "And I want it all in cash."

"Ross, you know damn well we don't have that kind of cash," Granger said.

"Well, tell me, gentlemen, do you know why you don't have that kind of cash?" Ross asked, and answered his own question. "Because Mr. Conway here continually pours all your profit into new projects." He looked at Si. "We decided it was a good idea for the pilots to wear uniforms, but you decided they shouldn't have to pay for it themselves; the company should pick up the tab. And what about—"

"—please, Ross, we've been all over that," Phil Granger said. "A dozen times."

Ross was undaunted. "And what about the ten thousand dollars you 'donated' to Billy Mitchell's defense fund?" he continued to Si. "And we won't even talk about what it cost for you to go to Washington and stay there a week while you testified for him."

"It was worth the publicity," Morris said.

All Si knew was that if he had to do it all over again, and if it cost twice $10,000, he would not hesitate. Brigadier Billy Mitchell had not only disobeyed his superiors' orders to stop lobbying for an independent air force, he had also refused to stop complaining publicly about the dangerously obsolescent condition of Air Service equipment. For this he was charged with insubordination and court-martialed.

Si had rushed to Washington to testify on Mitchell's behalf. To no avail. Mitchell was found guilty and dismissed from the service. In the end, however, the affair did much to clean up and improve the Air Service. Modern airplanes, including the Conair Conquerors, were ordered and new, younger, more imaginative officers appointed to run the service.

"... but that ten thousand was chicken feed compared to what you've thrown away on this plane you're building for the Atlantic flight," Ross Leonard was saying. "And how much of it's gone to Charlie Jensen for those 'magic' engines? How much—"

"—hold it, Ross," said Morris. "You're not suggesting we shouldn't enter the Orteig contest? My God, it will make this company famous around the world!"

"Of course I'm not suggesting we shouldn't enter," Ross said calmly. "I'm suggesting we not bankrupt the company to do it. Have you any idea how much this little adventure has cost us so far? Close to thirty-five thousand dollars!"

"Two hundred thousand, Ross?" Si said. "Is that what you want? All right, two hundred thousand is what you'll get."

The room fell abruptly silent. Morris and Granger regarded Si incredulously.

"Si—" Morris started to say, dismayed.

Si held up his hand to silence the protest. "We'll pay the son of a bitch his two hundred thousand."

"Cash," said Ross. "No notes, please, cash. And allow me to tell you what I'll do with that cash: I'll set up my own airline. So you'll not only lose the chance to merge on an equal basis with Boeing, you'll also end up with me as a competitor."

"We'll pay you in cash," Si heard himself saying. "If I have to go out and personally panhandle for it, we'll pay you. Now get the hell out of my sight!"

Ross looked at Morris and shrugged. "This is some 'forward-looking' individual running your company."

"It's his company," Morris said.

"Goodbye, Ross," Si said. "Talk to Phil in the morning about the arrangements."

Granger said, "Better go, Ross. I'll be in touch first thing tomorrow."

Si rose and turned his back on Ross. He stood at the window that overlooked Pacific Coast Highway and the ocean. Strings of colored electric light bulbs outlining the barnlike structure of the dance pavilion on Santa Monica Pier blinked red, white, and blue in the night. Beyond the pier, on the water, the red running lights of a small boat reminded him of his promise to Frank of a trip to Catalina on one of the excursion boats.

". . . all right, Si, where do we find two hundred thousand dollars?" Phil Granger was asking.

Si turned. Ross was gone. "A bank," Si said. "Any one of a dozen of them."

"We'll have to put up half the company for collateral," Morris said.

"So do it," Si said. "To get rid of Ross Leonard, it's worth it."

2.

If Meg could hardly tell the players without a program, not even players with numbers would have helped Si. In four years, Conair's airframe manufacturing division alone had grown tenfold. Three hundred and forty-seven people, from carpenters to tool-and-die makers, were now engaged full-time. One entire room was crammed with designers and draftsmen, and the Jensen engine division employed a work force of more than fifty. The airline division, CATS, employed two hundred people, including twenty-eight pilots. For Si, the four years had passed in a constant flow of new names and faces.

A pair of old names and faces, Ceil Bjornsted and Freddie Silcox, made Si's life considerably easier. Two weeks to the day following Si's arrival in Los Angeles with his new bride, Ceil and Freddie had driven to Tijuana and were married. Si threw a party for the couple, and as a wedding gift gave Freddie a whopping $25 weekly raise. Ceil met Meg for the first time at the party. Later, Meg confided to Ruth Tannen that Ceil looked at her as though she were a specimen under a microscope, and that she knew Si had had an affair with the woman.

Ruth had carefully replied, "Oh, no, Meg, I'm sure you're wrong."

Karl Eisler knew of Si's relationship with Ceil. Shortly after Ceil and Freddie's marriage, he had overheard a conversation between Si and Ceil.

". . . tell me something, Ceil," Si had asked. "Is it as good with Freddie as it used to be with me?"

"Si, as good as it was with you, it wasn't worth the trouble," she had said.

Karl was fond of Freddie, and as he came to know him better, he realized how utterly shattered Freddie would be if he ever learned about Ceil and Si. A few days after Ross Leonard's "resignation," Karl and Freddie were preparing to take off on a test flight of the Viking. Si was at the field with them. Si said Freddie looked lousy. Freddie said he felt lousy; he had a head cold. He said he caught it from Ceil.

"How's she feeling?" Si asked.

"Oh, she's all over it," Freddie said. "She gave it to me, instead."

Si jabbed Freddie's elbow playfully. "I think she's all over *you*! She's keeping you up too late at night! You tell her the boss said to give you a rest!"

Freddie laughed; he thought it was funny. Karl did not, and fought an impulse to take Si aside and tell him to ease off. But the conversation would have interfered with an unresolved problem of Karl's own with Si, something that had to be dealt with before the Atlantic flight.

Karl tried to concentrate on the work at hand, but several hours later, seven thousand feet over Santa Monica Bay, he was again reminded of Si. Freddie, in the Viking's left seat, began sneezing again. The outside air temperature read fifteen degrees below zero, and the Viking was unheated.

Freddie pulled a handkerchief from his hip pocket and blew his nose. "I think Si had a point!" He had to shout to be heard over the noise of the engines. "Maybe I should sleep in a different room!" But he grinned to show he was only kidding.

Si had a point, Karl told himself grimly. That was the whole damn trouble with Si. He always thought he had a point.

Freddie swung the control column over to the right side and locked it into position in front of Karl. "Okay, Karl, she's all yours!"

Karl gripped the wheel with one hand and closed the other around the three throttle knobs. He eased the throttles forward. The engines responded instantly. The powerful Jensen J-12s roared smoothly and steadily. The airplane surged ahead like a race horse under the whip.

Below, off to the left, was Catalina, a patch of brown in a vast blue-green carpet. Karl glanced out his window at the right engine. The oil-pressure gauge affixed to the nacelle was in the green. The nose and left-engine gauges all read normal.

So many instruments, he thought. They intimidated you. Mixture controls, temperature controls, voltage meters, rheostats, climb indicator, turn and bank indicator. In the old days you relied solely on your compass, tachometer, altimeter, and fuel gauge. This was why he enjoyed flying the antiques, the single-engined scouts. They were so much simpler.

"Try a left turn!" Freddie shouted.

Karl swung the wheel left and applied left rudder. The big airplane turned smoothly. Karl held her in the turn until he had almost banked a full 360 degrees, then leveled her wings. Ahead was the Santa Monica shoreline, and the city itself spreading east to the bean fields and citrus groves of West Los Angeles. Far to the right he could just make out Mines Field, the black asphalt runway and the sloping roofs of the Conair assembly buildings.

"She sure don't handle as easy as the 440!" Freddie shouted.

Ah, the 440, Karl thought, the Viking's progenitor, an extraordinary machine. With a range of nearly seven hundred miles, the 440 carried nine passengers in its heated cabin, and in relative comfort—if you overlooked the jackhammer pounding of the three Jensen engines. The 445, the Viking, with extra fuel tanks, would fly twenty-eight hundred miles nonstop.

It would fly the Atlantic.

"She handles like a truck, but who cares?" Karl shouted back. But he was thinking, I care, because flying these big airplanes makes me feel like a truck driver. A pursuit plane, now that was different; you were part of it, it was part of you, a mechanical extension of your body. Yes, and one of these days I will design a scout, a pursuit plane that will outfly and outfight anything in the sky. One of these days.

But tomorrow, in Herbert Fallon's movie, he would be flying a scout, a replica of a D-7. He was looking forward to it. He even looked forward to the elementary pleasure of shouting "Contact!" to start the engine.

Not so pleasurable was the thought of approaching Si and demanding once again to be part of the crew on the Atlantic flight. Si had flatly turned him down the first time he asked. Si wanted not an extra ounce of weight, not even an extra sandwich. He was actually considering removing the radio, 206 additional pounds.

For all that, Karl believed it was wrong of Si to deny him the privilege of going along. He had no argument with Si's choice of Freddie as copilot. Freddie was a far more experienced multiengined pilot. That at least made sense. But so did Karl's participation. Extra weight be damned.

". . . hey, come in, L.A., come in!" It was Freddie, shouting into the radio mouthpiece. "Viking zero-one calling L.A. Come in, L.A.! They can't hear me," he said to Karl.

"They should," Karl said. "You're screaming loud enough to be heard in San Francisco. You forgot to reel out the antenna!"

"Fuck it!" Freddie said. He ripped off his earphones and tossed them on the cockpit floor behind him. The mouthpiece, resembling an ordinary telephone mouthpiece, followed. They had been experimenting with the radio system for weeks. When it worked, even with the hundred-yard trailing antenna correctly deployed, you could hardly hear a voice through the interminable static. In theory, if you were close enough, you could contact ships at sea.

"All right, you take it," Karl said. He returned the control wheel to the left side. "Let's go home."

Freddie gripped the wheel. "I got it," he said. "So what do you think? Will she get us to Paris?"

"I think she'll get you wherever you want to go," Karl said. Or wherever *I* want to go, he thought, which after Paris was Vienna. Erika had said she would meet him anywhere, "anywhere" of course meaning outside Germany. He was still unable to return to his own country because of fear of reprisal from Nazi thugs.

Hitler was out of prison, and Göring back from exile in Sweden. Karl was confident he could deal with those two, but that still left Göring's pretty boy, Anton Moerzer, whom Karl knew would never forget or forgive what had been done to him and had sworn revenge. So now it was not Göring in exile, it was Karl.

They were over Santa Monica beach, descending south toward the field. "Hey, you coming over for supper tonight?" Freddie asked. He and Karl had become good friends, and Wednesday suppers were now almost a ritual. Ceil was a fine cook. And a fine woman, an opinion once shared by Simon Conway, Karl reminded himself.

Freddie came in slightly high but corrected and brought the big airplane down in a perfect three-point landing, a "grease job." He went off to check on the day's pilot assignments, while Karl entered the dispatch office to file his report. Si was waiting at the counter.

"That was a nice landing," Si said. "Freddie can really handle that baby."

"How do you know it was Freddie, Si?"

"Technique, Karl," Si said. "Technique. Let me see your performance notes."

Si scanned the notes and tossed the clipboard onto the counter. "Tommy Atkinson called in sick with a hundred and two temperature," he said. "So he won't be flying tomorrow for Fallon." Tommy Atkinson was a CATS pilot who, with Karl, had been hired to fly in the climactic one-on-one dogfight scene in Herbert Fallon's new movie.

"I'll find someone else," Karl said. "For ten dollars a day it won't be hard. Si," he continued in the same breath, "I want to go with you and Freddie."

"Go where?"

Karl glanced around the office. The dispatcher and two pilots were at the counter discussing a freight manifest. Karl, who had just lit a cigarette, stubbed it out in the brass propeller-hub ashtray on the counter. "Come outside, would you please?"

They left the office and stepped onto the tarmac, where two 110s were noisily warming up. "I want to make the Atlantic flight," Karl said.

"I thought we've already been through all that," Si said. "I thought you agreed with me about the weight."

"My one hundred and sixty pounds won't make that much difference."

"The hell it won't. It's thirty gallons of gasoline. Come on, Karl, do us both a favor and forget it. Please." Si's voice hardened. "Please."

"You owe me this, Si."

"I'm not taking three men, Karl. I'm taking two, period. I mean to fly that airplane to Paris and land at Le Bourget in one piece. My best chance for that is to have Freddie with me, not you."

Karl started to say, You'll have an even better chance with three of us, for God's sake! The words died in his throat. For the very first time, he understood why Si preferred Freddie as copilot. Because Freddie would be precisely that, a copilot, subordinate to Si, an employee. Si wanted no equal aboard, who might question or challenge a decision.

And, Karl decided, Si was right. It had to be that way. "Yes," he said, almost to himself, "you have a point. I'll not bring it up again."

"Good. I'm glad you see it my way."

Karl had to laugh. He knew Si better than Si knew himself. "You don't believe me, do you?"

"I'm waiting for the other shoe."

"It's dropped, Si. I surrender. *Kamerad!*" He changed the subject. "Any suggestions about Tommy Atkinson's replacement for tomorrow?"

"You're looking at him," Si said.

"You?" Karl said. "You'll fly in the movie?"

"Me," Si said, and added dryly, "That is, if you don't object."

"You and I, Si? In a dogfight?"

"Like old times."

"When was the last time you flew a Spad?"

"I haven't forgotten how."

"Don't you think you might be a little rusty?"
"Two minutes chasing you around, I'll be good as new."
"How 'good' was that, Si?"

3.

Nearly four years before, in the *Berengaria*'s first-class smoking room, Simon Conway and Karl Eisler had entertained Herbert Fallon with their wartime exploits. Their stories had inspired the first, successful Herbert Fallon war picture. Now he was making another "aerial extravaganza," *The Flying Circus*. The basis of the script was the Conway-Eisler rivalry, culminating in the duel over Monmedy.

The American ace's name was Ben Morton, played by Richard Barthelmess, who actually bore a slight resemblance to Si. Neil Hamilton played the German, Baron Franz Kessler. The actual flying was done by pilots doubling for the stars—Karl for Neil Hamilton, Tommy Atkinson for Barthelmess.

All but one of the film's aerial sequences were completed. Only the climactic duel remained. With the exception of the minor inaccuracy of substituting a Spad and a D-7 for the actual Nieuport and Fokker Triplane—the original aircraft were unavailable—Fallon demanded optimal authenticity. For audience acceptance, however, the events were slightly transposed: the American shoots down the German, and the German subsequently saves the American's life—at the cost of his own.

Fallon had always intended to film this final scene with the two wartime aces reenacting their real-life roles. On the day prior to the filming, Fallon offered Tommy Atkinson a fifty-dollar bonus to call in sick. Fallon, faced with this "emergency," asked Si to fly in Tommy's place.

The film company's location was a grassy meadow in the San Fernando Valley. An "airdrome" bearing a vague resemblance to Saint-Pol-sur-Mer had been constructed, complete with a false-fronted chateau and genuine tent hangars. At Si's insistence, Meg brought Richard and Frank to watch the filming.

If realism was what Herbert Fallon desired, then Si would damn well see to it that realism was what he got. The first take called for the opposing aces to meet at five thousand feet over the rendezvous. Both pilots were to approach each other like prizefighters in the ring formally acknowledging each other's presence, and then, as in a boxing match, the combatants would separate and commence the fight.

The day was clear and cloudless, pleasantly mild for February.

Even at five thousand feet, with the parachute and harness cramming him into the Spad cockpit like a cork into a bottle, Si was not uncomfortable. The wind, blasting into the windscreen, streamed past his goggled face. The smell of gasoline and oil wafted astringently into his nostrils. It smelled wonderful. The pounding of the engine deafened him. It felt wonderful.

Almost as a reflex, seeing the blunt-nosed D-7 in the distance, he charged his machine guns. The belts were filled with blank cartridges, every fifth one rigged to emit a tiny puff of white smoke when fired. Even as he cranked the gun charging lever, Si forgot this was make-believe. It was 1918, and twelve minutes earlier he had taken off from Saint-Pol-sur-Mer to engage Captain Karl Eisler over Monmedy.

The two airplanes raced toward each other. Fallon's instructions were for each man to salute the other, then bank away. Karl complied. Si did not. Instead, totally disregarding the rules, violating the neutral zone, he climbed straight up, turned ninety degrees, and reversed, which would bring him out above and behind Karl.

"You're dead, you Kraut bastard!" Si shouted into the wind, his finger on the control-stick gun trigger, his eye fixed on the Vickers gunsight, where he expected to find the D-7 lined squarely in the crosshairs.

Karl was not there.

Immediately, behind him, Si heard the staccato hammering of twin Spandaus. He whirled around in the cockpit and saw the D-7 glued to his tail. Karl Eisler touched a gloved hand to his helmet in a crisp, mocking salute. He had fully anticipated Si's opening maneuver and, an instant after banking away, had pulled straight up himself and rolled into a loop that brought him out on Si's tail.

Si pushed the Spad's stick forward and kicked right rudder. The little airplane, diving, skidded to the right. The D-7 followed. Si pulled the stick back into his stomach. The Spad shot upward, then arced over on its left wing in an almost complete loop that brought it out on the D-7's tail.

Karl rolled into a steep dive. Si followed, twisting and turning. Now Si was sure that the war had never ended. He was nine thousand feet over Monmedy, his heart thumping in that familiar combination of exhilaration and fear, matching his skill against the enemy's, his life against the other's. The years since France had never happened.

He was so immersed in the reality of the duel that he began wondering how he could explain this "dream" to the others at the squadron. This dream of having survived the war and gone on to head his own airline and aircraft manufacturing business. When he returned to the squadron—if he returned—he would tell Ledoux about it. Ledoux would understand and not laugh at him.

In the camera plane, Herbert Fallon watched, awed. The two "adversaries" dove and climbed, twisted and turned, neither gaining any discernible advantage. They had completely abandoned what Fallon called the Game Plan and had drifted miles away from the starting point to somewhere over the Santa Monica Mountains. Beyond the mountains the ocean sparkled blue and green in the sun.

Fallon did not know whether to be angry or pleased, but certainly intended to keep the camera rolling and preserve on film an incredible exhibition of flying. The audience would be screaming in their seats. For a crazy moment Fallon wished the guns were loaded with live ammunition.

As far as the pilots were concerned, the guns really did contain live ammunition. Both airplanes had leveled out, five hundred yards apart, facing each other. The D-7, throttle wide open, raced straight at the Spad. The onrushing D-7 loomed larger and larger in Si's windscreen. The red-painted tips of the D-7's whirling propeller blades formed a solid disk in front of the airplane. The disk grew larger. The two airplanes were milliseconds from colliding.

That son of a bitch! Si thought. He thinks he can frighten me into veering off. He thinks I have gotten soft and have lost my guts. He is wrong, a thousand percent wrong. I will not move. Again, they were over Monmedy, each determined to kill the other.

But this time Simon Conway refused to surrender control to that survival reflex that the last time had saved them both. The D-7 was so close Si could clearly see Karl Eisler's eyes behind the goggles. Cold, hard, resolute eyes. But Si knew Karl would give way. Si did not understand how he knew this, only that it would happen.

Si was right.

Fifty yards away, Karl broke off in a shallow diving turn. Si hurtled past, above the D-7, then rolled over and came out behind the Fokker. He lowered the Spad's nose and dove straight down at the D-7. He had forced Karl to break off once, he would do it again. Karl saw the oncoming Spad and pulled the D-7's stick back almost into his stomach. The D-7 rose on its tail almost vertically. It was so abrupt a maneuver and placed so much strain on the D-7's fragile wings that the entire top left wing buckled.

Carried by the momentum of the climb, the D-7 continued upward an instant. She resembled a huge stricken bird, fluttering helplessly, then flattening out and rolling over on her back. The collapsed wing, free now of both attaching struts, lay folded back against the

D-7's fuselage. The airplane, corkscrewing uncontrollably, fell toward the ground like a leaf caught in a downdraft.

Si had only glimpsed the shattered D-7 as he flew past it, climbing. Leveling out and banking around, he saw it clearly, and Karl's helmeted head slumped forward against the crash pad. It brought Si back to reality. This was not 1918, and it was no victory. It was murder. He had murdered Karl Eisler. He watched the D-7 spiral downward.

The buckled wing momentarily obscured Si's view of the cockpit. And then an object plummeted from the airplane. The image of another former Lafayette Escadrille squadron mate, Raoul Lufbury, loomed before Si. Luf had crawled out of his burning Spad and jumped to his death. Si remembered Lufbury's fear of burning alive. But Karl Eisler was not on fire and, unlike Lufbury, wore a parachute.

The figure tumbled downward, faster it seemed than the spiraling D-7. The airplane's other wings, upper and lower, had also folded and lay against the fuselage. More pieces broke away, a section of the empennage, and then the whole undercarriage.

"Pull the cord, Karl!" Si screamed aloud. "Jesus Christ, pull the fucking cord!"

The chute opened. First, a flash of white, then a narrow stream of white that widened and billowed out. Karl's body appeared suspended in midair and then, as the chute's shroud lines fully extended, was hurled almost violently upward. Si banked the Spad around and flew past Karl. Karl, conscious, was reaching up to grasp the harness. Si waved. Karl did not wave back.

Far below, a huge cloud of black dust rose from the ground. The D-7's fuselage had plowed into an open field not far from the highway. There was no sign of fire. Karl must have switched off the ignition. Si jockeyed the Spad closer to Karl. Karl had also been gazing at the splintered wreckage. Now he looked up at Si. Even at this distance, Karl's eyes behind the goggles were every bit as hard and resolute as they had been a few minutes before. More so, and cold with rage.

Karl's parachute came down in the middle of Roosevelt Highway, in Malibu, a mile from the village. As though playing out the final act in a comedy of tragic errors, the chute floated onto the road fifty feet in front of an approaching truck, which nearly ran Karl down. The truck driver, an Oxnard strawberry grower delivering a load of early-spring produce to town, was so flustered that he simply careened the truck around Karl and sped away. A passing sheriff's squad car picked Karl up.

Si witnessed all this from the Spad, flying low over the beach.

Knowing Karl was safe and apparently uninjured, Si returned to the movie airdrome. Word of the accident had already reached the set. Meg had sent the boys home with one of Fallon's drivers. By the time Si and Meg arrived in Pacific Palisades, Karl was sitting on the front porch steps, waiting. He still wore his flying clothes, helmet and goggles stuffed inside his half-buttoned leather jacket. He had borrowed a car from the Malibu sheriff.

Si whispered to Meg, "Now I'm in for it!"

"From what you told me, you deserve it," she said.

Si got out of the car and approached Karl. "Am I glad to see you! Let's go inside and have a drink." He grinned. "A lot of drinks! I think we need it, don't you?"

Meg started saying, "Karl, I'm so thankful you're—"

"—excuse me, Meg," Karl said. "I want to talk to Si."

"Sure, but let's go inside," Si said.

"Right here is fine," Karl said.

They waited in heavy silence until Meg was in the house. Si said, "Karl, I'd really like a drink—"

"—now I'm certain of it," Karl said quietly. "You really are insane. Mad as a hatter!"

"Come on, Karl, you're alive, in one piece. All's well that ends well."

"I want to tell you something," Karl said in the same flat, quiet voice. "I'm glad you're not taking me on the Atlantic flight. I think you're so obsessed with winning—and it doesn't matter what: the Atlantic, or a bloody make-believe motion picture!—you're so obsessed with it that you'll trample anything or anyone in your way. This afternoon convinced me."

The blandness of Karl's voice annoyed Si. It was like the pronouncement of some scientifically irrefutable fact. But what the hell was so bad about wanting to win?

He said, "You're only pissed off because I outflew you. I beat you, and you can't stand it!"

Karl said nothing. Si thought he had struck such a nerve of truth that Karl had no response. Si was wrong. Karl's silence was caused by his momentary inability to translate from German into English the angry words surging to his lips.

Si said, "Admit it, for Christ's sake!"

"You cheated," Karl said. "You always cheat. It's the only way you know how to win."

Si wanted to say, I always cheat? I suppose I cheated when I pulled you out of a burning airplane, and that time I saved your ass in Holland? And let's not forget Berlin!

Instead, he said, "All right, you said your piece. What else?"

Just then Richard dashed from the house. "Daddy!" he cried. "Tell me about the fight in the sky. You went so far away I couldn't see it!"

"Go back in the house!" Si told the boy.

Meg came striding after Richard. "Richard, I told you not to go out there and bother your father and Uncle Karl!"

Karl swept the boy up in his arms. "He's not bothering us, Meg. Tell him about it, Si. Tell him about our 'fight in the sky.' "

Si pulled Richard roughly from Karl's arms and pushed him toward Meg. "Go inside with your mother!"

Meg herded Richard back into the house. At the door she stopped. She had been about to offer Karl a drink, but one look at his face told her this was no time for social amenities. She entered the house and closed the door firmly behind her.

"I don't know why you're so rough on that boy," Karl said.

"You'd better go, Karl," Si said. "I'll see you tomorrow before I leave."

"Oh, yes, that's right," Karl said. "You and Meg are leaving for Europe."

"Yeah, it'll give you a little vacation from my 'obsession to win,' " Si said. He laughed suddenly. "You don't look so bad for all your troubles."

"No thanks to you."

"Go on home, huh? Go sit on the beach and drink some of that schnapps you smuggled in." Karl and Freddie Silcox had flown to Mexico a month before for a dozen cases of vintage brandy and schnapps. The liquor was kept in the wine cellar that Karl had built in the small cottage he had purchased on Venice Beach. "Go find a girl and get your pipes cleaned," Si said. "You'll feel better."

"You think so, eh?"

"Goddammit, Karl, you want me to say I'm sorry, is that what you want? All right, I'm sorry. I apologize!"

Karl's face tightened. He drew in his breath to speak, then stopped, as though he had decided that whatever he had planned to say simply was not worth the time or energy.

He said, "All right, Si, I accept your apology."

Si offered his hand. "Still friends?"

They shook hands. "Still friends," Karl said.

"We'll talk tomorrow," Si said.

"Yes," Karl said. He turned and left.

"Still friends," Si said dryly, aloud, watching Karl get into the car and drive off. He did not for an instant believe it, which saddened him. He wanted Karl's friendship, he needed it. He promised himself to somehow make everything right with Karl. But that would have to come later. Right now there were more important things to worry about.

To begin with, three thousand miles of Atlantic Ocean.

10

Saint-Pol-sur-Mer did not look the same. The tent hangars and tool shed were gone, replaced by a lush green lawn. The chateau's stucco walls fairly gleamed with fresh white paint. The copper roof, obviously brand-new, shone brilliantly in the morning sun. Beds of early-spring flowers zigzagged around the front of the chateau and in between the refurbished and repainted livery stables.

"It doesn't look anything like the movie set," Meg said. "Back in California, *The Flying Circus.*"

Si nodded in silent agreement. Beyond the poplars at the end of the field, for a moment he actually heard the raspy, uneven roar of a Fokker Tripe's Oberursel rotary and saw Karl Eisler's black Triplane swooping in low over the tarmac to drop the package containing Jimmy Forrest's helmet and goggles.

A large fenced riding ring occupied most of the area where the tarmac had been. Two horses cantered around the enclosure, one ridden by a young girl, the other by a boy not much older than Richard. Farther on, in the field where the airplanes had landed and taken off, four other horses grazed. The grass was trimmed as neatly as a golf fairway.

"Aren't you curious to see the house?" Meg asked.

"It won't be the same." He did not want to admit his disappointment at not finding the airdrome in its original state, preserved like some national monument, with the continual sound of blasting engines, and young men drinking at the makeshift dining-room bar where a crude-lettered cardboard sign reading *Ici on parle FRANÇAIS!* reminded them of the ten-centime fine levied upon any American speaking English in the mess.

"Besides, we can't just knock on the door and ask to come in."
He walked back to the car parked on the graveled road leading to
the chateau entrance.

The car, rented in Calais, was a 1924 Rickenbacker 8. Si felt almost
privileged to drive one of Eddie Rickenbacker's automobiles. Rick,
after all, was America's ace of aces, twenty-six victories. Si knew him
fairly well, and last year, when Rick's motorcar business failed, had
offered him a job with Conair. Rick appreciated the gesture but turned
Si down, explaining that he needed to be his own boss. Si certainly
understood that.

Si's original itinerary had not included a stop at Saint-Pol-sur-
Mer. From Calais, he had planned to drive to Le Havre, which was
where he expected to make his first French landfall on the New
York–Paris flight. From Le Havre he and Meg were to continue southeast to Rouen, paralleling the anticipated flight path. But because
Saint-Pol-sur-Mer was only a two-hour drive from Calais, Si had im-
pulsively decided to make a brief detour, which turned out to be a
fool's errand that only recalled unpleasant memories.

He glanced at Meg. She sat rigidly beside him in the car, lips
pursed, her face ash-white. He eased his foot off the accelerator.

"I'll slow up," he said.

"Thank you," she said.

"You wanted to go in the chateau, didn't you?"

"I would have liked to see it, yes."

"I know," he said. "But I didn't think the people that lived there
would appreciate a couple of strangers banging on their door."

"You've already explained, Si. I understand."

"I'll make it up to you in Paris. How're you feeling, by the way?"
He reached over with his right hand and patted her stomach.

"I'll be starting to show pretty soon," she said.

"But no problems?"

"No, Si, no problems."

"You didn't have any with the other kids, either."

"That's right, Si. I'm a regular brood mare."

They spent three days on the road, stopping overnight at small
hotels or roadside inns. The food was exceptional, and the April
weather perfect. At Rouen, while Si flew back and forth over the
countryside in a rented airplane, Meg visited the famous cathedral
and its museum. She would have liked to spend more time in Rouen;
there was so much to see. It was where Joan of Arc died. But Si
wanted to move on to Paris. Besides, he said, anybody who deliberately
set out to martyr herself couldn't have been too smart.

"That's right, Si," Meg replied. "And Joan never learned to fly a plane, either."

Meg enjoyed the trip. It was the first time since their marriage they had been really alone. They talked, more than Meg ever recalled them talking. At home, most conversations centered around airplanes and flying; obviously, one-way conversations. Here in France, they talked about everything, the war, politics, their children, the future.

They made love. Almost nightly, which Meg attributed to the change of scenery, and also found not at all disagreeable. Si was surprisingly tender and gentle. She began to look forward to Paris. She would buy some shameless lingerie and scandalous perfume. She had promised Ruth Tannen an ounce of that scent that was the latest rage, Chanel No. 5.

They arrived in Paris on a sunny Sunday morning and checked in at the Crillon. Extravagant, yes, but Si said since they were already splurging, they might as well do it right. Their 300-franc-per-day room, $15, was large and luxurious, with an enormous bed and the most comfortable mattress Meg had ever slept on. The next day she rushed to the Galeries Lafayette and purchased a half-dozen down pillows similar to the ones at the Crillon, and two comforters. Those comforters, satin and goose-downed, feather-light, kept you as warm as in a cocoon.

They stayed in Paris two weeks. Si's days were occupied with various French aviation officials at Le Bourget or reviewing details of the flight with American embassy functionaries. Meg busied herself like any other American tourist, seeing the whole city, from the Bois du Boulogne to Montmartre, and the Louvre, Versailles, Notre Dame, the Luxembourg Gardens, the Eiffel Tower, the Tuilleries, Les Halles. She loved every minute of it.

Evenings they dined at fine restaurants, the Tour d'Argent, Maxim's, Périgord, Père Jacques, always in the company of pilots or aviation manufacturers or newsmen. Endless talk of flying, dominated by the forthcoming Atlantic crossing. Anthony Fokker had entered the Orteig contest with his gigantic trimotor, *America*, to be flown by U.S. Navy Commander Richard Byrd, who last year had taken the same airplane over the North Pole. There were other serious contenders: the veteran Clarence Chamberlin, flying a custom-built Bellanca monoplane; and airmail pilot Charles Lindbergh who would attempt the flight in a tiny single-engined Ryan monoplane; and two more U.S. Navy pilots, Noel Davis and Stanton Wooster in their specially modified Keystone bomber, *The American Legion*.

But there was still time for the Folies, and for Josephine Baker at the Casino de Paris, and the revue Le Moulin Rouge. Another evening, Si casually guided Meg on a "walking tour" of Montparnasse, which included a stroll along Rue d'Odessa past the hotel where Andŕee had once lived. It was gone, the building torn down and replaced by an automobile-repair shop.

On the evening before their departure they were entertained at the home of Charles Nungesser, France's second-ranking war ace with forty-three victories, and himself a contestant for the Orteig prize. They returned to the hotel shortly after ten. Meg was not sleepy.

"Si, it's our last night. Let's do something."

"Do something? You've been everywhere. You've seen everything."

"Well, how about hearing some music? There are supposed to be some great American jazz groups here, colored musicians," she said. "They're wonderful."

"How about going into the bar for a drink, instead?"

"I'm sure you can get a drink wherever we go," she said. "Come on, do it for me."

The concierge knew exactly what the American lady wanted. "Ah, *le jazz hot*, eh? At Jason's, on Avenue Matignon. It is quite popular."

Either the concierge gave Si the wrong address or Si misunderstood. Si's French was fluent enough, but after nine years, rusty. The taxi driver could not find Jason's, but he knew another place, equally popular. They continued along Avenue Matignon to an apartment building on the corner of Rue Rabelais.

"Le Coin," said the driver. "Only the best people come here."

The small, posh cabaret was located in the apartment building's basement. A uniformed doorman escorted them through the canopied entrance, into the foyer, and downstairs.

Later, whenever Si thought about that night in Paris, he felt certain that it was not fate, luck, coincidence, or any other phenomenon that had caused it to happen. He even discounted the fact that they had walked into the club only because of Meg's desire to hear music. It happened because it was what he wanted to happen.

He realized this the moment they entered the cabaret's gleaming white leather-walled foyer. He felt as though he had been here before, in this very place, helping Meg off with her coat and handing it to the hatcheck girl at the Dutch-doored checkroom. Removing his own coat, folding it into the hatcheck girl's outstretched arms, placing his hat atop the coat, and all the while listening to the voice of a woman singing in the showroom. A jaunty, lilting song whose words he did not recognize.

He recognized the voice.

He never recalled entering the crowded, darkened room and

following Meg and the maître d' to a table. He only remembered seeing the white shirtfronts of tuxedoed musicians glowing in the dark behind a small stage, and a woman standing in the center of the stage in a bright white circle formed by the intersecting beams of four baby spotlights, and the silver and gold sequins of her gown sparkling under the light.

"What a beautiful woman," Meg said to the maître d' as he seated them.

"She is also the owner of the club, madame," the maître d' replied in accentless English, "and our one and only performer." He snapped his fingers for a waiter.

Meg said something, but Si heard only the voice of the woman singing. She had not changed. Older, of course, but the same silky-smooth complexion and chestnut hair, still bobbed but longer in the style of the day. The same perfect figure, perhaps slightly fuller, which, if anything, only enhanced her beauty.

The waiter arrived at the table and asked what they would like to drink. Si paid no attention. When the waiter asked again, Si spun around indignantly. "What the hell does he want?" he said to Meg.

"Our order, I think," said Meg.

"Armagnac for me and a split of champagne for the lady," Si said in French to the waiter, and immediately turned to the stage again. Andrée had begun walking slowly about the room, singing to one customer, then another. The spotlight moved with her.

Meg realized Si's interest in this *chanteuse* was more than casual, and more than sexual, and more than nostalgic. She had never seen him so absorbed in an entertainer. Usually, on the infrequent occasions she managed to cajole him into attending a theater or night club, he was quickly bored and would start to fidget or yawn or chain-smoke. He had not lit a cigarette or touched the glass the waiter placed before him. He was not even aware the drink had been served.

Andrée, who was just starting the second chorus of the song, "Les Amants de Paris," approached the table. She saw Si, and for just one instant they looked directly into each other's eyes. In that same instant, her voice briefly faltered. Then she moved on. Si's eyes followed her.

Andrée returned to the stage and concluded the song. The audience applauded enthusiastically. Andrée bowed, then left the stage. The house lights came on. The orchestra struck up a dance number. Si, who had not joined in the applause, turned to Meg.

"Want to dance?"

Meg said nothing. Her brain whirled with a thousand different thoughts. She felt humiliated, yet at the same time curious. The picture of Si and the singer looking at each other was unforgettable.

What had passed between them was not the uncertainty of strangers suddenly interested in each other, but the explicit familiarity of people who know and have been intimate with each other.

". . . snap out of it," Si was saying. He waved a hand before her eyes. "Do you or don't you want to dance?"

"You're a terrible dancer," she heard herself say. He did not reply. He drank down his Armagnac in one swallow and signaled the waiter. She studied him. She wondered how often he was unfaithful at home. "You're a terrible dancer," she said again.

"You're right," he said.

Unfaithful, Meg thought. What a quaint term. Of course he was unfaithful, probably with dozens of women, probably even with Freddie Silcox's wife.

"What's the singer's name?" she asked.

"What's the singer's name?" Si asked the waiter.

"Andrée," said the waiter.

"Andrée," Si said to Meg, and ordered another round of drinks. "One thing you can say about the French," he went on to Meg, "they're realists. They know better than to pass stupid laws like Prohibition."

Meg mumbled a meaningless reply. Andrée was surely older than herself, but more attractive, although comparisons were unfair. She and Andrée were two entirely different types.

She drank some of her champagne and said, "All right, let's dance."

Si was not at all surprised when the orchestra leader announced that Andrée would make no further appearances that evening. But Si knew he would see her again. He had to see her again, even if it meant a delay in returning to California to prepare for the Atlantic flight. Somehow he would explain it to Meg.

Meg saved him the trouble. Over breakfast in their room the following morning, she said, "You look dreadful. Didn't you sleep?"

"Off and on," he said. "Getting ready to leave for home, I'm jumpy, I guess."

"I didn't sleep well, either," she said. "Go and see her, Si."

He had just started lighting a cigarette. His hand, holding the match under the cigarette, froze. Then he lit the cigarette. "How did you know?"

"I'm not blind."

He said nothing; he did not know what to say. He mashed the cigarette out in the empty saucer of his coffee cup.

"It's all right, Si," she said. "Honestly. Go. We're not leaving until late in the afternoon. There's plenty of time."

"I knew her during the war," he said after a moment.

"So I assumed."

"I was in love with her."

Even as the words tumbled from his mouth, Si knew why he was saying them. This was too important for dishonesty. This was no fling, no hard-on for some woman you had seen crossing the street. This had been the love of his life. He wanted Meg to understand.

"I have to see her," he said.

Meg said nothing.

"I'm sorry," he said.

Meg walked to the window. The sky was bright and cloudless. The sun danced off the zinc roofs of the buildings across the boulevard. Behind her, she heard the metallic rattle of a coat hanger in the closet.

You must be a good sport about this, she told herself.

Why? she answered herself. Why must I be a good sport? Where the hell is that in the rules? But she knew there was nothing she could do about it. There was nothing she could do to change him.

Change him how? To what? From what?

To loving you, from not loving you.

But he never loved me.

Did you love him?

I married him, didn't I?

That is not what I asked you.

Behind her, she heard the door close.

2.

The cabaret was empty. A cleaning woman told Si that Andrée lived in an apartment above the cabaret. Si did not wait for the elevator. He hurried up the stairs to the first landing. There were two apartments. Si pressed the buzzer of the apartment nearest the stairwell.

The door opened almost immediately. Andrée, wearing a white silk robe and white mules, stood facing him. Clearly, despite the early hour, he had not awakened her. Not a hair of her freshly brushed hair was out of place. She looked up at him.

"I knew you'd come."

He swept her into his arms. They kissed. At first gently, hesitantly, and then with more passion. He felt drunk from the sweetness of her mouth, and her perfume, and the very fragrance of her body. Not a word was spoken, none was necessary. He picked her up and carried her into the living room and through the open door of her bedroom.

He lowered her onto the bed and opened her robe. She lay naked, gazing up at him. He kissed her breasts, first one, then the other, then back to the first. She grasped the back of his head and drew him down to her stomach. He kissed the smooth flesh of her belly and the hollow underneath.

"Wait," she whispered. She unbuckled his belt and unbuttoned his trousers, then reached into his fly and clasped her fingers around him, and then pulled him down on top of her and opened her legs for him.

She gasped as he slid inside her. The years in between had never happened. They were in her bed, in her room at the hotel on Rue d'Odessa, making love. Part of his mind told him they were not in any hotel room but in a large, luxurious, fashionably decorated bedroom. He was not sure how he had gotten there or when, only that it seemed natural and that he felt safe, warm, and secure. And knew precisely when, writhing under him, she would begin to cry, "*Je suis à toi! Je suis à toi! Mon amour! Mon amour!*"—her voice rising shrilly with each word, and her body heaving into his, until every muscle in her body stiffened, imprisoning him inside her. For a moment she remained absolutely rigid, clamping onto him so tightly he thought his whole body was immersed in hers. And then, with her, in a series of spasms, each one more intense than the other, he exploded.

For a few moments they lay wrapped in each other's arms, gazing into each other's eyes. And then her body went limp. He kissed her eyes, her nose, her mouth, her throat.

After a moment she pushed him gently away. She rolled over on her side and faced him. "*C'est toujours si bon, n'est-ce pas?*" she asked.

"It's not only still good, it's better than ever," he replied in English.

"Yes, better than ever," she said, and repeated it in French, "*C'est encore meilleur.*"

He suddenly realized that except for the cries of passion, these were the first words either of them had spoken, and he could not help laughing. She understood at once, and joined him in the laughter.

And now they talked, filling in the missing years. She, immediately after hearing he was shot down, believing him dead, had left Paris. She wanted to die herself. She went to Deauville, where she worked as a café singer, eking out a bare existence. Slowly, painfully, she allowed herself to return to the world of the living. She found a job in a better nightclub in Cannes. She saved her money and eventually came back to Paris and opened Le Coin.

In his turn, Si told her of his success. Yes, that was his wife with him last night. They had two boys, with another child on the way. He showed her photos of Frank and Richard, and told her how much the younger boy, Frank, loved airplanes. He told her of the New York–Paris flight, and that he expected her to greet him at Le Bourget with a bottle of Kristal. No, a case of it, and they would drink the whole damn case to celebrate.

They were seated at a garden table on the terrace, both fully dressed. They had been there nearly an hour, talking, drinking coffee, smoking. It was so much like old times that Si never wanted to leave. But it was after two. He had to get back to the Crillon to pack and leave for Gare Saint-Lazare by five. The Calais train left at six.

"In a few weeks you'll be making the flight, you say?" she asked.

"Unless we're ready sooner," he said. "Which I doubt."

"Oddly enough, Simon, I myself will be in New York late in May," she said. "I'm making a concert tour of your country. First stop, New York City."

"Postpone the tour," he said. He leaned across the table and kissed her. "Wait here until I make the flight."

"Until you make the flight," she repeated dryly. "And after that, then what?"

"Then you'll reschedule the tour, you'll come to the States, and we'll take it from there."

"Take what from where, Simon?" Her voice turned suddenly cold.

"You and I," he said. "You'll come to California."

"Ah, you and I," she said, her voice even chillier. "I'll come to California."

"It's beautiful country," he said. "It's just like the Riviera, only sunnier. You'll love it."

"Do you think your wife would approve?"

"I won't tell her," he said with the same irony.

"It should make a lovely *ménage à trois*."

"She knows about you," he said. "She knows I'm here right now."

She looked at him in disbelief. "You come back into my life and without the slightest hesitation believe I'll drop everything to be with you?"

"Is that such a bad idea?"

"My husband might think so."

The word "husband" rang in Si's ears. She was teasing him, of course. Yes, of course, he had hurt her by telling her about Meg. All right, he'd play along.

"You forgot to mention that minor detail," he said. "Where is he?"

"At the moment, in Spain. On business."

"Oh, I see. He travels a lot, does he? How long have you been married?"

"Four years. His name is Jean Fresnais. He manufactures railway cars. He's quite successful. I met him in Cannes. He helped me establish the club. In fact, he bought it for me. He has two sons himself, much older than your boys, of course. His wife died during the war."

"You're lying to me," Si said. "There's not a sign of a man in this place. No clothes, no pictures, nothing. Not even a razor blade in the bathroom." But even as he spoke he read the truth in her face.

"We have a home in Neuilly," she said. "I keep this apartment to rest in, and to stay in when he's away."

And to entertain former lovers, Si thought, although he knew better. But he could not suppress the anger and frustration rising within him. He said, "How many other old boyfriends do you invite up here when your husband's away?"

Andrée's hand flashed out and slapped Si hard across the cheek. She drew back her hand to hit him again, but he seized her wrist in midair and held it. After a moment, she pulled her hand free and sat back. She massaged her wrist. The flesh was still white from his fingers.

"You're a fool," she said.

He rose and looked down at her. "Why didn't you tell me you were married?"

"Please leave, Simon."

"Why didn't you tell me?"

"Would it have made any difference?"

"It would have been honest."

"We had a moment," she said. "We relived the past. We enjoyed it. Let it go at that."

" 'Let it go at that,' " he repeated. "And you talk about *me* coming back into your life! If you knew it couldn't go on, why the hell did you even open the door?"

"You want everything, Simon," she said. "That's always been your trouble. All or nothing."

"So it's nothing?"

"It has to be. I'm sorry."

"This?" he asked, waving his hand toward the open bedroom door, the rumpled bed. "This was 'nothing'?"

"It was everything," she said.

"Then why do you want it to stop?"

"Simon, I asked you to leave."

"I'm not going to lose you again," he said.

She got up and walked into the living room. He followed her. She gathered up his hat and coat from the divan and opened the apartment door.

"I love you," he said. His own voice startled him, for he realized that was the only woman to whom he had ever spoken those words. "I love you," he said again.

They stood looking at each other, and then he turned and left. Andrée listened to the hollow echo of his heels on the marble stairway. Tears brimmed her eyes. "I know," she said aloud. "I know."

3.

The rain started almost the moment they boarded the train. It was like an omen. For the first hour they rode in total silence. Meg read a magazine she found in the compartment, a six-month-old copy of *Vanity Fair*. Si chain-smoked and gazed out the window. The night was impenetrably black but for occasional pinpoints of light from some distant farmhouse or automobile. Now and then, high-pitched whistle shrieking, the train sped through a station. The dimly illuminated signs on the station walls rushed past in a blur.

Finally, Si mashed out his cigarette and said, "For Christ's sake, say something!"

She placed the magazine facedown on her lap. "I think you're the one who should say something."

"Look, you want me to say I'm sorry? No, I can't do that. I'm not sorry."

"Was it all you expected?"

"Jesus!"

"Was it?"

"What the hell kind of question is that?"

"An honest one," Meg said, telling herself the question was asked out of curiosity. She knew better; it was envy. "I'd like an honest answer."

He said nothing. He lit another cigarette.

"Don't you think I deserve an honest answer?"

"Yes," he said after a moment. "Yes, it was all I expected."

"Do you still love her?"

"She's married."

"That's no answer."

Her quiet, calm manner infuriated him. He wanted her to shout at him, insult him, attack him. He could handle that. "I don't know," he said finally. He drew on the cigarette. It tasted sour. His whole mouth tasted sour. He turned to the window again. "I don't know if I still love her."

The rain was coming down harder. The light from the compartment's domed ceiling fixture reflected opaquely off the window glass, mirroring his image. He felt helpless, and foolish. What had happened, had happened; he could not change it. He regretted having hurt Meg, but he was trying to be honest. With himself, and with her.

He forced himself to think of other things. The New York–Paris flight. He was ready for it, the airplane was ready. He had mapped the entire course, computed all the distances between checkpoints. The first thing to do in Los Angeles was put Charlie Jensen to work on a definitive fuel-consumption figure. Fuel consumption, yes. Nothing was more important than fuel consumption.

He sensed rather than saw the magazine hurled at him, but certainly felt it. The hard spine of the magazine struck him flush across the bridge of his nose. He gasped with pain.

". . . rotten bastard!" Meg was screaming at him. "Selfish, no good, thoughtless son of a bitch!" She was half leaning toward him, her face twisted in rage and humiliation, her eyes glittering.

Despite the lingering stab of pain, Si's first inclination was to laugh. It was the first time he had ever heard Meg swear or display such anger. "Emotion" was the word. Yes, "emotion." Why the hell didn't she use some of that in bed? He wanted to ask the question aloud but did not.

". . . been a good wife, damn you!" she was saying. "Loyal, patient, supportive! And faithful! That's a word you never heard of, isn't it? 'Faithful'!"

"Take it easy, Meg. The whole train'll hear you."

Meg drew in her breath to speak but then abruptly sat back. She started to speak again, and again stopped. She shook her head.

"All right," Si said. "I'm sorry. I honest to God am. I apologize."

Meg picked up the *Vanity Fair* that had fallen to the compartment floor. She flattened the magazine out on her lap and began aimlessly turning the pages. "Do you want a divorce?" she asked.

The question startled him. "What do you mean, 'divorce'?"

"That's the usual procedure, isn't it? When two people are unhappy or—"

"—who said anything about being unhappy?"

"—dissatisfied," she finished. She closed the magazine and held it firmly in her lap. She was proud of herself, of regaining her composure.

"I'm not 'dissatisfied,' either," he said.

"I see," she said. "You're not unhappy and not dissatisfied, but you don't know whether or not you're still in love with that . . . with another woman?"

"You asked me to be honest, goddammit!"

She looked at him again, then away, at the magazine. She resumed turning the pages. She had been reading an article in the "Arts & Artists" section about a new motion-picture theater in New York. The Roxy, said to be the largest theater in the world, a veritable "cathedral," according to the author, with a Kimball pipe organ so huge the keyboard required three organists. Meg had seen the building and thought it the epitome of tastelessness.

Tastelessness. This whole scene with Si was tasteless. And, of course, her own little tantrum had only made it more tasteless. Divorce, she thought, and wondered about the children, especially the one she was carrying.

"What kind of wife do you want, Si?" she heard herself asking quietly, and herself answering her own question. "A fantasy wife, that's what you want. A wife who'll give you everything and demand nothing. Someone who exists only in your imagination. That's your whole trouble, Si. You always want what you can't have."

My whole trouble, he thought wryly, the second time today a woman had told him what his trouble was, and both with almost identical views. They should get acquainted.

"Meg, you don't know what I want."

"Neither do you, Si," she said. "You never did. Oh, excuse me, you do know. You've told me a hundred times. You want to make the best airplanes in the world and own the biggest and finest airline in the world to fly the best airplanes. But you know something, Si? Even when you have all that, it won't be enough. You won't be satisfied. You'll never be satisfied. You're always reaching for something more than you have, something better."

"Is that bad?"

"When you don't know where to stop, it is," she said. "When you hurt other people doing it."

"Look, I'm sorry if I hurt you. And as far as always reaching for something better, why the hell shouldn't I?"

"The best airplanes and the finest airline," she repeated. "That's all that means anything to you, isn't it?"

"My family means as much."

"As much? Not more?"

"As much, I said!"

"Your 'family'? Your children, you mean?"

"Of course, my children," Si said. He touched his left cheekbone. The skin just below the eye felt tender, almost raw. "The children," he said again.

"Not your wife?"

"Those are your words, not mine. That's not what I said." He touched his eye again and thought about asking Meg for her mirror but decided to hell with it. So he'd have a black eye, so what?

Meg studied him. Hair rumpled as usual, in need of a haircut as usual, tie untied. Thank God for shirts with attached collars, although one point of the collar was curled like a piece of ribbon candy. The Frenchwoman, obviously, found no fault in his appearance.

"You say she's married?" Meg asked.

"Yes, she's married."

"That's too bad."

"Are you enjoying yourself with all this?" Si asked. "I'm not."

"I certainly hope not," Meg said.

"Then let's drop it," Si said.

"Why? Does it make you nervous?"

"That's right, Meg. It makes me nervous."

Meg wondered which made Si more nervous: not knowing if he still loved the Frenchwoman, or the prospect of divorce. At the same time she acknowledged her sense of relief that he apparently included her when he said that his family "meant as much" to him. Relief? she asked herself. What on earth are you saying? Are you saying you are relieved that he does not want a divorce? Are you saying that you want this marriage to continue? After all that has happened?

But all that has happened is that he visited a woman he was once in love with. Is that so terrible? She could not help thinking, And this is the man I was going to mold? The man whose rough edges I would polish, who was such an intriguing challenge? Mold, what a joke! And the joke was on her, for it was she who had been molded. The reason she wanted the marriage to continue was not any fear of losing the children. She would keep them with her, of that she was certain.

Simon Conway himself was the reason. Simon Conway, as from the very beginning, fascinated her.

Fascination, she thought, not love. Love was an entirely different commodity, and in this relationship a seemingly unavailable one. But then again was it "love"—in the classic sense—that she really wanted? For that matter, did she know what she really wanted? Simon Conway knew what he wanted. He wanted the world.

She listened to the metallic hum of the train's wheels on the tracks and watched the rain stream down the compartment's window. There was no doubt in her mind that Si would get what he wanted. But she, Margaret Taylor Conway, she wanted the same thing. She wanted the world, too.

And knew she would get it.

11

It began to look as though Simon Conway might have to eat his words. And memorable words they were, appearing in newspaper stories across the country and as a banner headline in the May 14, 1927, *New York Sun*: "WE GO, WEATHER OR NOT!"

If, as Morris Tannen said, the Conair Viking's Atlantic flight was a publicist's dream, it was a pilot's nightmare. Three days of solid rain had made Roosevelt Field a quagmire. You could not drive a wheelbarrow over the field, let alone an airplane with a full fuel load.

Si and Freddie Silcox had flown the Viking from Los Angeles to New York with only a single stop at Kansas City for refueling in a record-breaking twenty-three hours and twelve minutes. Karl Eisler, Morris Tannen, and Charlie Jensen had accompanied them on the flight, which was the first long-distance flight "riding the beam," a series of radio beacons marking the air route across the country. The airplane's radio tuned in the beacon's signal, which grew increasingly loud as the airplane approached, and then weakened as the airplane proceeded past it. The next beacon was then tuned in, and so on along the entire airway. An innovative idea, but still in the experimental stage.

Crossing the Atlantic, Si would have to rely on the Viking's compass and Freddie Silcox's ability to read the stars. Freddie was a competent navigator but a poor weather forecaster. On the record-breaking cross-country flight the weather had been clear all the way. Freddie predicted similar conditions for the Atlantic crossing.

The rain had started not five minutes after their landing at Roosevelt Field. It continued through that night. The weather bureau reported the front extending all the way to Halifax. Si agreed to wait another day.

More rain, no break up north.

But Si made up his mind to go, "weather or not!" His mood was as foul as the weather. What had begun as a head cold and sniffles now seemed to have settled heavily in his chest.

Tony Fokker pleaded with him to hold out one more day.

"Don't be a fool, Si," Fokker said. "You'll end up in the drink like Nungesser."

Si was thinking, Sure, it's fine for you to talk. You're not making the flight. Your airplane is a pile of junk! Fokker himself had been at the controls last week when the trimotored *America* crashed. Fokker walked away from the wreck, but the pilots, Commander Byrd and Floyd Bennett, were both seriously injured.

Byrd and Bennett were not the only casualties of what the news-papers enthusiastically labeled "Mayhem in May." Davis and Wooster had been killed test-flying their trimotored Keystone bomber, *The American Legion*. And the venerable Nungesser, flying east to west— Paris to New York—had vanished at sea. Lindbergh was still in Cal-ifornia waiting for the weather to improve.

Si, Fokker, and Karl Eisler were in Conair's "command post," the drab coffee shop of the Garden City Hotel. Fokker, who only recently had moved his manufacturing facilities to the United States, had driven up from New Jersey to see Si and Karl. For a while the three rehashed old times. More accurately, Karl and Tony Fokker did the rehashing. Si kept getting up and walking to the restaurant window to observe the weather.

He had sent Freddie to the field with instructions to glue himself to the weather bureau telephone. At the first word of a break, no matter what time of day or night, they would leave. As always, the weather panicked Freddie. And Freddie's wife, Ceil, certainly did not help, constantly exhorting him not to be stampeded into something he might regret. Ceil and Ruth Tannen were in Long Island at the hotel. The women had taken the train a week before. Meg had re-mained in California.

Although Meg used the baby as an excuse—six months pregnant, she simply did not feel strong enough for another long trip—Si knew better. The day before he took off in the Viking for New York, Meg had shown him an item from a month-old *New York Daily Mirror*. She said she had bought the paper at the pier the day they arrived in the United States and saved it as a surprise for him.

Si remembered the item by heart, from the "My Broadway" col-umn by Danton Walker:

**... French chanteuse Andrée, the rage of Paris, checks in
at the Astor Hotel next month. The lovely songbird starts
her American tour with an appearance at the Latin Quarter
on May 16.**

Today was May 16.

Si remained at the rain-splattered coffee-shop window another
moment, wondering what Morris would think of a publicity photograph featuring Simon Conway and a lovely French chanteuse. He
mashed out the cigarette he had just lit. Each time he inhaled he could
hardly breathe.

He walked back to the table and sat down. Tony Fokker said,
"Relax, Si. There's nothing you can do."

"Where's Morris?" Si asked.

"He went to take a telephone call," Karl said.

"From the field?" Si asked. "From Freddie?"

"Long-distance," Karl said. "California."

"Goddammit!" said Si. "When the hell will this rain stop?"

Karl said, "Almost reminds you of the Western Front, doesn't it?"

Si spun around to face Karl. "You know something? I almost have
the feeling you're glad we can't go."

"That's a strange thing to say," Karl said.

"You are, aren't you?" Si asked. "You're glad."

"When was the last time you had a decent night's sleep?" Karl
asked.

"Don't worry about my sleep, Karl," Si said. "Worry about the
weather."

Just then Morris returned. He looked grim. "Lindbergh left San
Diego at six this morning. He's due in St. Louis before dark. They
expect him in New York late tomorrow afternoon."

"If the weather breaks," Fokker said. "Otherwise he'll wait in St.
Louis."

"It'll break," Si said. "Morris, drive me out to the field." And
without another word, not even a goodbye to Tony Fokker, Si strode
from the room. Morris shook hands with Fokker, expressed a hope
to see the Dutchman again, and followed Si out.

"Are you a betting man, Tony?" Karl asked. "Simon Conway will
take off for Paris tonight, 'Weather or not.' "

Karl would have lost the bet, but only by chance. Si did in fact
order Freddie to prepare the Viking, and announced their imminent
departure to the newsmen gathered around the airplane inside the
Shell Oil Company hangar.

The moment Si finished talking to the reporters, Freddie Silcox took him aside and showed him the latest weather report. Still-heavier rain was forecast for the entire Atlantic seaboard and, worse, hurricane-force winds paralleling their route all the way to Newfoundland.

"We'd be crazy to go," Freddie said. "Even if we made it to Halifax, we'd have used up a quarter of our gas against that wind."

They were in a small toolroom at the rear of the hangar. The rain hammered down on the corrugated-iron roof. Ceil was also there, the first time Si had seen her in months, and even in his anger and frustration he thought she looked wonderful. For a brief second he was back with her in that little room in the Hotel Monica. He missed that kind of love. He needed it.

Yes, he needed Andrée. And oh, yes, he did want to telephone young Frank before he left, say goodbye to the kid and listen to him wish his father good luck. That's what Frank had shouted at the airport in Los Angeles. "Good luck, Daddy!" And with no prompting from Meg. She had brought the boys to the field to see Si off. Richard was another story: he had stayed in the car and wouldn't get out, not even to say goodbye.

". . . please, Si, listen to Freddie," Ceil was saying. "You know he's right."

Si's legs felt suddenly wobbly. He sank down onto a tool chest and drew in his breath. His chest ached. He ran his fingers across his forehead. He was sweating. He forced a grin. "You're a goddam good-looking woman, Ceil."

"I'm a smart one, too, Si. I can read a weather report."

"Okay," Si said. It seemed too much trouble to argue. "We'll wait."

Ceil placed her hand on Si's forehead. "You're running a fever."

"I'm fine." Si pulled himself up. "I'll go on back to the hotel and take a nap. You too, Freddie. You'd better get some rest if we're taking off tonight."

"I'll see he does," Ceil said. She slipped her arm through Freddie's. "He'll be in top shape, believe me."

"Tonight," said Si. He gripped the doorjamb. He felt dizzy. "We leave tonight."

2.

Si's first inclination was to hang up. The old saw about if a man answers, hang up. Especially a man with a French accent. The man was Jean Fresnais, Andrée's husband. But what the hell, there was no time for games. So Si introduced himself and said he only wanted to say hello to Andrée and wish her good luck.

Fresnais promised to give Andrée the message and said that he knew he was speaking for her—and most definitely for himself—when he wished Si good luck. The French newspapers were filled with stories of the Viking's forthcoming flight.

Fresnais also expressed the hope that someday they might meet. He had heard much about the famous Simon Conway. After they hung up, Si, who was feeling better after a long nap, wryly wondered exactly how much Jean Fresnais had heard. He doubted Andrée had told him how, when she and Si made love, she always screamed, "*Je suis à toi!*"

Si had called from a pay phone in the hotel lobby. He started into the coffee shop but saw Morris and Ruth seated in a booth with Karl. He did not want to talk to Karl. He felt a little foolish for having behaved so badly earlier in front of Tony Fokker. He also did not care for another lecture from Karl about the hazards of flying in such bad weather.

In truth, no lecture was required. The nap had cleared Si's head. One glimpse of the angry gray sky told him no airplane would leave for Paris tonight. It was at that moment he decided to go into Manhattan to see Andrée.

Si stepped back to the lobby telephone booth to call a taxi. Through the hotel's revolving door he saw Charlie Jensen driving up in one of the three sleek sedans that the Auburn Motor Car Company had made available to Conair. Stamping his feet and slipping out of his yellow oilcloth rain slicker, Charlie entered the lobby, his thick silver hair plastered tight to his scalp from the rain.

Si called to him, "Charlie . . ."

Charlie hurried over to Si. "I ran up the engines. I was afraid the plugs might be fouled from all the dampness, but those engines never sounded better." He nodded gloomily at the rain outside. "It ain't letting up, Si, not a bit."

"I can see that," Si said. Little rivulets of water dripped from Charlie's hair onto the linoleum floor.

"How you feeling?" Charlie asked. "They said you were a little under the weather. Hey, 'under the weather.'" He grinned, pleased with the play on words. "I guess to hell we're all of us under the weather, all right!"

"Charlie, give me the car keys," Si said.

"No sense going out to the field," Charlie said. "You can hardly see your hand in front of your face."

"The keys, Charlie."

Charlie slapped the keys into Si's outstretched hand. Si thanked him and started toward the stairs, intending to go to his room for his coat and hat. But seeing Morris and Ruth Tannen and Karl emerge from the coffee shop, he wheeled around and went out the revolving door.

The Auburn's self-starter felt sluggish. At first, even flattening the pedal to the floor did not turn the motor. Finally, carefully working the choke, Si got the car started. The Auburn's vacuum-operated wiper blade swept furiously back and forth across the windshield as Si drove through the city to the Jericho Turnpike, followed the direction signs to Jamaica, and settled down for the long ride through the rain.

He gripped the steering wheel and shivered. He should have worn a coat. He fished in his pocket for a cigarette, brought it out, and, eyes fixed on the road, lit it. His lungs did not hurt drawing in the smoke. Good, the chest cold was not so bad after all.

He asked himself why he was driving into Manhattan to see Andrée. She was married, and he was married. What the hell was the point? And why the hell was the sweat rolling down his back? A second ago he was cold, now he was hot. His eyes ached. He rolled down the window and threw out the cigarette.

One instant the car was traveling smoothly over the asphalt road surface, tires sloshing rhythmically, big twelve-cylinder engine purring. The next instant it was coasting to a dead stop in the middle of the highway.

He floored the starter pedal. The engine turned over with a sound like an asthmatic old man. Goddam plugs, he thought. The goddam wires had gotten wet in the rain. He tried the starter again. Now the engine would not even turn. The battery was gone, too. He got out and pushed the car off the road, onto a shoulder. The rain was coming down even harder.

He got back into the car. He'd have to watch for approaching cars and get out and wave them down. He waited. Five minutes, ten. Not a single car passed in either direction.

Finally, after another few minutes, he decided the smartest thing was to find some help. He started walking back to Garden City. His first thought was to get dry, his second to reach a telephone and call Andrée. He continued walking and suddenly saw oncoming automobile headlights. He waved for the car to stop. The car sped past.

Si's whole body felt warm, and then cold, then warm again. He thought he might vomit. His churning stomach and the bile surging up into his throat reminded him of a funny story told by Morris Tannen.

Where the hell was Morris?

Sure, warm and snug back at the hotel.

The funny story? Something about vomiting. Oh, yes, now he remembered. Not a story but a discussion between Morris and Karl concerning the installation of a chemical lavatory in the next 440 series. The 440's present lavatory was in the rear, a canvas-enclosed cubicle containing a metal commode that "flushed" by pulling a lever that popped open a small door on the bottom of the fuselage. To date, although now and then there were whimsical reports of passenger "blowbacks," no one on the ground had complained.

Si plodded through the rain, wondering why he thought the story so funny. Hey, talk about funny stories. Tony Fokker could hardly stop laughing when Morris told him about a CATS sales promotion back in the early days of the 330. Morris had learned that many wives, fearful of the danger, discouraged their husbands from flying. He offered a free ticket to any woman who accompanied her husband. The promotion was so successful that Morris sent each wife a note of thanks and an invitation to fly CATS again. Shortly thereafter, the program was abruptly terminated. In the space of a single week four different women appeared in Morris's office, each irately informing him that *they* had never traveled as a CATS passenger and demanding to know who had.

Si tried to concentrate on the road in front of him, but his mind wandered. He thought of Meg, and the boys. Of the Viking, and Karl Eisler. Perhaps he should change his mind about Karl joining Freddie and him on the flight. How much fuel would Karl's weight represent? Twenty gallons? Thirty? Those extra gallons might damn well mean the difference between a safe landing and a wet one.

He walked on, soaked through to the skin. He walked and walked, and then remembered nothing. A black cloud seemed to descend on him and envelop his whole body, head to toe, like a shroud.

3.

They brought him into the hospital in Mineola with a temperature of 105 and a raging case of pneumonia. A carpenter from Hempstead had spotted the figure lying by the road and at first thought it was a corpse, another rum-runner.

For two days Si lapsed in and out of consciousness. Each time he awoke he remained alert long enough to peer across the room at the window. Each time, satisfied the rain had not stopped, he fell back to sleep. He was vaguely aware of someone else always in the room, if not a white-uniformed nurse then Morris Tannen or Ceil Silcox, or Karl. In that first day he remembered Morris saying something about

Meg arriving in the next thirty-six hours. A special CATS 440 was flying her to New York.

"Am I that bad?" Si had asked.

"No, no," Morris had replied. "You're fine."

"You're full of shit, Morris," Si said. "Where's Lindbergh?"

"Will you please stop worrying about that?"

"Where is he, goddammit?"

"He's still in St. Louis," Morris said, "waiting for the weather to clear here."

"Good," Si said, and fell back to sleep.

Simon Conway, as the hospital spokesman informed the daily gathering of newspaper reporters in the hospital lobby, was a very sick man. Si's doctor, a prominent Park Avenue pulmonary specialist, confidentially told Morris that only a miracle would save this patient.

A miracle did occur.

Late in the evening of the second day the rain stopped and the sky cleared. Next morning the sun shone bright and warm. The private night nurse brought Si a cup of beef broth and a telephoned message: Mrs. Conway was expected to arrive that evening.

"Isn't that nice, Mr. Conway?" the nurse asked. A stout, motherly woman who worked the eleven-to-seven shift, she was pleased at having such a celebrity for a patient. "I have a feeling that seeing your wife will do wonders for you," she went on.

Si happily noted the sun streaming into the room and went to sleep again. At nine, when the doctor arrived, the fever had broken. It was down to 101.2. This was no miracle. It was an act of sheer will. With the weather improving, Si knew he had to find the strength to get up, to leave the hospital and go to the airport.

"When can I get out of here?" he asked.

The doctor smiled professionally. "You're still a very sick man, Mr. Conway."

The doctor's caution was justified. As he told the day nurse, a young frizzy-haired girl with a bad complexion, a drop in temperature did not necessarily indicate recovery. The patient's chest still sounded like the East River.

At noon, the day nurse placed an exclamation point after the temperature notation on the patient's progress chart: 99.1! Si asked for some solid food. She brought him a chicken sandwich. He devoured it, and a cup of black coffee. The nurse also brought him a newspaper, a *New York Tribune*. The headlines were bold and black: CONWAY ON DANGER LIST; LINDBERGH STAYS ST. LOUIS

The story went on to say that with Simon Conway hospitalized and at least temporarily out of the race, Charles Lindbergh was in no hurry to leave St. Louis. He would wait there until assured of decent flying weather over the Atlantic. It was yesterday's paper, before the weather had so unexpectedly improved.

Si knew Lindbergh would not wait now.

Neither would Si. He reminded the nurse of his wife's anticipated arrival and sent her downstairs to phone a florist for some flowers for Meg.

Thirty minutes later, in clothes still damp from the rain, Si drove into downtown Mineola in a black Lafayette coupe with a green-and-white caduceus emblem attached to the front bumper. The car, keys in the ignition, had been parked in the "Physicians Only" area in the rear of the hospital near the emergency-room entrance.

In Mineola, a postman gave him directions to Roosevelt Field. He addressed Si as "Doc." Si raced to the field and pulled up at the Shell Oil Company hangar where the Viking was parked. The hangar doors were fully open. The airplane's wingtips nearly touched the building's walls.

Ceil Silcox and Karl Eisler stood under the Viking's nose engine chatting with two reporters and a newsreel cameraman. All stared at Si in disbelief. The reporters immediately began shouting questions. "Hey, Mr. Conway, you're supposed to be at death's door!" "Are you going?" "Is that why you left the hospital?" "Are you going?"

Si ignored them. "Where's Freddie?" he asked Ceil.

Karl said, "Si, what the hell are you—"

"Where's Freddie, goddammit!"

"Over at operations," Ceil said.

"Si, are you crazy?" Karl said.

Just then, Freddie entered the hangar. The newsreel cameraman tapped Si on the shoulder. "Come on, Mr. Conway, just give us a statement."

Si turned to the newsmen. "Listen, all of you, get out of here for five minutes," he said. "When you come back, I promise you the biggest scoop you ever had!"

Si forced himself to hold on until the newsmen left. Then he gripped the Viking's propeller blade and clung to it for support. Immediately, Karl slid a mechanic's combination stool-stepladder under Si's knees. Si sank gratefully down on the seat.

Freddie said, "Jesus, Si, you shouldn't be here!"

"We're taking off for Paris," Si said. "Now!" He started to rise but his legs felt leaden. "Just let me catch my breath."

"Si, the only place you're taking off to is back to the hospital," Karl said gently. He touched Si's forehead. "You're burning up!"

Si did not need Karl to tell him that. He knew he could not fly, and that he had to get back into bed. He drew in his breath. Even to talk was an effort.

"You wanted to fly the Atlantic, Karl? Okay, you'll fly. You and Freddie. Now, right away! Okay?"

Freddie and Karl exchanged glances of incredulity. Freddie said, "Si, we just got the latest weather." He brought a folded piece of lined yellow paper from his hip pocket. The paper was covered with scribbled sentences in Freddie's handwriting.

Si tried to focus on the words; they swam before his eyes. He pushed the paper back to Freddie. "So what?"

"So what?" Freddie asked. "Did you read it?"

"Of course I did," Si lied.

" 'Halifax reports heavy rain and severe icing,' " Freddie read from the paper. " 'Condition not expected to improve for at least next twelve hours.' Si, I copied this exactly as they gave it to me over the phone—"

"—you take off now, by the time you reach Halifax it'll be clear." Si was speaking to Karl, as though Freddie were suddenly unimportant.

Karl shook his head. "We would never make it to Halifax."

"Goddammit, Karl, this is what you wanted, isn't it?"

"I also want to stay in one piece," Karl said. "No, Si, forget it. No one goes until the weather clears."

"You damn fool, Lindbergh'll be on his way any minute now!"

"On his way here to New York, perhaps," Karl said. "But I guarantee you that he won't start for Paris until he knows he has a chance."

"Si, listen to Karl," Ceil said. "Please, Si."

Si ignored her. "I'm ordering you to go," he said to Karl.

"I'll go, Si, I'll be only too happy to go," Karl said. "But only when it's safe. Now let me help you get back to the hospital."

Si pushed Karl away. He said to Freddie, "You go without Karl, then. Hire another pilot for the right seat. There must be a hundred guys who'll jump at the chance."

"Forget it, Si," Freddie said. "I'll go, with Karl, when the weather's right."

"Lindbergh'll beat us!" Si shouted. "You want some goddam mail jockey to beat us? Is that what you want?"

"What we want, Si, is a half-way decent chance—" Freddie started to say.

"—you're yellow!" Si shouted. "That's what it is! You lost your goddam guts! No, you didn't lose them; you never had any! For the last time, Freddie, I'm telling you to go!"

Karl brushed Freddie aside and faced Si. "You'll never change," he said. He spoke quietly, almost sadly. "I knew it back in California in that 'dogfight,' when you nearly killed me. It's just as I said, Simon: you're obsessed with winning. Nothing means anything to you except to win." He paused for breath, started speaking, then stopped and walked quickly from the hangar.

Ceil, and then Freddie, spoke to Si. Si did not hear a word they said. He was still hearing Karl's voice. It was old stuff, all of it, and Si possessed neither the strength nor the inclination to argue the point. If Karl could not understand the significance of being first to fly the Atlantic, no amount of talk would help.

Si said to Freddie, "You go, Freddie. It's worth fifty thousand dollars if you do. Cash up front." Si had directed this last sentence not to Freddie, but to Ceil. He knew Ceil, and knew her ambitions. "Fifty thousand, Ceil. Think what the hell you can do with that kind of money."

Ceil said, "Si, take the money and stick it in your ass." She gripped Freddie's arm. "Let's get out of here. I can't stand the stink."

For the rest of his life, those next few minutes would remain engraved in Simon Conway's brain.

"Let me tell you what she means when she says she can't stand the stink, Freddie," he heard himself saying. He rose unsteadily, one hand flattened on the stool seat for support. "She wants to get back at me because I threw her over. She's never forgiven me."

Ceil said, "Si, you low-life bastard!" She tugged at Freddie's sleeve. "Pay no attention, honey—"

"—you 'threw her over'?" Freddie said to Si. "What does that mean?"

"It means she and I were once very good friends," Si said. "But I dumped her when I got married. So she picked you up on the rebound. Ask her."

Freddie did not have to ask Ceil. The answer was written in her expression of rage and humiliation. Freddie nodded tightly, knowingly. "I always figured something like that went on. I just never wanted to believe it."

"It's been over for years, Fred," Ceil said. "Long before we were married."

"But it was going on all that time I was chasing you like a lovesick little puppy, wasn't it?" Freddie said. "All those times I'd take you home from a date so horny I couldn't see straight, and you'd push me away and whisper, 'Relax, relax, you'll live longer.' Sure, and then you'd run over to him and jump in his bed. That's what happened, didn't it?"

Ceil said nothing. She had turned away, weeping.

"Sure," Freddie said softly. "Good old Freddie. I'll bet you two had some good laughs over how crazy I was for you. How I used to beg you to marry me—"

"—damn you, Freddie!" Ceil cried. "I love you! What does it matter what happened a hundred years ago? All that matters is now! Please, darling, please!"

Freddie said to Si, "All right, Si, tell you what: you had your fun with her, so now maybe it's time you paid for it. Let's talk about a hundred thousand, not fifty. A hundred thousand. Plus the twenty-five thousand Orteig money. That's what it'll cost you for me to fly that airplane."

"Done," Si said instantly.

"But after that, Si, you and I are through."

Si nodded, yes.

And with that, Freddie stepped past Ceil and strode from the hangar. She gazed after him a moment, then looked at Si. "Why?" she asked. "Why?"

Si never did reply. He thought it was too stupid a question to dignify.

Afterward, they told him he had collapsed in the hangar and an ambulance had returned him to the hospital. As he was wheeled in, he kept shouting, "We beat Lindbergh! Goddammit, we beat him!"

Simon Conway's relapse nearly cost him his life.

For a day and a half he hovered near death, comatose the entire first night and most of the following day. On the evening of the second day, he opened his eyes to find Meg at his bedside.

"You're going to be all right, Si," she said.

"Like hell," he replied, and fell unconscious again.

Meg was still sitting there ten hours later when Si awoke, but she had dozed off. On her lap was a late edition of the *New York Daily News*. Even through his blurred vision the headlines were too big to misread:

FLIER SILCOX LOST AT SEA!

Si demanded the truth, so they had no choice but to tell him. The Paris-bound Conair Viking had last been sighted over the ocean twelve miles east of Portland, Maine. From all indications the airplane had flown directly into, first, a squall line south of Portland, and then into an early-summer thunderstorm. The U.S. Navy had launched a search and located pieces of the Viking's wreckage. A Coast Guard cutter on Prohibition patrol found the Viking's life raft. There was no trace of the pilots, Frederick Silcox or Gordon Grant, an American Airways captain who had signed on as copilot.

Si fell into a series of hallucinatory dreams. In one, he was back in Saint-Pol-sur-Mer, in the chateau in a room that resembled his old quarters except it had no furniture. Jimmy Forrest was there, saying in a pleasant, conversational voice, "Si, you're a murderer."

"Now hold on just a second, kid," Si said to Jimmy in the dream. "You wanted to be a hero. You went out there and faced Eisler on your own. I didn't send you."

"You're a murderer, Si," Jimmy said.

And then Jimmy's face became Freddie Silcox's face. Si said to him, "Now, listen, Freddie, you had to go. Jesus, guy, we had no choice! You had to do it!"

Freddie Silcox said nothing. He stood there looking at Si, which made Si angry. "Yeah, well, I know just what happened, you son of a bitch!" Si said to him. "You fucked it up. I told you it'd happen someday like that. All that cautious, by-the-book bullshit. Sure, you ran into a situation that never was in the fucking book, so you didn't know how to handle it! It's called 'airmanship,' old buddy. You didn't have it when you needed it, when it counted. I knew you'd goddam well kill yourself one of these days. And you went down with the finest airplane ever made, you dumb prick! Goddam your soul!"

This dream recurred in various forms over the whole three days before it was replaced by a far more pleasant dream. At his bedside, of all people, was Andrée. This he knew was a dream, one he desperately hoped would recur, but of course it did not.

On May 22, he came out of it. They said he had achieved another miracle. He knew it was no miracle. He had refused to die, it was that simple.

On that same May 22, Charles A. Lindbergh landed safely at Le Bourget airfield in Paris.

PART THREE

THE 660

12

Morris Tannen did not recall any car ever giving him as much pleasure as his brand-new 1934 Packard. He invented errands simply as an excuse to drive it. He loved the sheer naked power of the huge twelve-cylinder engine, and the satiny feel of the polished walnut steering wheel. He loved the smooth ride and the envious glances of other motorists. He loved the very smell of the car, that unique new-car smell of virginal rubber and fresh paint.

More important, especially on this muggy July evening, was the sense of security it provided. Tonight, if anything went wrong, Morris was confident the big car would speed him to safety, or, more accurately, away from the scene of the crime.

He drove past the darkened theater and turned into the adjoining parking lot. Even in the dark he could make out the letters on the theater marquee.

Cathay Circle Theater Presents
LITTLE WOMEN
Starring K. Hepburn
Free Auto Park

He drove all the way across the grassy field of the empty parking lot to the wood fence at the far end. He parked parallel to the fence, switched off the headlights and motor, and lit a match to see his wristwatch. It was 1:43. In two minutes, at 1:45, he would flash his lights.

Morris had chosen this spot for the rendezvous because he had parked in the same lot only three nights before and noted how deserted it was after the movie. He had taken Ruth to see *Little Women*, one of her favorite childhood books. Halfway through the film, he had dozed off. Ruth shook him awake during the Pathé News when they showed pictures of President Roosevelt presenting an NRA flag to the head of some small Midwestern steel mill. That goddam Roosevelt, Morris remembered thinking, he'll be the destruction of us all! If you didn't paste a little decal of the NRA eagle in your office windows, or fly an NRA flag from the factory mast, you were considered unpatriotic. NRA, National Recovery Act. National *Ruination* Act was more like it.

Morris sat listening to the loud, rhythmic chirping of crickets and, from Olympic Boulevard, the occasional swish of automobile tires on the newly paved road surface. He closed his fingers around the thick brown envelope on the velour upholstered seat beside him. The bills, fifty $1,000 notes, were stuffed tightly inside the letter-sized envelope.

He lit another match, checked the time, and counted slowly to sixty. Then he switched the headlights on and off three times. Immediately, from the opposite end of the parking lot, like two yellow eyes in the night, automobile headlights blinked on. A moment later the other automobile, a Plymouth coupe, pulled up alongside the Packard. The driver switched off the lights. Morris could just make out the boxed outline of the driver's straw hat.

"Mr. Tannen . . . ?"

"Yeah, Walter, it's me," Morris said. He hoped no one else was in the car, slouched down beside the driver. "Come into my car."

Although Morris could not see him clearly in the dark, he thought Walter Driscoll looked thinner than when they had last met. But that was three years before, in Washington, during a Republican administration when Driscoll was Assistant Postmaster General of the United States, and before a young Alabama senator named Hugo Black had decided that the Post Office was rotten with corruption.

Walter Driscoll got into the Packard on the passenger's side. Morris handed him the envelope. "What about the ticket?" Walter Driscoll asked.

Morris held his breath a moment, waiting for someone else to jump out of the Plymouth to arrest him.

Driscoll said impatiently, "The ticket?"

"It's in there with the money."

Driscoll jammed the envelope into his inside coat pocket. "I'm curious," he said. "Did Conair foot the whole bill?"

"As a matter of fact, no," said Morris. "All the airlines chipped in. All except Trippe. He said Pan American didn't fly domestically so why the hell should he contribute? Make sure you're on that boat, Walter," Morris went on. "It leaves at noon today from San Pedro."

"I'll be on it," Walter Driscoll said. He got out of the car, closed the door, and spoke to Morris through the open window on the passenger's side. "Tell Mr. Conway he's got nothing to worry about. He should be in Washington by now, shouldn't he?"

"He'll be phoning me from Kansas City," Morris said, deciding not to wait for Si's call but instead to send him a message on company radio. "Enjoy your trip, Walter."

"Don't worry, I will," said Walter Driscoll. He got into the coupe and drove away.

Morris, watching Walter Driscoll's headlights cut through the dark, debated phoning the message into the CATS dispatch office at the airport instead of driving all the way there. There was an outdoor public phone booth near the theater. No, to make sure it was sent correctly, he'd have to handle it personally.

" '. . . deed is done,' " Morris said aloud, reciting the message he had composed. " 'Relax and enjoy our nation's capital.' "

Our nation's capital, he repeated to himself, thinking that not once since the day four months ago when Walter Driscoll first approached Conair with this proposition had anyone—himself, Morris Tannen, included—questioned the morality or ethics involved. They simply accepted it as a normal way of doing business. Procedures and policies practiced by the entire industry. It was that, or perish. Now, having justified this to himself, he felt better.

2.

Si, Phil Granger, and Ross Leonard were seated in the last two rows of the 550. Tom Blanchard came back into the cabin to tell them they had picked up a 30-mile-per-hour tail wind. He had decided to overfly Kansas City and land instead at Indianapolis, which would get them their final destination, Washington, between 5:30 and 6:00 A.M., a little earlier than scheduled.

"Sure, Tom," Si said. "Whatever you say." He brushed his fingers over the two gold stripes on the sleeve of Tom's natty blue uniform. "You're the captain."

Tom Blanchard, young, handsome, articulate, was Hollywood's idea of an airline captain. A University of Michigan graduate, he had learned to fly as a U.S. Army Air Corps cadet and had been with CATS nearly seven years, hired by Freddie Silcox shortly before the ill-fated Atlantic flight. Tom did not know it yet, but Si planned to appoint him CATS chief pilot.

Tom nodded hello to Philip Granger who sat across the aisle from Si, then to Ross Leonard in the seat just ahead of Si's. "What do you think of this airplane, Mr. Leonard?"

"I like it."

"So do we," Tom said. He winked at Si, then proceeded back to the cockpit, stopping to chat briefly with each passenger. All eleven of the remaining seats were occupied. This exercise of the captain introducing himself to the passengers and engaging them in casual conversation was now standard CATS procedure. Customer relations, Morris Tannen termed it.

When Ross Leonard said he liked the airplane, the 550, it was not entirely true. The 550 was a biplane version of the 440, bigger, more powerful, and much improved. In appearance the 550 bore a vague resemblance to the Curtiss Condor, but with three engines to the Condor's two. Ross actually considered the Condor a better passenger vehicle, but he had purchased and put into service eight 550s for his Intercontinental Airways merely to make peace with Simon Conway. Peace with Simon Conway meant a first crack at the Conair 660, a truly new and innovative airplane.

The 660 prototype was scheduled to be flown in the next three months, no later than October. A sleek, all-metal, twin-engined, low-winged monoplane that would carry eighteen passengers coast to coast in no more than two stops, the 660 had been designed by Pete Dagget, Karl Eisler's brilliant young protégé. Cruising at 140 mph, it would be the first airliner to earn a profit solely from carrying passengers. Speed, after all, was the secret. The faster you delivered the passengers, the more flights you could make.

The 660 would also be the first CATS airplane with a third crew member, a registered nurse. A stewardess. Si had resisted this new trend but finally relented. What the hell, if passengers were attracted by the idea of a pretty girl distributing packets of chewing gum to relieve the pressure on their ears when descending, and holding a burp bag for them, why not? Besides, it was a golden opportunity to get a jump on Eddie Rickenbacker's Eastern Air Transport Service. Rick said the only way a woman would ever wear an Eastern uniform was over his dead body.

Si leaned forward and tapped Ross's elbow. "If you like the 550 so much, Ross, why don't you put in an order for a dozen more?"

Ross and Si both knew the 550 was obsolete almost before it flew, completely outclassed by Boeing's new all-metal transport, the 247, and Douglas's DC-2. Like the 660, these two new airplanes were twin-engined, retractable-geared, low-winged monoplanes.

Ross said, "I'll wait for the 660, thanks."

Phil Granger said, "Ross, you're one of Conway Air Transport Service's biggest competitors. Why the hell should we sell you equipment that'll help you compete with us?"

"You didn't mind selling me 550s, did you?"

"We wanted to help you out," Granger said.

"Yeah, I just bet," Ross said. "You made so many 550s you didn't know what to do with them. Listen, young man, if you don't sell to me, Boeing or Douglas will."

"Douglas is committed to TWA for their new plane," Granger said. "And Boeing will never sell to you. You're competing with their airline, too." Boeing Air Transport Service, with CATS, was the only other large airline owned and operated by an aircraft manufacturer.

"But you will," Ross said. "You'll sell to me, because I'm prepared at this very minute to write a check for a hundred thousand dollars for an option on six 660s against a full purchase price of sixty-five thousand each. I happen to know how much cash you've already plunked into developing the airplane." He twisted around to face Si. "You haven't changed, Si. You still haven't learned how to balance your books."

Si had not heard a word Ross said, not since the first mention of the 660. He hated all the business talk. He left all that to Granger and Morris. He would not even be going to Washington if he had not been served with a subpoena to appear as a witness before a Senate committee.

He gazed out the window at the fuzzy little green and white halos of the navigational lights on the 550's upper and lower wingtips. They were flying just above a layer of thin clouds that completely obscured the ground. He wondered where they were. Somewhere between Albuquerque and Kansas City, he estimated.

The voices of the others blended with the pounding of the engines, almost as a faraway echo. They were still talking about the 660, the Skybus, as Pete Dagget had named it on the drawing board. Pete, whom Karl had hired the day the boy graduated Cal Tech, was a genius. Pete's presence left Karl free to concentrate on a project closer to his heart, a pursuit plane to be called the Hunter.

The Hunter, at present, was nothing more than an idea of Si's and a vague concept in Karl's head, a head that at the moment was halfway around the world. After assurances from the new Nazi government that he was more than welcome, Karl had returned to Germany to visit his critically ill mother.

Karl had never forgiven Si for Freddie Silcox, and Si had never asked forgiveness. Expressions of remorse or confessions of guilt would not bring Freddie back. What was done was done. In the seven years since that terrible day, whenever Si and Karl spoke, their conversations were mainly confined to business. Even when Karl congratulated Si on Meg's giving birth to Janet—three months after Freddie's flight—it was in an almost grudging monotone. He sent flowers to Meg in the hospital but never visited her at home. Si could not recall when Karl had last come to the house, and Karl was especially fond of Richard.

Freddie, in Karl's view, was not the only one Si had destroyed that day. Si knew that Karl held him responsible for Ceil, too. Shortly after Freddie's disappearance, Si presented Ceil a company check for $125,000, Freddie's "bonus." Ceil tore the check into four neat pieces and hurled the pieces into Si's face. But each Christmas thereafter, Si gave Phil Granger an envelope containing $2,500 in cash which Granger then delivered to Ceil, swearing to her that the money came from his own pocket, not Si's.

Last December, ironically on the day Prohibition officially came to an end, Lucille Silcox was found dead in a Los Angeles skid-row hotel room. The direct cause of death was attributed to the ingestion of a large quantity of denatured alcohol—bad bootleg gin.

Si liked to think, and it was not untrue, that Freddie Silcox had helped pave the way for others. In the seven years since Freddie crashed into the sea, more aviation progress had been made than in all the thirty years since Kitty Hawk. A woman, Amelia Earhart, had flown alone across the Atlantic. Wiley Post had flown around the world in seven days. U.S. Army Major James Doolittle had flown coast-to-coast in under eleven hours—with three stops for fuel.

Aviation was big business. One glimpse of the Conair factory told you that. The old dirigible hangars were gone, replaced years ago by two huge, sawtooth-roofed buildings longer and wider than football fields. A glittering blue-and-white electric sign on the roof displayed the Conway logo: the American eagle with the letter C. And this new assembly area was already too small. Another had to be built for the 660 so the existing facility could keep up with the military contracts, the CT-5 trainers, the 0-17 army observation airplanes, and the Cloud King, a trimotored, high-winged army and navy transport that should have been more aptly called Super Viking.

Precisely because aviation was big business, and getting bigger, Simon Conway and these other executives were traveling to Washington. They had been summoned to testify before a Congressional committee chaired by Hugo Black, the young Alabama senator. Mr. Black possessed hard evidence of collusion between the Post Office Department and the big airlines in the awarding of mail subsidies.

Ross Leonard was only half joking when he said that if the full story ever came out, he, Si, and a dozen other airline executives might spend the next hundred years in Leavenworth—with time off for good behavior. A former Assistant Postmaster General, Walter Driscoll, had agreed to reveal details of how thoroughly the airlines had corrupted the Post Office Department.

". . . excuse me, Mr. Conway." Jerry Skaggs, the peach-fuzz-faced copilot, was gently shaking Si's shoulder. He handed Si a slip of paper. "This just came in for you on the company radio."

The message was written in pencil in large block letters: DEED IS DONE. RELAX AND ENJOY OUR NATION'S CAPITAL. TANNEN. Si handed the paper to Phil Granger. Granger read it, pleased, then passed it to Ross Leonard.

Ross said, "Well, with Senator Black's star witness gone, it looks like we'll keep carrying the mail after all."

"We'll still have to answer questions," Granger said.

"Listen, probably the only thing they don't know about us is what we tell our wives when we've been out all night," Ross said. "And I wouldn't be too damned sure about that!"

Our wives, Si thought. He and Meg were enjoying a kind of sexual awakening that had started on a July Fourth weekend two years ago when they were guests of Herbert Fallon at the Palm Springs Racquet Club. It might have been Si's sudden awareness that other men were interested in Meg, and his twinge of unexpected jealousy, coupled with a feeling of possessive pride. Or it might have been nothing more than a new appreciation of Meg's poise and charm, or just a simple matter of his realizing that she had matured into a very lovely woman. Whatever the reason, he found their new passion quite pleasant.

Yes, much was to be said for marriage, an institution Si recommended for Karl Eisler. Si, knowing of Karl's long and unfulfilled relationship with a German general's daughter, had always entertained the whimsical hope that marrying the lady might settle Karl down enough to restore their friendship.

Karl had no knowledge of the Walter Driscoll affair. Si was glad Karl was away and not involved in this latest piece of "corporate creativity," as Granger termed it. Karl would never have approved.

3.

Erika von Kurzfeld's maternal great-grandmother, who was still alive, had seen her own white satin wedding gown passed down to three generations of von Kurzfeld women. Although Erika and Karl Eisler were not married in a church by a priest—the ceremony was conducted in the office of the mayor of Berlin, and by the lord mayor himself—the venerable old lady insisted that Erika wear the gown anyway. The bridegroom's best man was the Reich Commissioner for Air and Speaker of the Reichstag, Hermann Göring.

Immediately after the wedding, in a car loaned to them by Göring, the newlyweds drove to Wiesbaden, where they remained through the weekend. Now, on the first morning after their return to Berlin, in the cavernous marble-floored lobby of the main Berlin-West Post Office on Fasanenstrasse, Erika waited for Karl to finish sending a cable to America.

She watched him move up to the counter behind an impeccably dressed old man leaning on a malacca cane. The old man's militarily erect figure reminded Erika of her father, who had once told her that she was his whole life. Well, that life had been finished for nearly six months. Stefan von Kurzfeld simply went to sleep one night and never awakened. At least his death had freed Erika to marry the man she loved.

When Karl learned of his mother's illness, he had contacted Göring for permission to return home. Göring not only unhesitatingly guaranteed Karl's safety but personally greeted him at Tempelhof with the pronouncement that "all is forgiven."

Apparently, more than forgiven, as evidenced by Göring's generosity not only in arranging the marriage—cutting through the usual maze of license applications and posting of banns—but himself standing as Karl's best man. But then, about love and marriage especially, Hermann Göring was an admitted sentimentalist. His own wife, to whom he was devoted, had died two years before, and only recently had the *Reichsminister* begun to recover from his grief.

The sight of Karl was like a tonic to his mother. She recovered, and two hours after he had placed her in a comfortable rest home, he rang the doorbell of Erika's apartment. It was like a film. She opened the door and they gazed at each other, and then they were in each other's arms, weeping and laughing at the same time.

After the tall old man who reminded Erika of her father left and Karl had sent his cable, Erika slipped her arm into his and they started out of the building. "Let me see what you said in the telegram." She snatched the copy of the cable from him. The message was in English:

CONAIR LOSANG 22 JULY 1933 MARRIED STOP ON HONEYMOON
STOP RETURNING LOSANG TWO WEEKS STOP EISLER

"It's a kind of private joke," Karl said. "There's a famous story about my partner, Simon Conway, sending the same cable when he got married."

"Believe me, Herr Eisler, your marriage to me is no joke," Erika said with mock sternness. "And you haven't told me where we'll live in Los Angeles." She folded the paper and tucked it into his jacket breast pocket. "Nor have you asked me what kind of house I want."

"I'll build you a castle," he said. He snapped his fingers in sudden frustration. "Damn! I forgot. We're meeting Göring for lunch."

"I thought we were having dinner with him tonight."

"I know, but he says he has something very interesting to show me. I'll cancel the dinner engagement, I promise you."

What Göring wanted to show Karl turned out to be something very interesting indeed, although Karl had to wait until after lunch to see it. While Erika went shopping on the Kurfürstendamm, the *Reichsminister* and Karl drove fifty miles north of Berlin to a brand-new airdrome with five large corrugated metal hangars, a control tower, and two intersecting one-mile-long concrete runways.

The tarmac was crowded with Ju-52 trimotored transports, some smaller liaison planes, and, lined wing to wing in front of the control tower, twelve of the biggest fighters Karl had ever seen. Single-engined biplanes with the black iron cross decaled on the silver fuselage and the Nazi swastika emblazoned in black on the vertical tail fin.

"Heinkel 51s," Göring said proudly. "Ugly brutes, aren't they? They'll do three hundred and twenty kilometers per hour full out and climb to five thousand meters in twelve minutes."

As he spoke, overhead, three more HE-51s appeared. Flying abreast, they swooped down and raced straight toward the open Opel sedan parked on the tarmac near Göring and Karl. Karl had to fight every instinct not to hurl himself to the ground. The three airplanes, engines screaming shrilly, came straight on and then, as one, zoomed up and banked speedily away.

Karl swiveled around to watch. The Heinkels, climbing, were almost out of sight. Göring said, "All right, so what do you think of that?"

"I think it's a sight I was afraid I'd never live to see."

It was the perfect response. Göring beamed with pleasure. "We don't have many. What you see is all of them, fifteen. But soon we'll have hundreds more. Hundreds, take my word for it! And I'll bet you're thinking, How the hell does he think they can get away with this?"

"It did cross my mind," Karl said. "It's a direct violation of the treaty."

"Very few people know of the existence of this airfield," Göring said. "Or that half of Heinkel's Bavarian factory that is supposed to be turning out stoves is instead manufacturing airplanes. But, my friend, in a year, two at most, it will all be academic. We'll have fifty fighter squadrons and twenty heavy-bombardment squadrons. Then we will simply, and officially, inform the Allied Commission that we no longer recognize the Versailles Treaty and do not consider ourselves obligated to comply with its terms."

"And two days later Berlin will be occupied," Karl said.

"By whom?" Göring asked. "The Swiss navy? I guarantee you that when we reveal our new Reichsluftwaffe, the British and French won't dare oppose it. They'll skulk away and do nothing."

Karl was not so sure about that, but knew Göring was not seeking a debate. Göring had a definite motive for bringing him out here, a motive which Karl sensed was about to be revealed. He was right.

"Karl, we need an entirely new design, a pursuit plane twice as fast as these big fellows," Göring said. "I want you to build it for me."

"I beg your pardon?"

"I am inviting you to design a new fighter for us."

Far in the distance the three HE-51s were coming in to land, not on the concrete runway but within a wide grassy infield between the runways. Karl wondered why so much effort had been put into concrete surfacing, then realized the runways were designed for the future, for larger, heavier, and faster airplanes. Yes, these Nazis were certainly thinking ahead.

"Did you hear me, Karl?" Göring asked. "I said we would like you to build a plane for us."

Karl said dryly, "I somehow doubt the United States government would approve."

"I hadn't intended to ask their permission," Göring said, and dropped the subject entirely, almost as though he felt he had said too much. Karl knew better. Göring was a salesman. A good salesman knew when to stop selling and leave the next move to the customer. Hermann Göring was a good salesman.

Karl was unable to keep his promise to Erika to cancel the dinner engagement. Göring said he had some vitally important matters to discuss, and Karl and Erika were leaving in the morning for a five-day Monte Carlo holiday, and then on to Southampton to board the *Saturnia* for New York.

They dined that evening at Göring's home outside Berlin, a small, almost modest villa on the lakefront in Wannsee. The *Reichsminister* had only recently moved into the house from his bachelor suite at a Berlin hotel.

After dinner they went out to the terrace and sat at a garden table where Karl and Göring sipped brandy, smoked cigars, and discussed aviation in general. Although Göring had not once referred to the conversation at the airfield, Karl knew that this was the important matter the *Reichsminister* wanted to discuss and that it would be brought up before they parted. "Closing the sale," as he once had heard an automobile dealer in Santa Monica describe it. Karl hoped Göring took the answer graciously, for he had already decided he could not—more accurately, would not—accept the offer.

Despite his differences with Simon Conway, Karl was eminently satisfied with his life in America and looked forward to the future there. At the same time, the sight of those handsome pursuit planes at the secret airfield had thrilled and inspired him. He believed Germany should by all means renounce the Versailles Treaty, a question of simple justice, no more, no less. He could only hope that Göring was right, that the Allies would not march back into Germany and the country once again be thrown into chaos and anarchy.

The sleek image of the still-embryonic Hunter flashed into Karl's mind. The Hunter, the airplane that Karl and Si planned to build, the fighter that would outfly and outfight anything in the sky. The Hunter, with a white-outlined black iron cross on its fuselage and, on its rudder, a swastika.

Perhaps some arrangement might be made, a licensing agreement for foreign manufacture of the Hunter. Why not establish a Conair plant in Germany? Ford made cars here, as did General Motors.

Göring poured more brandy into Karl's snifter. "Rémy Martin," Göring said. "We make better airplanes and guns than the French, and turn out finer soldiers, but can't hold a candle to them for their wines and liqueurs. Does that tell you something?"

"It tells me I'm getting drunk," Karl replied, noticing Erika managing to stifle a yawn; she was getting bored listening to them. And you are gaining weight, Herr Reichsminister, he thought, noticing the jiggling jowls and decided protuberance under the tweed jacket. Earlier in the day at the airfield, in uniform, Göring had looked thinner.

Just then a maid came out to the terrace and whispered in Göring's ear. Göring looked at his wristwatch. "Right on time," he said. "Tell him to wait in the study."

Genuinely apologetic, Göring asked Erika to please excuse Karl and him a few minutes. He said to Karl, "Someone's here I'd like you to meet."

Karl reached across the table for Erika's hand. "I love you," he whispered, and followed Göring into the house.

The foyer was cluttered with unopened boxes, pieces of luggage, and wardrobe containers. Göring was still in the process of unpacking. He opened a door off the foyer and entered the study, a large room with a broad oak table that served as a desk, a leather sofa, and several ornately carved wooden lounge chairs. The room was in disarray, crowded with stuffed animal heads, cartons of books, photographs, paintings. Two of the paintings were formal portraits, one a life-sized oil of Göring as a young Imperial Air Service lieutenant, the other a rendering of his late wife, Carin, a fair, delicate, beautiful woman.

A tall well-dressed young man with curly blond hair and deep-blue eyes rose from one of the chairs. He turned toward Karl, arching his head so that the left side of his face, which had been shadowed, was now fully exposed in the light of the desk lamp.

From eye to mouth the skin was crisscrossed by angry red scars. The flesh itself was flat and nearly pink. Karl's first thought was that the poor son of a bitch had been burned, and what a tragedy for so handsome a man to be burdened with such a handicap. And then he recognized the man.

Anton Moerzer.

". . . you two met many years ago," Göring was saying. He seemed almost nostalgic. "Do you remember, Karl?"

Karl remembered all too vividly that night in 1923 at the Nazi Party offices in Berlin, when Simon Conway had broken Anton Moerzer's nose. But the nose seemed fine, straight, unmarked. What the hell had happened to the face?

"You're looking well, Herr Eisler," Moerzer said. As though reading Karl's mind, he added, "But I'm not looking so well, am I? The injury, you see, was not so much to the nose as to the cheekbone. It was fractured, smashed to bits. It required plastic surgery. The doctor—a Jew, what else would you expect?—botched the job, and then attempted to repair the damage with a skin graft." He ran his fingers over the scars. He appeared to enjoy Karl's discomfort. "This is the result."

"I wanted you to hear from Anton's own mouth that he bears you no ill will over the incident," Göring said. "I asked him to personally repeat my invitation to you."

Moerzer shook Karl's hand now. "We need you, Dr. Eisler. Germany needs you."

"There, Karl, the final obstacle," Göring said. "Now let's all sit and have a drink and discuss the matter." Immediately, Göring poured brandy from a cut-crystal decanter into three glasses. He raised his glass in a toast to Karl.

If Karl had been drunk, he was sober now. The sight of the grotesquely disfigured Anton Moerzer was enough to sober anyone. And he resented this little game of Göring's, confronting Karl with Moerzer as though presenting an overdue bill.

". . . so, Karl, what do you say?" Göring was saying. "Are you with us?"

"Hermann, I need time to consider," Karl said. He hated himself for his cowardice but knew an outright refusal would only antagonize Göring.

"Take whatever time you need," Göring said. "I realize you have obligations to your associates in America."

Göring had addressed this last sentence directly to Anton Moerzer, as if to remind him that Karl's "associates" included Simon Conway. The scars on Moerzer's face stood out like strands of red wire.

"Yes," Moerzer said as though on cue, "I understand Mr. Conway is in serious trouble with the American government. Some business about bribing Postal Department officials?"

"I'm afraid I can't tell you much about it," Karl answered truthfully. "You probably have more information than I."

"The word I get is that your airline—along with many others, of course—is in danger of losing its mail subsidies," Göring said.

"As I said, Hermann, I can't tell you much about it."

Göring said, "If Conway loses the mail subsidies, is it fair to assume he'll concentrate more on manufacturing? Specifically, military aircraft?"

Ah, Karl thought, now I understand. "Hermann, to begin with, I'm confident that whatever trouble Simon is in, he'll extricate himself."

"That doesn't answer my question."

"It's too hypothetical a question."

"Answer it hypothetically, then."

"Yes," Karl said after a moment. "The answer is probably yes. If the mail subsidy is lost, Conair will probably concentrate on military aircraft. Now, exactly what military aircraft are you interested in?"

Göring laughed. "You're not much on discretion, are you, Karl?"

"I'm taking a leaf from your book, Hermann."

"Dive-bombers," Göring said. "Curtiss is experimenting with a machine for the United States Navy, the Goshawk. I'd be interested to know how it compares with what Junkers is developing for us, the *Sturzkampfflugzeug*. The Stuka. My people are quite interested in dive-bombing as a prime tactic. I've seen pictures of the Goshawk but no performance figures."

"Curtiss is not Conair," Karl said. "They're hardly likely to offer me a look at their figures."

"The U.S. Navy might," Göring said. "If Conair were to build a dive-bomber."

Moerzer leaned over the side table for the decanter and refilled Göring's glass and Karl's. Karl nodded his thanks and said dryly to Göring, "Herr Reichsminister, what is it you want of me? To design airplanes, or become an espionage agent?"

Göring's eyes narrowed angrily; it was as though he thought Karl was making fun of him. But then he smiled. "Perhaps both, Karl." He touched his glass to Karl's. "Perhaps both."

It was true that Hermann Göring knew more about Conair's difficulties with the U.S. government than Karl did. But the *Reichsminister's* intelligence sources were unaware of the existence—or, as U.S. Senator Black learned to his chagrin, the non-existence—of Walter Driscoll. In testimony before the Black Committee, Simon Conway steadfastly denied ever bribing or attempting to bribe any Post Office official.

But there was enough evidence of collusion to persuade President Roosevelt to cancel all airmail contracts. New contracts would be awarded, but not to airlines that had previously held them. In the interim, Roosevelt declared an emergency and ordered the U.S. Army Air Corps to fly the mail. In the space of a single week, five pilots were killed and eight airplanes destroyed. Shortly thereafter, the new airline mail contracts were awarded.

Karl learned all this long after the fact, and not from any intelligence source. He read about it in *Time* magazine on the train from New York to Los Angeles. He had not flown, because he wanted Erika to see the vastness of the country. In Chicago, boarding the *Super Chief*, he purchased the September 4, 1934, issue of the magazine.

What immediately caught his eye was a quarter-page ad in the business section, a line drawing of a Conair 550 flying above the clouds. The familiar blue, blocked letters on the airplane's fuselage bore an unfamiliar name: CONWAY NATIONAL AIRLINES.

Conway National Airlines?

The brief ad copy was only slightly more enlightening:

Our name may be changed, but not our dedication to safety, service, and comfort. When you fly CNA, you fly with our "million-mile" pilots in the world's finest airplanes. Since 1922, we have served the traveling public with distinction. We will continue to do so.

The explanation of the name change lay in the magazine's aviation section, in a story of how both the Post Office Department and the airline industry had managed a face-saving restoration of airmail contracts.

Complying with the Presidential order, the contracts now had to be given to new companies, and they were. New companies, that is, solely by virtue of new names.

Overnight, American Airways had become American Airlines. Eastern Air Transport Service became Eastern Airlines. Conway Air Transport Service became Conway National Airlines. Intercontinental Airways became Intercontinental Air. The corporate name changes, a patently transparent device, technically met the Department of Commerce's mandate. More important, the mail would get through.

And keep the airlines in business.

When Karl read the article he could not help being amused. Actually, the last part of the article was what amused him. The corporate-name-change scheme had been termed the Tannen Plan, after its creator, Morris Tannen, a Conway Aviation Industries vice president.

Karl could almost see the scene as it must have unfolded in Conair's conference room—Morris proposing the name change, and Si criticizing it as just another of Morris's wild ideas; but, in the end, Si deciding it might work and praising Morris's genius.

He placed the magazine on Erika's lap. "Darling, read this story. It's about how business is done in this country."

13

It was like reliving the past, that bright sunny day in Holland when Simon Conway had flown Tony Fokker's F-8 and shouted into the wind, "You are the most beautiful lady in the world!" The same words floated to his lips now.

". . . hey, Mr. Conway!" Tom Blanchard, in the right seat, called out.

Si pushed the battered old fedora to the back of his head. "What the hell are you looking at?" he asked.

"Your face," Tom said. "You looked like you were in a trance." They spoke in almost normal tones. Even with the 660's twin J-800s roaring steadily and smoothly you did not have to raise your voice to be heard. The cabin and cockpit were soundproofed with a new fiber compound.

"Turn on the radio," Si said.

The radio transmitter and receiver, a bulky apparatus that resembled a large filing cabinet, was anchored to the wall behind the copilot's seat. Tom switched it on. "Anytime you're ready," he said. "This new Philco rig warms up fast."

Si held the control yoke with one hand while he removed his hat, placed it on his lap, and put on his earphones. He plucked the candlestick-like microphone from its wall hook, squeezed the transmitter button, and spoke into it.

"Hello, Conair tower, this is six-six-zero. Come in." He listened a moment, then said to Tom, "Nothing but a lot of goddam static!"

Tom put on his own earphones and rotated the receiver frequency knob. "There they are," he said to Si.

The Conair tower operator's voice boomed loud and clear in Si's earphones. "This is Conair tower, six-six-zero. Go ahead, sir."

"Six-six-zero approaching Venice Beach," Si said into the microphone. "We are at eight hundred feet. She flies like a dream. Over."

Although all commercial operations at the airport were controlled from the Department of Commerce tower, Conway Aviation Industries maintained its own control tower. Painted in gaudy red and white checkerboard squares, and used solely for company aircraft, the Conair tower was located on the roof of the original factory on the opposite side of the field, which had recently been renamed Los Angeles Municipal Airport.

In the cramped glassed enclosure, Morris Tannen, Philip Granger, Karl Eisler, and young Pete Dagget clustered anxiously around the loudspeaker.

Morris jubilantly pounded Pete's shoulder. "'... flies like a dream!'" Morris said, and quoted the advertising slogan he planned to use in newspaper ads: "'Luxury with speed! Coast to coast in twenty-six hours without changing planes!'"

The Conair operator was saying into his microphone, "Six-six-zero from Conair. Hey, Mr. Conway, that's great!"

Great, Karl thought, a word that hardly did the 660 justice. Incredible was more like it. With her eighteen passenger seats she not only was the first airplane with the potential to make a profit purely from carrying passengers but also, truly, a pilot's dream. An all-aluminum stressed-skin monoplane, the 660 cruised at 150 mph, with a maximum range of 950 miles. She had a fully retractable landing gear and extendible wing flaps for additional lift on takeoff and landing. Her propellers were two-speed Hamiltons that set the blades at the most efficient angle for takeoff and then readjusted them at cruising altitude for fuel-efficient flight.

Her state-of-the-art instrumentation included a Sperry artificial horizon and directional gyro, and a Kollsman pressure altimeter. The 660 could fly anytime, anywhere, in any weather. Already, Tom Blanchard had organized a complete 660 ground-school program for CNA pilots. No pilot would sit in the left seat until fully certified. This included the boss himself, Simon Conway.

In the 660, Si removed the earphones and clamped his hat back on his head. Directly ahead was the amusement park on Venice Beach pier, the roller coaster, the Whip, the Bamboo Dragon Slide, and the captive airplanes, the ride Frank most enjoyed. Si had taken both boys to the park the previous week. Frank would have ridden the captive airplanes all day, while Richard refused to step into them. He said they made him dizzy.

Si had brought the boys to the airport last summer for the National Air Races. Richard could not have cared less but Frank, as always, was thrilled, although disappointed that no Conair racer was entered. Si explained that he and Karl simply did not have time to spend building a racer.

Frank, all of eleven years old, understood at once. Si could still hear the kid, that choirboy-soprano voice proclaiming, "We want them to know we make the biggest and best planes in the world, not toys. Right, Dad?"

The big silver 660 flew directly over the roller coaster. The people in the cars waved gaily. A few minutes later, well over the water, Si pulled the yoke gently back and asked Tom to increase power. "Forty inches manifold, keep the props at low pitch," Si said. "We'll take her up to eight thousand."

The airplane climbed effortlessly. Ahead, glistening blue in the early afternoon sun, the waters of Santa Monica Bay stretched on into the horizon. Beyond the pier a large deep-sea-fishing vessel had just passed the red-tipped buoy marking the breakwater. Fishermen on the deck gawked at the airplane.

At eight thousand feet, Si set the propellers at cruise pitch, synchronized both engines, and trimmed the elevator and aileron controls. He removed his hands from the yoke and folded them across his lap. The airplane flew serenely on.

"How about this!" Si said elatedly. "We won't even need that new automatic pilot Sperry's supposed to come out with! This thing'll fly by itself!"

Tom, who had been relaying a continual stream of flight reports into the microphone, grinned at Si and said, "Amen!"

Si gripped the yoke again, but only lightly. He felt not the slightest tremor. She really was a marvel. Pete Dagget deserved a bonus for this one. So did Karl for discovering Pete.

Karl. Ever since the hardheaded Kraut came back from Germany he was more distant and standoffish than ever. He and his new wife had settled in a rented house in Brentwood, and Meg had invited the couple to dinner several times. Karl and Si had talked, but mostly business. Karl said little about his trip to Germany, only that he had seen Anton Moerzer and that Göring was very interested in dive-bombers and it might be a good idea for Conair to play around with a dive-bomber design. Si told him to do whatever he wanted, as long as it did not interfere with their plans for the fighter, the Conway Hunter.

The Hunter, which Si was determined to have in the air within the next two years, would make every other military pursuit plane look like an old Nieuport. The army and navy would lick Simon Conway's toes for a chance to bid on that airplane.

Yes, they'd build the Hunter and he and Karl would make peace; they were getting too old for a silly feud. Old, he thought, glancing at Tom furiously jotting notes on the clipboard and talking to the field at the same time. Si, at thirty-nine, was ten years older than Tom, but what the hell was so old about thirty-nine? Not even a gray hair in his head. Well, perhaps a few little strands here and there on the sideburns.

". . . want to take her up to ten?" Tom was asking.

"We've done enough for the first day," Si said. "Let's go home."

Si flew over the field at fifteen hundred feet. The hardstand in front of the terminal was crowded with airplanes: Ford Trimotors, Curtiss Condors, Stinson Trimotors. More and more of the major airlines had moved here from Burbank and Glendale. New hangars and new administration buildings were springing up so fast you could hardly recognize the place from one day to the next.

On downwind leg after completing the landing checklist with Tom, Si removed his hat, put on the earphones again, and spoke into the microphone. "Gentlemen, this is Conair six-six-zero, gear down and locked, turning final."

In the tower, Morris nudged the radio operator aside and shouted into the microphone, " 'Luxury with speed! Coast to coast in twenty-six hours without changing planes!' "

"Try twenty-*four* hours!" Si replied. "Get the champagne ready! Six-six-zero over and out." He whipped off the earphones and tossed them carelessly aside, kicking them out of the way as they caromed off his knees and fell to the floor at his feet. He put his hat back on and gripped the yoke. He intended to grease this airplane in, land her so gently no one would even hear the crunch of rubber on the runway.

In the tower, watching the 660 bank gracefully around into final, her angle of descent so steady you might think she was sliding down an invisible chute, Karl Eisler could not repress a little nod of admiration. You could always measure the skill of a pilot from his approaches. The good ones made it look easy. Simon Conway was a good one. Whatever else he was, Karl thought—selfish, bad-tempered, egotistical, narrow-minded—Simon Conway was a natural pilot. Give the devil his due.

The airplane flew over the end of the runway, nose still down. Karl waited for Si to flare out. At one hundred feet the angle of descent remained unchanged.

All right, Si, Karl said to himself, that's enough showing off. Pull up the nose and land. Si did not pull up. The airplane hurtled downward, silver nose aimed at the black asphalt runway surface like an arrow speeding toward its target.

In the airplane, Si heard Tom Blanchard's voice shouting words that made no sense. The black runway surface loomed larger and larger in the windscreen. Si pulled the yoke back with all his strength.

The yoke would not budge.

Everything seemed impossibly slow. Everything sounded hollow and distorted. Tom's voice, the incongruously smooth purr of the engines, Si's own voice trying to form words. In his brain the words were clear. The controls are frozen! Cut the main switches! Grab the wheel and help me! But as slow as it all seemed, he knew it was all happening in a few split seconds, two or three blinks of the eye.

The blackness of the runway was so close he could make out individual little creases in the tar shining dully in the sun. He continued trying to move the yoke, although he knew it was too late. But he had to try. He had to.

In the control tower, listening to the voices behind him crying out in shock and horror, Karl Eisler experienced that same sensation of time suspended. Someone else, not he, not Karl, was watching the beautiful silver airplane smash nose-down into the runway, the right wingtip scraping the surface, the right landing wheel collapsing, the right engine grinding into the asphalt, breaking the propeller blades off at the hub and sending both blades tumbling along the ground. Yes, it was someone else who watched the right wing buckle and fold back into the fuselage, the wingless fuselage cartwheel and skid off the runway and, spewing bits and pieces of metal, plow a deep, twin furrow along the grass infield before finally coming to a lurching, shuddering, stop.

There was absolutely no sound in the control tower. The wreckage of the 660 lay before them, a giant metallic bird struck down in flight, shorn of one wing and both legs, the right side of its head half buried in the ground.

Then, like a tableau coming to life, the men in the tower were shouting and rushing out the door. On the field, ambulances, private cars, and fire engines all raced toward the crashed airplane.

Karl remained in the tower. He did not want to see the broken bodies in the cockpit. More than once he had envisioned Simon Conway dead and himself, Karl Eisler, not at all regretful. Not pleased, but certainly not mourning the great man's passing.

Although the crash site was more than a quarter mile from the

tower, through binoculars Karl could clearly see the rescue team pulling a figure from the smashed cabin. A tarpaulin covered the figure's
face. Karl did not want to see them bring out the second man and
instead focused in on Morris Tannen shuffling about the wreckage,
his face contorted in grief. He held a small object in his hand, but
before Karl could identify it, Morris stepped behind the fuselage.
Karl put the glasses down and left the tower.

He climbed carefully down the rickety wood stairway and walked
to his car, a new Ford coupe whose V-8 engine he considered as
technologically advanced as the J-800, Charlie Jensen's superb new
engine developed specifically for the Conair 660. The 660 that had
killed Simon Conway.

Karl got into the car. Just as he turned the ignition key he realized
what Morris had held in his hand. Si's battered old gray fedora, his
lucky hat.

All the way to Brentwood, Karl rehearsed his speech of condolence to Meg and the boys. Si had died the way he would have chosen,
doing what he loved most. Karl wondered if there would be a funeral
service. Si, he knew, had not been inside a church in years, but Meg
was an Episcopalian. Karl hoped Episcopalians did not ask the de-
ceased's friends to speak. If they asked him to speak, what could
he say?

All right, if they ask me, I will say a few words for him, Karl
thought. It will make me feel like a hypocrite, but I will do it. I will
say, "Simon Conway died doing what he loved most. . . ."

A few days later, recalling that moment, Karl felt more hypo-
critical than ever. He stood in the doorway of a private room at
Hollywood Presbyterian Hospital gazing at a bandage-swathed figure
on the bed.

The figure laughed humorously. "Disappointed you again, didn't
I, you Kraut bastard?"

2.

Tom Blanchard was the unlucky one. His side of the airplane
had taken the full impact. Si was seriously injured. Internal bleeding,
facial lacerations, a concussion, broken collarbone, broken right arm
and compound fracture of the right leg, in addition to assorted
cracked ribs and other lesser complications. But the Conway luck held.

He recovered completely, and in a relatively short time. Seven
weeks in the hospital, another two months at home. The first days
were bad. The broken bones and bruised body would mend and be

forgotten, but not those final seconds in the airplane. He blamed himself for Tom Blanchard's death. His brain swam with ifs and buts and maybes, all punctuated with physical pain that only reinforced his guilt.

He had hoped that a thorough inspection of the 660's wreckage might vindicate him. He had ordered every possible piece of debris salvaged. It was like a jigsaw puzzle: put all the pieces together, you find the answer. Until that answer was found, the answer of why the controls had jammed, Si knew that the accident would be attributed to Pilot Error. The mark of Cain.

By the time of Karl's second visit, five days after the crash, the wreckage had been assembled in a hangar. Morris accompanied Karl on this second visit. They met Meg in the corridor outside Si's room. She looked pale, with great dark circles under her eyes.

Morris said, "When's the last time you had any sleep?"

"If I'm not here to quiet him down, the nurses threaten to quit," Meg said. "He's driving them crazy. He wants to see the newspapers. He wants to know what they're saying about the crash."

"He won't like what they're saying," Karl said. The *Los Angeles Times* reported a rumor of the two pilots engaging in a fist fight in the cockpit. The *Express* claimed an empty whiskey bottle was found on the cabin floor.

"Please, tell him there isn't too much press coverage on the accident," Meg said. "The doctor doesn't want him excited."

Si, his face taut with pain, lay in bed, right arm and leg suspended in traction, both limbs encased in heavy plaster-of-Paris casts. His first words to Karl and Morris were "Don't ask how I feel. I feel like shit."

"You look like it, too," Karl said.

"Thanks," Si said. "What've have you found out?"

"Nothing," said Karl. "Not a bloody thing."

Morris said, "We're going over the wreckage with a fine-tooth comb. We'll find out what happened."

Si said to Karl, "What do you think it was?"

"I haven't the slightest idea," Karl said. "I wasn't there."

"You think I fucked it up, don't you?"

"I don't think anything, Si."

"Cancel the 660 program," Si said, after a long moment. "Shut it down."

Morris said, "Si, do you know how much money we've poured into—"

"—I said shut it down!" The effort of talking formed beads of perspiration on Si's forehead and upper lip. He fell back against the pillow.

Alarmed, Morris moved toward the door. "I'll call the nurse . . ."

"Fuck the nurse!" Si said. "Just get the hell out of here and leave me alone." To Karl, he said, "Do what I told you. Cancel the program."

"Whatever you say," Karl said.

"When I'm back on my feet, and after we find out what happened the first time, I'll reactivate the 660," Si said. "When I can personally direct it."

Morris said, "Please, Si, listen to reason. Ross Leonard says the 660 is fundamentally sound. He wants us to go ahead on his order. Fifteen firm, with options on a dozen more. We counted on those sales, Si. We have to have them!"

"Sure, that son of a bitch Ross thinks the crash was my fault," Si said. He leaned up and pointed a finger at Morris. "No, Morris, the airplane is not 'fundamentally sound.' It will be, but until it is, it's not for sale!" He fell back against the pillow again, exhausted.

Morris glanced at Karl for help, but Karl only shrugged indifferently. Morris said quietly, "All right, Si, if that's how you want it."

But Si as usual had paid little attention to Conair's finances. To cover the 660's development costs, Si had blithely drained the company's cash. More than once, Philip Granger had been forced to obtain short-term bank loans to meet payrolls and subcontracting bills. Now, with the anticipated cash from 660 sales no longer a possibility, Conair was broke.

In April 1935, the third month of Si's convalescence, Morris Tannen and Philip Granger, independently, reached identical conclusions. Conair, to survive, must go public. Several eastern banks and underwriters were eager to assist. The first stock offering could bring at least $2 million.

Si would not hear of it.

"You've been preaching this 'we're broke' story ever since the days of the 110. Maybe we are, maybe we aren't. But one thing for sure, gents, I am not—repeat, not—selling stock in this company to outsiders."

The three men were in the library of Si's Pacific Palisades home. Si had listened impatiently, rising continually from his comfortable leather lounge chair to stomp around the parquet floor with a cane, testing the strength of his leg.

"That's your final word?" Morris asked. "You won't even talk to these underwriters?"

"Morris, Conair is my company, *I* am Conair. I'm not selling it to outsiders. Period, end. Okay?"

Granger took a deep breath. "Si, there's another piece of news you won't like—"

Just then Meg brought Janet in to kiss her father good night. The little girl, an eight-year-old diminutive replica of her mother, climbed up on Si's lap.

"Daddy, I love you!"

"I love you, too, honey," Si said. He kissed her and gently put her down. "Say good night to everybody."

Janet, giggling, said good night to Morris and Granger, and left with Meg. Morris said, "That young lady will be a killer when she grows up. How are the boys?"

"Frank keeps reminding me that I promised to take him up in one of the new trainers," Si said. "Don't tell Meg, but I rigged up a dummy cockpit in Janet's little playhouse out in the backyard. I've been giving the kid lessons." His pleased expression faded. "But Richard's a whole other story. I honest to God think he'd rather play with Janet's dolls."

"He'll come around," Morris said. "He's only eleven."

"Nearly twelve," Si said sourly. "And how does Paul like his car?"

"Paul doesn't 'like' it, Si, he's *married* to it!" Morris said. "We can't pry him loose from the seat. Thanks to you," he added good-naturedly. Paul Tannen's bar-mitzvah gift from Si and Meg was a working model of a Duesenberg coupe with a one-cylinder gasoline engine. The little car, built by a Conair mechanic who constructed such miniatures as a hobby, had originally been a tenth-birthday present for Frank Conway. Meg had refused to allow him to keep the car. It seemed that Frank enjoyed chasing his older brother, Richard, up and down the driveway with the car. Paul Tannen became the lucky recipient.

"Every time you two come here, it's with bad news," Si said. "The first week I was home it was the Marine Corps canceling an order for a dozen CT-5s. The next week it was a hundred people being laid off at the factory."

"Because you stopped the 660 program," Morris said.

"We'll build the 660, as soon as I'm ready to tackle it again," Si said. "Besides, if we're as broke as you say, we couldn't have afforded to keep going with it right now anyway."

"What we said, Si, was that we can get all the money we need," Granger said. "But we'll have to go public for it."

"The country's in the worst depression in history," Si said. "Five million unemployed. Bankers are selling apples on street corners. And you're telling me we can have all the money we want?"

"If we go public," Granger said.

"Forget it," Si said. "Next case."

"Hugo Black," Granger said.

"Him again!" Si said. "What now?"

"The Black-McKellar Act," Morris said. "Congress is determined to enforce it. O'Neil gave me the word this morning."

"He's some character, our friend Mr. Senator Black," Si said with a touch of resentful admiration. "He was hell-bent to get even with us for the airmail contracts, wasn't he?"

"And he has," Morris said. "Black-McKellar makes it a violation of antitrust laws for an airline to be owned or controlled by an aircraft manufacturer. Boeing, I know, is giving the whole Boeing Air Transport Service to their United Airlines division. We have to make the same choice, Si: the airline, or the factory."

"Can't O'Neil do anything?" Si asked, but he knew the answer. U.S. Senator Kenneth O'Neil, Conair's "friend in Washington," was of little help to them in a Democrat-controlled Senate. O'Neil himself admitted that he doubted he could fix a traffic ticket.

"How much can we get for the airline?" Si continued in the same breath.

"Not enough," Granger said. "Not the two million we need."

"But it'll give us enough to keep going a while, won't it?" Si asked. "Until we can rebuild the 660?"

"Probably," said Granger.

"Get rid of the airline," Si said.

It was not a difficult decision. Anybody could fly an airplane. The challenge and, ultimately, the money lay in building them. CNA was sold to Ross Leonard's Intercontinental Air for $1,350,000, one third in cash, the remainder in interest-bearing notes. Although Granger had already earmarked every dollar, Si immediately diverted $100,000 for another 660 prototype.

It would be a year before the second 660 rolled out. A momentous year for aviation, for the industry in general, and Conair in particular. In January of 1936, the same month Simon Conway's pilot's license was recertified—which was the same month Hermann Göring announced the existence of his Luftwaffe—two of Conair's most important executives resigned from the company. The first was Morris Tannen.

In neither case was the separation amicable. In Morris's case it was particularly bitter.

3.

Phil Granger said he had something important to discuss with Morris and suggested they do it over lunch. Since Morris would be in Hollywood that day they agreed to meet at Musso & Frank's Grill, one of Morris's favorite places. He was especially fond of the abalone steak, sautéed with lemon butter and capers. Musso's was out of abalone that day—none had been delivered all week because of the unseasonably stormy weather. Later, Morris said he should have known it was an omen.

He was a few minutes early, so he sat at the bar and ordered a plain tomato juice. Drinking during the day made him drowsy. He sipped the tomato juice and idly listened to the conversation of two men on his left. Writers, he guessed, from their talk and their clothes.

". . . so he says, 'I'm the producer, you work for me, and that means we do it my way,' " said one writer, a young man wearing a brass-buttoned blue blazer with a red polka-dotted ascot tucked into a white shirt.

"That's Marty, all right," said the other. "He wouldn't know a good story if it was tattooed on the end of his dick!"

A familiar voice behind Morris said, "How about buying me a drink?" It was Si.

"What the hell are you doing here?" Morris asked.

"Joining you for lunch."

"The last time you came into town for lunch must have been back before Prohibition," Morris said. "And why the long face?"

"Goddam leg aches." Si rapped a fist against his right leg. "Damp weather always does it." He ran his hands through his unruly brown hair. For the first time Morris noticed a few strands of gray.

"You're getting gray," Morris said.

"I'm getting old," Si said.

"Yeah, let's see, you must be all of what? Forty?"

"Forty-one. You're still five years my senior, old fella."

Just then Granger appeared and the three moved to a booth. Si ordered a martini, Granger a ginger ale. They joked about Si's resurgent health until the waiter served the drinks. As soon as the waiter left, both Si and Granger fell abruptly silent. Morris suddenly realized that Granger's "important discussion" was of a personal nature and concerned him, Morris.

Morris said to Granger, "The two of you look like you're going to a funeral. What's it all about?"

"I thought we should talk about this trip to Washington you're planning next week," Granger said.

Morris had made appointments with high War Department officials about an army contract for fifteen YC-6s, the military transport version of the rebuilt 660, an airplane yet to make its first flight.

"I thought we already did talk about it," Morris said. "And we agreed I'd guarantee delivery within fourteen months, no later than March of 1937. That's the date you gave me, isn't it, Si?"

"Give or take a few months," Si said, and in the same breath continued, "Listen, you're being promoted. From now on you're executive vice president. How's that sound?"

"It sounds great," Morris said. "What does it mean?"

"Phil can explain it better than me," Si said.

"It means Si thinks I should take over sales and marketing," Granger said.

Morris felt his heart beating rapidly. Just stay calm, he told himself. He said, " 'Si thinks.' " He faced Si. "Has anybody asked what I think?"

"You have a new job, executive VP," Si said. "You won't have time for sales and marketing."

The waiter returned to ask if they were ready to order. Morris said to him, "Come back in five minutes!" He said to Si, "Why won't I have time, Si?"

Si, uncomfortable, looked at Granger. Granger said, "Morris, we think the company's gotten so large and important, especially in the next two or three years with the 660 . . ."

Granger paused. Morris was studying him so intently he had momentarily lost his train of thought. Morris wanted to say that they didn't even know if the next goddam 660 would fly. It already had killed one good man, hadn't it? But he realized his silence was making Granger nervous, which pleased him.

Granger went on now, ". . . well, let's say we think Conair needs . . . well, it needs a more sophisticated sales approach."

" 'Sophisticated'?" Morris said. "What exactly does that mean? And you keep saying 'we' think. Who's 'we'?"

"Both of us," Granger said. "Si and me."

"Both of you," Morris repeated. "Both of you think I'm not . . . what was it? Oh, yeah, I'm not 'sophisticated' enough. You haven't told me what that means."

Si drained the remainder of his martini in a single swallow. He slammed the empty glass on the table. "I don't understand you, Morris. Why are you making this so hard on all of us?"

Morris forced himself to stay calm. "I'm making it hard on *you*? You just told me I'm being demoted, for Christ's sake!"

"Executive vice president is hardly a demotion," Granger said.

Morris said, "Yeah, well, I'm also an officer and general partner in this company, so I'm regretfully declining the 'promotion.' I appreciate it, understand, but I'm turning it down. So let's eat." He tried to attract the waiter's attention.

"It's for the good of the company," Granger said.

"What is, Phil?" Morris asked. "What is good for the company?"

Granger said, "A new look, Morris. That's what's good for the company."

"A new look," Morris repeated. "You as sales director instead of me? That's your new look?" He faced Si. "Why?"

"Goddammit, Morris, it *is* for the good of the company!" Si said.

"I asked you why," Morris said. But he knew why. He had known for years, at least as far as Phil Granger was concerned. Si, however, was another story. That Si shared Granger's feeling came as a total surprise. But then he should have realized Si was no different.

When the waiter returned for their orders, it was Si who waved him impatiently away, at the same time gesturing with his empty glass for a refill. He said to Morris, "This is how it has to be."

"When did you decide all this?"

"We've been talking about it awhile."

"Si, why don't you just tell me the truth and stop pussyfooting around?" Morris said. He had no intention of letting them off easy. "What's behind all this?"

Si drew in his breath, exasperated. He looked at Granger, then at Morris, then Granger again, his face mirroring relief as the waiter approached with the new drink. Si snatched it off the tray.

"Are you gentlemen ready to—" the waiter started to ask.

"Later!" Si said.

Granger said to Morris, "All right, I'll give it to you straight. The national marketing director represents the company. He's the company's symbol. We don't think it's good business anymore for a Jew to represent the company."

Morris, who was sitting opposite the two men, studied them a moment. Both resembled doctors who had just informed the patient he was terminal. What horse's asses! Morris thought.

He said to Si, " 'We' don't think it's good business for a Jew to represent the company? 'We'? That means you, too, Si?" Before Si could reply, Morris turned to Granger. "Or should it be *'Et tu, Brute'*?"

"Morris, why can't you be reasonable?" Si said.

"Fifteen years ago, Si, you didn't mind a Jew representing the company!" Morris said. "Fifteen years ago, you needed a Jew." He jabbed a finger toward himself. "You wouldn't have a company without a Jew. You'd still be flying that Jenny around, scrounging for five-dollar rides!" He jabbed the same finger toward Granger. "Him, I always knew he was a Jew-hater. But you, Si, you're the last one I'd have suspected. Honest to God. I never would have figured you for one."

Si seemed astonished. "Me? You think I'm a Jew-hater?"

Morris almost laughed. It reminded him of the army, when the good old country boys who had never seen a live Jew expressed genuine surprise that you couldn't hardly tell Morris apart from any other real American.

"... all I give a damn about is this company!" Si was saying, pounding the table with each word. "It's a plain and simple matter of image. Image! Phil Granger will present a better image. It's as simple as that."

Morris almost felt sorry for Si. He was certain that the last thing Si ever considered himself to be was a Jew-hater.

"... but okay, you want to get right down to it," Si was saying, "Granger is right. Those idiots in the War Department might not be too happy about handing out contracts to a Jew. You know how goddam prejudiced some of those bastards are."

"That's right, Si," Morris said. "Everybody knows how prejudiced they are."

Si caught the sarcasm but apparently chose to ignore it. "All that matters, Morris, is the company. Conair. Someday you'll be able to put out an ad that says, 'The Sun Never Sets on a Conway Airplane!' That's what we said we wanted, isn't it? All right, so that's what we'll damn well have. And believe me, nothing, nobody, is going to stop us."

Morris nodded absentmindedly. The flashily dressed writers were still at the bar. He thought he might go over and talk to them. They looked Jewish.

4.

Si recognized the driver of the green Ford V-8 phaeton convertible that pulled up outside the house, a kid named Finberg or Finkelstein, Morris Tannen's personal attorney. Finberg/Finkelstein wore an open-collared polo shirt, white flannel trousers, and white buck shoes. No jacket or sweater. It was a sweltering day, eighty-five degrees at ten in the morning, thanks to the Santa Ana winds. The radio predicted a scorcher that might break all January records.

Si was sitting with Frank in the driveway, in Meg's La Salle coupe. Frank was at the wheel, propped up by two pillows borrowed from the maid's room. Of course the kid was only eleven, but he had a flair for machinery that Si, at the same age, certainly never had. As Si told Meg, he wanted to nurture such a talent, not discourage it.

Meg had replied, "Yes, and the next thing I know you'll be teaching him to fly."

"Oh, no, Meg," Si had said with a straight face. "Not until he's sixteen, not a day before."

The young lawyer strolled up the driveway and spoke to Si through the La Salle's window. "Mr. Conway, forgive my disturbing you on Sunday—"

"—which Mr. Conway are you talking to?" Si asked. He pretended not to know the lawyer. He ruffled Frank's hair. "This is Mr. Conway, too."

The lawyer smiled solemnly and extended his hand to Frank. "How do you do, sir?" He shook Frank's hand and said to Si, "I'm Mel Forbstein, Morris Tannen's attorney. We've met before."

Si snapped his fingers in recognition. "Oh, sure," he said. "What's up?"

"Can we talk? It's important," he added, as Si frowned. "It won't take more than ten minutes of your time."

It took less than seven minutes. Six and one-half minutes after Melvin Forbstein arrived, Si angrily asked him to leave. But then, in truth, Si realized that any anger toward Melvin Forbstein was misdirected. Melvin Forbstein had merely delivered a message. The villain in the piece was Morris Tannen. Morris Tannen, in Si's mind now a traitor of world-class proportions.

Morris had decided to sell his Conair stock.

In accordance with company bylaws, the stock first had to be offered to the corporation. The purchase price of Morris's 120,000 shares was $11.60 per share—$1,392,000.

The price had been verified by a bona fide tender offer from a consortium of New York underwriters, led by the prestigious firm of Lehman Brothers. Conair had fifteen business days in which to exercise its first-refusal option.

They were fifteen of the most hectic days in Simon Conway's memory. To begin with, as Morris Tannen well knew, the company's available cash did not total one tenth of the amount required. Therefore, as Morris Tannen also well knew, the company would be forced to borrow the necessary funds, pledging as collateral all its assets. With the nation's economy in so precarious a state, any business setback, even the most temporary, could result in Simon Conway losing control of his own company.

Si had no intention of allowing the stock to fall into the hands of outsiders. His only recourse, as both Meg and Philip Granger pointed out, was to personally appeal to Morris and ask him to accept company notes in lieu of cash.

Si flatly rejected the suggestion. He would never lower himself. Besides, Si was certain this was exactly what Morris wanted of him: to beg.

Never.

But Si had an idea that might achieve the same result.

For lunch, Si occasionally enjoyed bringing a sandwich and coffee to a promontory overlooking the airport. He had been coming here since the field was little more than a grassy area in need of constant mowing, and had watched it grow into today's three asphalt runways, one of them nearly six thousand feet long.

It was not so long ago that the ramp was lined with TAT's Ford and Stinson trimotors, American Airways' big twin-engined Curtiss Condor biplanes, and, of course, the Conair 330s, 440s and 550s. Now, although a few of those old airplanes still operated, the airport was crowded with Boeing 247s, Lockheed Electras, and Douglas's DC-2s and the new eighteen-passenger DC-3s.

And, soon, Conair's 660. No amount of treachery by the likes of Morris Tannen could prevent it. It was to discuss Morris Tannen that Si had asked Karl Eisler to join him for lunch on the promontory.

The day, which started out bright and sunny, had turned gray and chilly, the fringe of a storm front from the north. Showers and low visibility were forecast by nightfall. In the meantime the airplanes continued landing and taking off, one every ten or fifteen minutes. Taking off, they rolled down the runway, silvery noses pointed straight ahead until all at once they were in the air, metallic monsters whose very existence defied the law of gravity.

Landing, they came in from the east, wheels extended like the incongruously slender legs of some giant winged creature, settling down onto the pavement with a crunch of rubber and puff of smoke, speeding along the runway another few moments and then, as though reluctant to have come down to earth, rolling more and more slowly, turning onto the access strip, taxiing to the terminal and, abruptly, stopping.

"Not much like France, is it?" Si said. He and Karl were sitting on the running board of Si's Lincoln Zephyr sedan. Karl's Ford was parked nearby.

"Nothing is much like France," Karl said. "Thank God."

The mention of France had reminded Si of Andrée. She was a big international star now. Only a few days ago her picture had been in *Look* magazine. He wondered if she ever thought of him. He doubted it.

"All right, so what do you say?" he asked.

"About going to Morris as your emissary and asking him to take company notes instead of cash for his stock?"

"That's the idea," Si said.

When Karl had arrived a few minutes before, Si greeted him with that request: go to Morris on Si's behalf. Karl and Morris were very friendly. Their wives were close, too. Ruth treated Erika like a daughter. If Karl spoke to Morris, Morris might listen. Moreover, Karl had as much to lose in this as anyone else.

"No," Karl said. "The answer is no. Do your own dirty work, Si."

"It's him who did the dirty work."

"Ask him yourself."

"I told you, Karl, I won't play his game."

"Then don't ask me to do it for you."

Si laughed harshly. He remembered a remark of Morris's. He repeated it now to Karl. *"Et tu, Brute?"*

Karl shook his head sadly. "There's only one way for you, Si. If we're not for you, we're automatically against you."

"That's right. And speaking of being against me, what's this I hear about you going back to Germany?"

"I thought we were talking about Morris."

"I know all about your little jaunt to San Francisco last week to see the German military attaché," Si said. "A personal message from Göring. He wants you back."

"Your spies have been busy, I see."

A speck in the distant eastern sky quickly became an approaching airplane, a DC-3. Karl watched it a moment, then said, "I'm thinking about it, yes."

"Well, stop thinking about it," said Si.

"Is that an order?"

"Before the 660 goes into production I want her to have every test in the book, a dozen times over. And we're supposed to get started on the Hunter, aren't we? You're needed here."

"They need me there, too," Karl said. He spoke quietly, almost to himself, listening to the DC-3's engines, the solid steady hum of the P&W Twin Wasps.

Later, whenever Si thought about that moment, he remembered how the word "treachery" had seemed so appropriate. If Morris was a traitor, then Karl was doubly so.

Si said, "In that case, Karl, why don't you put your stock up for sale, too? You can clean up just like Morris."

Karl's whole face tightened. "You treated Morris very badly. Stupidly, I mean. You treated him stupidly."

"Maybe so, but you know damn well that what he's doing is wrong."

"You left him no choice."

"He stabs us in the back, and you say it's 'right.' "

"Were you right in doing that to him because he's a Jew?"

"Now I've heard everything. Those Nazis of yours are beating the shit out of every Jew they can find!"

The DC-3 was just touching down. It was a TWA airplane, *The Lindbergh Line* inscribed across the top of the fuselage. It wheeled onto the access strip and taxied toward the terminal. Karl faced Si again.

"First of all, Si, they are not 'my' Nazis. Secondly, those stories are exaggerated. German Jews are not being persecuted. A few thugs went crazy one night and beat up some Jews. The government put an immediate stop to it."

"You haven't answered my question. Why don't you sell your stock, too?"

At the airport, a portable stairway ramp was being pushed up to the DC-3's door. A crowd of reporters waited behind the Cyclone fence separating the ramp and the canopied passenger terminal entrance. Some celebrity was arriving. A movie star.

". . . you want eleven bucks a share, too?" Si was asking. "I'll give you twenty. How's that?"

"I don't want your money, Si," Karl said, still watching the DC-3. The newsmen were rushing toward the airplane. A woman nestling a bouquet of flowers stood posing in the cabin doorway. Karl did not recognize her. "I only want you to wake up and see what's happening to you."

"I am awake," Si said. "That's why I want to buy you out. How much?"

Karl reached up behind him. He grasped the Lincoln's door handle and pulled himself to his feet. He looked down at Si. "One dollar," he said. "One dollar per share, Si."

"I'm serious."

"I, too," said Karl. "I have thirty thousand shares. Thirty thousand dollars. That's a fair price, isn't it?"

"Why the bargain?"

"Do you accept the offer?"

"You bet I do. Now what's the catch?"

"No catch," said Karl. "Just have the money ready by five o'clock." He started toward his car. He stopped suddenly and wrestled with his key ring. Finally, removing two keys, he tossed them to the grass at Si's feet. "Keys to my office and file cabinet, Si. Go through it all carefully to make sure I don't run off with anything that belongs to you."

Karl got into his car and drove away. Si did not move; he sat on the running board, staring at the keys. He felt no anger, which surprised him, only a vague sadness and a strange sense of relief that something he knew was inevitable had finally happened.

When Si returned to the factory, his first act was to order Karl's office sealed. As he explained to Granger, "I don't want him taking anything out of there."

"What could he take out?" Granger asked.

"Blueprints, sketches, whatever. Plans for the Hunter, for all I know! You want him bringing those back to the Krauts?"

"Si, any plans for the Hunter are locked up in Karl's head."

"Yeah, I suppose," Si admitted grudgingly. "But at least it makes the point."

"What point?" Granger asked.

Hours later that same day Si asked himself the same question. He was sitting alone at the bar of the Miramar Hotel in Santa Monica, getting drunk. He had come there directly from the factory after signing the $30,000 check for Karl's stock.

"I think I know the point," he said to Chuck, the Miramar's bartender. Chuck, who had spent three seasons with the Hollywood Stars as a utility infielder, looked more like a professional wrestler than a professional ballplayer. Si enjoyed talking baseball with him.

"What point is that, Mr. C?" Chuck asked.

"Never mind," said Si, and drank down his scotch. He tapped the empty glass for a refill. The point, he thought, is that in less than one week I have parted company with two of my closest friends and business associates. And, in the process, painted myself into a $1,392,000 corner, the price of Morris Tannen's stock.

Si's wristwatch read 7:35, which he knew was impossible. He had arrived here shortly before 7:00, hours ago. He placed the watch to his ear. He had forgotten to wind it. When Chuck served the new drink, Si asked him the time.

"Ten past ten, Mr. C."

Si wound the watch, then set the hands. It was his favorite watch, a gold Gruen Curvex, a Christmas gift from Meg and the children. Meg, he thought. He wondered what she would say when she heard about Karl.

She had had plenty to say regarding Morris, mainly that Si was intractable and ungrateful. Si chose not to debate the issue, let her believe what she pleased. He knew she would feel the same in Karl's case: Si was intractable and ungrateful.

Now, at 10:11 P.M., on Thursday, the 30th of January, 1936, Simon Conway realized that the only way to avoid mortgaging Conair to the banks for Morris's stock was to personally ask Morris to accept company notes in lieu of cash. Ask, meaning plead. Talk about Jews and their pound of flesh.

The insight immediately sobered him. He paid his bill, left a $2 tip, and hurried outside to his car. He drove south along Ocean Avenue. Only when he passed the Santa Monica Bay Club's handsome new three-story brick building did he realize he was headed the wrong way. Morris's house was in the opposite direction.

He remembered Meg's saying that when you really did not want to do something, your subconscious mind tried to help you avoid it. Either that, he told himself, or I am still drunk. Or both.

By the time he had doubled back through downtown Santa Monica, turned into Lincoln Boulevard, and pulled up outside Morris's darkened house, he needed a drink. Yes, the first thing he would do was ask Morris for a drink. It would relax them both.

No lights were on downstairs, only the front porch lamp, but a light shone through the drapes of the room directly above the porch, which he knew was Morris and Ruth's bedroom.

All right, so he'd get Morris out of bed. He strolled to the front porch and rang the bell. He waited, then rang it again. A shaft of light suddenly illuminated the lawn on both sides of the brick-inlaid walk. The heavy oak front door squeaked open.

"Yes . . . ?"

Ruth stood in the doorway. She wore a flannel bathrobe and flat-soled leather slippers. Her hair, taken down, hung in pigtails over her shoulders.

"Oh, Ruth," Si said lamely.

"Si?"

"I wanted to see Morris."

"Oh, my God, Si, look at me!" Ruth touched her face in dismay. "Morris isn't here. He went to San Diego to meet with Ross Leonard."

Ross had moved Intercontinental Air's headquarters from San Francisco to San Diego several years before. Si almost asked why in hell Morris was meeting Ross but then realized it no longer was any of his business.

"He'll be back tomorrow afternoon," Ruth continued.

"Ruth, do you have a drink in there?"

"Drink? Liquor, you mean?"

"Yeah, liquor."

"Si, the way I look—"

"—you look fine," he said, and brushed past her into the house.

Ten minutes later Si sat comfortably on the floral-patterned glazed-chintz divan in the living room, smoking a cigarette, drinking scotch over ice in a heavy, squat old-fashioned glass, waiting for Ruth to finish "putting on some lipstick."

Upstairs, seated at her dresser mirror, Ruth's hands trembled. What is wrong with you? she asked herself. You are acting like a schoolgirl primping for her first date. But Ruth knew what was wrong. It was as though some wicked, long-secret fantasy had at last come true. Her husband away on business, her son away at boarding school, and Simon Conway sat in her living room. He was alone, she was alone.

Simon Conway, a man whom not one week ago she cursed. A man who had tried to destroy her husband. A man who for years had been the center of her erotic dreams and masturbatory reveries. A man whose wife had once been her dearest friend and confidante, and whom she still considered close.

Simon Conway, anti-Semite.

It was a compulsion, she told herself. A sickness. Which did not mean she should hurl herself at his feet and beg him to undress her. She was a mature, intelligent woman—"mature," she thought dryly, at thirty-seven one is certainly mature—who could most definitely control herself.

When she finally came downstairs, hair combed and falling over her back and shoulders, face freshly powdered and rouged, wearing a black silk negligee with high-heeled white silk mules, Si had helped himself to a second drink.

"You look beautiful," he said.

"No, it's just that I look better than I did a few minutes ago, but thank you, anyway." She fixed herself a small brandy and sat opposite him.

"And that perfume," he said, crinkling his nose pleasurably. "What is it?"

"It's cologne, Si," she said. "Good old-fashioned drugstore cologne."

"It smells better than the stuff Meg uses. Twelve bucks an ounce!"

"How is Meg?" Ruth asked. "I haven't seen her in weeks. And the children?"

He said Meg and the children were fine. She said Paul was doing well at Carlsbad, a military academy near San Diego where many motion-picture moguls sent their sons. You can imagine how spoiled rotten those boys were. But then Paul was no slouch in that department, either.

"They'll make him shape up, believe me," Si said. "Listen, I'm sorry for barging in like this."

"Don't be silly. You're always welcome here, you know that."

"Don't tell Morris you said that."

"Frankly, I think you're both acting like children."

"Yeah," Si said slowly. "Well, that's what I wanted to see him about."

Ruth shook her head. "Si, Morris won't change his mind. He really wants out. He doesn't want anything to do with Phil Granger."

"Or with me," said Si. "I don't blame him." He leaned forward and rested his hand lightly on her knee. "But, Ruth, two wrongs don't make a right. He's forcing me to hock up the company to pay him. I don't have to tell you that that's the one thing we promised ourselves never to do again. Not since the time we got rid of Ross Leonard. You remember how that almost wiped us out?"

"Then what is it you want Morris to do?"

"Instead of cash, I want him to take company notes, IOUs. With interest," Si added. "Four percent. It'll keep us in business, and make him rich."

The pressure of his hand on her knee seemed heavier, warmer. She felt her heart beating rapidly. "Here, let me freshen that for you," she said. She got up and poured him another and added a small amount of brandy to her own glass. She started to sit down beside him but changed her mind and sat opposite him again.

He raised his glass in a toast, then drank. "Well, that's my sad story," he said. "And you know how much chance I have of your husband doing it? Tell me about ice cubes in hell."

"Would you like me to talk to him for you?"

Si said nothing a moment, then suddenly laughed, a quiet, nostalgic little laugh. "I just remembered the time we stole those tires from old Fred Thompson. When you 'fainted' in the night watchman's office. Remember?"

"How could I ever forget?"

"Those were good days. We had fun."

"We were young, Si. Things were much simpler."

"I'll say," he said. "Ruth, do you think it would do any good if you did talk to Morris?"

"It might."

Si drank the rest of his drink. He placed the empty glass carefully down on the marble-topped coffee table. "If you did that for me I'd be forever grateful," he said.

"Then I'll do it," she said. She knew she could get Morris to agree. She would even tell him how Si came to the house and virtually pleaded. Morris would enjoy that. And Si was right: the company was solid. The notes were good as gold. Better than gold, with what Roosevelt was doing to the economy.

She looked up to see him standing over her, his face close to hers. Then she felt his lips on hers, tentatively at first and then more confidently. Somehow she was on the divan, in his arms, his body pushing gently down upon hers, the pressure forcing her legs apart. She could feel his hardness against her groin and one hand cupping her breast, his fingers kneading the nipple, which was stiff and swollen and throbbing. She closed her eyes and let her head fall back against the divan cushion.

". . . this is wrong, Si," she heard herself whispering.

"It sure is," he said. "But who gives a damn?" His mouth was nuzzling her chin, her throat. He had spread open her negligee and his tongue was caressing first the nipple of one breast, and then the other.

In her mind she reached out and touched him, that hardness she could feel pulsing through the fabric of his trousers. In her mind she was unbuttoning his fly and drawing it out, cupping it in her hand, fondling it, guiding it inside her. She wondered idly how big he was and thought it did not matter because she was so wet it would slide in like a pencil.

His hand crept in under her belly to unbuckle his belt and unbutton his top trouser button, then his fly. She held her breath and waited. In an instant she knew she would feel him smoothly inside her, the feeling she had wanted since the first moment she had seen him so many years ago. When they were young, and poor, and Morris had a dream.

A dream, she thought, and cried, "No, Si! No!" She pushed him roughly away. He looked at her, bewildered.

"What's wrong?" he asked.

She sat up and caught her breath. She clutched the edges of her negligee with one hand, and with the other hand arranged her hair. She strained to keep her voice steady.

"Do me a favor, Si. Get out of here. Just get out."

He said nothing. He seemed confused and looked almost comical, seated awkwardly on the edge of the divan, his hand placed palm down on the carpet to prevent himself from falling, his fly bulging.

"Please, Si," she said.

He slumped back against the divan cushions. "Why did you let me go this far?"

It occurred to her that she should be frightened. That notorious Simon Conway temper. But not only did she feel no fear, she felt an unfamiliar sense of power. She had simultaneously overcome her own desire—no, not desire, something far more difficult to control, lust —and defeated him, the Jew-hater. And now she knew she would never have allowed him to make love to her, not if he were the last man on earth.

"Go home, Si," she said. "Go home."

"You enjoyed teasing me, didn't you?"

"No," she said. "I apologize for that."

"You're not sorry one bit, and we both know it. You did it deliberately. It's your way of getting back at me for Morris." He got to his feet and tucked in his shirt, buttoned his fly, buckled his belt, and smoothed his suitcoat. "Thanks for the drink," he said, and walked to the door.

He had opened the door when she called after him, "I'll talk to Morris about the notes. I'll see what I can do."

Si stopped, frozen. He stood with his back to her and then, slowly, turned. His face was taut with anger and humiliation. The veins in his throat stood out like steel cords.

"Don't do me any favors, Ruth."

"Don't be so proud, Si."

"Pride is a word I doubt you know the meaning of, Ruth."

"Pride, Si, is why you're on your way home now and not in my bed," she said. "It wasn't necessary for you to try to make love to me. I'd have talked to Morris anyway."

"That's not why I did it."

She knew he spoke the truth, which both flattered her and made her victory all the more gratifying. Hers and Morris's. "Si, I will speak to Morris," she said. "I can't promise results, but I'll try."

They both knew this meant it was done. She could handle Morris. Si shook his head. "You're a strange woman, Ruth."

"I know. Good night, Si."

She stood in the living room, gazing at the door long after it had closed behind him and she had heard his car drive off. Finally she stepped back to the cellarette and poured herself a stiff drink.

"Congratulations, Ruth," she toasted herself. "You put a rotten, Jew-hating son of a bitch in his place, and it feels good." The brandy warmed her whole body. It felt marvelous. She felt marvelous.

14

Si could not help comparing it to a Hollywood movie premiere. *". . . from the people who in 1927 gave you the unforgettable 440, and in 1933 the incomparable 550, now in 1936 comes an even greater airplane . . . the airplane the whole world has awaited . . . the Conair 660!"*

Never mind the whole world, he thought, no one had waited more impatiently for the 660 or worked harder for it than he, Simon Conway. As though a reminder of that anxious year—and of the crash of the first 660 prototype—he felt his right leg suddenly cramp. It would rain soon. It always did when the leg ached. If the 660 failed he could always get a job with the weather bureau.

From the Conair control tower, Si watched the big airplane turn base leg and start its final approach into Los Angeles Municipal. He thought he saw a small white cloud momentarily envelop the 660. The cloud vanished almost as soon as it appeared. Si knew it was his own imagination, the terrible memory of that last flight. To this day the cause of the accident had never been determined.

". . . ah, Conair Tower, six-six-zero on final." Mike Doyle's deep voice boomed over the tower loudspeaker. Mike, twenty-seven years old, was Conair's new chief test pilot. "Si, she's a marvel. She gets better every time I fly her!"

"Tell him thanks," Si said to the radio operator.

The radio operator said into his microphone, "Roger, six-six-zero. Mike, Mr. Conway says 'Thanks.' Six-six-zero, you are clear to land."

"Congratulations, Si!" Phil Granger said. "In two years I guarantee you it'll really be 'The sun never sets on a Conair airplane.' Every airline in the world will be flying the 660!"

The reconstructed 660, although identical in design and appearance to the original, was an entirely new airplane. She had been built with new, lighter and stronger metal alloys, and equipped with new instrumentation and a new and truly efficient radio system. The 660's twin J-850s, improved Jensen engines, gave her a cruising speed of 185 mph, with a 1,600-mile range.

She would carry twenty-one passengers in parlor-car comfort, which included a small electric oven to heat already prepared full-course meals, a far cry from the box lunches of the late twenties and early thirties, and the "hot" meals served from giant thermos jugs on the Conair 550s.

The 660's successful completion of months of test flying had all but erased the stigma of its predecessor's crash. Today's performance was the new airplane's first official public appearance, primarily for Ross Leonard's benefit. Ross had agreed to purchase twenty-five 660s. Si had to laugh whenever he thought of Morris Tannen signing the purchase order on behalf of Intercontinental Air. The chagrin Morris must have felt: Morris had gone to work for Ross Leonard.

Ironically, it had been for that very purpose—a job with Intercontinental Air—that Morris was out of town the night of Si's memorable visit to Ruth Tannen. Si had not seen her since. The Tannens had moved to San Diego. Good riddance. All Si wanted to do now was pay off the outstanding Conair notes held by Morris. The success of the 660 would certainly help achieve that.

". . . tower, six-six-zero," came Mike Doyle's voice. "How do we look, fellas?"

Pete Dagget snatched the microphone from the radio operator's hand and shouted into it, "You look great!"

Si wished again that he sat in that left seat. But Phil Granger had put the kibosh to that by threatening to resign if Si flew the 660. Granger said Si's place was in the "executive suite," not the cockpit of an untried airplane. No one was more surprised than Granger himself when Si, almost meekly, gave in.

Granger did not know that Si had long ago realized that the company was now too big and complicated for him to run alone. After losing Morris and Karl, Si could not afford to lose anyone else, especially Phil Granger. It was called, Si told himself at the time, getting smart. Now he regretted it. Test-flying the 660 was his job, his obligation.

". . . for the audience's delight, shall we execute another single-engine climb-out?" Mike Doyle asked over the loudspeakers. On a previous touch-and-go landing, he had shut down an engine and feathered the propeller. The airplane climbed, as Mike announced, "like a blankety-blank fighter!"

The radio operator looked to Si for a reply to Mike's question. Si said, "No, tell him to come on in. He's shown the audience enough for one day."

The "audience," which was gathered at the ramp in front of the control tower, consisted of newsmen and newsreel photographers, observers from the U.S. Army Air Corps and U.S. Naval Air Service, and a number of airline executives, including Eddie Rickenbacker. Rick had promised Si that if he liked the 660 he would order ten for Eastern Airlines with an option for ten more, at $72,000 per unit, which added up to $1,440,000. It was like finding gold in the streets.

". . . what do you think they're talking about?" Phil Granger asked in Si's ear, nodding down at the ramp where Rickenbacker was engaged in a deep conversation with Morris Tannen and Ross Leonard.

"Five gets you twenty Rick's trying to muscle in on Intercontinental's order," Si said. "I told Rick we were so backlogged we couldn't promise him delivery until summer of '37 at the earliest."

Granger said, "Sure, and at the same time he's talking to us about building Eastern a 660 with four engines, a plane half again as big as this one."

"Why not?" Si grinned. "Call it the six-six-*four*!"

Granger returned the grin. "No, we'll call it the Skybus," he said. "Make Pete happy."

"Skybus it is," said Si, who at the moment would have done anything in the world to please Pete Dagget. Si had vetoed the use of Pete's term "Skybus" for the 660. Too tempting for some wiseass to call it Sky*bust*. Now, though, Si felt so good about the 660, for all he cared Pete could name the next one after his mother.

Mike Doyle's voice floated ebulliently over the loudspeakers. ". . . turning final, gents!"

"Come on in, six-six-zero," said the Conair radio operator. "Champagne's waiting!"

"Shit!" It was Mike Doyle's voice over the loudspeakers again, this time tense, almost frightened.

"Six-six-zero, Mike, what's wrong?" the operator shouted into the microphone.

". . . control column is frozen!" a voice cried over the loudspeakers. It was the copilot, Dusty Evans, a veteran Conair test pilot.

Si turned to the window again. The 660, a quarter mile from the end of the runway, was plunging downward.

". . . can't raise the nose!" Dusty Evans's anxious voice continued.

The nightmare was being repeated. The white cloud again enshrouded the airplane. Si knew he was imagining it, and himself in the cockpit, pulling back on a yoke that would not budge, watching the glittering black asphalt rush up at him, awaiting the metallic grinding sound of the airplane smashing into the runway, and not even feeling the slightest pain, although he knew his bones were being crushed.

He remembered it all, so vividly that he even saw the black cloth insulating cord of the earphones that had fallen to the cockpit floor, and his shoes kicking them out of the way. The earphones on the floor. *The earphones on the floor!*

Si dashed across the control tower to the radio and tore the microphone from the operator's hand. He shouted into it, "Evans, did Mike take off his earphones?"

"Affirmative!" Dusty Evans answered over the loudspeakers.

"Are they on the floor?"

"Yes!" the copilot replied after a moment. "They slipped down under the floorboards"

"Pick them up!" Si shouted. "Yank them out of there!"

For another instant the 660 hurtled toward the runway. And then, as though lifted by unseen hands, the nose abruptly rose. The airplane flared out. Her wheels skimmed the runway, touched down. She bounced once, then again, and then settled smoothly onto the surface.

Si did not hear the cheers of the men around him or feel the hands clapping his back; he saw only those earphones on the cockpit floor. They had slid neatly into the aperture between the floor and the control column and, wedged against the column, completely jammed it. The impact of the crash had shaken the earphones loose and thrown them back onto the floor, erasing the evidence.

"Si, you saved them . . ." It was Pete Dagget. The young man's face was streaked with tears.

"First thing you do," Si said slowly, enunciating each word, "you block up that hole in the floor. You understand, son? Close up the fucking thing!"

"Yes sir," Pete said. "I will close up the fucking thing. First thing."

Within eighteen months, by the spring of 1937, the fortieth Conair 660 had been delivered—to the Dutch airline, KLM—and by then the sun truly never did set on a Conair airplane. The familiar American eagle clutching in its talons the letter C was emblazoned on the rudders of aircraft on every continent on the globe, from the blue-and-silver 660s of Intercontinental Air in the United States to a dozen small stubby fighter planes parked in sandbagged revetments on a field outside the city of Hankow, China.

Even Karl Eisler had to admit the truth of the sun never setting on a Conair aircraft. He happened to see that fortieth 660 at the KLM gate at Tempelhof Airdrome on the morning of April 23, 1937.

2.

The sleek little all-black fighter with the white engine cowling and silver propeller spinner taxied past the giant 660 parked at the canopied passenger gate. The fighter, the KE-1, bore Luftwaffe markings but no other identification. It was the prototype model, which Karl had flown into Berlin from the factory at Stuttgart for publicity photos—propaganda photos, more accurately. Propaganda to bluff the Allies into believing the Luftwaffe was invincible.

But, in truth, in two years the Luftwaffe would be more than invincible. The factories were working three full shifts producing airplanes of all types—bombers, transports, fighters. Already the frighteningly effective Junkers dive-bomber, the J-87 *Sturzkampfflugzeug*, the Stuka, was in service in Spain, along with Wili Messerschmitt's fine new fighter, the Bf109. And Focke-Wulf's FW-190, still on the drawing board, would soon outclass anything in the air, except Karl's KE-1.

The KE-1 was a low-winged, all-metal stressed-skin monoplane with two wing-mounted 7.92mm machine guns and a 20mm nose-firing cannon. Her liquid-cooled twelve-cylinder Daimler-Benz engine pulled 1,050 horsepower. In its first speed trial Karl had flown the KE-1 at 350 mph in level flight. The only word he could find for this airplane was awesome.

"Awesome," he hoped, was the same word his eminence Feldmarschall Hermann Göring would use to describe the KE-1 later today when he inspected it at Carinhall, his hunting lodge fifty miles east of Berlin, where Karl was expected for lunch.

He wheeled into takeoff position and held at the top of the runway while an Air France Potez 62 lumbered in for a landing. The Potez 62, a fourteen-passenger high-winged monoplane with a nicely designed monocoque fuselage, was an interesting airplane but no match for Simon Conway's 660.

Simon Conway's 660? Karl thought as the control tower fired a green flare: no radio equipment was yet installed in the KE-1. Karl locked the Plexiglas canopy and eased the throttle steadily forward. The little airplane accelerated down the runway and flew into the air. Karl cranked the undercarriage control lever into the *auf* position and thought again, *Simon Conway's 660?* The 660 was as much Karl's creation as Si's, and more Pete Dagget's than anyone else's. Simon Conway's 660. Old habits were hard to break.

He leveled out at eight thousand feet, reduced power, brought the needle-sharp nose around to 082 degrees, and settled back to enjoy the brief flight. Göring expected him to remain overnight, but Karl had already decided to return to Stuttgart before dusk. He had promised Erika dinner in the elegant dinning room of the Hotel Schondorf, whose fifth-generation Jewish owners were rumored to have signed away half their interest in the hotel for the privilege of remaining in business.

It reminded him of his last conversation with Morris Tannen, the day Karl and Erika sailed from New York aboard the *Bremen*. Morris and Ruth, in the city for a week's holiday, had come to see them off, and Morris had expressed his concern at the reports of Nazi persecution of German Jews.

Karl had assured Morris that the stories were unfounded, a frustrated response to German rearmament. Even being here and seeing it with his own eyes, Karl was still convinced that only a handful of street thugs were responsible for the worst atrocities. The government for its own good reasons looked the other way. These Nazis might at times behave crazily, but they had resurrected a defeated nation and restored its self-respect.

The KE-1's airspeed indicator read 275, and she was not even breathing hard. He loved the feel of this airplane, its power, its grace, its very smell. Of course it was his, his own creation, the first Eisler Allgemeinmaschinenwerke product, the first of a long, illustrious line. Yes, say what you will about the Nazis, they had treated him well, giving him his own factory, unlimited resources, and a free hand. They needed him as much as he needed them, a satisfactory quid pro quo. He had never been happier or more content.

Seventeen minutes later, flying over Carinhall, Karl thought that Hermann Göring also had everything a man could want. From the air the "hunting lodge" looked more like a small duchy, with vast open fields and thick wooded forests, several sizable ponds and streams. In the center was the main house, a rambling, two-story stucco-and-wood structure resembling an English country manor.

Carinhall, named after Göring's first wife, also resembled a fortress. At least two armored cars and two motorcycles were patrolling the immediate area, and helmeted soldiers manned a guard post at the only road leading in from the highway.

As instructed, Karl landed in a flat grassy field behind the house, not far from a swimming pool larger than any he had ever seen in

California. Göring, wearing *Lederhosen* and a rakish felt hunting cap, was at the field to meet him. Two other men, also in civilian clothes, accompanied Göring. One, a slight, balding man of middle years, was Erhard Milch, a Luftwaffe general. The other was Anton Moerzer, the scarred, splotched side of his face turned toward Karl like a badge of honor.

Moerzer was now Göring's "special assistant," which meant he performed whatever distasteful tasks the *Feldmarschall* preferred not to be involved in. The young man was kept quite busy.

"A gorgeous landing, Karl," Göring said, pumping Karl's hand. "Believe me, if I could wire my jaws shut for just one month and lose this pot"—he patted his stomach—"I'd like nothing better than to fly this beauty." He blew a kiss toward the KE-1.

Karl opened his leather jacket and unbuttoned his shirt-collar button. A half hour of the sun beating down on him through the cramped cockpit's glassed canopy had drenched him with sweat.

"You're looking well," he said to Milch. He almost greeted Moerzer with the same words but caught himself in time and only nodded politely.

Moerzer returned the nod in cold silence, which Göring noted with disapproval. "I'm determined," he said, "that one of these days you two will be friends, even if I have to make it a direct order!" He draped an arm over Karl's shoulder. "You'll stay with us until morning, of course?"

"I'd rather not, if you don't mind, *Feldmarschall*," Karl said. "My wife is expecting me back this evening."

"You'll miss some very interesting entertainment."

Yes, Karl thought, if smoking hashish or whatever it was they smoked or swallowed could be called interesting entertainment. He said, "Another time, perhaps."

"As you wish," Göring said. "Let's get you a cool drink and then you can demonstrate this airplane for me."

A mess-jacketed Luftwaffe sergeant served cold beer. Karl drank only half a glass. Too much beer made him logy. He climbed back into the KE-1, signaled the two Luftwaffe mechanics to wind the crank of the inertial starter, taxied out, and took off. For forty minutes, he put the KE-1 through every conceivable aerobatic maneuver. The airplane performed flawlessly.

When Karl landed, Göring asked a number of intelligent, probing questions. It was one of the most thorough grillings Karl could recall. When it was over, Göring's rotund face brightened, and he jabbed his fist triumphantly into Milch's shoulder.

"Well, Erhard, was I right?"

"It would seem so," Milch replied.

" 'Would seem so'?" Göring's voice hardened with annoyance. "How in the hell would you know, anyway?" He turned to Karl. "General Milch's knowledge of aviation is unfortunately confined to production."

Milch reddened. "What I meant, *Feldmarschall*, was that the plane hasn't yet been tested in actual combat."

"Actual combat?" Karl asked Milch.

Anton Moerzer replied for Milch. "In Spain, with the Condors," he said, referring to the Condor Legion, the volunteer Luftwaffe squadrons fighting on the Nationalist side in Spain.

Milch said to Karl, "We'd like you to check out two or three of our best young pilots in the machine. They'll take it to Spain. We'll know soon enough if it lives up to expectations."

"Don't worry, it will," said Göring. "But we should try to enlarge that damned cockpit. We're not taking midgets in the Luftwaffe yet!" He laughed, pleased at his own joke.

Karl was thinking about Milch's words, "two or three of our best young pilots," and wanted to shout at Göring, No! If anyone is to test the airplane in combat, it will be me! Combat. The very word quickened his heart and tightened his stomach.

Ever since the day Karl and Simon Conway first discussed a fighter, the Hunter, long before Karl conceived the KE-1, the prospect of once again flying in combat had intrigued him. Often, lying awake at night, he would relive the old days in his black triplane, an enemy airplane in the cross hairs of the gunsight, the feel of his thumbs on the machine guns' firing levers. The airplane vibrating nose to tail with the recoil. The acrid smell of cordite stinging his nostrils. The pitting of his skill and courage against another's.

Karl waited until he was ready to leave before raising the subject. As they were walking across the field to the parked KE-1, he told Göring he wanted to discuss a certain "discreet matter." Göring, as Karl had correctly predicted, assumed it concerned a woman and jocularly ordered Milch and Moerzer to remain behind.

"Respectfully, *Feldmarschall*, I suggest to you that the most practical and efficient method of testing the airplane in combat is for its designer to do it himself."

"You?"

"Why not?"

"What on earth is wrong with you, Karl? You're older than I am, and I'm forty-four! Must I give you that boring but true lecture about combat flying being a 'young man's game'? No, Karl, I won't hear of it. Not another word!"

Göring resumed walking briskly toward the KE-1. Karl hurried to keep up. "Hermann, you must listen to reason—"

But to Göring the matter was closed, and he was dealing with an entirely new one. "You once confided to me your concern about your former associate, Simon Conway, building a fighter similar to yours—"

"—the Hunter," Karl said, alarmed. "Have you some information on it?"

Göring said, " 'A compact, low-winged monoplane, the Hunter combines the speed and agility of a GB racer with the sturdiness and clean lines of the Northrop Alpha and Gamma mailplanes.' " He was quoting verbatim a military attaché's description of the Hunter. He continued, " 'While performance figures are not yet available, with its twelve-hundred-horsepower Jensen engine and four .30 caliber wing- and cowl-mounted machine guns, the aircraft is considered a most formidable weapon.' "

Göring, reading the dismay in Karl's face, paused. He raised his hand in a signal that the news was not all that bad. "The airplane was rejected not only by the U.S. Army," he went on, "but by the Chinese government as well."

Karl shook his head, bewildered.

"It seems our friend Mr. Conway went ahead and, on his own, manufactured ten or twelve of the machines, which he then attempted to sell to Chiang Kai-shek. The Generalissimo agreed to accept them on a trial basis."

"What do you mean, 'trial basis'?"

Göring was silent a moment, enjoying the suspense. Then, "If the airplanes proved reliable, the Chinese would purchase them. It turns out that after only three sorties the Chinese canceled the agreement and ordered the remaining planes—I believe one was shot down and another two destroyed on the ground—returned to the manufacturer, along with a group of American pilots Conway recruited to fly them."

Karl did not know what to say. He was embarrassed at having to hear this from Göring. He, Karl, should have made it his business to keep informed. China, he thought. American pilots. That bastard Simon Conway, you had to admire him. Nothing slowed him down.

". . . so as far as the Americans producing some incredible new fighter, there's little fear of that," Göring was saying. "How long will it take you to deliver the three KE-1s?"

"Six months," said Karl, his brain far ahead of his tongue. What he wouldn't give to see Simon Conway's face when Si learned of the KE-1's success. He must make certain that the word reached Si. "Five months, if engines and instrument components aren't delayed. Herr Feldmarschall, I have to tell you now that unless I am permitted to take this airplane to Spain myself—and personally test its combat-worthiness—I will withdraw completely from manufacturing additional models."

Göring stopped in his tracks. It was like a dump truck braking to a halt. His eyes narrowed into little slits of anger. He looked away, past Karl's shoulder, at the two enlisted men waiting attentively at the KE-1. When he faced Karl again, he seemed almost amused.

"Is that an ultimatum, Karl?"

"A statement of fact, sir."

Göring saw Karl's determination. "You're too fucking old, Karl," he said quietly.

"We've already been through that, Herr Feldmarschall."

"Give me three more KE-1s in three months, and I'll agree," Göring said after a moment.

"You'll have them in two months," Karl said.

"But only one sortie for you, Karl. You fly no more than one combat mission." Göring held up his index finger. "One," he said, and walked away.

Hermann Göring's information regarding Conair Hunter fighter planes in China was somewhat inexact. Only one of the twelve Hunters had been shot down—and that one accidentally, by antiaircraft fire from its own Chinese batteries—and only one destroyed on the ground, another accident. Moreover, the airplanes had not been returned to the manufacturer, they were taken out of service, although the Chinese government did order the pilots to leave China. And both of these actions came not as the result of any unreliability, but from Japanese diplomatic pressure on the U.S. State Department.

As for the report that the U.S. Army had rejected the Hunter, this was true, but for no other reason than cost. At $40,000 per unit, the airplane was too expensive for an air corps whose annual $75 million budget was already deemed excessive and threatened with Congressional reduction. So Si had developed the airplane with Conair's own funds and offered the Hunters, and the pilots to fly them, to the Chinese government on terms too attractive to ignore.

Göring's information also lacked certain salient details regarding the American pilots, or "Conway's Eagles," as they came to be known. The *Feldmarschall's* Japanese sources were unaware that on one of the three combat sorties flown, one of the pilots was forty-two-year-old Simon Conway himself.

3.

Carol Harris said she made two great mistakes in her life, and one intelligent decision. The intelligent decision was leaving her home town of Adrian, Michigan, immediately after graduating high school. The mistakes, in order of importance, were (1) passing up a Metro-Goldwyn-Mayer starlet's contract in favor of a New York model's career, and (2) marrying Duke Harris.

Why she allowed him to sweep her off her feet was the mystery of the ages. When she met him in 1934, three years ago, she was twenty-two years old and hardly fresh off the farm. Four years as a single girl in New York and a Powers model with three *Vogue* magazine covers to her credit should have taught her something.

But there he was, tall and handsome in his blue U.S. Navy officer's uniform with gold pilot's wings and the two gold stripes of a full lieutenant. Handsome, of course, purely in the eye of the beholder. Ralph Harris was no talent agent's idea of a matinee idol. For one thing, his face looked carved out of a piece of granite. "Weatherbeaten" was the word. It reminded her of the craggy face of the bronze statue of a fisherman in Gloucester, Massachusetts, where she had once spent a weekend with a Broadway theatrical producer.

So Duke, whom she met at a Walgreen's Drug Store coffee counter, swept her off her feet. They made an attractive couple. She, nearly as tall as he, with the flaxen hair, wide-set blue eyes, high-cheekboned face, and fine firm body of her Norwegian forebears. He, with that rugged masculinity and mischievous Irish charm.

She went to bed with him on their first date and married him on the third. Then she accompanied him to Pennsylvania Station, where he boarded a train for San Francisco and his new duty station aboard the aircraft carrier *Lexington*. In the next two years she saw him exactly seven times, each time for never more than three days except once for two weeks when the ship put in at Newport News, Virginia, for repairs.

By then, no longer in love with him, she asked for a divorce. He took the news calmly. He had been expecting it. But he had news of his own. He was leaving the navy, resigning his commission to take a flying job with a salary five times his navy pay.

". . . and with that kind of money, we might be able to live a more normal life," he said. "Look, this company I'm going with has agreed to bring you out to the West Coast, all expenses paid, and put you up in an apartment in Hollywood. What do you say?"

Hollywood, she thought. All expenses paid. Her modeling career was over; she had not had a magazine assignment in nearly a year.

They were always seeking fresh faces, and hers was too familiar. She knew people in the motion-picture business. Perhaps MGM might give her a second chance. After all, she was still young and attractive.

"This new job?" she asked. "What is it?"

"A better question is *where* is it."

"All right, where is it?"

"In China," he said.

Duke Harris and Mike Doyle, Conair's chief test pilot, had been classmates and close friends at Pensacola. Mike, after completing the four-year obligatory tour, resigned his commission to take the Conair job. Duke stayed in the navy. Over the years the two remained in contact. In the late winter of 1936, Mike was approached by his boss, Simon Conway, with a most unusual request.

Si had sold a dozen Conair Hunters to the Chinese. The airplanes were to have been shipped to Shanghai and turned over to the Chinese Air Force. But after learning that China's air force was composed of incompetent and undisciplined foreign adventurers who had destroyed every decent airplane the Chinese possessed, Si decided to take the Hunters to China himself, and the pilots to fly them. American pilots, military-trained, and each checked out personally by Simon Conway.

Si asked Mike Doyle to recommend a pilot with a military background who would be qualified to command this latter-day Lafayette Escadrille. Mike himself was disqualified: Si needed him at the factory. Mike recommended Ralph Harris.

The moment Si saw Duke Harris he knew he had found his man. In truth, Si repressed an almost irresistible urge to drag Duke home to Pacific Palisades and introduce him to thirteen-year-old Frank. Duke Harris was the man Si wanted Frank to grow up to be.

Duke also coined a new name for the unit which Si had already christened Conway's Hunters. No self-respecting pilot, said Duke, could resist the temptation for a play on words transforming Conway's Hunters to Conway's Cunters. Duke suggested Conway's Eagles, an alternative Si gratefully accepted.

Within four weeks, Duke had recruited fifteen more fighter pilots, all with extensive army or navy backgrounds. After another month of transition, the sixteen pilots of Conway's Eagles crated their airplanes, packed their bags, and boarded a steamer for Shanghai.

One week after they departed, Simon Conway announced that he himself would fly to Shanghai and then go on to join the group at their base in Hankow. He tried to make it appear as if the decision were sudden. He fooled no one, especially not Meg.

"Si, you planned this from the start!" she said. "Don't bother denying it. I knew it weeks ago when you began telling everybody how well the factory could operate without you."

"But it's true," he said lamely. "All these college boys with their engineering degrees and newfangled technology look at me like I'm some fossil they found frozen for two thousand years in a cake of ice."

"Si, I don't mind your running away like this—"

"I'm not 'running away.' "

"—I only wish you'd be honest about it."

He started to say that, dammit, he *was* being honest, but realized she was too smart for that. "All right," he said. "It's something I want to do. Something I have to do."

"That's better."

But Si knew that she, and all his associates, considered this Chinese adventure if not insane, at the very least childish. The only person who seemed to truly comprehend why Si wanted to go to China was young Frank. He was a nice-looking boy, with his mother's fair hair and fine features, although probably destined to be not as tall. Richard and Janet had inherited their parents' height.

But Frank had been gifted with his father's love of flying, and Si's innate ability. Before he was twelve, Frank had nearly fifty hours of dual flying time and could easily have passed a CAA test for a private pilot's license. Si, who had flown with him during most of those hours, gave the boy a special thirteenth-birthday gift: permission to solo, which Frank did, flawlessly, like the natural he was.

Of course, it had to be in secret: Frank's mother would never have had allowed him flying lessons in the first place, not until he was at least sixteen. She had extracted a promise from Frank, and from Si at the same time. Si had given his word and sternly instructed the boy to stop pestering him for lessons. The moment Meg turned away, the father winked conspiratorially at the son.

Shortly before leaving for China, Si took Frank up to the promontory overlooking the airport. They often came here to talk, usually aviation or baseball, but more often just to watch the airplanes. Frank's older brother, Richard, never accompanied them; he had still not outgrown his fear of airplanes. Si had all but given up on him.

That Sunday, they sat on the running board of Si's Lincoln Zephyr, gazing at the airplanes on the field below, and Si said to Frank, "At the end of this week, I'm going away for a while."

"Business?" Frank asked.

"Sort of," Si said, and told him about Conway's Eagles.

Frank's eyes widened and his imagination soared. When Si finished, Frank said, "You're lucky, Dad."

"Why?"

"Because you're getting in another war."

"And you call that 'lucky'?"

"Don't you?"

"Frank, it's purely a matter of business," Si said, and changed the subject. The truth of it was that, yes, he did consider himself lucky to get into another war. He simply lacked the courage to admit it to his son.

Coincidentally, only the very next day he again had occasion to question his moral courage. Or lack of it. That was the day he met Carol Harris.

She had arrived in California too late to see her husband off but had visited the factory to pick up a note from Duke, the keys to the apartment, and her $300 monthly allowance.

She instantly reminded Si of Ceil Silcox. The same hair, the same satiny complexion, the beckoning body—those breasts and thighs that could conquer the world—and the same invitation in her wide blue eyes. It had been years since a woman excited him so.

But Carol was no Ceil. The first three minutes of their conversation made that intoxicatingly clear. This was a bright, witty, sophisticated woman. Furthermore, Si had no intention of repeating his mistake. For one thing, he had too much regard for Duke Harris.

He saw her again, twice, before he left for China. Both times, their conversation carefully centered on Duke and how much each of them respected him. But Si knew Carol was not fooled. She knew how taken he was with her.

She popped in and out of his mind throughout the long flight to Shanghai. After all, there was such a thing as being too noble. Only after he arrived at the airfield outside Hankow and shook hands with Duke did Si finally decide he was glad he had not met the challenge.

Hankow was an endless series of problems. From the day-to-day availability of fuel and ammunition, to the competence of the Chinese mechanics and armorers. From the miserable living conditions in tents on the muddy airfield, to the quality of the food. There was even a question of whether the gin in the Gordon's bottle was genuine, indeed, if the bottle itself was genuine.

For all that, China was one of Si's most gratifying experiences. For him, it was France all over again. Never mind that the pilots wore civilian clothes and their airplanes bore the flaming-sun disk cockade of the Chinese Air Force. It was the Escadrille, this time with infinitely superior equipment and far-better-trained pilots. Not to mention far-better-paid pilots: $600 monthly, plus a $1,000 bonus for every Japanese airplane destroyed.

Everything changes but nothing changes.

Duke scheduled the first patrol six days after the Eagles settled in. Si wasted no time announcing that he, Simon Conway, would fly one of the Hunters.

Duke wasted less time disabusing Si of the notion. Simon Conway would fly no operational missions. "End of discussion," said Duke.

"For Christ's sake, Duke, I'm more qualified to fly this airplane than anybody else here!" Si said.

"Not in combat, Si," Duke said. "You hired me to command this outfit, and I'm doing it. You're not flying."

"I'm too old, is that what you're trying to say?"

"That'll do for openers."

"Tell you what," said Si, who knew he had to be careful not to force Duke into a corner. "I give you my word not to engage in combat. If we see any enemy planes, I'll turn around and scoot right back here to the field."

Duke thought about it and finally agreed. "Okay, Si, but you're crazy. No," he added quickly, "I'm crazy . . . for letting you do it!"

As he clambered up onto the Hunter's wing and into the cockpit, Si himself could not help thinking, Yes, of course I am crazy. I have to be crazy doing this. But once inside the cocoonlike glassed enclosure, the smell of leather and oil wafting over him, he knew that while he might be crazy, he was happier than he'd been in years. He was back where he belonged, doing what he did best.

The flight of six Hunters had hardly reached ten thousand feet when word was radioed of incoming Japanese bombers. Duke ordered the Hunters to arm their guns and switch on the electric gunsights.

The bombers were spotted a few minutes later. Nine twin-engined Mitsubishi G3Ms, approaching Hankow from the east at seven thousand feet. The formation was almost directly below the Hunters.

"Stovepipe Six," Duke called over the radio to Si. "I have to ask you to turn back now. Over."

Duke's voice was loud and clear in Si's earphones. He picked up his microphone and started to say, "Negative, Stovepipe One," but then decided to simply not respond.

"Stovepipe Six!" Duke called again.

Si did not reply.

". . . goddammit, Si, I know you can hear me!" Duke shouted over the radio and then, disgusted, addressed the flight. "Okay, Stovepipes Two through Five, let's go get 'em!"

Immediately, Duke rolled his Hunter over and dove on the Mitsubishis. All five Hunters followed, Si in the number-six slot. In an instant the Hunters were racing in and out of the bomber formation in a wild, gun-chattering melee. In that same instant, racking the fighter around, crushed into his seat by G forces even young men found intolerable, attempting to take in the whole sky with eyes no longer sharp and reflexes maddeningly slow, Si regretted disobeying Duke.

You are one damned fool, he told himself. One damned, conceited old fool. He caught a glimpse of a Mitsubishi exploding in midair, disintegrating in a ball of orange flame and black smoke. He rolled the Hunter around and suddenly, startlingly, the nose and cockpit of another G3M filled his gunsight. He snapped open the spring-loaded trigger guard on the control stick and curled his finger around the trigger. But something was wrong. The unique feeling of exhilaration he had anticipated was not there. Instead, as the G3M lay exposed in his gunsight, Si was thinking, I am about to kill the men in that airplane. They are men I have never seen, and have nothing against. Oh, yes, they are the same people who have burned cities and killed children. I have seen some of that with my own eyes. But what in the hell have these Japs ever done to me?

All he knew about them was that their skin was yellow and their eyesight poor, that they manufactured inferior toys and machinery but were excellent gardeners. Si thought of his gardener back in Pacific Palisades, a nice little man named Sam Takahashi, with whom he sometimes talked baseball.

"Si, break left!" Duke's voice crackled into Si's earphones. "Break left!"

Si jerked the stick left and kicked left rudder. Simultaneously, above his head, half the Hunter's canopy vanished. Pieces of Plexiglas showered down onto his lap and onto the cockpit floor. The wind screaming in through the shattered canopy blotted out the sound of engines and gunfire. Instinctively, Si pulled his goggles over his eyes. Slightly above him, to his right, the GM3's rear gunner was swiveling the gun barrel around to fire again.

Sam Takahashi was trying to kill him. Si dove the Hunter away from the G3M, rolled her half over, then pulled the stick into his stomach. He was directly under the G3M. The bomber's belly loomed huge in his windscreen. He vaguely realized that the electric gunsight had no backlight—it must have been hit in the same burst that smashed the canopy—but the target was so close no gunsight was needed.

He fired. Shells from the four .30 calibers punched a neat line of holes along the length of the bomber's fuselage from the tail wheel to the wing root. Si whipped the Hunter around in a tight, climbing right turn. He came out straight and level two hundred yards behind the G3M. She was breaking apart in the air. Pieces of aluminum fluttered away, a propeller, a gun turret. And then it exploded.

He felt no elation. He felt hollow, completely drained. It was an effort to move the stick, to push the rudder pedals, to handle the engine controls. And he was hardly aware of the express-train roar of the wind through the open canopy.

All he could think of on the way back was that he had killed six men, and that in the other war this had never disturbed him, and that the only possible reason it disturbed him now was that he was getting old.

Duke Harris put it straight to him. If Si planned to fly again, then he also should plan to find a new squadron commander. Si assured Duke that the one flight was the one and only flight. In truth, Si was relieved. That moment of hesitation before he fired on the bomber, that moment of reflection, of doubt, had been nearly fatal. He had no desire for a repeat performance.

In the end it turned out to be academic, anyway. The Eagles flew only two more missions. Despite the group's success—eight Japanese bombers shot down, no Eagle pilots lost—the Chinese government, at the insistence of the U.S. State Department, reluctantly disbanded the unit. Si agreed to allow the Chinese to purchase the twelve remaining Hunter fighters.

Si went to Shanghai to catch another Pan Am clipper back to America. His first evening there, at the bar of the Empress Hotel, he was joined by a thin, sharp-featured, middle-aged man wearing a rumpled seersucker suit. Si recognized him.

"Chennault," Si said. "Claire Chennault. Bolling Field, 1933. You tested my O-17 observation planes. Are you still in the army?"

"I retired," said Chennault. He tapped the lobe of his left ear. "Seems the service isn't too anxious for an overage captain with hearing problems." He grinned sourly. "Too many years of open cockpits."

"What the hell are you doing all the way out here?"

"Believe it or not, I was on my way to Hankow to talk to you. The Generalissimo's wife saw me in Washington and asked me to get my ass over here and help you."

"Help me do what? Pack up?"

"Help you mothball those airplanes," said Chennault. "My job is to sit tight until things cool down, and in the meantime to set up a proper ground-support unit—mechanics, communications, medical —and then very quietly put another volunteer group together."

Si slammed his empty glass on the bar. " 'Another volunteer group'! What the hell does that mean?"

"Take it easy, Mr. Conway. I wasn't sent here to replace you. Roosevelt—" He paused abruptly. Si's irate expression told him that he had used precisely the wrong word. He rephrased the sentence.

"It's a diplomatic problem. The U.S. isn't ready to buck the Japs yet. But they want another American volunteer group in China as soon as the time is ripe. Another year, two at most."

"You mean Roosevelt wants one," Si said. The initial surge of anger was gone. He realized Chennault was merely following orders.

"Yes, of course, Roosevelt," Chennault said. "But believe me, it's nothing personal. It's what they call 'diplomatic expediency.' You were in the right place, but at the wrong time."

"Tell that to my guys," Si said. "They broke their backs to make this thing work. Eight Japs shot down, for Christ's sake!"

Chennault shrugged helplessly. "What can I say?"

"You can hire Conway's Eagles back," Si said, and added, " 'As soon as the time is ripe.' "

"They'll be welcome, believe me. But if it's all the same to you, we'll be known officially as the American Volunteer Group. Unofficially, how does Chennault's Tigers sound?

"Not as good as Conway's Eagles," Si said. But he smiled when he said it to show there were no hard feelings, and offered a suggestion. "Make it Chennault's *Flying* Tigers."

"Flying Tigers," Chennault repeated. "I like it."

"You owe me a drink, then," Si said.

"My pleasure." Chennault signaled the barman for refills, and said to Si, "You're taking the clipper in the morning?"

"Straight home, and damned glad to be there."

"I'll bet," said Chennault. "By the way, I don't suppose you heard about Guernica?"

"Guernica? Is that a person or a place?"

"A city in Spain," Chennault said. "The Germans leveled it yesterday. There aren't a dozen buildings left standing. Dive-bombers did most of the damage. Those JU-87s. 'Stukas,' I think they're called."

"Yeah, I heard they're pretty good with those things," Si said. "Well, believe me, captain, there are ten times as many 'Guernicas' here in China."

"I'm sure of that," Chennault said, then clicked his glass against Si's. "To a safe journey."

"To the Flying Tigers," Si said.

"And to Conway's Eagles," Chennault said. "May they fly again."

"I'll drink to that," Si said.

They drank to it. Neither had the vaguest idea that within two years Conway's Eagles would indeed be flying again, not in China but in Spain.

15

Phil Granger told Si the story would appear in the business section of tomorrow's *Times*. It was the kind of bad news, said Granger, that made you want to kiss your worst enemy—or even your wife, he had added half seriously. Western Airlines had placed a firm order with Conair for seven 660s. The "bad" part was that it created an even bigger 660 production backlog, possibly as long as a year.

The next morning, with the housekeeper off, Si went outside to get the paper himself. The day was chilly and gloomy-gray. The newspaper, damp from the overnight dew, lay front page up on the grass. It was the early edition of the July 2, 1937, *Los Angeles Times*.

EARHART LOST AT SEA!
MASSIVE U.S. NAVY SEARCH UNDERWAY

Si picked up the newspaper gingerly, as though hoping he might have misread the headline. No such luck, and luck was precisely the right word. Amelia Earhart, the only woman to have flown solo across both the Atlantic and Pacific oceans, had run out of it attempting to establish a new round-the-world record.

He cringed guiltily, unable to repress a flash of selfish relief that she had chosen a Lockheed Electra for the flight instead of the specially modified 660 he had almost persuaded her to use.

"Dad . . . ?"

Frank, fully dressed in a short-sleeved blue shirt with red-and-white-striped tie, white flannel slacks, and white tennis shoes, stood watching him curiously.

"What's the matter?" Frank asked.

Si held the paper up for Frank to see.

"Jesus!" Frank said.

"How many times have I told you not to use that language? Go back in the house and I'll talk to you in a minute."

"You said you were taking me for a lesson this morning."

Si ruffled the boy's hair affectionately. "I forgot to tell you, kid, I have an early meeting today with a man from Spain."

"Spain, where they're having that civil war?" Frank asked. "Isn't that where Duke went?"

"Yes, and that's what the meeting's about. About what Duke went there for. That's why I can't give you a lesson today."

"We don't have to fly for a whole hour. Half an hour, how's that?" Now, with summer vacation, Frank worked at the factory as a messenger boy but spent most of his time either talking with the test pilots or helping the mechanics. Two or three times weekly Frank went up in a CT-5 trainer, most recently under Duke Harris's tutelage. With Duke away in Spain, Si had promised to fly with Frank.

"Not today," Si said.

"I wanted you to see how good I'm doing."

"How 'well' you're doing," Si said gently. "I know how well you're doing. I'll take you up Saturday."

"Yeah," Frank said. His voice had taken on a whining tone that annoyed Si. "Sure."

Si pointed at the sky. "For one thing, this overcast won't burn off for hours. You couldn't fly this morning anyway."

"How about when it clears up, then?"

"I told you, I have a meeting."

"It's this morning, you said."

"I'm having lunch with this man, too. Now go inside and have breakfast," Si said, and immediately resumed reading the newspaper account of Earhart's disappearance in the Pacific. Her last radio contact had reported her position as a hundred miles west of her scheduled stop, Howland Island. After that, she and her navigator simply vanished.

Another one bites the dust, Si thought, and wondered how it had happened, and why. A hundred possible reasons, from engine failure to a navigational error. A one-degree miscalculation, not at all unusual, could result in a fifty-mile difference, leaving you lost—with a thousand miles of ocean in all directions and no gasoline.

He lit a cigarette and sat on the porch steps for a long time, thinking, and by the time he returned to the house, Frank had already finished breakfast and gone off on his bike. Richard and Janet were still at the table in the breakfast room. Si poured a cup of coffee for himself, listened impatiently to Richard's version of a squabble with Frank, then went upstairs to shave and dress.

When Si came downstairs again he brought the newspaper into the garden. Meg, trimming rose bushes, looked up from under the floppy brim of her hat.

"Have you had breakfast?"

"I don't have much of an appetite this morning," Si said, and displayed the newspaper front page.

Meg read the headline. "Oh, my God!"

"They might find her," Si said.

"That poor woman." Meg placed the garden shears on the ground, removed her heavy work gloves, and took the newspaper from Si. She read the brief story. "It's always only a matter of time, isn't it? Until the percentages catch up with you."

"When you're doing that kind of flying, yes," he said. "But somebody has to do it."

"Of course," Meg said tightly. " 'Somebody has to do it.' I understand all that. I just feel sad for their families."

What she meant, Si knew, was her anxiety over Frank's flying. Not long ago, awakened from a sound sleep by Meg's screaming, Si found her sitting up in bed, weeping. She had had a dream about Frank. In the dream she saw him dead in the wreckage of an airplane. It was then that she confessed having known for some time of the lessons Si was secretly giving the boy.

Si was not surprised that she had had such a dream; it was the same week of the *Hindenburg* disaster. The newspapers were filled with pictures of the German dirigible exploding and burning, killing thirty-three of its ninety-seven passengers and crew. He repeated now what he had said to her then.

"For a woman whose whole life is centered around airplanes and flying, I wish you wouldn't live in such fear of it."

"So do I, Si," she said.

To change the subject, Si pointed to a small item on the lower left front page of the newspaper. " 'Pioneer airline executive Morris Tannen today announced his candidacy for the U.S. Senate seat left vacant by the death last month of Kenneth O'Neil,' " he read. "What do you think of that?"

"I think it's wonderful."

"I think it's sad. If he gets ten thousand votes, he'll be lucky." Si folded the newspaper and tucked it under Meg's arm. He started back into the house. "I'm not sure if I'll be home for dinner," he said. "I'll call you."

Meg felt bad for him. She knew he was upset about Amelia Earhart and was trying not to show it, trying to protect her. It was his way of expressing tenderness and affection, a strange way, but she had come to understand it and accept it. Part of the price, she supposed, for her having accepted him and wanting the world, which he had given her. Everything had a price.

"Somebody has to do it," she said quietly, to herself.

Si's meeting that morning was the result of a letter Duke Harris had recently received from an old friend, Frank Tinker, flying for the Loyalists in Spain. Tinker had written that the Loyalists were paying pilots $1,000 per month plus $1,000 for every Rebel plane shot down. The problem was that the Loyalists' antiquated Breguets and Nieuport-Delages—and even the new Russian fighters that had begun trickling in, the I-15s and I-16s—were no match for the Rebel's Messerschmitts and JU-87s. What the Loyalists really needed were Conair Hunters.

Si sent Duke to Spain with an offer: Conair would sell the Loyalists twenty-four airplanes if they agreed to employ the services of an additional group of American pilots, Conway's Eagles.

The Spaniards balked. As a matter of honor, they preferred to have their own pilots fly the new equipment. Si said honor had nothing to do with it: as far he was concerned, it was a matter of not wrecking one fine airplane after another. The Spanish Air Force dispatched a senior officer to Los Angeles to negotiate with Si.

The officer, Colonel Augustín Liano, booked a room at the Carmel Hotel in downtown Santa Monica and arranged to meet Si there. Si arrived on time, eleven o'clock, and stopped at the newspaper stand in the hotel lobby to buy an early-afternoon edition of the *Herald*. The headline read EARHART S.O.S REPORTED! But that story, as he had heard on a news flash on the car radio, was false. He jammed the newspaper into his suitcoat pocket and started across the marbled lobby floor to the desk.

"Mr. Conway . . . ?"

Si turned to face an aristocratic young man wearing an impeccably tailored double-breasted blue covert-cloth suit and thirty-dollar-hand-sewn patent-leather loafers.

"Captain Ramón Sanjuro at your service, sir."

"You're from Liano?" Si asked.

"Colonel Liano," the young man delicately corrected. "I am the colonel's aide. I'll phone him that you're here."

Si and Captain Sanjuro waited for Colonel Liano in a corner booth of the darkened Carmel Hotel lounge. Sanjuro, who spoke perfect BBC Oxford English, enjoyed talking. He was a Spanish Air Force pilot, he said, although his talents admittedly lay more in fund-raising than flying.

". . . listen, pilots are a dime a dozen, but a good fund-raiser, now that's hard to find," Si said, thinking that if this man was an example of the Spanish Air Force, no wonder the Rebels were winning.

Colonel Augustín Liano, however, was another story. Short, swarthy, with thick jet-black eyebrows, a huge bulbous nose and sandpaper complexion, he looked more like a stevedore or a ditch digger than a fighter pilot. He was as laconic as Captain Sanjuro was loquacious.

But he and Si spoke the same language. Augustín Liano was forty-five years old, a former Aéropostale pilot with thousands of hours of grueling South American flying. He had paid his dues. He and Si had a few drinks, exchanged stories about the old days, and then, almost reluctantly, began discussing the present situation.

As Si had anticipated, the meeting went on for hours, through lunch at the new Riviera Country Club in Pacific Palisades, and well past three in the afternoon. Although Colonel Liano considered the financial terms generous enough—$37,500 per airplane, the money to be deposited in a Swiss escrow account—he was adamant in his refusal to allow American pilots to fly them as an autonomous unit.

Si was equally adamant. Whenever he felt himself weakening it required only a glance at Captain Sanjuro's tanned face and manicured fingernails to restore his determination. No, the Hunters would be flown by Conway's Eagles or not at all. And then, with the utterance of a single word, the issue was resolved.

"Mr. Conway, we need your planes," Liano said. He was growing impatient. "The Germans have brought in a new fighter that is flying rings around our Russian planes. This KE-1—"

"—KE-1?" Si repeated.

"Yes, the KE-1," Liano said, unaware of what the KE-1 meant to Si. "The plane was first seen in June, over Teurel, and before the end of the year we expect an entire squadron to be stationed at Seville."

Si heard the words, and understood, but all that really mattered to him, all that he wanted to prove, was that his Hunter could outperform Karl Eisler's KE-1.

"I'll do it," he said, before Colonel Liano had even finished speaking. "You'll have the Hunters. But I want at least twelve of my own pilots flying them. For the other twelve, I want your personal guarantee that whoever flies them, I don't care who—Americans, Englishmen, Frenchmen, Russians—I want your assurance that they'll be checked out by Mr. Harris."

"Agreed," said Liano, and they shook hands on it.

There were all manner of other details. The airplanes, disassembled, would be crated as "farm equipment" and sent by ship to Barcelona. The twelve Eagle pilots would also travel by sea, but to Marseilles. From Marseilles the French would allow them to proceed overland into Spain. Si promised to order the airplanes into production within a month, and delivery of all twenty-four units, with spare parts and engines, before January 1, 1938.

Following the meeting he went directly to his office at the airport. He composed a cable, addressed to Ralph Harris in care of the American Embassy in Madrid: DEAL SET STOP HUNTERS HUNT STOP EAGLES FLY AGAIN STOP.

He instructed the night clerk in the Conair mailroom to dispatch the message immediately. The clerk, an acne-faced teenager wearing a plaid bow tie and Harold Lloyd horn-rimmed glasses, read the message and said, " 'Ralph Harris'—that's old Duke, ain't it? His wife just phoned up and said she'd be down here in a little while to pick up a letter. I saw her a couple of weeks ago. Boy, is she a good-looker!"

Good-looker, Si thought, was the understatement of the year. He had not seen her since before leaving for China but certainly remembered her. He decided to hang around a few minutes and perhaps bump into her, maybe take her to dinner. He had told Meg not to expect him home.

And it would be no betrayal of Duke, for Duke had confided to Si that the marriage was practically over. He and Carol had reached an understanding. As soon as he returned from Spain she would file for divorce.

Jesus H. Christ! Si told himself. You sound like an idiot, a horny old idiot. Well, so what's wrong with that? he answered himself. And please, he added to himself, don't give me any lectures on morality. Besides, I'm not looking for a meaningful relationship, only a deep one. Yes, at least seven inches deep.

"... hey, Mr. Conway?" It was the mailroom clerk, on his way to the airport communications room to send the cable. "You feeling okay, sir?"

"I feel fine."

"You looked kind of funny."

"I was just thinking about—" Si started to say, and stopped abruptly. He almost had said, I was just thinking about fucking Duke's wife. "—about something," he finished lamely. "Go ahead and get that cable off."

A half hour later, when Carol had still not appeared, Si gave up. In truth, he was almost relieved. It was a bad idea to begin with, a fantasy that could lead only to Trouble, capital T. Inadvisable, that was the word. Inadvisable.

He hurried out to the parking lot, got into the Lincoln, and drove straight home. By the time he had pulled into the driveway and given Richard hell for leaving his bicycle on the lawn, he decided to take Meg to dinner at the Riviera. Fridays, the club's Mexican chef made a fish stew Si liked, Siete Mares. Hardly a satisfactory substitute for Carol Harris but definitely safer, certainly more advisable.

2.

A fool's errand, Karl Eisler thought, ordered by fools and undertaken by bigger fools. Karl realized that this last category, bigger fools, unfortunately described him. But he had been given little choice. The order came directly from "Der Grosser Hermann," who, according to rumor, soon would be promoted to *Reichsmarshall*. One did not, or at least should not, ignore orders from a *Reichsmarschall*, even a *Reichsmarschall* who was a fool.

Below, directly ahead, was the crowded tarmac of the Cádiz airfield. The Spanish-speaking voice of the control-tower operator boomed loud in his earphones. ". . . you are clear to land, Condor Able George Dog."

Karl picked up his microphone and spoke into it in halting Spanish. "Thank you, tower. Able George Dog turning onto final."

He slipped the KE-1 smoothly down onto the runway. God, but he loved the way this airplane handled! He wondered how the Conair Hunter performed. Probably every bit as well as the KE-1, if young Pete Dagget had supervised the Hunter's design, which Karl suspected was the case. As a designer, Simon Conway would win no prizes.

But what remained of the Hunter—a burned-out frame and some charred engine parts strewn over two square kilometers—had revealed nothing. Inspecting the Hunter's wreckage was the first of the fool's errands: the *Reichsmarschall* naively believed that a detailed examination of the wreckage might disclose some new, secret manufacturing technique or metallurgic advance. Karl knew better. The Hunter was a well-designed, soundly constructed, powerfully engined airplane but essentially simple, as were all fine machines.

Karl had seen enough photos of the Hunter to know it bore no resemblance, not even familial, to the KE-1. What would be interesting was an encounter between the two airplanes. A battle of titans. But it was unlikely to happen, not with the KE-1s based in Seville, five hundred miles from the Hunters' airfield at Valencia.

The apron at Cádiz was packed with trimotored JU-52 transports and bombers, their corrugated metal wings gleaming brightly in the hot afternoon sun. Two rows of biplane fighters, HE-51s and Fiat CR-32s, were parked behind the JU-52s, along with a smattering of other German and Italian airplanes. All bore the black painted X of Nationalist Spain on their vertical fins.

No Condor Legion personnel were based here, only Italian and Spanish pilots, which always posed a language problem for Karl, whose Spanish was strictly rudimentary. But on this errand, the second fool's errand Karl was performing for Göring, English would be spoken. And this second errand, interviewing the captured pilot of the downed Hunter, at least promised to be more interesting.

The pilot had parachuted to safety after being hit by a Nationalist antiaircraft battery while escorting a flight of MB-210 bombers attacking Rebel positions south of Madrid. Unfortunately, a number of civilians had been killed or injured in the raid and the pilot was accused of committing war crimes against the people of Spain. A military court had tried him, found him guilty, and sentenced the poor bastard, an American mercenary named Ralph Harris, to die before a firing squad.

The commandant of the base, Colonel Emilio Cruz, was on the phone when Karl brushed past the sergeant major and stormed into his office. Cruz, a thirty-six-year-old fighter pilot who had served as a captain under General Franco in the Army of Africa, immediately terminated the conversation and rose to greet Karl.

Cruz and Karl had met once before, and despite Karl's being German, Cruz rather liked him. But what the hell was Karl doing in Cádiz? He looked tired. A cigarette dangled from his lips. His black leather flying jacket was slung over one shoulder of his sweat-stained khaki Luftwaffe short-sleeved shirt. He also looked very annoyed.

Cruz forced a smile and extended his hand. "Herr Eisler, this is a surprise." He spoke in English; his German was as limited as Karl's Spanish.

"Look, Cruz, I just came from town," Karl said as they shook hands. The impatient tone of his voice told Cruz this was no social call. "Have you ever seen what they call a 'jail' at the central police station?"

"I beg your pardon?"

"The central police station, goddammit!" Karl said. He paused as the sergeant major, standing uneasily in the open doorway, cleared his throat discreetly. Cruz waved the sergeant major away. Karl went on, "You're holding an American pilot there. The conditions in that place are shameful! What in the hell is wrong with you people?"

"Now just a minute, please—"

"I want that man put in a decent cell, with decent facilities. And I want it done now, Cruz! Today! Do you understand?"

Important industrialist or not, Cruz's first instinct was to have this arrogant German thrown out on his ear. On the other hand, arguing about comfortable quarters for a condemned man was an obscene waste of time.

"I'll see to it immediately, Herr Eisler," Cruz said. "I'll have the man placed under twenty-four-hour-guard at the officers' quarters here at the field."

The question that occurred to Colonel Cruz, but that he never asked, was why Karl Eisler had taken such an interest in the affair. Karl might have replied that Duke Harris, or for that matter any captured combat pilot—especially one condemned to death—deserved better treatment at the hands of his captors. But that did not explain why, in the week Karl remained in Cádiz, he visited Duke daily, making certain the prisoner received only the finest food and was treated by his captors with utmost courtesy.

Duke Harris was no ordinary pilot. Karl's very first glimpse of Duke told him why Simon Conway had delegated so much responsibility to the young man. In Duke, Si saw himself and, more important, the man he wanted his two sons to be. Indeed, Duke Harris was the man Karl would like his own son to be. If he had a son, which he did not have and would not have. Erika was unable to bear children.

Once again, Simon Conway had bested Karl Eisler.

Each day, Karl and Duke talked, sometimes for hours, mostly about flying and occasionally about their mutual acquaintance Simon Conway. Of his personal life, Duke spoke little. He was married, no children; his wife resided at the moment in California. Duke was far more interested in hearing about Karl's wartime experiences and his early days at Conair.

The more Karl came to know Duke, the more determined he was to save his life. If the Nationalists intended to execute pilots for crimes against the Spanish people, then they had best begin with the Condor Legion. The ruins of Guernica and Madrid bore witness to that.

Karl had asked the Condor Legion commander himself, General Sperrle, to intervene on Duke's behalf. It was a mistake. Sperrle had resented Karl's presence from the start, suspecting him of being Göring's personal spy. Karl's detailed report to Göring criticizing Luftwaffe tactics in the first battle of the Ebro merely confirmed Sperrle's suspicions. The general not only refused to help Duke, he ordered Karl back to Seville.

The afternoon before he left, Karl paid Duke his daily visit at the temporary "prison cell" in the officers' quarters at the airfield. Karl brought a basket of food, grilled sardines, an onion salad, two loaves of crusty white bread, and a bottle of Gewürztraminer, the last of a case Erika had sent him.

"Looks like a picnic," Duke said. He was sitting propped up in bed, reading a dogeared copy of a travel guide, *1926 In Europe.*

"It's more of a farewell party," Karl said, and told him about having been ordered back to Seville. "Here, open this bottle while I set the table."

"Open it with what, Karl?" Duke asked. "My teeth? Condemned men aren't allowed any sharp objects. That includes corkscrews. Hey, Carlos!" he shouted. Immediately, the guard opened the door. In Spanish, Duke asked him to open the bottle.

Karl placed the basket on the table and began unpacking. To make room for the food he pushed aside a glass-framed photograph, the only object on the otherwise bare table. It was a large, shadowed head shot of Carol.

"I haven't seen this before," Karl said. "Your wife?"

"That's her," Duke said. "They sent me some personal stuff from Valencia. I only got it this morning."

"She looks like a movie star."

Just then the door opened. Blindly, Karl held his hand out to the guard for the bottle. "*Gracias*," he said.

The bottle was placed in his hand not by the guard, but by Colonel Cruz. "My pleasure, Herr Eisler," he said.

Duke said, "The colonel looks as though he has bad news." He took the bottle from Karl and began filling the two wineglasses Karl had removed from the basket.

"No news," Cruz said. He accepted a glass and sat heavily on the cot. "In this instance that is not necessarily bad, but neither is it good. Frankly, the longer the appeal is delayed, the bleaker the prospect."

"What about the U.S. State Department?" Duke asked.

"Not a word from them," Cruz said.

"That figures," Duke said. He gave Karl the second wineglass and poured some for himself into a water tumbler.

Karl said, "This is absurd, Cruz, and you know it!"

"This whole bloody war is absurd." Cruz raised his glass. "*Salute*," he said, and drank. The others also drank. Cruz noted the bottle label. "A shade too dry for my taste, perhaps, but very nice." Speaking, he had reached over to the table and picked up Carol's photograph. "And so is this pretty lady."

"My wife," Duke said.

"As you can see, our American friend has excellent taste," Karl said.

Cruz, who seemed intrigued with the photograph, suddenly snapped his fingers. "It might work," he said quietly, really thinking aloud. "It just might work! Look here," he said to Duke, "General Franco is a romantic. He admires beautiful women. If your wife were to send him this picture"—he tapped the photograph's frame—"along with a personal plea to save the life of the man she loves, it just might persuade the Generalissimo to grant a pardon. What do you think?"

Duke laughed harshly. "Excuse me, colonel, but this isn't a Hollywood movie."

"Try it!" Karl said. "What do you have to lose?"

Duke laughed again. "Only my life," he said.

3.

As a foreign correspondent, Bill Macon had few peers. Not without reason was it said that when Bill Macon could not find a good story he invented one and then somehow made it happen. At forty-nine, he was as cynical and thick-skinned as a man could be after twenty-three years of covering wars or insurrections for the *St. Louis Post Dispatch*, the *Chicago Times*, and now the *New York Sun*. The byline "Exclusive from Our Special Correspondent William H. Macon" had appeared on stories from Pancho Villa's raid on Columbus, New Mexico, to the siege of Madrid—with the slaughter at Verdun and the rape of Nanking in between.

Bill Macon did not have to invent the story he filed on the morning of November 5, 1938. He had happened onto it the previous week in the nearly empty dining room of the Palace Hotel in Barcelona, Spain. More accurately, the story happened onto him in the person of Simon Conway, whose face he had last seen in Hankow, China, more than a year before and some ten thousand miles from Barcelona.

Macon, in Barcelona for a well-deserved rest after five grueling days in besieged Madrid, had just finished a fine dinner of *paella* and almost a whole bottle of a 1932 Marqués de Riscal *rioja*. He felt a little guilty knowing that while he ate, the people of Barcelona were starving. The Nationalist advance had all but cut off the city. But what the hell, he thought, if the Loyalists could shoot priests and nuns, why couldn't he enjoy a black-market meal?

He was pondering the morality of all this when he saw Simon Conway, accompanied by a stunning blond woman, entering the candlelit dining room. Conway looked his usual unkempt self, hair rumpled, double-breasted suit jacket unbuttoned, tie askew, trousers unpressed. But the woman, considerably younger, was the height of chic fashion in a tailored black pinstriped suit. Under a pert black straw hat her fastidiously coiffed hair gleamed in the candlelight.

A year and a half ago in China, Simon Conway had given Bill Macon an exclusive story on Conway's Eagles. In return, Macon agreed not to reveal Simon Conway's presence in that theater of war, or that he had recruited the pilots flying the warplanes. Macon's only regret was that he could not print Simon Conway's description of his pilots.

"They take very seriously their flying, drinking, and fucking."

"In that order?" Macon had asked.

"I think the fucking comes before the drinking," Simon Conway had said. "But not before the flying."

Watching the maître d' escort the couple to a nearby table, Bill Macon thought he knew exactly where "fucking" fit into Simon Conway's personal scheme of things here in Spain. But in the same thought, Macon became aware of the truth behind the rumors of a new, devastating fighter plane shipped to the Loyalists by the American government and flown by U.S. Army pilots.

The planes were Conair Hunters, flown by Conway's Eagles.

Macon, although correct on both counts, never even remotely suspected that the real story revolved around the good-looking blond woman and was, of all unlikely things, a love story.

Two weeks before, when Si received the transatlantic telephone call from Karl, he had at first thought it was a joke. Karl's voice was tinny, almost unintelligible, shouting into the phone, ". . . I'm in Spain, Si. I'm calling you from Spain!"

Si went along with the joke. He shouted back, "Seen any bullfights lately, Karl?"

"Si, listen to me. Please listen carefully," Karl said, and explained the importance of Carol Harris writing a letter to Francisco Franco, to be sent with her photo.

So Carol wrote the letter—glamorous photograph enclosed— which was promptly delivered to General Franco at the Nationalists' temporary capital at Burgos. Carol's plea did impress the Generalissimo, not enough to grant the clemency she asked but enough for him to invite her to Spain to visit him personally, and to see her husband before the sentence was carried out.

General Franco's romanticism notwithstanding, the U.S. government forbade travel in Spain to all American citizens. Si, however, was determined that Carol Harris would go to Spain even if he had to carry her there on his back.

It required considerable swallowing of pride on Si's part, for he was forced to seek the assistance of newly elected U.S. Senator Morris Tannen. Morris bullied the State Department into issuing Si a diplomatic passport that allowed its bearer to be accompanied by one staff member, in this instance a secretary, Carol Harris.

Carol called Si's attention to Bill Macon. "That man's coming over here," she said. "Do you know him?"

Si not only recognized Bill Macon, but saw in the war correspondent a way to convince Francisco Franco to spare Duke Harris's life. The Generalissimo aspired to sell the world an image of himself as a leader of vision and compassion. If the whole world knew how he had heeded the plea of a beautiful young American woman to spare the life of the man she loved, Francisco Franco would be universally admired.

Who better to tell that story to the world than a writer of the stature of William H. Macon?

Si introduced Carol to Bill Macon. "She's Duke Harris's wife," Si said. "You remember Duke? You met him in Hankow."

"Sure, I remember him," Macon said. "And he's here in Spain, isn't he, along with the rest of your fliers?" He banged his fist elatedly into his palm. "I knew it!"

"Look, Mr. Macon, I'll give you the scoop of your life," Si said. "But I need a favor."

"Name it."

"We want to get down to Cádiz—"

"—from here?" Macon said.

"That's right, from here."

"They've sealed the lines up tight," Macon said. "On both sides, it's shoot first, ask questions later."

"Come on, you must know the right people to see," Si said. "Or the right buttons to push."

"Am I supposed to ask why?" Macon asked. "Or do I wait until you're ready to tell me? That's the big scoop, isn't it? The why?"

"That's it," Si said. "All right, so can you or can't you help us?"

The "us" seemed to hover in the air as Macon's eyes devoured Carol. Si could read Bill Macon's mind, more accurately, Bill Macon's dirty mind. If only it were true.

It might have happened, it could have happened, but did not.

By mutual agreement, Si and Carol's, nothing happened. Neither ever articulated this pact, each just implicitly accepted it. Not since Andrée had Si been so drawn to a woman, and two weeks of close, constant contact with Carol had nearly driven him crazy. Airplanes, trains, buses. Meals together, drinks, talks, laughs and, most frustrating of all, forty-three hours in each other's company aboard that most luxurious of flying boats the *Dixie Clipper*.

The giant seventy-passenger Boeing 314 featured a convenient rear stateroom called the Honeymoon Suite. Even more conveniently, on Si and Carol's flight—a trial flight of Pan American's scheduled New York–Marseilles service—the compartment was unbooked. It remained unbooked. Now was not the time, Si had told himself. Later maybe, when all this was over, after Duke was pardoned and Carol obtained her divorce.

". . . probably can do something for you," Bill Macon was saying. "It might cost a few dollars."

"Whatever it takes," Si said.

"But I'll have to tag along," Macon said. "I mean, all the way to Cádiz."

"Sure, how else would you get the story?" Si said.

Later, he claimed he could actually see the story forming in Bill Macon's mind, the heart-warming, tear-soaked saga of the beautiful, sophisticated New York and Hollywood actress-model journeying six thousand perilous miles to visit the supreme commander of an army at war to plead for the life of her husband.

William Macon's story of how Carol Harris met and charmed the Spanish general ran for three consecutive installments in the *Sun* and was picked up by the London *Times* and *France Soir*, and might or might not have been what motivated Francisco Franco to pardon Duke Harris. Certainly, the Generalissimo was lauded as a humanitarian, and a romantic. Best of all, the story had a happy ending.

Franco pardoned Duke on condition that Duke leave Spain and never return. Duke and Carol departed together, arm in arm, a pair of star-crossed lovers. The story ended there, a perfect ending, but only because Bill Macon omitted the final chapter, the account of Carol's divorce in Reno, Nevada, after the required six weeks residency.

There was another angle to the story, which Bill Macon never knew. This other angle, while certainly not a love story, might have been sold to Hollywood as the aviation epic of the decade. A thumbnail synopsis of the movie could well have read, "Twenty years after the Great War, former aces face each other in the blood-drenched skies over Spain!"

4.

The taproom of El Cortés, Cádiz's finest hotel, was crowded with uniformed Spanish Nationalist officers and civilian-clad Italian technicians of the Regia Aeronáutica. On a small dais near the American-style bar a slick-haired young man played a guitar and occasionally sang, his tenor voice all but lost in the clamor.

Adjoining the bar, separated from the taproom by a narrow service window, was a small private lounge. From the bar, through the serving aperture, one could see into the lounge, where an attractive blond woman and three men, all civilians, were seated in tufted leather armchairs arranged around a large tile-topped coffee table.

Although the four conversed in English, except for a brief appraising glance at the woman, no one paid them any special attention. To be sure, no one suspected that the youngest of the men was a former enemy pilot.

Karl had returned to Cádiz to say goodbye to Duke and, more from curiosity than anything else, to see Si. Their meeting was not at all unpleasant, in fact was almost like old times. Si was enjoying himself so much that only when Duke and Carol announced they were going to bed did he realize it was past midnight.

". . . sure, see you in the morning," he said, annoyed at being interrupted in the middle of the story of the earphones that had jammed the 660's control column.

"No later than six, Si," Carol said.

"Make it quarter to," said Duke. "That's one plane I damn well mean to be on!" He and Carol, with Si, were scheduled to depart for Lisbon on a 7:00 A.M. Lufthansa flight.

"Karl, thank you for everything," Carol said. She kissed Karl on the cheek and hurried away.

Duke and Karl shook hands, then embraced affectionately, and Duke followed Carol out of the lounge. Karl said to Si, "It just occurred to me: she's your type."

"I know you won't believe this," Si said, "but I never gave it a second thought."

"You're right, I don't believe it," Karl said. He signaled the waiter for another round. "But I also don't think you ever had a chance with her."

"You're probably right about that, too," Si said, and completed the earphone anecdote. He hardly paused for breath as he continued, "Tell me about this KE-1 of yours."

"Tell me about the Hunter," said Karl.

"You first," said Si.

"We'll toss a coin," said Karl.

They tossed. Si lost. He told Karl about the Hunter. Karl told Si about the KE-1. They sounded like two men bragging about favorite children. Shortly after one, Si realized that if he was to be up before six he needed some sleep. He pushed himself up out of the chair. The room began spinning.

"Karl, are you as drunk as I am?"

"Drunker," said Karl.

Si studied Karl solemnly. "Yeah, I guess you are drunker." He flipped Karl a snappy salute and started to leave. "I'll see you around sometime."

Karl said, "There's one way to find out which airplane is best."

Si, whose back was to Karl, froze. Karl's words danced before his eyes, each word as crisp and clear as though displayed on an illuminated sign. It sobered him instantly. He turned. He faced Karl.

Karl said, "We finish what we started back in Monmedy. You remember Monmedy?"

Si saw that Karl, too, was absolutely sober. Karl's eyes were cold and hard, the same eyes Si had seen over Monmedy that morning in 1918, the eyes of a hunter stalking his prey.

"At Monmedy, we were trying to kill each other."

Karl's face was bland, but his eyes shone colder and harder than before. "It will settle the question once and for all," he said.

"What question?"

"Of which airplane is the better."

Just then the waiter came over to ask if they wanted another drink. The waiter's voice startled Si. In the few seconds since Karl had issued the challenge, it seemed as if all sound and movement in the room had suddenly ceased.

Si told the waiter to bring them two more, and said to Karl, "Karl, you don't care which fucking airplane is better, you want to prove which *man* is better!"

"It's all one and the same, isn't it?" Karl said.

"You must think that because you've been flying and I haven't, you'll have an advantage," Si said. "Is that why you're so anxious for this?"

"I never considered it," Karl said. "I'm sorry. I withdraw the challenge."

Si said, "Duke told me you shot down six Loyalists."

"Seven," Karl said. "I got two I-16s in one day."

"He said you got a couple of heavies, too."

"They were Potezes," Karl said. "Twin-engined. Very slow. The stupid bastards didn't even jettison their bombs when we attacked."

"You must have enjoyed that."

"As a matter of fact, I felt quite bad about it. But you're right, it wouldn't be a fair match between us. I withdraw."

Si said, "I'll need a few hours' transition time. They put a whole new weapons system on these Spanish Hunters. I have a friend, Colonel Liano. I'm sure he'll give me some time in a Hunter."

"We'll need to set a time and place, and rules of engagement."

The waiter brought the fresh drinks. Neither Karl nor Si touched his glass. When the waiter left, Si said, "Whatever you arrange, I'll go along with."

"The Hunters are based in Valencia. That's four hundred miles from here. How will you get through the lines?"

"Something tells me you can fix that," Si said.

Through the Hunter's windscreen the high early-morning sun on the surface of the Guadiana River reflected glaringly back into Si's eyes. The river, twelve thousand feet below and thirty miles to the southwest, snaked in a nearly perfect U around the city of Valdepeñas, which lay like a white bowl in a broad green valley surrounded by high hills, and was located almost in the center of the part of Spain still in Loyalist hands.

Other than the area immediately around Barcelona, this increasingly shrinking patch of territory in the southeast corner of the country was all that remained of the Republic. Karl had selected the Valdepeñas sector for the rendezvous because military activity was all but nonexistent there. The appearance of aircraft from either side was unlikely.

Si looked around the clear cloudless sky for any sign of Karl, who was to approach from the mountains, ten miles south. They were to meet over the sparsely populated plateau twenty miles west of the city. He nudged the Hunter's throttle. The blunt-nosed little airplane accelerated upward. For the Spanish version of the Hunter, Charlie Jensen had developed his most powerful engine yet, a 1250-horsepower monster. Charlie called the airplane a flying engine. He was right.

Si reached for the earphones hanging on a hook below the instrument panel, then remembered that both the radio and the antenna had been removed for repairs and never reinstalled. It made no difference; what the hell could he and Karl talk about, anyway? Wish each other luck?

Luck helped, but firepower was more important. He switched on the electric gunsight, pushed in the gun-charging levers, and, in a single upward sweep of the flat of his hand, flicked on the four gun-arming toggles. He squeezed the gun trigger on the stick. All four .30 calibers hammered rhythmically. Si marveled at the airplane's stability: other than a slight tremor the Hunter hardly vibrated with the guns firing. It had cost him a $100 bill plus trading his Gruen wristwatch for a dollar Ingersoll pocket watch to make sure the four Brownings were fully loaded. He hoped the Spanish ordnance sergeant at Valencia enjoyed the watch and used the money wisely. He fired another burst of five rounds. The barrels, open now with the muzzle tape shot off, whistled hollowly in the wind.

Si had waited four days in Valencia for Karl to send word to him. Four days to reconsider, to analyze motives, to decide whether this so-called duel was madness, childishness, egocentricity, or just plain foolishness.

He had used the time in Valencia well, logging enough Hunter hours to prepare himself adequately. And practice was what he needed, no easy task, not with gasoline in such short supply and Colonel Liano increasingly suspicious. It was one thing for Si to request some brief flight time simply to keep his hand in, quite another to remove an airplane from active patrol duty for what appeared to be Simon Conway's daily personal pleasure.

But Colonel Liano made a Hunter available. It was not that difficult, not after Si committed himself to ship twelve more Hunters to the Loyalist air force. If a Loyalist air force still existed by the time the promised Hunters were ready for service. Barcelona's fall was imminent, and the fulfillment of Franco's vow to spend New Year's Eve in Madrid seemed more than probable.

The sight of a distant speck in the sky to the south sent Si's heart racing. Not once since the challenge was issued had he considered backing down. He was crazier than Karl. Two crazy old men determined to prove which of them was the better.

It reminded him of his conversation with Meg the night he told her he was going to Spain. They had just gone to bed. Meg had shut off the bed lamp and started to turn over. "Listen, I've decided I have to do something for Duke," he said, and went on to explain that he believed himself responsible for Duke's situation. He felt obligated to do what he could to save the man's life.

"Very noble," Meg had said. "Especially when you'll be traveling with that pretty young wife of his."

"She's got nothing to do with it," Si had replied and, as though to prove it, kissed her and proceeded to make love to her. A quite satisfactory performance, as he recalled, although he could not help wondering now, as then, if it had not been to prove his denial of interest in Carol more to himself than to Meg.

The distant speck became an oncoming airplane that rolled out of its turn in a wide sweeping curve, giving Si a full profile view of the rapier-slender fuselage. The KE-1, painted entirely black but for the white cowling and silver propeller spinner, bore no identification other than the white Nationalist X on the rudder.

It was Si's first glimpse ever of a KE-1 in flight. It was a beautiful machine, graceful in appearance, in contrast to the Hunter's solid, sturdy configuration. Comparing a ballerina to a stevedore. But the Hunter was designed for power: the airframe had been built around its huge radial engine.

A similar thought ran through Karl's mind. He recognized, and appreciated, the brute strength of the Hunter. Now, seeing the airplane, Karl realized that Simon Conway had created it after all, a reflection of his own personality. Naked force and raw power. Karl had expected no less. He fired a short burst from the cowl guns to clear them, then racked the KE-1 around and came straight on at the Hunter. The Hunter's big round nose filled Karl's whole windscreen, and then was gone.

Behind him, Karl heard the thud of machine guns. In his rearview mirror he saw the winking yellow of Si's four .30 calibers. He pumped the stick, stood on the right rudder and flicked the KE-1 into a porpoising, skidding, violent snap roll to the right. The Hunter was five hundred feet below, climbing back toward him.

The son of a bitch could still fly, and the airplane was good. But Karl was better and always had been, and the KE-1 was better than both of them. He knew the Hunter's radio was inoperative: no antenna wire was visible on the radio mast just behind the Hunter's cockpit. He would have liked to ask Si two simple questions.

Si, do you have a parachute?

Si, did you make out your will?

In the Hunter, Si was not thinking about parachutes or wills, only that he had committed a stupid, almost amateurish error. He had underestimated the KE-1's speed and not compensated with his own. By the time he had fired, Karl was out of range. If he had taken proper advantage of the Hunter's power, its four guns might have sawed the KE-1 in half. Might have sawed Karl in half, too, which was not the object of this exercise. Or was it?

As Si lowered the Hunter's nose and punched the throttle forward, Karl stood the KE-1 on its left wing and hauled it into a tight left turn. Si pulled the stick back into his stomach and, trading speed for altitude, sent the Hunter into a nearly vertical zoom climb. He knew he could not turn with the KE-1. But he could fight vertically, with diving attacks and zoom recoveries back to altitude. Below, on the right, the KE-1 shot past like a blurred black line drawn in the sky.

Si rolled over and came out straight and level. Karl was a quarter mile below, passing astern in a left turn, swinging around to the south. Si rolled to the right and hung the Hunter on its nose. His left wing momentarily obscured his view of the KE-1, but he was confident that Karl would continue turning to put the sun at his back and remain below the Hunter. Si was wrong.

When he brought the Hunter back straight and level, the KE-1 was heading directly toward him. A small gray puff of smoke erupted from the silver nose spinner, and then another, and yet another. The Kraut bastard was firing the 20mm cannon! The shells rocketed past overhead, so close Si could smell their burning phosphorus. He jinked right, then left, then right again. The KE-1 mimicked his every move, but in an instant had streaked past, overhead.

Although Si's outside air temperature gauge read minus twelve degrees, under the leather jacket his shirt was soaked with sweat. His parachute pack cushioned his back from the constant pounding against the seat in the abrupt turns, but his arms and legs ached, and his gloved fingers curled around the control stick felt numb. He knew Karl was faring better, not because of a superior airplane—Si was satisfied that the KE-1 and Hunter were reasonably well matched— but because Karl had been flying combat and Si had not. A lucky, point-blank shot a year and a half ago at a lumbering Jap bomber hardly constituted combat experience.

Karl was thinking the same thought. He should have given Si a handicap, as in a golf match. He watched the Hunter's nose drop as both airplanes commenced turning toward each other again. He knew now where and how to defeat the Hunter: finesse Si into committing to a steep trajectory with no maneuver options, then pick him apart at long range with the cannon.

Si was halfway down the slide into his approach when Karl abruptly tightened the radius of his own left turn. To retain the KE-1 in his sights, Si was forced to steepen the Hunter's dive. Karl, already applying almost full back pressure to hold the turn, suddenly lowered the KE-1's nose and rolled in the opposite direction. The airplane virtually stopped in midair. The G forces slammed Karl forward into his shoulder harness and momentarily blacked him out. An instant later, when his vision was restored, the Hunter lay dead ahead, one hundred yards off the KE-1's nose, framed like a painting in Karl's gunsight.

Si felt the Hunter shudder as 7.92mm slugs pounded into the airplane's horizontal stabilizers, fuselage, and wings; and then he

heard the hard thump of Karl's thin-walled cannon shells. Bits and
pieces of the Hunter's fuselage began flying off. Fist-sized holes appeared in both wings. The right wingtip vanished. Part of the aileron
flapped uselessly against the shredded metal of the wingtip.

Si put the nose straight down and pushed the throttle wide open.
The jagged chunks of metal trailing from the fuselage and wings
shrieked in the slipstream. He knew Karl was close behind and only
hoped the Hunter could outdive the KE-1.

But the Daimler-Benz's direct fuel injection system allowed Karl
to drop the KE-1's nose in a negative-G pushover that would have
stopped the engine of any other fighter. The KE-1 accelerated instantly, guns firing, scoring more hits on the Hunter.

To spoil Karl's tracking—and hoping the Hunter stayed in one
piece—Si threw the airplane into a clockwise vertical spiral. He caught
sight of the KE-1 barrel-rolling behind him, opposite to his turn. Si
knew that Karl would immediately be back on his tail, and that he
needed all his strength just to move the controls. His whole body felt
numb from the battering it had taken. And there was more to come.

In the rearview mirror Si saw the silver propeller spinner closing
like a relentless, pursuing cannon shell. He reversed sharply up and
to the left. Karl counterturned, but the Hunter slid from left to right
above and ahead of the KE-1, too fast and at too acute an angle to
provide Karl a shot.

But the altimeter was against Si. The diving, twisting airplanes
were passing through six thousand feet, now five thousand. The
Hunter was in danger of running out of sky. This would cost Si the
option of the vertical, making him an easy target in a turning contest
on the deck. Karl needed only to keep on top of the Hunter so Si
could not escape back up to altitude.

And then, almost unexpectedly, Karl had him. The Hunter's
entire forward section was in Karl's gunsight. He fired, 7.92mm guns
and the cannon. The first explosion rocked the Hunter from side to
side and nearly flung Si from the seat. More explosions followed,
carrying away engine cylinder heads, seals, oil lines, pieces of electrical
harness. The throttle was jarred from Si's left hand with the force of
a sledgehammer blow.

The big Jensen sputtered, crackled, and intermittently cut out
altogether. Thunderous detonations shook the whole airframe. The
needle of every temperature and pressure gauge was in the red,
pegged against the stop bar. Oil streaked the Hunter's windscreen.
Yet another explosion filled the cockpit with smoke.

In the KE-1, Karl tapped the left rudder pedal and closed to
within a hundred yards astern of the limping Hunter. Karl throttled

back, offsetting himself slightly starboard to avoid the smoke and debris trailing from the Hunter. Si looked as though he was going down. Karl felt no elation but rather a sense of guilt. It had not been a fair fight.

Si was thinking the same thing, but with no anger, only chagrin. He had only himself to blame for being suckered into the duel. It was like entering a home-run contest with Joe Dimaggio or Mel Ott, or getting into the ring with Joe Louis.

He had retarded power and reduced manifold pressure, and cracked open the canopy to clear the smoke. At thirty inches of manifold pressure his IAS indicator read 254, which was as fast as he dared to push her. It stopped the detonations and brought the cylinder-head temperature back below the red. Although she was vibrating from nose to tail, the Hunter—and Charlie Jensen's engine —had absorbed all that punishment and was still flyable.

On his left, the KE-1 suddenly appeared. Karl had slid up beside him to look him over, astonished that the Hunter was still in the air. It was a smoking, leaking, metal-shredded wreck. Si waved to signal that he was unhurt. Karl nodded curtly, and then pointed ahead and downward. For a moment Si did not understand. Then, glancing at the compass, he realized they were headed southwest. Karl wanted him to land at a Nationalist field, like a trophy bagged in a hunt. Si shook his head, no.

Karl rolled to the left, climbed shallowly up and around, and came back in behind Si. Karl centered his target pipper on the Hunter's left wingtip, tapped left rudder, and fired three cannon shells past the Hunter's wing.

Si gripped the Hunter's bucking control stick and waited for the KE-1 to come alongside again. They studied each other across the forty feet separating the Hunter's left wingtip and the KE-1's right wingtip. Again, Karl pointed down, and this time he lowered his wheels and flaps. Si knew that despite the Hunter's damage the Jensen had some power left, perhaps as much as 70 percent, which might give him a few miles on Karl but not nearly enough for a sustained run. Karl would eventually catch him and either shoot him out of the sky or the airplane would simply break apart.

"All right, you son of a bitch, I'll have to do what you want!" Si shouted, knowing of course that it was impossible for Karl to hear. He raised his hands in surrender.

Karl acknowledged with another curt nod and throttled back to slip in directly behind the Hunter. To match the crippled Hunter's slow speed, Karl had to keep the KE-1's gear and flaps down. Si had no idea where Karl intended to land. He hoped it was not the Condor

Legion base at Seville. He doubted the Hunter would hold together that long.

In the rearview mirror he saw the KE-1 close behind. He could just imagine the expression on Karl's face. So smug, so pleased, so cocksure of himself. And complacent, Si thought. The word fluttered in the air above the mirror and then, letter by letter, seemed to print itself across the mirror in large black capital letters, C O M P L A C E N T.

The letters vanished in the mirror, replaced again by the KE-1. With its wheels and flaps down it had slowed to Si's speed of 140 knots. It resembled a long-legged bird awkwardly fluttering in to land. A bird.

A sitting duck.

Si slammed the Hunter's throttle through the emergency boost seals and the engine responded with all its remaining power. Si knew the sudden surge might blow the cylinder heads that were still intact, might even rip the entire engine loose from its mounting or tear the airframe to pieces. But he also knew it was his last and only chance.

Vibrating, detonating, gushing smoke, the Hunter swung around in a savage ninety-degree left turn. Karl was helpless. The Hunter, gunports flashing, was broadside on Karl's left almost before he could flip the gear lever and ram the throttle open.

The instrument panel disintegrated before Karl's eyes. Shards of glass stabbed into the lower half of his face and his hands. The entire cockpit canopy flew off. Bullets tore into the KE-1's engine, drenching Karl's legs and shoes with oil and coolant.

Through the open canopy the wind blasted into Karl's face. He hunched down behind the windscreen. He could clearly hear the rasping, choppy cough of the Hunter's faltering engine as Si swept past the KE-1's starboard side and banked around to come back in for another attack from above and behind.

Si did not know how badly he had hurt the KE-1, or if the burst had hit Karl. The KE-1, gear and flaps up now but propeller wind-milling, was already more than a thousand feet below the Hunter. Si throttled back to stop the Hunter's detonations. He marveled again at the engine's endurance.

So did Karl, cursing himself for underestimating not only Simon Conway's skill, but Charlie Jensen's engine. Grimly, he surveyed the KE-1's smashed instrument panel. The compass and a few engine instruments, although splattered with red hydraulic fluid, were intact. Karl arched his neck back and stared up at the Hunter hovering five hundred feet above. Even at half power Si had closed rapidly on the windmilling KE-1.

On the instrument panel Karl's gun-arming light was now only an empty, jagged hole. Karl pressed the machine-gun button. The guns fired, but the recoil transmitted from the stick handle into his gloved fingers felt soft, almost spongelike. The glove itself felt spongy. He realized that the red fluid dripping from the windscreen and instrument panel was not hydraulic fluid.

It was blood. From his face and neck. He was soaked in blood. Superficial but painful wounds, as though someone had scraped the flesh raw with a steel brush. He raised his right hand to eye level. Blood from the glove cascaded down onto his lap. Now he became aware of pain, radiating like an electric shock from his fingers all the way to the elbow. A metal fragment from the instrument panel had sheared razorlike into the glove and neatly sliced a layer of flesh off the back of his hand.

The Hunter drew abreast. Si's face was expressionless. Karl cursed himself again, this time for not finishing the Hunter when he had the chance, leaving Si no choice but to abandon the airplane and bail out. Instead, he had foolishly decided to force the Hunter down, capture the machine intact, further humiliating Simon Conway.

As though reminding Karl of who had been humiliated, a puff of dark greasy smoke, spewing from the KE-1's engine, became a cloud of black smoke that swirled blindingly into the windscreen and into the exposed cockpit. Karl nosed the KE-1 into a shallow dive.

Si followed Karl down. He watched the black smoke pour past the KE-1's white cowling. He moved in closer, so close he clearly saw the smoke eddying around Karl's helmeted head and shoulders in two separate streams.

Now, from a hundred yards, in the glowing red light in the center of Si's gunsight the KE-1 was tantalizingly large and unmoving. Si's finger tensed on the gun trigger. In his mind he saw the yellow tracer lines from his guns converging on the shattered cockpit, tearing into Karl's body. In his mind he saw the body slump forward, the airplane nose over. In his mind he saw it hurtle into the ground and explode in a ball of orange flame.

The KE-1's cockpit filled the gunsight's entire frame. Si relaxed his grip on the gun trigger. Killing Karl would prove nothing and accomplish less. A victory over a cripple.

No victory, an execution.

He snapped the security cover back over the trigger guard. To hell with it. To hell with Karl Eisler. To hell with everything. He gingerly increased power and crept alongside the KE-1, his smashed right wingtip so close to the KE-1's left wing that he thought they might collide.

Si raised his hand in a mock salute. Karl's face was wrinkled with surprise and skepticism, as though he did not quite believe that Si was disengaging, and that any moment he expected Si to finish him off. He did not return Si's salute. They gazed at each other another moment before Si banked sharply away and raced off. He steered left until the compass needle swung around to 45, then he leveled out and headed for Valencia.

The day Si boarded a New York–bound Pan American clipper at Lisbon was the same day Barcelona fell. He wondered if Karl was marching in the victory parade. Probably not. In Cádiz, Karl had said that Göring wanted him to return to Germany to work on a new form of turbine propulsion.

"Picture a balloon," Karl said. "You blow it up and then, with the valve still open, you toss it into the air. The air escaping propels the balloon, pushes it forward."

Si had said, "The British are working on it, too."

"We'll have it before they do," Karl said.

Maybe you'll have it before they do, Si thought now, maybe not. Maybe I'll have a jet before all of you. He'd talk to Charlie Jensen about it. The idea of a jet engine intrigued him. You didn't have to be an MIT graduate to understand the possibilities.

And there was money available to finance jet experimentation. Si removed a cablegram from his pocket. It had been awaiting him in Lisbon. From Phil Granger: NAVY TRIPLING ORDER FOR DEFENDER.

The Defender, the PB-7, a midwinged, twin-engined long-range patrol plane, had been designed by Pete Dagget for the U.S. Navy and Coast Guard. The navy had initially ordered eight. Now, with an order for twenty-four, the project was automatically in profit.

Yes, things were going well. Eddie Rickenbacker had asked Conair to develop the 665, a forty-passenger, four-engined transport with a pressurized cabin. *Forty* passengers, seven more than Boeing's new pressurized 307, the Stratoliner. Equally gratifying was word from the Spanish Nationalists that the remaining Eagle pilots would be repatriated to the United States.

Everything was falling into place, especially when the Clipper reached its eight-thousand-foot cruising altitude and an attractive red-headed woman settled into a seat on the aisle opposite Si. She looked vaguely familiar. Drinks had just been served. Si raised his martini glass to her. She smiled politely at him.

"I've seen your picture in the newspapers," she said. "Something to do with aviation. You're not the one who took off for California and ended up in Ireland?"

"Corrigan, you mean?" Si said. " 'Wrong-Way Corrigan.' No, that's not me." He raised his glass to her again and drank. "I'm the guy that flew around the world in three and a half days. Howard Hughes is the name."

"No, I know Howard. It was something about Spain." She snapped her fingers. "Conroy. No, Conway! Conway, that's it! Simon Conway."

"You got me," he said. She might have been in her late thirties, well built with very brown, very discerning eyes. She wore a blue knit dress that did wonders for her breasts and that marvelous, slightly rounded little belly bulge. He remembered young Russ Lewis, one of the Eagle pilots, insisting that on women between the ages of thirty and forty those little stomachs came from continual, enthusiastic fucking.

". . . and I'm going to California, too," she was saying. "They've decided I'm finally good enough to make a movie." She extended her hand. "I'm Irene Sinclair."

Now he recognized her, Irene Sinclair, a well-known Broadway actress. They shook hands and began chatting. Two martinis later she and Si were sitting together, studying the dinner menu. Si ordered the Steward's Special, Lobster Thermidor. Irene Sinclair decided on a grilled New York steak.

The Boeing 314 Clipper, plowing along at 150 mph at eight thousand feet, was as stable as a railway dining car, and you dined at real tables in a spacious dining room. Si and Irene Sinclair remained at the table long after dinner, sipping brandy and talking.

They landed at Horta, in the Azores, for refueling and then took off again on the long fifteen-hour flight to New York. This time Si promised himself to make use of the airplane's Honeymoon Suite. Irene Sinclair, in fact, had herself suggested it. Nothing old-fashioned about that lady and, clearly, she had had previous experience with this unique feature of the Clipper.

"I'm a charter member of the Mile-High Club," she said. "Give me ten minutes." She gathered up her suede overnight bag and cosmetic case and headed for the suite in the rear cabin.

In the main cabin, the stewards had already made up the Pullman-style bunks. Most of the passengers were asleep, or at least trying to sleep. Si remained in the dining room, impatiently glancing at the new Rolex wristwatch he bought in Lisbon to replace the one he had donated to the Valencia ordnance sergeant.

"Mr. Conway . . . ?" It was Mac, the steward, a grizzled, middle-aged man with a thick Scottish burr. Mac held a small white envelope: PAN AMERICAN AIRWAYS SYSTEM RADIOGRAM.

"A man can't hide anywhere these days," Si said good-naturedly. He took the envelope and started opening it.

"Yes, I'm afraid that's so, sir," Mac said. Something in the somber tone of the man's voice alerted Si. He tore open the envelope and removed the radiogram. The message was neatly typewritten in capital letters.

SIMON CONWAY PAX PAN AM DIXIE CLIPPER EN ROUTE PT WASH-INGTON 26 JAN 1939

REGRET INFORM YOU DEATH OF FRANK CONWAY STOP AUTOMO-BILE ACCIDENT STOP FUNERAL IMMEDIATELY UPON YOUR AR-RIVAL STOP SIGNED PHILIP GRANGER STOP

"I'm so terribly sorry, Mr. Conway," Mac said.

Si looked at the steward but saw nothing. He heard nothing, only the smooth steady beat of the four engines. He did not know how long he sat there, the paper clenched in his hand, nor did he recall Irene Sinclair coming out to see why he had not joined her. All he thought about was the end of the dream, the great dream of his son making the Conway name the greatest name in the aviation industry. Frank was gone, never to return, and no one could replace him.

He completely forgot the existence of his other son, Richard.

PART FOUR

RICHARD

16

Everybody said if you were old enough to fight and die for your country, you should be old enough to buy a drink. The club-car waiter apparently agreed. He had responded to Richard's order for a beer with a fast "Yes sir, general, one Pabst coming right up."

Every seat of the club car was occupied and people were three deep at the tiny bar, the majority of them servicemen, mostly officers. One, a navy two-striper with a submariner's badge and a row of impressive ribbons, clearly resented Richard's beating him to the only empty parlor chair. An AAF corporal should know enough to offer his seat to a navy officer.

The sounds of voices, ice clinking in glasses, and laughter blended with the metallic clickety-clack of the train's wheels on the tracks. Richard closed his eyes and listened. The hollow rushing sound of roaring air was like holding a seashell to your ear. Bits and pieces of conversation drifted into the seashell.

". . . you hear about Patton? They say he makes his guys wear long sleeves and field jackets even in the middle of the desert! Claims it makes them tougher soldiers. Jesus!"

". . . this Nazi, Rommel, he's on the run."

". . . so he says, 'Two more months, we'll be in Rome.' I said, 'Two more months, we won't even be in Rome, *New York*!'"

". . . you didn't hear about it? Where the hell you been, for Christ's sake? That's right, Eddie Rickenbacker, can you imagine, him of all people! After all he's been through, he's on this B-17 on an inspection trip to the Pacific and the plane goes down smack in the middle of it. But after three weeks drifting in a raft, they find him! And alive!

They made it by eating raw fish and raw birds, the poor sons of bitches!"

Richard opened his eyes. The navy two-striper continued to regard him glumly. Richard swung his chair around to the picture window. The New Mexico flatlands, vast and endless during the day, seemed not at all foreboding now at twilight. The setting sun cast soft golden hues across the desert. Shadows were beginning to form behind rocks and small bushes. It all looked quiet and peaceful.

It would be far from quiet and peaceful when he arrived home. Janet had seen to that. Richard could hear his father's voice as clearly as he had heard it on the telephone last week when he called collect from a phone booth in the PX. Si, in his office at the factory, had answered the phone himself.

The operator had said, "I have a collect call from Smyrna Army Air Field, Tennessee. Will you accept charges?"

"Yes, all right, put him on," Si had replied, and without an instant's hesitation continued, "Richard, have you reapplied for cadets?"

"Dad, I called to tell you that I've graduated the advanced radio operator's course here. I'm coming home on a ten-day furlough before they ship me overseas."

"What about cadets?"

"I haven't reapplied."

"You told me you would!"

So Richard had to remind Si that twice in as many months he had reapplied and both times failed the initial aviation cadet physical, for the same reason: 20/50 visual acuity in the right eye, 20/70 in the left. Well, goddammit, give it one more shot, Si said, and then told him about Janet.

Janet. It was hard to believe. He shook his head and chuckled and, behind him, heard a deep baritone voice ask, "What the hell is so funny?"

Richard swiveled the chair around to see a marine captain looking down at him. "Nothing, sir, I—" Richard stared at the captain. "I don't believe it! Paul Tannen!"

The marine, a tall, solid young man whose gray-green uniform tunic was crowded with two rows of real service ribbons, including a Purple Heart, stuck out his hand.

"I'll say it first," he said. "Small world."

"I heard you were on Guadalcanal," Richard said as they shook hands. He pointed at Paul's ribbons. "You did okay, I see."

"Everybody did," Paul said. "They gave you a medal for just stepping off the boat. Never mind that crap. You're on your way home?"

"Ten-day furlough," said Richard.

Paul, too, was on his way home, but only because "home" happened to be San Diego, near Camp Pendleton, his new assignment. Paul suggested they find a quieter place to chat. They left the club car and went out to the platform between cars.

Richard said, "You asked me what was so funny. Well, you won't believe this, but my sister just ran off and got married!"

"Janet? Little Janet, married?"

" 'Little Janet' is nearly as tall as me," Richard said. "And everybody says she's the spitting image of Linda Darnell. In fact, she's been offered a movie contract. RKO, I think. My father said if she even thought twice about it, he'd send one of his bombers over the studio and blast it to bits!"

"I don't blame him," Paul said. "She's still a baby."

"She just turned seventeen," Richard said. "But get this: the guy she married is at least thirty. An RAF pilot. He was over here talking to my father about a new attack plane. Janet sees him one night at the house. Two days later they drive to Las Vegas and get married."

"Your folks must be fit to be tied."

"My mother raised hell about it, but my father thinks it's great," Richard said. "Of course, the fact that this guy is a genuine hero—in the Battle of Britain he knocked down something like a dozen Germans—had something to do with it."

"Stand still a second," Paul said. He stepped back a few paces and studied Richard. "Talk about 'spitting images'—my God, you're your father's twin!"

"That's what everybody says," Richard said. "I think that's maybe why he's so disappointed I couldn't make cadets, and that I'm not an officer."

"Believe me, you're better off as a GI," Paul said, and went on to tell him about his own parents. Morris had just been elected to a second term in the U.S. Senate. Ruth was busy with her Red Cross work.

By the time they reached Los Angeles and parted—Paul had to catch another train for San Diego—Paul's stories of combat in the Pacific had convinced Richard that he indeed might be better off as an air force GI.

A Conair company car met Richard at Union Station. The driver, an elderly Mexican whom Richard remembered as a part-time handyman, said that Si's instructions were to take Richard straight to Conway Field. Si wanted to see his only son the moment he arrived.

"Was that how he said it, 'only son'?" Richard asked.

"That is exactly what he said," the driver said. " 'I want to see my only son.' "

They were driving through downtown Los Angeles. The department-store windows and the big red electric trolley cars were decorated with Christmas lights and "Merry Xmas" signs. The streets bustled with holiday shoppers. If not for all the uniforms and the A, B, or C gasoline stickers on automobile windshields, you would never know there was a war on.

The driver was saying something about the Christmas lights being on only for a few minutes at twilight because the city was supposed to be blacked out, but Richard was not listening. He was thinking about being Si's "only son."

He would never forget the day four years ago when Si returned from Spain. Si had gone directly from the airport to the Pierce Bros. Mortuary on Montana Avenue in Santa Monica. Frank had been driving a Ford convertible that belonged to a Palisades Academy classmate and smashed it into a tree near the Beverly Hills Hotel. The three people with Frank, the classmate and two older girls, were seriously injured but recovered. Frank and his friend had picked up the girls in Hollywood and were taking them out to the beach. They said Frank was driving ninety miles an hour on Sunset Boulevard. He was so drunk he thought the park opposite the hotel was the beach.

When Si finally arrived home after seeing Frank at the mortuary, he had tried to embrace Meg but she pushed him away.

"Are you satisfied now, Si?" she had asked. "Your son grew up as you wanted him to, in your image. He wanted to emulate his dashing, glamorous, world-famous father! Flying, racing cars, chasing women—oh, yes, Si, even at fifteen he did that! A fifteen-year-old boy with the morals of a thirty-five-year-old man. No, the morals of his forty-four-year-old father! It had to end up this way! I always knew it would!"

When Richard saw the expression of unexpected, abject pain on Si's face, he wanted to cry, the first time throughout that whole week he had wanted to cry. And not for his dead brother, but for his grief-stricken father.

That day, Si had looked at Richard, ruffled his hair, and said, "You're my only son now. You'll carry on for Frank."

"I will, Dad," Richard had said. "I promise you, I will."

But Richard was not Frank and never would or could be. He loved his father and would do anything to please him, even learn to fly. At eighteen, after a year at Harvard, and with parental permission, he enlisted in the United States Army Air Force as a flying cadet.

Aware of his poor eyesight, he purchased a standard optometrist's eye chart and memorized the bottom, crucial lines. It did not help. The army optometrist, recognizing the tactic, substituted an entirely different chart.

At the time there were no openings for bombardier or navigator cadet training, and Richard did not want to ask Si to pull strings on his behalf. He requested radio operator's school, vowing to become the best radio operator in the air force. Ironically, by graduating at the top of his class he automatically disqualified himself as a B-17 or B-24 radio operator-gunner. Radio operators with the most potential were immediately assigned to AACS, Army Airways Communications System, to man the air force's point-to-point radio circuits. Richard already knew he was to be sent to an AACS station somewhere in England.

". . . here we are," the driver was saying. "Conway Field."

Conway Field.

An entirely new facility on the other side of the promontory overlooking Los Angeles Municipal Airport. In 1940, when President Roosevelt ordered the air corps to triple its size, Conair had purchased a small private airfield in Culver City and moved all its operations there. A huge new factory was built, as well as a four-story administration building topped by a stanchion-supported sign containing hundreds of red and blue electric bulbs that formed the Conway American eagle. When illuminated—in peacetime, of course—the sign was visible for miles in all directions.

Within a year, a second, much longer runway was added, and the company acquired adjoining land to erect still another assembly building. By then the complex encompassed six square miles, with a row of five cavernous corrugated-metal hangars facing a quarter-mile-long hardstand, machine shops, power plants, garages, warehouses, a gigantic red-and-white-checkerboard-painted water tower, and a fifty-foot-high concrete control tower that resembled a lighthouse.

Outside the Cyclone-fenced factory area, as far as the eye could see, an asphalt-topped parking lot was packed with automobiles. The elderly Mexican drove the car around the parking lot, past the Union Pacific Railway siding, and entered the factory through a barbed-wire enclosed gate. Two armed MPs waved them through.

Richard hardly recognized the place. Since his last visit, eleven months before, two additional assembly buildings had sprung up on either side of the first factory structure. These new buildings dwarfed the old one, which itself was longer than a football field. Little diesel tractors pulling carts laden with aircraft parts or tools rumbled out of one building and into another. The ramp was crowded with trucks, jeeps, automobiles, and other vehicles.

On the airfield's two parallel runways, Conair 660s in USAAF olive-drab paint, CT-5 trainers, and an occasional Hunter fighter with blue-and-red RAF roundels were constantly landing and taking off. And just taxiing out to the run-up pad was one of the first production models of the 770, the enormous four-engined, tricycle-geared, twin-ruddered transport designed to carry a hundred fully equipped combat troops.

"My God, when did all this happen?" Richard asked.

"Hey, it's always happening," said the driver. "Every day it gets bigger."

Bigger, Richard thought, did not do it justice. He knew the plant had expanded in the past year—some ten thousand employees at Los Angeles alone—but had never dreamed of this vast scale. And now, in December of 1942, Conair had opened two more plants, in Dallas and Atlanta, manufacturing B-17s on license from Boeing in Dallas, and P-51s and B-26s in Atlanta.

Si had left word for Richard to be brought to the research and development building, a structure the size of a dirigible hangar. From fifty feet away, Richard heard a shrill, almost eerie high-pitched whistle or hum, ever louder, ever more reverberating. The sound reached a crescendo and then seemed to wind down, like a generator grinding to a halt.

Inside the R&D building, Si and three other men stood on a catwalk peering at an object bolted to the floor. The object, which Richard recognized as some type of engine, resembled a long, fat, open-ended torpedo.

"Hey! Up here, kid!" Si waved and hurried along the catwalk to the stairs to wait for Richard. He draped an arm around his son and hugged him, then stepped back and looked him over. "Well, you don't look too bad. For a GI," he added sourly.

"Dad, believe me, they're not accepting nineteen-year-olds in OCS."

"You're almost twenty. And I can get you in."

"No thanks, I'll do it on my own."

Si guided Richard toward the other three men clustered on the catwalk. Richard knew two of them: Pete Dagget and Charlie Jensen. They shook his hand and remarked on how great he looked. The third man, an RAF squadron leader, younger than the others, was tall, sandy-haired, very lean. Si introduced him.

"Rich, this is Gordon Hall."

"My new brother-in-law?" Richard said, liking him on sight.

"One and the same," said Gordon Hall. He said something else but his words were lost in the constantly increasing shrill whine of the engine on the test stand that had started up again.

"It's a new engine we're experimenting with!" Si shouted to Richard. "A gas turbine!" He nodded at Gordon Hall. "The RAF wants us to redesign the Hunter for jet propulsion!"

"How fast will she fly with this . . . this jet?" Richard asked.

"The engineers figure at least four hundred, four-fifty," Si said. "Depends on what they call 'thrust.' I'll explain it to you later when we're—"

The banshee howl of the jet had become so loud it totally muffled Si's voice. The men all clamped their hands over their ears. The engine belched a solid yellow sheet of flame. Richard watched, fascinated, and was thinking, I am looking at the future.

He promised himself to spend the ten days of his furlough learning more about the engine. But the ten days flew past, and it was Christmas, and a day later he was on a train bound for Presque Isle, Maine. The only jarring note about the whole furlough was Janet's anger at Si for not using his influence to cancel the RAF's orders recalling Squadron Leader Gordon Hall to active duty.

"Did you ask him to?" Richard asked.

"Of course I did," Janet said. "He said he couldn't interfere."

Janet did not know that Gordon Hall had declined Si's offer to arrange for Gordon to remain on temporary duty at the Conair Los Angeles factory. And Si had respected Gordon's request not to reveal this to Janet.

Si respected Gordon, period. Their relationship was similar to the one between Si and Duke Harris. Gordon had met Duke in 1940 when Duke was flying with the RAF Eagle Squadron in the Battle of Britain. Gordon said Duke always maintained that the Eagle Squadron, composed solely of Americans, was not Conway's Eagles but almost as good. "Almost" because Conway's Eagles held their liquor better.

Duke was killed on September 23, 1940, over Romney Marsh when his Spitfire collided head-on with an ME-109. Si had learned of Duke's death in a phone call from Duke's ex-wife, now married to a Washington, D.C., attorney and the mother of twin girls.

Si said that he wished Duke had been flying a Hunter, and the German had been flying a KE-1, and its pilot was Karl Eisler. Richard thought it a strange thing for his father to say. Of course, Si was always saying strange things about Karl, but Richard believed that despite their business differences, and the war, his father and Karl still retained some bond of friendship.

On the day of Richard's departure for Presque Isle, he and Si
were in Si's office on the top floor of the administration building. The
telephone rang constantly. Si would pick up the receiver, listen briefly
to his secretary screening the call, then hang up.

"I'm waiting to hear back from Hap Arnold," Si explained to
Richard. "I put the call in early this morning. He's pretty good about
returning calls to me. So I have to wait. Otherwise, I'd drive you to
the train myself."

"I didn't expect you to, anyway," Richard said. "It's okay."

"Relax. You don't have to be at the station for another hour.
Maybe I'll get the call before then. I want to talk to him about a report
I saw on German war production. A month ago the RAF hit Karl
Eisler's factory at Stuttgart and claimed they put him out of produc-
tion for at least six months. This report says he relocated the factory
underground, and he's *doubled* production!"

As Si paused, Richard noticed for the first time a definite shade
of white in the gray of Si's temples. He wondered if his own hair
would start turning white at forty-seven.

". . . but I think this story of doubled production is a lot of bull.
I know those Nazis. They pulled the same stunt back in the thirties,
when they wanted to bluff the Allies into believing the Luftwaffe was
five times bigger than it really was. They *let* you find out this 'secret'
information. Karl told me so himself. I'll bet a thousand dollars to a
dime that Karl's not making KE-1s in that underground factory." Si
paused again, this time for emphasis.

"Jet fighters," he continued. "That's what that Kraut bastard is
making. Jets! And that's what I want to tell Hap. So he can bury
Karl and his goddam factory under a million tons of good German
dirt!"

"I feel bad about Karl. I always liked him," Richard said, and
immediately wanted his words back.

Si's eyes narrowed, the corners of his mouth turned down, and
his jaw tightened—all the signals of an impending explosion with
which Richard was all too familiar, and which still frightened him.

"Where the hell are your brains, boy?" Si pounded the desk. "Karl
Eisler is the enemy!"

"But you still can't be sure that he's making jets."

"But I am sure of it! I know Karl Eisler, don't I? When it's about
Karl Eisler, I'm sure!"

Richard knew that expressing any further doubt would only further ignite his father's temper. He said, "Well, even if he is making
jets, he can't be too far along. Gordon said the RAF will have a jet

fighter flying in another year, two at most. The Germans can't be that much ahead of us."

Richard was wrong.

2.

One look at Karl's face when he emerged from the conference room told Dieter Bauer the meeting was not going well. Of course, a blind man could have known that. You needed only to hear Hermann Göring's angry voice. In the half hour since Göring and Karl had entered the room the *Reichsmarschall* had done nothing but shout.

Karl brushed past Dieter and strode down the corridor to the W.C. Probably not to pee, Dieter thought, but to vomit. Dieter, Karl's assistant and a brilliant engineer in his own right, momentarily considered entering the conference room to offer the *Reichsmarschall* a drink or refreshment of some kind. This was Göring's first visit to Karl's Stuttgart factory and the first time Dieter had ever seen him in person.

Dieter flattened his ear to the door. Inside the room he heard the *Reichsmarschall* chatting with his aide, a Luftwaffe lieutenant colonel, a man with a scarred face and cold eyes that had looked right through Dieter when they were introduced.

Dieter moved away from the door and debated whether or not to enter the conference room. It would not hurt to get to know Göring a little better, and for the *Reichsmarschall* to know that Dieter, a graduate of the Berlin Polytechnisches Institut, had worked with Dr. Hans von Ohain on his remarkable turbojet engine. Following that, he had spent a year helping Ernst Heinkel develop the HE-178, the world's first serviceable jet fighter. Such a background had made Dieter Bauer, at twenty-eight, Karl Eisler's chief consultant on jet propulsion.

Just as Dieter decided to go ahead and talk to the *Reichsmarschall*, Karl returned. Dieter nodded at the closed conference-room door. "What's been happening in there?" he asked.

"Can't you hear?" Karl replied. He prodded Dieter in the stomach. "You're getting too flabby, my boy. Pretty soon you'll be giving the *Reichsmarschall* competition."

Dieter stepped to the window. The June day was dull and cloudy, like the faces of the people walking past the rubbled block directly across the street. Two months ago an American B-17 on a daylight raid on the marshaling yards at Mannheim had become separated from its formation and wandered more than a hundred miles off course. Approaching Stuttgart, the plane was shot down by antiair-craft fire. The crew bailed out, but the plane and its entire bomb load crashed into an apartment building and destroyed the whole block, killing more than one hundred people, mostly women and children.

Not six weeks before, Karl had moved the administrative offices of Eisler Allgemeinmaschinenwerke into the city. Karl appreciated the need to relocate his production lines underground, but insisted that he and his design staff work aboveground like human beings, not hunted animals. Perhaps the Americans had intentionally sent the B-17 to Stuttgart to kill Karl and his engineers. It was not im-possible.

From the conference room, more shouting. Dieter had warned Karl not to take issue with the *Reichsmarschall's* decision to convert the KE-2 jet fighter into a bomber. But Dieter believed Karl was right, and that the *Reichsmarschall* was not thinking clearly. The KE-2 was de-signed as an interceptor, a defensive weapon, not an offensive bomber. Properly used, the KE-2 could change the whole direction of the war. Dieter lit a cigarette and sat on the hard wood bench. From the sound of Göring's voice, the meeting might go on quite a while.

Hermann Göring was giving Karl hell, but not for the reasons Dieter Bauer thought. Göring agreed with Karl that the KE-2 should be deployed defensively. The problem was Hitler. Hitler had ordered the new airplane converted to an attack bomber. Karl, naively, had sent Hitler a note demanding recision of the order. Luckily, Göring had intercepted the note and rushed to Stuttgart to personally ac-quaint Karl Eisler with certain facts of life. To make sure that word of Karl's insubordination never reached Hitler, Göring left his usual retinue of ass-kissers and opportunists in Berlin and came accom-panied only by Anton Moerzer.

In the conference room, Göring sat at the head of the long table with Karl directly to his left. On the table before them cigarette butts overflowed from a large circular glass ashtray set into a miniature rubber tire. Surrounding the ashtray, like soldiers at attention, were two half-filled water tumblers and three empty mineral-water bottles that wobbled precariously as Göring banged his fist on the table.

". . . damn your soul, Karl, why can't I make you understand this!"

"Hermann, your best pilots, those who have flown the KE-2, tell you she'll wipe the sky clean of Allied bombers," Karl said. "Werner Ramsch himself said so, as did young Galland. Are you suggesting that Hitler is unaware of the hundreds of B-17s and B-24s that each day penetrate deeper and deeper into Germany?"

"I am simply informing you that his mind is made up."

"Then why haven't you told him he's wrong? No, better, why don't you tell the people of Hamburg? What were the figures I read on the three RAF raids last month? Forty thousand dead? The city a pile of rubble? And what about Schweinfurt, and Regensburg?"

The corners of Göring's mouth turned down petulantly. His lips glistened red. Karl wondered if the *Reichsmarschall* used lipstick. "Why are you doing this?" Göring asked in a quieter voice. "Why are you making it so difficult for all of us?"

"I speak the truth, and to you it's 'difficult,' " Karl said. "You're more interested in kowtowing to our revered leader than in winning the war."

"That's enough, Karl!"

"I'm sorry, Herr Reichsmarschall," Karl said dryly. "For a moment I lost my head."

"That might well prove to be more than a figure of speech, Dr. Eisler," Anton Moerzer said.

Göring laughed. "Very aptly put, Anton."

Karl wanted to say, Yes, Anton, very aptly put, and we both know damn well where you would like to aptly put *my* head. Instead, he said, "Yes, Anton, very clever."

"Thank you, Dr. Eisler," Moerzer said. It was the first time he had spoken since the meeting began. He sat in a straight-backed chair near the window, his head half turned so that the sun highlighted the deep scars on his face. The sight made Karl uneasy, but then he knew that this was precisely Göring's purpose in having Moerzer present.

Karl said to Göring, "Why are you paying no attention to your own intelligence reports? And I know you've seen Speer's evaluation of American bombing." He quoted Albert Speer's most recent memo: " '. . . unless daylight precision bombing is stopped, or at the very least radically curtailed, it will systematically destroy our entire industrial capability.' "

"It will be stopped," Göring said. "I guarantee it."

Karl had to fight an almost overwhelming urge to say, Yes, Meyer, just as you guaranteed that no enemy bomb would ever fall on Berlin. Göring had once boasted that if Berlin was ever bombed he would change his name to Meyer.

Karl said, "The way to 'guarantee' it, Hermann, is to commit five groups of jet fighters to the defense of Germany. Defense, I said, *not* offense. What the hell are we going to bomb with KE-2s, anyway? Blitz London again, for Christ's sake?"

Göring was clearly straining for composure. His face was beet-red. "We'll bomb the troops on the beaches," he said.

Karl said, "What beaches, *Reichsmarschall?* In Sicily? It's too late. In Salerno?"

Göring overlooked the sarcasm. The American and British divisions that had come ashore at Salerno were already three miles inland, the first Allied troops on European soil. Hitler had ordered a fighting withdrawal north to Naples.

"I'm talking about the real beaches," he said. "The French beaches, next year, or the year after that, when the Allies finally decide to invade. We'll blast them to pieces with our jet bombers." Göring enjoyed the ring of the words. He looked at Moerzer. "Correct, Anton?"

Moerzer said, "Absolutely, *Reichsmarschall.*"

Karl realized further argument was useless. Göring, no matter how much he agreed with Karl, feared Hitler or, more accurately, feared losing command of the Luftwaffe. "All right," Karl said wearily. "The KE-2 will become a bomber. I only hope you'll allocate sufficient parts and material for mass production."

"You'll have whatever you need." Göring clapped Karl fondly on the shoulder. "If you were to see the new weapon, the V-1, I think you might not be so skeptical about the Führer's—" He glanced cautiously at Moerzer, then lowered his voice and continued to Karl, "—about his understanding of offensive versus defensive tactics. This V-1, I tell you, will change our fortunes! I'll arrange for you to go to Nordhausen for a demonstration."

"Nordhausen?" Karl said. "I thought the thing was being assembled in Peenemünde."

Göring sighed. "Two days ago the RAF practically blasted Peenemünde off the map. But thank God we were prepared for such an eventuality. We've moved the whole factory, lock, stock, and barrel, underground, a thousand miles from Peenemünde. Believe me, they'll never find it this time."

Underground, Karl thought. Soon the whole country would be living underground. He said, "I'm looking forward to it."

Karl also looked forward to going home that evening and relaxing for a few blissful hours, forgetting the war and Hermann Göring and the stupidity of a certain Bohemian corporal. He had rented a small house for himself and Erika in Kornwestheim, a lovely little town near the factory. Erika, who enjoyed gardening, had planted roses and begonias in the front yard and a vegetable patch in the rear. Some cucumbers and a few tomatoes and scallions were almost ready. For the summer months at least, the Eisler table would not lack fresh produce.

Driving home, he was thinking about this, a crisp salad, a Niçoise perhaps. He was also thinking that his car, a 1934 four-cylinder Opel cabriolet, sounded as though it needed new valves. He would discuss it with one of the mechanics at the factory tomorrow. He had just swung off the main road onto the graveled path to the house when he saw a Luftwaffe staff car parked by the fenced gate. A general's standard flew from either fender of this car, which several weeks before had been parked in the same spot. Karl had hoped to never see it or its occupant, Werner Ramsch, again.

3.

Generalmajor Werner Ramsch, age forty, a fighter pilot credited with ninety-seven victories, proud holder of the Ritterkreuz mit Eichenlaub, commander of the Stuttgart-area fighter defenses, was the first man to have flown the KE-2. After the flight, immediately upon opening his canopy, the young general had yelled down to Karl, ". . . no piston engine vibration, no torque, no deafening propeller blast! All you hear is a soft whistling sound! Dr. Eisler, this airplane is a dream to fly!"

But after their encounter at Karl's house the previous month, even the sight of the staff car made Karl's stomach turn. He wanted no part of Ramsch and the insane plans of the people he claimed to represent. He thought he had made this abundantly clear at Ramsch's last visit.

Karl pulled up behind the Mercedes and got out. The Luftwaffe chauffeur clicked his heels and came to attention. "I'm not an officer, sergeant," Karl told him. "Relax."

"Yes sir," the sergeant said but remained at attention.

Erika met Karl at the door. She brushed his cheek with her lips and whispered, "That handsome young general is here again. I gave them some coffee."

" 'Them'?"

"He's with two other officers," Erika said.

"Bring me some coffee, too, darling." Karl kissed her and went into the living room.

The room was pleasant and comfortable. On either side of the large brick fireplace and on both walls, ceiling-to-floor bookcases were crowded with books, photographs, bric-a-brac, and dozens of model airplanes. Ramsch and two colonels sat primly on the sofa and lounge chairs. All three immediately rose to greet Karl.

"Karl," Ramsch said. He grasped Karl's hand. "Please forgive the unannounced visit. It's important we talk." He introduced the two colonels, neither of whom was Luftwaffe. One was armored corps, the other infantry. Both wore the red-and-blue ribbon of the Russian campaign and silver wound badges—indicating at least three combat injuries—and both looked considerably older than Ramsch.

Ramsch wasted no time on amenities. "It hasn't gotten out yet, but yesterday the Russians recaptured Smolensk. Had Hitler allowed von Paulus to withdraw from Stalingrad, none of this would have happened. I've seen the casualty figures. The numbers are appalling! And now he's ordered southern Italy held. Mussolini's government has been overthrown, the Italians have surrendered, but our peerless leader is determined to save their gutless hides! If this isn't madness, I don't know what is."

As Ramsch drew in his breath to continue, Erika entered with Karl's coffee. Karl placed his arm around her shoulder and drew her close. "My wife's late father was an Imperial General Staff officer, Ramsch, did you know that?" Karl asked.

Ramsch bowed to Erika. "My compliments, Frau Eisler."

"Thank you, *Generalmajor*," Erika replied. She looked at Karl again. He smiled reassuringly at her. "If anyone wants something, please let me know," she said, and left.

Karl said to Ramsch, "Let me save you a lot of trouble, Herr Generalmajor. I am not—repeat, not—" He paused, chagrined at using Göring's favorite phrase. "I am not interested in your . . . problem. I'm sorry."

"It's not 'my' problem," said Ramsch. "It's the entire nation's problem. Unless we sue for immediate peace, we will eventually lose the war. But by then this whole country will be nothing but a pile of rubble. Have you seen Hamburg? Bremen? Frankfurt? And now when we finally have the opportunity to do something about it—" He got up, reached behind him to the bookcase, and plucked a little model airplane from the first shelf. "When we finally have a weapon worth its name, what happens? The genius in Berlin says it shouldn't be used for what it was designed to do."

Karl did not want to waste time or energy recounting his conversation with Göring earlier in the day. He took the model from Ramsch and replaced it on the shelf. It was a lacquered wood replica of an all-black KE-2, finely detailed, with the two jet-engine nacelles slung from the wings, the four wing guns and single nose cannon, even little rubber tires on the main wheels and nose wheel.

Karl said, "Ramsch, I haven't changed my mind. You're talking treason. I am not interested."

"I'm talking," Ramsch said, "of the salvation of our country."

"Not by assassinating the legal head of the government," Karl said.

"How else, then?" It was the infantry colonel, a tall, heavy man with close-cropped gray hair. Karl thought he bore a vague resemblance to the late revered Feldmarschall Paul von Hindenburg.

The other colonel, the tanker, said, "Dr. Eisler, we have come to you because of your contacts with important people in America. We need assurance that once the government is reformed, the Allies will be amenable to an armistice. You can approach these people."

"Please, gentlemen, I want to hear no more of this," Karl said. "I will pretend that none of these conversations ever happened. No more, I beg of you."

"That's your final word?" Ramsch asked.

"Yes," said Karl. He knew they did not fear his betraying them. No matter how innocent he was, even the very whisper of such a plot would automatically implicate him.

Karl walked them to their car. They drove off. As Karl started back into the house, Erika came out to meet him.

"I heard," she said.

Karl said nothing.

"They're mad," she said.

"Perhaps."

" 'Perhaps'? My God, Karl, you can't possibly be taking them seriously?"

"No," he said quickly. "Of course not."

"These 'important contacts in America'?" she asked. "Simon Conway?"

"No, Morris Tannen," Karl said. "Morris is on the Senate Armed Services Committee."

Erika said nothing a moment. Then, abruptly, she gave a brittle little laugh of irony. "That's funny," she said. "He's a Jew."

"Yes, that is funny," Karl said.

17

M ajor Shaeffer, driving his own jeep, had picked Richard up outside the main gate. Shaeffer was the new CO of the Prestwick AACS detachment, and the last person Richard wanted to see.

"Going into town, sergeant?" the major asked.

"Yes sir," Richard replied. "I'm off until oh seven hundred."

"Get in." It was an order, not an invitation.

They rode in silence. Overhead, a Conair 770, the bottom of its olive-drab wings streaked black with engine oil, roared in for a landing. Richard could clearly make out the big block printed letters atop the fuselage door: AIR TRANSPORT COMMAND, and the ATC emblem, a pylon superimposed on a lineal projection of a world globe.

The instant the 770's tires crunched on the runway another airplane, a C-54, appeared in the landing pattern. Round the clock, a constant stream of transports, bombers, and fighters landed and took off. All came from the States. The transports carried soldiers and material; the bombers and their crews would join the 8th Air Force at bases throughout the U.K. It was said that each month in this year of 1943 the 8th Air Force, like a pregnant woman, had doubled in size. Now, in August, she was enormous.

". . . hot date, sergeant, I suppose?" Major Shaeffer was saying.

"Sir?"

"I said you must have something good going for you in town. I mean, running in at this time of day."

"Yes sir, I guess it is late at that," Richard said. It was past nine o'clock, although the sun was still high in the western sky. It had rained earlier in the day, and the land sparkled green. In the eight months he had been in Scotland, Richard recalled hardly a morning when he did not wake to find the air damp and the sky cloudy, and then a few hours later see the sun burn through the overcast. By late afternoon the day was bright, and the air crisp and clean with the fresh smell of the sea.

". . . wanted to talk to you, anyway," Shaeffer was saying.

"Sir?"

"Goddammit, Conway, are you hard of hearing?"

"Sorry, sir, I was thinking of something."

"I said, sergeant, it's good I ran into you, because there's something we should discuss." Shaeffer looked away from the road to peer at Richard over the rim of his glasses. He was a big man, with thick reddish hair and a freckled face. The horn-rimmed glasses gave him a certain professorial appearance.

Richard fixed his own glasses firmly on the bridge of his nose, wondering what in the hell he had done now to piss Shaeffer off. "What is it that you wanted to discuss, sir?"

"Mrs. McLennan," Shaeffer said slowly, "Mrs. Catherine McLennan."

Richard's stomach sank. What could this fucker want to discuss about Kay? Was it possible Shaeffer had known her before Richard? No, impossible. Until five weeks ago Shaeffer had never been in Scotland.

Richard said, "I beg your pardon?"

"You heard me," said Shaeffer. He swung the jeep onto the left road shoulder as a convoy of half a dozen GI six-by-six trucks rumbled past on the narrow two-lane highway.

"She's a friend of mine," Richard said.

"Yes, so I understand." Shaeffer steered the jeep back onto the road after the convoy had passed. "A pretty good friend, too, from what I understand, although she's probably ten years older than you."

It was incredible, Richard thought. Of all the piss-poor luck, of the ten million soldiers in the U.S. Army the one to find out about Richard and Kay had to be Major John A. Shaeffer. From the day five weeks before when Shaeffer arrived in Prestwick, transferred from the 58th AACS Group in North Africa, he had had it in for Richard. Luckily, Richard had already received his promotion to buck sergeant. Shaeffer's very first words to him were "I know you're a big shot's son. That's why you made sergeant so fast. Don't expect any more special treatment."

Master Sergeant Clarence Pribble, Richard's friend and mentor, assured Richard that he had made sergeant strictly on merit as one of the most gifted high-speed CW operators to come along in years. Pribble advised Richard to pay no attention to Shaeffer, but certainly to keep out of the major's way. Pribble also told Richard why the major had a hard-on for him.

Pribble knew Shaeffer from the peacetime army. Both were lifers who had been stationed at various stateside army airfields as point-to-point AACS radio operators. In 1940, when the Army Air Corps expanded, a small cadre of technically qualified regular army men were offered temporary commissions. Pribble had turned the offer down; he did not want the responsibility. Shaeffer was more ambitious.

Four years earlier, at the conclusion of his first hitch in 1936, Shaeffer had briefly returned to civilian life as a radio operator in Conair's newly established communications division. His first night on the job he showed up slightly drunk. It proved to be his last night. To his credit, he never took another drink, but Conair did not give him a second chance. Shaeffer reenlisted, eventually to be promoted out of the ranks to major, but he never forgave Conair.

So when Simon Conway's son turned up in Shaeffer's new command, the major ragged him mercilessly and unfairly. On several occasions Pribble had to rescue Richard. But Pribble, wise old dogface that he was, also advised Richard to transfer the hell into another detachment. Johnny Shaeffer sooner or later would have Richard's ass.

Richard hated the idea of transferring. He liked Prestwick and his AACS buddies, especially Pribble, who had made Richard his special protégé and taught him everything he knew, which was a lot.

AACS's task was to provide short- and long-distance in-flight communication facilities, operate airport control towers and airways approach control centers, and man point-to-point radio stations between air bases around the world. Prestwick, radio call sign WYY, was the busiest of all. The station was located on the second floor of a stately old manor house that had been requisitioned from its wealthy proprietors. The slate roof of the house, which stood adjacent to the airfield, bristled with wire and antenna poles.

At WYY, a bank of fourteen point-to-point radio receivers and transmitters handled aircraft arrival and departure messages, weather information and endless reams of low-priority, nonoperational data. Millions of words daily. The messages, all encoded, were sent and received in International Morse Code, dots and dashes.

Each operator, seated at his typewriter and listening to the Morse code through earphones, handled a separate station. WYY to WYTU in Iceland; WYY to WYQN in Goosebay, Newfoundland; WYY to WYQR, Presque Isle, Maine; and so on, to more than a dozen other large and small stations.

Richard enjoyed the work and was good at it. Airways communications was an entirely new science. Each day brought a new problem, demanding an innovative solution. Richard's expertise steadily increased. He knew Si would be proud of him. In a way it would make up for not being a pilot.

But now, thanks to a total stranger, everything was falling to pieces. A month ago Richard had had the world by the balls. He had just been promoted to sergeant and shift chief, overseeing seven other operators, and was earning a network-wide reputation for speed. Pribble had taught Richard how to use the manual speed key, the "bug," and as a gift presented his own personal bug to Richard. Richard had become so proficient that hotshot operators from other stations often expressly asked to work "RC," Richard's call sign. A request to work a certain operator was the mark of excellence.

". . . yes, she's a good friend," Richard was saying to Shaeffer, deciding nothing was to be gained by continuing the cat-and-mouse game. To hell with Major John A. Shaeffer. "What point are you trying to make, major?"

Shaeffer seemed to smile. It was as though he had succeeded in provoking Richard to insubordination. "Keep a civil tongue in your head, soldier! You're talking to a superior officer!"

"Excuse me, sir."

"That's better. The point, sergeant, is that Prestwick is a small town and your little dalliance with a married woman has come to my attention. A married woman, I might add, whose husband is a disabled veteran of the 8th Army."

The landlady, Richard thought, that bitch of a big-mouthed old woman from whom he rented the flat on Clyde Street. He paid her thirty shillings a week, plus a carton of Old Golds, for one dreary furnished room where he and Kay could be alone on the nights Richard was off. She must have blabbed to someone who in turn had relayed the gossip to Shaeffer.

". . . so what do you have to say for yourself, sergeant?" Shaeffer was asking.

Poor Kay, Richard was thinking. Her husband, the disabled 8th Army veteran, supervised the graveyard shift at the Royal Clydebank tank factory in nearby Ayr. "What do you want me to say?" Richard said.

" 'Goodbye,' " Shaeffer said. "I want you to say goodbye to the lady, sergeant, because I don't intend to have a scandal on my hands. And I'll tell you right now that if it causes me or the U.S. Army any embarrassment you'll be a buck private so fast you won't know what hit you!"

They had just driven across the little stone bridge over the Ayr

River and were in Prestwick, on High Street. Outside the Gaumont, the town's only theater, a crowd milled about waiting for the late show to start. The marquee read:

"DARK VICTORY"—B. DAVIS & G. BRENT
Plus
"TOTTINGHAM STATION"—ALISTAIR SIM

Most of the men were in uniform, U.S. Army olive drab and RAF blue. Many were with girls, some also in uniform, WAAF blue or ATS brown. ATS: Auxiliary Territorial Service, known more familiarly as American Tail Society. The girls in civilian clothes all carried topcoats or jackets over their arms. The wind from the Firth of Clyde was chilly, even in summer.

"Do you read me, sergeant? Do we understand each other?" Shaeffer had pulled up to the curb a few feet from the theater. He flipped the gearshift lever into neutral and gunned the engine impatiently.

"I heard what you said, sir."

"That's not what I asked."

"Yes sir," Richard said after a moment. He slid out of the jeep and stood on the sidewalk. "Yes, sir, we understand each other."

"Good," Shaeffer said. He jammed the jeep into gear and drove away.

2.

Karl watched the V-1 roar off its launching pad. It reminded him of sky rockets in America at July Fourth fireworks displays, except that this was no rocket but a small, unmanned aircraft with short, stubby wings attached to its long cylindrical body. A pilotless bomb, powered by a jet-pulse engine and guided by a gyrostabilizing device, it was designed to carry two thousand pounds of high explosives 150 miles.

Through binoculars, Karl followed the little airplane as it arced upward, climbing faster than a KE-2 before gracefully leveling out. He tracked it until it vanished into a cloud bank. In a few seconds, when it reached the vast deserted area of the Nordhausen test range, the engine would stop and the V-1 would nose over and dive into the ground. When deployed, fired from launching pads in France, its target would be the city of London.

". . . is she everything she's said to be, or isn't she?" a jolly voice beside him boomed. It was Max Clausen, Project Cigar's deputy chief engineer. Clausen himself had coined the phrase "Project Cigar." The V-1s, he claimed, would knock the cigar right out of Winston Churchill's mouth.

"Very impressive, Max," Karl said truthfully.

Far in the distance a cloud of black smoke rose, followed almost instantaneously by a sharp thud. Beneath their feet the ground trembled. The V-1, which had plunged to earth some four miles away, carried no warhead. Otherwise the ground would have rocked as in an earthquake.

They were in a concrete bunker fifty yards from the launching pad, accompanied by two white-jacketed civilian technicians and a uniformed Luftwaffe major, a nonflying officer. Everyone was in high spirits. This was the flying bomb's twenty-first consecutive successful test.

"She's in mass production now," Clausen said, anticipating Karl's question. "The Führer wants the first ones in operation by May 1, but we'll be ready earlier. Now come along and join me in a glass of champagne."

Clausen, a stocky, compact man of fifty with wispy gray hair and a complexion someone said resembled the surface of the moon, opened the bunker door for Karl. The entire area was barren except for the launching ramp, which was now being disassembled. The factory, laboratories, offices, and living quarters were all underground. Allied photo reconnaissance would reveal only a few stone farmhouses and large spaces of open ground in the foothills of the Harz Mountains, one hundred miles west of Leipzig.

Göring had arranged special clearance for Karl to enter the facility and observe a V-1 in flight. The *Reichsmarschall* had sent his own plane to Stuttgart to pick up Karl and fly him to Nordhausen. A day's sightseeing, Karl told Erika; he would be home in time for dinner.

She was still nervous over the visit of young General Ramsch and the two colonels. But then, so was Karl. Until now, despite the setbacks in Russia, he would not have agreed that Germany was losing the war and was convinced that the Allies could never successfully mount a cross-Channel invasion. He had seen the Atlantic defenses. On the other hand, the Allies continued to inflict incredible damage upon German industry, and even with proper deployment of the two jet fighters, his own KE-2 and Wili Messerchmitt's ME-262, Karl doubted the enemy air raids could be stopped. The jets might make the Allies pay an agonizingly high price, but they would never stop them.

The destruction of German industry guaranteed the eventual destruction of the state itself. Hermann Göring knew this, Albert

Speer knew it, the young officers on the line knew it. The only person who seemed ignorant of the fact was Adolf Hitler.

Camouflaged netting had been erected over an area extending fifty yards on either side of an innocuous cottage, which was the entrance to the underground factory. Dozens of trucks, fuel carriers, and cars were parked under the netting, which also concealed a series of large ventilation fans. From the air one could see nothing more than an open field that blended perfectly with the terrain.

Inside the cottage, Clausen led Karl through a narrow corridor to an elevator that took them down to the second level. A single passageway branched off into other, similar passageways. An endless stream of uniformed soldiers and white-coated civilians rushed busily about. What struck Karl most was the noise, a cacophony of whirring ventilation fans, clanging metal, rumbling machinery. The din was overwhelming, as was the odor, a stifling combination of unwashed bodies, burned rubber, and dust.

Clausen noticed Karl's appalled expression. "There are three thousand people down here!" he shouted. "You'll get used to it!" He guided Karl into a brightly lighted corridor to a steel door. Stenciled white letters on a placard taped to the door read ABRIKHALLE #3.

"I want you to see this," Clausen said. "And then we'll go down to the officers' dining salon for lunch."

They entered a massive, low-ceilinged room where hundreds of men sat crowded on narrow benches. Some, wearing jeweler's loupes, painstakingly adjusted sections of the V-1's gyroscopic steering mechanism. Others, assembling the gyroscope itself, plucked pieces of the device from a slow-moving belt, put the pieces together, tested the fully assembled unit, then replaced it on the belt where, farther down the line, it was removed for additional inspecting and testing.

The workers wore identical uniforms, ill-fitting gray-and-white-striped shirts and trousers with matching skullcap. No one talked, no one laughed, all eyes were dull. Without exception every face, young and old, seemed shrunken, the skin sallow and parchment-tight.

". . . every one of them is a former watchmaker or jeweler!" Clausen shouted into Karl's ear. "What precision, eh?"

"They don't look too well fed," Karl said.

Clausen laughed, as though Karl had made a clever, witty remark. He clapped Karl on the back and guided him from the room. In the corridor, as they started back toward the elevator, he said, "Now for some lunch."

"Those are slave laborers, aren't they?" Karl said.

"They're Jews," Clausen said. "And some Poles, and Russians."

"I thought the stories were only rumor, Allied propaganda. But it's true, isn't it?"

Clausen seemed almost offended. "Who's been doing the work in your factory, Dr. Eisler? I'm sure Eisler Allgemeinmaschinenwerke employs more than a few of these foreign workers."

"We don't put convict uniforms on them, and we don't starve them," Karl said. "My workers are well fed, well housed, and well treated."

Clausen replied, but Karl was not listening. He was thinking that he had no right to criticize Nordhausen's slave laborers, for Clausen was correct. Karl used them, too. The fact that his workers were better treated made him no less guilty. He had accepted the foreign workers willingly, yes, even eagerly, without a second thought.

Karl remembered little of his lunch with Max Clausen and other Nordhausen technicians, except that their conversation was sprinkled with conviviality and the expectation of miracles to be achieved with their new weapons. He did recall clearly, however, part of a conversation at a table behind him.

Two Luftwaffe flight surgeons were discussing a series of experiments conducted in a high-altitude pressure chamber. The tests would provide information on precisely how to treat aircrewmen stricken with anoxia, oxygen deprivation. The physicians discussed the matter quietly but intently, like two college professors at a faculty cocktail party analyzing a Shakespearean play.

Not until the two had risen to leave did Karl turn to look at them. One was fairly young, quite good-looking. The other was older, white-haired, his face blotched with liver spots.

". . . so this afternoon, we'll put them in at sea level and get them up to forty thousand feet in ten minutes," the younger one said.

"How many do you have?"

"Three," said the younger. "Two men and a woman."

"Jews?"

"Oh, yes."

"Don't use the woman," the older said. "For some reason—metabolic or hormonal difference, I suppose—females seem able to withstand more pressure. Your data should be based solely on male reaction."

"I would be inclined to dispute that theory, but we'll see how long these two males last. Not long, I'm sure, but it should be informative."

"I don't know about 'informative,' but I guarantee you it will be messy," the older one said.

That evening when Karl arrived at Stuttgart, he did not go directly home, nor did he stop at the factory. He went instead into the city, to the Goldener Hirsch Hotel. There, he removed a slip of paper from his wallet. The paper contained a Munich telephone number. He asked the hotel telephone operator to connect him and waited outside a booth adjoining her switchboard.

A few minutes later the operator informed him the call was ready. He stepped into the booth, closed the door, and spoke into the phone.

". . . this is Karl Eisler. I'd like to leave a message for General Ramsch. Tell him, please, that I have changed my mind."

3.

Kay McLennan would have been flattered had she heard Major Shaeffer describe her as probably ten years older than Richard. She was thirty-four, fifteen years Richard's senior. She was slight, almost petite, but with a full, fine figure. Chestnut hair framed an oval face whose brown eyes and perfect nose matched a flawless complexion and nearly perfect mouth and chin.

Kay, the daughter of a professor of Romance languages at Edinburgh University, was herself a graduate of that school. In 1934 she had met and married a young construction-company engineer, Robert McLennan. They purchased a small cottage in Prestwick and enjoyed a comfortable life, until the war. A captain in the Royal Engineers, McLennan was one of the first casualties of the Italian incursion into Egypt in 1940. Mustered out of the army, he returned to his job at the Ayrshire arsenal.

Kay and her husband were devoted to each other. Their sexual relationship, however, which had begun deteriorating when Robert discovered Kay was unable to bear children, had ended long ago. But she had remained steadfastly faithful until she met Richard Conway one windy May evening on the beach promenade.

She was taking her nightly walk, after dropping her husband at the tram station where he boarded the last bus to Ayr and his all-night job. Kay saw a lone figure huddled on a bench, legs outstretched, gazing out at the sea. He appeared to be trembling. She asked him if he was all right.

"I would be," he had replied. "If I'd remembered to bring an overcoat. I'm freezing."

"Then may I ask why you continue to sit here?"

"I like to watch the waves, the whitecaps, and listen to them crash on the beach."

"Next time don't forget your coat," she said, and continued on her way.

A week later she saw him again. Same time, same place, and now he wore the coat. They began chatting, innocuous small talk. He said he loved the way she spoke, that Scotch burr. She invited him to join her for a drink. She saw no harm being escorted into the pub at Kilmarnock House by an American almost young enough to be her son. It was nearly closing time anyway and the family room was empty.

They sat on a divan facing the flames crackling in the fireplace. He talked. Oh, how he talked! A torrent of words, as though he had just been rescued after months on a desert island and she was his first human contact. He talked about himself, his family, the United States Army, his work at the airfield.

No, he had no girlfriend. Yes, he had met a few nice girls at Red Cross dances and, on a tour of Robert Burns's birthplace, one very pretty WREN. He had made a date with her but she never showed up. Richard reminded Kay of a puppy—well, he *was* a puppy—so anxious for attention, so eager to please.

"Tell me the truth," Kay said that night at the pub. "Have you ever been with a woman?"

Even in the glow of the flames from the fire his face reddened. "Sure I have. A lot of times."

"A lot of times?" she asked teasingly. "How many is a lot?"

"All right, a few times." He blushed even deeper. "Once," he said, blurting the word. "Just once! Okay? It was in Boston a week before I quit college to join the army—"

Kay touched her fingers to his lips to silence him. "You've answered the question." She touched his cheek; his skin was soft and smooth. She wrapped his hand in hers and said, "How would you like to be in bed with me right now?"

And it was not love that landed her in bed with this nineteen-year-old boy. It was a very simple matter of mutual needs fulfilled. It was for a purpose and served a purpose.

Now, three months later, waiting for him in the room she had insisted he rent, she was thinking that she had enjoyed every single moment of their time together. She lay atop the bed, clad only in her bra and half-slip, gazing at the blue-red flame of the gas heater in the fireplace hearth. She hated this room. It was cold and dark, and smelled of light housekeeping, but she could not bring Richard to her own house. She felt no special guilt about her child lover, but her house was also Robert's and she respected her husband too much to demean him further.

Respected, she thought, not loved? No, she loved Robert. This physical relationship with Richard could be called lust, gratification, satisfaction, fulfillment, but not love. Oh, she was fond of him, a mother's fondness for a child, which made it incest, she thought, and smiled uncomfortably to herself.

The door opened and Richard entered. He tossed his hat on the table, came over to the bed, and kissed her. She threw her arms around him and drew him to her. She knew he liked her to hold him in her arms. She liked it, too.

"Roll over," she whispered, and as he obediently complied, she unbuckled his belt and unbuttoned his top trouser button. Then, button by button, she opened his fly. He gasped as she closed her fingers gently around him.

"Jesus . . . !" he moaned.

"Jesus can't help you now, laddie. Only Catherine can," she said, bending down and enveloping him in her mouth.

"Jesus . . . !" he moaned again.

She knew precisely how far to bring him, and herself, before she pushed him away and instructed him to undress completely and, naked, stand in front of her. She leaned up on one elbow and reached out for him, cupping his testicles. His enormous erection throbbed in her hand.

"My God, that is so beautiful!" she said, and pulled him down on top of her and gently slid him into her. "Now pump, darling!" she whispered, kissing his mouth, his nose, his eyes. "Pump!"

She enjoyed telling herself that she had taught him all he knew, which was not untrue, for in the beginning he was innocence personified. He knew how to satisfy himself, yes, but all animals instinctively did that. She taught him patience and consideration. He had proved a most adept pupil.

When it was over, she fell back limp and drained, her body soaked with sweat. She kissed him. "You get better all the time."

"Thank you."

"May I have a cigarette?"

He reached out to the night table for a package of Old Golds and a book of matches. He lit one cigarette, then lit the other from the tip of the first.

"Did Mrs. Collins see you come in?" he asked. Mrs. Collins, the landlady, lived on the first floor.

"Is that what's bothering you?

"What makes you think something's bothering me?"

"I know you well enough by now, laddie. No, she did not see me come in. And what difference does it make? She doesn't know who I am."

"Somebody does," Richard said, and told her of his conversation with Major Shaeffer. Kay listened quietly. "What are we going to do?" he asked when he finished.

"Nothing," she said. "We'll just be more careful."

The next morning Richard bicycled over to Pribble's office at the transmitter site in Redbrae. Six miles from the airport, Redbrae was little more than a mark on a map, a few farmhouses scattered among the hills rising up to the east of Prestwick. The AACS antennas were located here, a maze of hundred-foot-high radio towers and wire, a forest of steel trees.

Master Sergeant Clarence Pribble was a leathery, white-haired Kentuckian. He wore six hash marks on the sleeve of his army blouse, twenty-four years of service. He was sweating out the remaining six. He planned to retire on his pension and do nothing but drink, smoke good cigars, and maybe find a young good-looking wealthy widow.

He liked Richard because Richard tried so hard, and because Richard was the only rich man's son Pribble had ever known who wanted to make a success on his own. In short, the kid had balls. But when Richard told him of Shaeffer's order to dissolve the relationship with Kay McLennan, Pribble knew Richard's time was up. Especially since the lady apparently did not want to let go.

" 'We'll just be more careful,' that's what she said?" Pribble asked Richard that morning at Redbrae. They were outside the transmitter shack, seated in Pribble's jeep, drinking coffee from GI canteen cups. "What the hell does that mean, 'more careful'?"

"Making sure the landlady doesn't see us," Richard said.

"Look, I know you got the sweet-ass for this lady, but if Johnny Shaeffer told you to break off with her, you'd better fucking well do it. You, Sergeant Conway, are what they call a marked man." Pribble bit off a cigar end and spit it out. "On the other hand, if it wasn't this, he'd find something else to hit you with. I told you that before."

"So what do I do?"

"I told you that before, too," Pribble said. "Transfer the fuck into another outfit."

"And let the bastard win?"

"He's an officer." Pribble lit the cigar. "Officers always win."

As usual, Pribble was right. Not three days later Richard was summoned to Major's Shaeffer's office and informed that his off-base privileges were suspended until further notice.

"... and I don't think I have to tell you why," Shaeffer said.

"Furthermore, sergeant, I am issuing a direct order: you will give up that room of yours in town."

Richard said, "Respectfully, sir, I'd like to transfer to another unit. I'll submit my request in writing to the first sergeant."

"Save yourself the trouble," Shaeffer said. "I won't endorse the request. You're staying right here, Sergeant Conway." The major smiled. "Right here, with me. Dismissed!"

Richard remained standing at attention. All he could think was that from now on, for him, duty at Prestwick would be like a condemned man waiting for the ax to fall. Sooner or later, as Pribble said, Major Shaeffer would have Richard's ass.

"Is there anything else, sergeant?"

"No sir, nothing else." Richard saluted, about-faced, and started for the door.

"Hold it," Shaeffer called out. Studying a sheaf of mimeographed orders fixed to a clipboard, he motioned Richard back to the desk. "How badly do you want a transfer?"

"Very badly, sir."

"Tell you what," said Shaeffer. He tapped a manicured fingernail on the clipboard. "This came in the other day: a request from SHAEF for an experienced CW operator to volunteer for a special mission. Now I happen to know this special mission has something to do with commando training. You ever had commando training, sergeant?"

"No sir."

"I didn't think so. All right, you want out, here's the only way you do it." Shaeffer tapped the clipboard again. "Volunteer for this special mission, whatever it is."

"Whatever it is, I'll volunteer," Richard said. Anything was preferable to continuing to be at Shaeffer's mercy and unable to see Kay.

"I'm sure your family will be very proud of you," Shaeffer said. "Make a great PR thing for Conair Aircraft Company, don't you think? Special mission volunteers usually end up as heroes. Good luck, sergeant."

"Thank you, sir," Richard said. He wondered why Major Shaeffer had not added, "dead heroes."

18

Richard Conway was convinced that Sergeant Major Arthur Fellows, who stood six feet five and weighed 230 pounds—not an ounce of which was fat—was a direct descendant of the chief warden at the Tower of London's torture chambers. Richard was lying flat on his face in a mud hole on the approach side of the twelve-foot-high greased wood fence halfway through the obstacle course. The knotted climbing rope dangled near his ear, the same ear into which Fellows's voice was bellowing.

"Off your dead arse, Yank! Move!"

No way, Richard told himself, no way could he move. Every muscle in his body ached. His fatigues were soaked through. The muddy water stank. Each day of the five days he had been here at Shrivenham he had tried, and failed, to complete the two-mile-long obstacle course.

"Come on, Richard, you can do it!" It was a classmate, one of the two women in the program, both of whom had successfully negotiated the fence, as they always did, which made it especially galling. This particular girl, Blair Moffet, a WREN lieutenant, was not much older than Richard.

". . . keep going, miss!" Fellows shouted at her, his voice never missing a beat as he seized Richard's collar and hauled him to his feet. Blair hurried on to the next obstacle, a series of barbed-wire barriers. You had to crawl under the wire to avoid live ammunition fired some two inches over your head.

". . . have at it again!" Richard felt his elbow clamped in the steel vice of Fellows's fist. This time Richard nearly made it over the fence, but the insides of his fingers were so raw from rope burns he let go of the rope and tumbled to the ground. Again, he lay facedown in the mud. The brackish water felt cool and soothing on his hands.

"Shit!" Fellows cried. "Shit, shit, shit!" He planted the toe of his combat boot under Richard's belly and rolled him over on his back. The sergeant major's tree-trunk legs straddled Richard's body as he gazed disgustedly down at him. "All right, pack it in for today. Tomorrow you do it *three* times. Three! Get on to the next station."

Shrivenham was all Major Shaeffer had promised, and worse. A former Royal Army disciplinary barracks in Oxfordshire, seventy miles west of London, it was now a combined U.S. Ranger-British Commando training center. Any chagrin or self-deprecation Richard might have felt for running away, for not standing up to Shaeffer, vanished on his very first day at Shrivenham. He found that he had leaped not into the fire but into the inferno.

". . . sergeant, have you any idea why you're here?" The question had been put to him that first day by a young U.S. Army captain named Roger Chalmers.

"I'm here for some kind of special mission," Richard had replied.

"Do you know what OSS is?"

"Office of Strategic Services, I believe."

"That is correct, sergeant, Office of Strategic Services. Do you know what its function is?"

"Counterintelligence."

"Also correct, sergeant. You're batting a thousand. You have been assigned temporary duty with OSS. You'll be a member of a five-man team—excuse me, a three-man-two-woman team—which is a joint OSS-SOE project. SOE, sergeant, stands for Special Operations Executive and is the British counterpart of our OSS. Your 'special mission' is to be dropped into Yugoslavia."

"Yugoslavia?" Richard said. " 'Dropped'?" The image it conjured was as ominous as the word sounded.

"Dropped," Captain Chalmers repeated. "Dropped by parachute. You do know what a parachute is?"

"What am I supposed to do there?"

"You're an experienced radio operator, aren't you?"

"Yes sir."

"Then that's what you're supposed to do. Report to Sergeant Major Fellows," Chalmers said.

Richard needed five more days to successfully negotiate the obstacle course. By then, as sore muscles healed and hardened, he began feeling stronger and surprisingly self-confident. Successful completion of the commando program required nine intense weeks of combat

training and technical instruction. The days passed in a blur of 5:00-
A.M. reveilles, fifteen minute breakfasts, ten minute washtime periods,
two hours of rifle range, four of radio and cryptographic procedure,
then three more hours of hiking with a thirty pound pack.

At night, Richard and his four classmates, all radio operators,
were too tired to do more than collapse onto their bunks and sleep.
But gradually they settled into the work, and after the third week it
had become routine. Richard and Blair Moffet spent more and more
free time together.

"You've become a different person," she said when they were
strolling through the quadrangle one evening. Blair had been telling
him of a phone call from her father, a retired Royal Navy warrant
officer. In the past few weeks the Germans had mounted nightly air
raids on London, called by Londoners the Little Blitz. Last night's
raid had obliterated an entire block on Nottingham Hill Road where
the elder Moffets lived. Not only were Blair's parents uninjured, their
house was untouched. Luck of the Irish, she said.

"You're not Irish," Richard said.

Which prompted her remark about his being a different person.
"You're not the same little boy I met three weeks ago," she said.

"What do you mean?" But he knew full well that he had matured.
That goddam sadist Sergeant Major Arthur Fellows had seen to that.
But now he had to thank the son of a bitch.

". . . I mean, you're a man," Blair was saying, and abruptly turned
to him, drew his face down to hers, and kissed him. A light, delicate,
almost indecisive kiss. Kay had kissed him with that same indecisive-
ness when he said goodbye to her the night before he left for Shrivenham. He had been a little ashamed of the relief he felt, but had
sensed the same relief in her.

In the dark he looked at Blair. The touch of her lips still lingered
on his, and the smooth sweetness of her lipstick. If the kiss reminded
him of Kay, it was also different, less urgent, less desperate.

He said, "I think that's what's known as a 'brotherly kiss.' "

"That's all we're allowed here, isn't it? 'Brotherly' feelings for
each other." She quoted a statement from their project officer, a
British brigadier general named Rowland, perfectly mimicking the
general's public-school lisp. " 'In our business there is no room for
emotion.' "

"What's happened to General Rowland, by the way?" Richard
asked. "He hasn't been around since that first week."

"He's always traveling between here and London," Blair said.
"They say he reports directly to Winston."

Early on, back in October, Rowland had sent for Richard to say that he, Rowland, had been in a German POW camp with Richard's father. Someday he must tell Richard a little story of his father's escapades in that camp. Yes, said the general, Simon Conway was quite a character.

". . . and as General Rowland says," Blair continued, "we must take care not to form emotional attachments with each other." She mimicked Rowland's voice again. " 'Any, ah . . . well, let us say, ah . . . emotional attachments . . . might well interfere with good judgment which in turn might well cost you your lives.' Those are the rules, aren't they?" she said.

"They certainly are," said Richard, and swept her into his arms. What good judgment? he asked himself as they kissed again.

Three days before graduation Richard and Blair were summoned to Captain Chalmers's office to meet an American civilian who had just arrived from Washington.

Craig Olney was balding, on the far side of fifty, and very businesslike. "Your orders have been changed," he said. "You won't be going to Yugoslavia after all."

He waited for someone to ask the obvious question and when no one did, he continued, "You'll be going into France. We selected you, Lieutenant Moffet, because of your fluency in French." He turned to Richard. "Sergeant Conway's personnel records indicate straight A's in high school French and two semesters of college. You'll be given a brush-up course in the language in any event."

"What exactly is our mission?" Richard asked.

"We'll be dropped into France to make contact with a certain Maquis group. You and Lieutenant Moffet will establish communications with London for them."

"Sir, you said 'we'll' be dropped in," Blair said. "Does that mean you'll accompany us?"

"That is precisely what it means," Olney said. "I realize I might look a little ancient for this, but I've done it before. I'll not be a burden to you. I don't mean to sound melodramatic, but this is an extremely vital mission. Excuse me, I *do* mean to sound melodramatic. The whole course of the war could turn on this mission."

Bullshit, Richard thought, and waited for the usual disclaimer: anyone desiring to withdraw was free to do so. Captain Chalmers made that announcement. Blair said nothing. Olney looked at Richard, who was sure everyone could read his mind. OSS casualties in France approached 50 percent. When you went into France they issued you a single cyanide tablet.

". . . sure, okay," he heard his own voice saying. Even as he spoke he was thinking, Gutless bastard! You're afraid to say no. You're afraid of what Blair will think of you.

No, not afraid of her, in love with her.

Not until later that same evening, lying on his bunk staring at the crystal-domed light fixture in the ceiling, did he realize that something about the mission was wrong. Very wrong. At least three of the radio operators in other teams were French, born in, raised in and, until Dunkerque, residents of France. They spoke the language and knew the country.

He could understand why Blair was chosen. As a woman her presence cast less suspicion on the team. But if the mission was as vital as claimed, why had he been selected over the Frenchmen? He pondered the question until early morning, when he finally fell fitfully asleep.

That same gray drizzly morning of December 15, 1943, seventy miles to the east in London, another man woke from an equally fitful sleep. This man knew the answer to Richard's question because he personally had requested that Richard participate in the mission.

The man, whose bedroom was twenty feet below the surface of the city streets in a supposedly bombproof vault adjoining what was called the War Room, shouted for his valet.

"What time is it?"

"Half after six, sir," said the valet, who had rushed into the room with the man's silk bathrobe—the man preferred sleeping nude—and a pot of tea.

"Are last night's damage reports in yet?"

The valet, whose name was George Archer, a thrice-wounded veteran of the 1914–18 war, told him the reports were on the desk and added, "General Allen is waiting, sir."

"What the devil for?"

"To brief you on the oh-eight-hundred staff meeting."

"Does he mind if I pee first?"

While Winston Churchill shuffled into the W.C. that had been specially installed in this small bedroom, George Archer set about laying out the Prime Minister's clothes, pouring the tea, and placing a cigar and box of matches on the night table.

Five days earlier, in this same room, George Archer had brought a dispatch notifying the PM that Operation New Broom was underway. New Broom was the British code name for Generalmajor Werner Ramsch's plan to assassinate Adolf Hitler, and the key to New Broom's success was Karl Eisler.

Karl, via Swedish intermediaries, had contacted U.S. Senator

Morris Tannen, who in turn notified General William Donovan of OSS. Karl agreed to meet with Craig Olney, an OSS representative, to discuss the implementation of New Broom. The meeting would take place in Paris, arranged by a French Resistance leader known only as Cricket.

Immediately after receiving word of Karl's agreement, Churchill instructed his military aide, Lieutenant General Sir William Allen, to schedule a lunchtime meeting that day with Wally Rowland of SOE and Craig Olney of OSS. The War Room chef, through his connections with a U.S. Army Quartermaster Corps first sergeant, obtained three one-and-one-half-pound T-bone steaks, which he grilled to perfection and served with steamed brussels sprouts and French-fried potatoes.

Churchill's first words to the two men had been "Well, gentlemen, I take it that the game is on."

Craig Olney said, "It is, sir. Karl Eisler believes we'll consider a negotiated peace with a new German government."

"Let him believe whatever he wants," Churchill said. "Promise him whatever he wants. The question is, will he trust us?"

"If he doesn't now, he certainly should when he sees young Conway," Rowland said. "After all, sir, that's why we're sending the boy in, isn't it?"

"Yes, it's a stroke of luck that the son of Eisler's former business partner volunteered for Shrivenham," Churchill said. "Have you told him he'll be meeting Eisler?"

"I don't believe we should, Prime Minister," Olney said. "Not until we're further along with the mission."

Churchill nodded his approval. "The presence of Simon Conway's son in the operation should demonstrate our sincerity. Otherwise, why would we risk exposing the lad to such danger? I'm certain Eisler will trust us."

"I only hope we can trust *him*," Rowland said.

Now, five days later, while the Prime Minister relaxed with his morning tea and cigar, his military aide reviewed the day's agenda. Before commencing, General Allen had some news regarding New Broom.

"Eisler will be in Paris exactly one month from today, on January fifteenth," he said. "The team will be dropped in on the fourteenth, young Conway included."

"Good."

Allen's face suddenly clouded. He handed Churchill a piece of white paper torn jaggedly from a teletype machine. The Prime Minister read it.

"Last night?" he asked.

"Yes, sir. At Cologne."

Churchill folded the paper neatly in half and slipped it into his robe pocket. "All right, get on with the rest of it, please."

They discussed the forthcoming staff meeting for another twenty minutes. Allen moved to leave but Churchill motioned him to remain. The Prime Minister drew on his cigar and waited until the ash glowed red before reaching into his pocket for the teletyped message. He reread it.

"Has the family been notified?" he asked.

"I phoned our embassy in Washington myself," Allen said. "I asked the ambassador to make the call personally."

"You know, Allen, that if any harm comes to this young man, Richard Conway, it will fall to me to make the next personal telephone call to the Conway family."

"Well, sir, let's hope and pray it all works out."

"Yes, but I doubt there is a bookmaker in England who wouldn't give you at least four to one against New Broom's success," Churchill said. "Do you know that of the some six hundred agents we have dropped into France in the past three years, nearly two thirds of them—two thirds, Allen!—have not survived? If not through their own incompetence, then through French treachery! Every damned time a Frenchman is arrested, the Nazis turn him around by offering him his life. And now we come up with this fanciful scheme!" He clamped down hard on the cigar. "The damn trouble is that we have no choice. We *have* to try it."

After Allen left, Churchill started to dress. He removed his robe and tossed it carelessly on the bed. The white edge of the paper protruded from the pocket. It was part of a report of the previous night's RAF operations. Six aircraft lost, including a Lancaster bomber that had taken a direct hit from antiaircraft fire and exploded in midair. The Lancaster's pilot was Squadron Leader Gordon Hall, Richard Conway's brother-in-law.

2.

The noonday sun flashed off the gold dome of the Avalon casino and off the decks of the small boats moored at the pier. From ten thousand feet, Catalina was a patchwork of colors, blue water, beige beach sand, green lawns, red-tiled roofs on the whitewashed business buildings in the center of town and, up into the hills, the brown of winter foliage.

". . . I'm going to turn back now, Mr. Conway!" the pilot, Art Hamel, shouted. Art, Conair's new chief test pilot, had replaced Mike Doyle, who was back in the army as an ATC lieutenant colonel, at last report flying C-46s over the Hump.

"Yeah, Art, let's do that!" Si shouted back. "Let's take this goddam cow home!"

Si, in the flight engineer's jump seat directly behind the control pedestal, was already hoarse from shouting. The roar of the four 2,400-horsepower, eighteen-cylinder Jensen J-24 compounds obliterated all other sound. They had been in the air more than an hour, the first extensive flight test of the 775, or, as everyone called her, the "Seven-seventy and a half." With good reason. The new airplane, half again as big as the 770, was an otherwise exact replica of that model. Whenever he looked at the 775, Si had to wonder how she ever got off the ground. With the exception of Howard Hughes's giant plywood flying boat, the 775 was the largest airplane ever built.

Si himself had flown the 775 on her first flight. He thought she handled like a rowboat caught in a riptide. He had toyed briefly with the idea of modifying the design as a test bed for Charlie Jensen's jet engines, but Charlie's jets, in this January of 1944, were no farther along than a year ago.

The 775 was not a good airplane, yet Si knew the Army Air Force would buy it. As a long-range transport capable of carrying 280 fully equipped troops, the 775 fit the army's specifications. Well, damn the army's specifications. The only specifications that mattered were Simon Conway's, and this underpowered, overweight mongrel airplane called the 775 did not come close to them.

". . . want to land her, Mr. Conway?"

"No, Art, the pleasure is all yours!"

Art Hamel, in his late twenties, possessed wrists the size of baseball bats. You needed that kind of muscle to manhandle the 775's controls. That was another problem, the power boost system. Sluggish as the airplane itself.

You are getting old, Conway, he told himself, thinking that next year was the magic number, fifty. But he did not feel old. On the contrary, he felt young, as strong as he ever had been; and, except for the reading glasses he increasingly reached for, healthier. More pep and vitality, more ambition. More to look forward to.

Janet, for example. She was coming home today. Meg would already have picked her up and driven her back to Pacific Palisades.

Poor Janet had looked like hell when he saw her a week ago. Thin to the point of emaciation, no color, the long, lustrous black hair dull and frizzy. And so unhappy. But how could you be happy after a month at the Pasadena Oaks? Pasadena Oaks, a clever name for a sanatorium.

". . . don't know what you plan to tell the army people about this airplane," Art Hamel was saying. "Or that senator."

"I'll tell them the truth, Art," Si said. "The airplane is a dog." And as for "that senator," he thought, he'd inform that senator in no uncertain terms to put away the hatchet and go back to Washington. The senator had somehow learned of the 775's problems and rushed out here hoping to quash the air force's order. Si would save him the trouble. More accurately, deny him the satisfaction. That senator was, of course, Morris Tannen.

"Gear down!" Art Hamel shouted. "Flaps ten degrees!"

Immediately, the whole airplane began vibrating with the descending gear. The four truck-sized main wheels and double nose wheel slammed into place with a shuddering thump that nearly wrested the control yoke from Art Hamel's grip.

"Down and locked!" the copilot shouted.

Art Hamel shook his head sadly. "I'm sorry, Mr. Conway, but this son of a bitch has got to go back to the drawing board!"

"Not the drawing board, Art," said Si. "The junk pile!"

Art Hamel landed the big airplane smoothly enough. He taxied to the ramp and switched off the engines, slumping back in his seat and sighing with relief. Si patted him on the shoulder, mumbled, "Nice work," and hurried from the flight deck. For the first time in memory he was ashamed of a Conair product.

Si avoided the AAF officers and the cluster of Conair people waiting to greet him. He especially wanted to duck Morris Tannen. He went into his office and closed the door. He removed his hat—a grease-streaked gray fedora that only a few months ago had been brand-new—and leather jacket, tossed both on the couch, then removed a bottle of Chivas Regal from a bottom desk drawer. He poured himself a large drink and carried it over to the window.

In the midst of the mechanics and engineers swarming around the parked 775, Si saw Morris Tannen with a younger, taller man, a marine officer. They were walking toward Phil Granger, who was chatting with three army officers under the 775's fuselage. Morris and Granger exchanged a few words, and then Granger shook hands with the marine and introduced him to the army officers.

Si drank the drink down in a single swallow and told himself, Relax, for Christ's sake! All right, so the 775 was a disaster, but just last week Granger had given him the figure for Conair's gross revenue in 1943: $500 million, a half billion, capital B! Si remembered back in '39, only five years ago, when the figure was $22 million.

Behind him, he heard someone enter the office. "Si . . . ?"

It was Meg. With her was Janet.

"Daddy!" Janet rushed across the room and embraced him. Si held her close, then placed her head on his shoulder as he had done when she was a little girl. She always said it made her feel safe and secure. She stepped back. "How do I look?"

"You look fine," he lied. "I wasn't expecting you."

"She made me bring her straight here," Meg said.

"I wanted to see you," Janet said.

"I'm glad you came here instead of going home," Si said, which was not untrue; he had promised himself he would help her get well. He owed her that much. He would never forget the morning four weeks ago when she learned of Gordon Hall's death. The doctors called it a nervous breakdown. Si called it no guts. He cringed now, remembering his own fatuous words, the stupid bromides he had hurled at her.

Goddam you, he had yelled, stop feeling sorry for yourself! You're not the only wife who lost a husband! Grow up, goddammit! And more of the same, and more, until she rushed out to her car and drove recklessly away. Luckily, a Malibu sheriff stopped her, probably saving her life. He said he clocked her at ninety-five miles an hour on Pacific Coast Highway.

So instead of a traffic-court appearance, Janet got four weeks at the Oaks. It seemed to have helped, and with no fancy treatment other than daily chats with her psychiatrist, a German refugee named Feldman, who wanted to try a new treatment on Janet, insulin shock therapy. Si refused him permission. She's grieving, Si said. Everybody grieves, and everybody gets over it. But he also went out of his way to make sure Janet knew, despite his initial reaction, that he was on her side.

"Why don't we go home and celebrate?" he said. "I'll cook some steaks. One of the pilots brought in a box of two-inch-thick filets from Omaha." He patted Janet's cheek. "What do you say?"

"I say yes," she said.

"Then let's go," Si said.

They were in the parking lot when Morris Tannen called to them. The young marine officer, a captain, was with him.

Meg said quietly, "My God, that's Paul!"

"He's gorgeous," Janet said.

Morris kissed Meg and Janet, guardedly shook hands with Si, and went through the motions of reintroducing Paul. They chatted briefly, mainly about how well everyone looked and what a long time had passed since they had seen each other.

Morris took Si aside. "That's quite a piece of machinery, that 775," he said. "A little bigger than our old 110, I'd say."

"That's right, Morris, just a little."

"The rumors have it that the airplane is in trouble."

"The army wants to buy it," Si said. "It meets their specifications."

"I'd like to see the initial flight test reports."

"They're confidential."

Morris shook his head, amused. "Don't ever change, Si. The shock might kill me."

"In that case, I'll do my best to accommodate you."

"That, Si, I'm sure of. But I still want to see those reports."

"What for?"

"To begin with, because I'm a member of the Senate Armed Services Committee."

"Then go through channels," Si said. "Ask the Pentagon."

"Si, you know damn well I've a right to see those reports. In fact, that's why I'm here."

Before Si could reply, Meg walked over to them and said to Morris, "We're having a little party this afternoon at the house, just the family. Why don't you and Paul join us?"

To Si's dismay, Morris said, "We'd love to, thank you."

Later, at home, Meg explained her motive for inviting Morris and his son. "I think Paul would be good for Janet. She needs someone to be with, Si, someone close to her age. Paul is a very nice young man."

"He's Morris's son, for Christ's sake!"

"Yes, Si, so he is."

Meg's hunch was sound: the two, Janet and Paul, spent most of the afternoon together, talking. Si had to admit that this was the first time since Gordon had returned to England that he had seen Janet so animated.

After the conversation at the field with Morris—and for no other reason than to defy Morris—Si had changed his mind about canceling the 775. He had decided to redesign the airplane, no matter what the cost. But now, seeing his daughter so cheerful and vibrant, the pleasure of defying Morris Tannen seemed quite trivial.

". . . that's correct, senator," Si said. "I'm canceling the program. I've explained why. Do you want me to go over all of it again?"

"What about the development funds?"

"They'll be returned to the government."

"You can't use the money on something else, you know."

"I said the money will be returned."

They were in Si's library, Si on the leather couch nursing a scotch and water; Morris, with a schooner of beer, opposite him on a lounge chair.

"Anytime you do something honorable, Si, something's fishy."

"Thank you."

Morris raised his glass in a gesture of wry acknowledgment. At least they understood each other, Si thought. And what the hell, they should understand each other, they went back a long enough way. And Morris was beginning to look his age, which did not displease Si, although he wondered if Morris was well. He looked wan and haggard.

Jesus H. Christ, Conway! he told himself. Here you are, feeling almost friendly toward this little bastard who gave you a $1,392,000 fucking. And without the loving, yet—$1,392,000, at a time when Si did not have $1.39 to call his own. And on top of it, he had wrongly accused Si of anti-Semitism.

Si said, "I was just thinking that it's a shame you didn't hold on to your Conair stock. Today, it'd be worth ten times what you sold it for."

"I'm not complaining," Morris said.

"Last year we grossed a half billion," Si said. "That's 'B,' like in 'banker.' "

"That's 'B' like in 'before,' Si. Before taxes."

"You always have to get the last word, don't you?"

Si opened the hammered-silver humidor on his desk and extracted two cigars, Upmanns, from one of five boxes Ross Leonard had picked up in Havana as a gift for Si. The Intercontinental Air president was now, and for the duration, Colonel Ross Leonard, USAAF, functioning as a kind of roving troubleshooter for Air Transport Command in the Caribbean region.

Si handed Morris a cigar. Morris peered at the band, impressed, but then examined the tip with mock suspicion. Si took him half seriously. "It won't explode," Si said. "You don't trust anybody, do you?"

"But I do, Si," Morris said. He leaned over for Si to light the cigar. "*Almost* anybody."

"Thank you again."

"Don't mention it," Morris said. He drew on the cigar. "What do you hear from Richard?"

"I got the craziest letter from him." Si plucked out a piece of tissue-thin blue V-mail stationery from the papers stacked haphazardly on the desk and gave it to Morris. "See what you make out of this, the last sentence."

Morris read the last sentence aloud. " '. . . volunteered for some kind of special duty. I can't say what it is yet but maybe you'll be reading about it in the newspapers. Love, Rich.' " Morris returned the letter to Si. "I don't know what to make of it. I could probably find out."

"No, maybe it's better I don't know."

"Talking about 'special duty,' " Morris began, and stopped abruptly. "Forget it."

"What were you going to say?"

"Something I shouldn't have," Morris said. "Nothing about Richard, believe me. Forget it." Morris had come close to telling Si that he had been contacted by Karl. But even revealing that much was too dangerous. "I'm sure Richard is fine. He's probably on some hush-hush air force radio project."

"Another beer?" Si asked.

"Still have that cognac I always liked so much?"

"It's Armagnac, not cognac," Si said.

"It's the same thing, Si, only with a fancy name."

Not in his wildest dreams could Morris Tannen have imagined that the operation he had set into motion with Karl Eisler, and the "special duty" mission Richard Conway had embarked upon, were one and the same.

3.

They jumped low, from twelve hundred feet. Richard was second out the door, behind Craig Olney and ahead of Blair. He caught a glimpse of Olney's chute billowing below him but he could not see Blair at all. In the blackness, a blinking pinpoint of yellow light marked the center of the landing area.

Richard hit the ground hard. The impact drove his lower jaw into his upper with a sharp jolt of pain. He flexed his knees and held the lines stationary while he released the harness buckles. Voices were shouting excitedly in French, and then he heard his name called.

"Richard . . . ?" It was Blair.

"Over here!" he called back.

"Be quiet, damn you!" a man called out in French. This same man gripped Richard's arm and, in English, said, "Get rid of your harness. We'll take care of the parachutes!"

Richard could make out three other men rushing across an open field to the equipment canisters that had been dropped with them. The man who had spoken to him was barking orders. He wanted the entire area cleared in ten minutes.

Tall and heavy-framed, the man wore a coarse wool pea jacket and corduroy work cap. A Sten gun was slung over his shoulder. In heavily accented but grammatically perfect English, he said to Richard, "Get out of your flight suit." As Richard began unbuttoning the flight suit, the man continued, "What's your name?"

"Who are you?" Richard said.

The man laughed harshly. "You'd better hope I'm who I'm supposed to be. I'm Cricket."

"I'm Conway."

Cricket trained the flashlight on Richard's face. Quietly, almost to himself, he said in French, "You're so damned young . . ."

"Excuse me?" Richard asked.

In English, Cricket went on, ". . . and you're bleeding. Open your mouth." He shone the light into Richard's mouth. "It looks like you broke a tooth." He switched off the flashlight. "Do you know where you are?"

"Étampes, forty miles south of Paris," Richard said. He saw Blair approach, carrying her flight suit bundled in her arm. She wore a shabby cloth coat over a dark wool dress. Even in the dark Richard could read the distress on her face.

"Olney is dead," she said. "A broken neck, the accident they told us could happen only once in a million times. Well, this was the millionth time!"

"Yes, and we must get away from here fast!" Cricket said. "We'll take the dead man with us and dispose of his body somewhere in the village. Not a very promising way to start a mission, is it?"

Dispose of his body, Richard thought. Jesus Christ! The whole thing seemed suddenly unreal. But the voices arguing angrily in French were real enough: ". . . it's too dangerous now!" one voice cried.

"You fool, there's no choice!" replied Cricket. "Where am I supposed to take them? Into Paris, for God's sake?"

"That's your problem!" said the first, a squat barrel-chested man whose features were almost entirely obscured by lampblack.

Cricket and the man moved away to continue their heated discussion. Blair explained the problem to Richard. "They're arguing about us. We were supposed to be billeted at a safe house near here. But only Olney knew where, and with whom. This man"—she indicated the man talking to Cricket—"lives in Étampes but says it's too risky taking us with him."

"And Cricket says he has no place to put us up in Paris," Richard said. "I got that much of it."

A few minutes later Cricket ordered everyone into a disreputable old Renault furniture van whose motor ran on alcohol and spewed a constant cloud of sickly-sweet fumes. They drove to a nearby farm. There, in an empty barn, Richard strung an antenna wire between two roof eaves, set up his radio, and tapped out a brief coded message reporting Olney's death to London.

The response came directly from Brigadier Rowland: the mission was to proceed under Cricket's supervision and at his discretion, which, as Cricket dourly commented, left him no option but to take Blair and Richard into Paris. The entire group spent the night in the barn. In the morning the truck, Olney's body, and the three Maquis were gone.

The daylight offered Richard and Blair their first clear look at Cricket. With thick gray hair, deep piercing eyes, and a leathery face, he exuded authority and looked like a man accustomed to an outdoor life, although Blair remarked that his hands were smooth and uncalloused.

"Never mind his hands," Richard said. "Who is he?"

"He's the man in charge of the mission," Blair said.

"That's what I mean," said Richard. "What the hell *is* the mission?" They were at the Étampes railway station, waiting on the platform for Cricket to purchase the train tickets to Paris. "And what in the hell are we doing here?"

"I'm sure we'll find out soon enough." Blair shifted her heavy leather valise from one hand to the other. With her free hand she smoothed the lapel of Richard's suitcoat. "You look strange in civilian clothes," she said.

"In these civilian clothes, I do," he said. The suit, issued in Shrivenham along with appropriate personal documents, was old and shiny-smooth from wear; a black worsted jacket, vest, and trousers. He brushed his hand over the ruffled white collar of Blair's navy-blue wool dress. "I wouldn't call this the height of fashion, either."

"The idea, dear boy, is to be inconspicuous."

"I sure don't feel like it in these clothes," Richard said. "On the other hand, maybe the guys in Shrivenham knew what they were doing: if any Germans see us they'll laugh themselves to death before they can arrest us."

But of the dozens of people milling about the platform, not a German uniform was in sight. While it made Richard feel no easier, it relieved some of his anxiety about the battered leather valises he and Blair carried, each with a false bottom that concealed a radio transmitter, receiver, earphones, antenna wire, and telegraph key.

They rode in a second-class compartment, crammed in with three nuns and a young boy. The boy continually munched on a sandwich that stank of rank cheese. Other than a brief exchange between Cricket and the nuns about the unexpectedly mild winter weather—which the nuns insisted presaged a chilly, rainy spring—there was little conversation.

Now and then the train passed burned-out freight cars on adjacent tracks, which themselves were torn and twisted. Once they passed the charred, skeletal hulk of a bomber, the faded outline of a French roundel still visible on its wings and fuselage.

The quaint little villages and towns soon turned into an urban sprawl of larger buildings, busier streets, and, for the first time, German soldiers. Richard looked at Cricket, who nodded grimly.

"Welcome to Paris," Cricket said.

19

The ornate lounge was noisy with the sound of ice clinking in glasses and the constant buzz of chatter and quiet laughter. The women, all in elegantly fashionable evening gowns, wandered invitingly in and out of the room, or sipped champagne with customers at the glass-bricked illuminated bar or on the velour settees. Near the arched, colonnaded entrance a tuxedoed trio played soft string music. The air was heavy with the heady aroma of expensive perfume and body powder that blended not at all unpleasantly with male cologne and tobacco smoke.

The Sphinx Club at 32 Rue Edgar Quinet, a legendary address, was the residence of some of the most beautiful and accomplished prostitutes in Paris. Most of the establishment's "clients," as the management preferred to call them, were German officers. As the prominent French industrialist had said, the Sphinx Club was inconspicuous in its conspicuousness. A perfectly logical place for the Frenchman to conduct business with an equally prominent German aircraft manufacturer.

Karl, who had arrived ten minutes early, had just ordered a glass of wine but was momentarily considering switching to a martini. The barman had just mixed one for a young, bearded Kriegsmarine officer, a submarine captain. It looked deliciously dry, every drop as crisp and tangy as those concocted by the bartender at Wally's, the speakeasy back in Santa Monica.

Karl decided it was too early in the day for a martini. He drew on his cigar and sampled the wine while he watched the submarine captain summon a tall, buxom blond in an exquisite black sheath gown.

Karl felt a presence behind him. He turned. A man in a well-tailored business suit stood regarding him blandly. The man's husky body and craggy features gave him the appearance of a manual laborer, not a captain of industry.

"Monsieur Fresnais," Karl greeted him.

"Herr Eisler," replied the other, whose name was Jean Fresnais, although Karl also knew him by his Maquis code name, Cricket.

Their only previous meeting had been held in the offices of Industrie Fresnais in the grimy Paris suburb of Billancourt. Industrie Fresnais before the war had manufactured railway cars, but now assembled various aircraft parts for the Luftwaffe. Karl and Jean Fresnais had actually reached a genuine agreement on the production of the KE-2's Plymax wing assembly.

It provided the perfect cover for them to work together. The Frenchman was considered by many of his countrymen a *collabo*, a collaborator; the German was a man whose position and prestige left no question as to his loyalty to Fatherland and Führer. No one would ever suspect these two of conspiring to kill that Führer.

They now nodded formally and shook hands. "You were absolutely right about this place," Karl said in French. " 'Inconspicuous in its conspicuousness.' "

"Yes, but please don't think me a habitué," Fresnais said. "I'm a happily married man and faithful husband. I must confess, however, that my sons—" Fresnais's face tightened. "Both my boys were . . . initiated . . . here in the Sphinx. As was I," he added with a faint smile.

"Not an unpleasant family tradition," Karl said. He knew that Fresnais's sons, army officers, had been killed in 1940, within days of each other.

"No, not at all unpleasant," Fresnais said. "Look, we have much to talk about and not much time to do it. A glass of the red, please," Fresnais said to the barman, and for the barman's benefit, went on to Karl, "You'll be gratified to know that my engineers say they anticipate no problem retooling for your plywood-and-Duralumin wing assembly."

"How soon can you deliver?"

"How many units?"

"Five hundred to start."

The barman served Fresnais's wine. Fresnais raised his glass in a toast. They drank. Fresnais said, "Just get me a matériel allocation and in two to three weeks we're ready to go." He nodded toward the windowed doors at the far end of the room. "Let's take a walk."

The doors opened onto a terrace and a flight of white-bricked stairs leading down to a tree-lined courtyard. In the center of the courtyard was a small hexagonal ceramic-tiled pool that in prewar times had contained tropical fish. The fish were long gone and the pool, bone-dry now, was strewn with dead leaves and branches.

Fresnais placed his wineglass on the smooth glazed rim of the pool. "The agents were parachuted in the night before last," he said. "Olney was killed."

Karl sighed with dismay.

"The project will proceed as planned," Fresnais continued. "The other two, the radio operators, landed safely. Rowland informs me that you might know one of them, an American named Conway."

"Conway?" The very sound of his own voice repeating the name startled Karl. "*The* Conway? No, how could it be?"

"His son."

"Richard?"

"I never thought to ask his Christian name."

"It has to be Richard," Karl said. "But of all people, why on earth send him? It certainly can't be a coincidence." In the same breath, he answered his own question. "Yes, of course: I'll know the boy and will trust him. You are all going to great lengths to assure me of your sincerity, aren't you?"

"The objective is as important to us as it is to you."

"Does the boy—my God, how old can he be? Nineteen? Twenty at most. He's a baby—does he know what this is all about? Does he know of my involvement?"

"He doesn't know a thing yet. It would be too dangerous. But I think you're right: they sent him here as proof of sincerity. Now tell me, are there any new developments?"

Karl did not reply. Richard, he was thinking. My God, how was it possible?

"Eisler . . . ? Please, we haven't much time."

In the past two days, wherever he went, whatever he did and said, the words "Treason" and "Traitor" had flashed into Karl's mind. Treason, Traitor. And, perhaps, Fool.

Even as he began speaking, he was asking himself the same question he had pondered from the moment he first met Jean Fresnais. Could the Frenchman be trusted? Was the man a double agent luring Karl ever deeper into a trap? Of Fresnais's personal life, Karl knew little beyond the tragedy of the two sons and that his wife, to whom he had been married seventeen years, was not their mother.

Of course, concerning trust, it worked both ways. Why should Fresnais trust him? Never mind that they were brought together on arrangements made in Washington and London, Fresnais had no guarantee Karl was not a Gestapo plant.

And now, Richard.

It was inconceivable that the Americans would have sent Simon Conway's son if the slightest possibility of betrayal existed. But Karl had only Fresnais's word that Richard was in France. Before proceeding one step further, he would demand to see Richard for himself.

He said, "No, nothing has changed from what you already know. Sometime in the next few days Hitler will visit the Atlantic fortifications. He'll fly in his personal airplane to Paris, to Villacoublay airdrome, and then be driven to a nearby rail siding to board a special train for Calais. I will be at the airfield when he arrives. I am sure that no one will question my being there, and that I'll have no trouble learning the time of the train's departure. I'll telephone the information to your radio operators, who will relay the message to London. A squadron of Mosquito bombers will attack the train."

Fresnais said nothing. He appeared dissatisfied.

"It's the same plan we discussed," Karl said. "I know you would prefer something more substantial, but this is what I believe will work and what London has approved."

Fresnais said, "Even if the train is destroyed, we have no assurance that Hitler will be killed. A bomb on the train is the ideal solution. Set it to blow at the approximate time the RAF planes reach the train. The attack would then conceal the actual cause of the 'accident.' "

"And who places this bomb aboard the train?" Karl knew the answer before he asked the question.

"You," said Fresnais. He swirled the remaining wine around in his glass, and then drank it down. "Not a bad vintage for a *maison d'amour*." He pointed the empty glass at the house. "Perhaps you'd like to partake? I'll be happy to introduce you to the madam."

"Some other time, perhaps." Karl knew the suggestion was facetious, but it brought Erika to mind. She was in Stockholm, supposedly as a representative of Eisler Allgemeinmaschinenwerke to facilitate delivery of a shipment of Duralumin. She had phoned from Stockholm to inform Karl of her safe arrival. Dieter Bauer had taken the call and relayed the message to Karl.

Erika, as Dieter was well aware, would not know a piece of Duralumin from a thumb tack. He was certain that Karl had sent Erika to Sweden to escape the interminable Allied bombing, in Dieter's mind an utterly unpatriotic act. Karl wanted Erika out of harm's way, all right, but not from fear of Allied air raids. He wanted her safely out of Germany while he, Karl, set about the business of assassinating Dieter's beloved Führer.

The new government would probably put Dieter—along with other fanatical Nazis—in front of a firing squad, which in a way was regrettable. Dieter was on the verge of developing a jet engine with five thousand pounds of thrust.

Karl faced Fresnais. "The bomb will need a very sophisticated timer. And it must be small enough to hide in a package, or a briefcase."

"Why not an overcoat?" Fresnais asked.

"An overcoat?"

"An overcoat, Herr Eisler. It's wintertime. Everyone wears an overcoat."

2.

When Karl first saw Richard, he thought he had been thrown back in time, and that it was 1918, or 1923, and he was face to face with Simon Conway. The resemblance, however, ended there. Richard conveyed none of Si's brash self-confidence or arrogance, and he was clearly anxious for acceptance. Si, of course, had never cared one way or the other. And most important, one liked Richard immediately. The same could hardly be said of his father.

They were in the unheated parlor of a small flat on the ground floor of a five-story tenement on Rue Froissart in Billancourt, not far from Jean Fresnais's factory. The apartment was the residence of the elderly widow of a toolmaker who had worked at Industrie Fresnais for twenty-five years. She lived there rent-free, thanks to the generosity of Jean Fresnais, who owned the building. As a favor to Fresnais, she had agreed to provide Richard and Blair her spare bedroom for a few days.

". . . it's a rather simple assignment actually," Fresnais was saying. "Sometime in the next twenty-four hours Herr Eisler will telephone you. He will say, 'Could we meet at the Café Étoile at two-fifteen?' Or he might say, 'Could we meet at three-twenty?' Or 'three-thirty.' Whatever time he fixes for the 'appointment' will be the text of the message that you will radio to London."

For a moment no one spoke. Then Richard said, "That's it? That's all?"

"This is what they sent us here for?" Blair asked. "To answer the telephone?"

"It's probably the most important call you will ever receive," Karl said.

"There's more to it than that, isn't there?" Blair said.

"You know all you need to," Fresnais said. "It's for your own protection."

"In case we're captured, you mean?" Blair said.

"Exactly," said Fresnais. "Now, are there any questions?"

"Why are there two of us?" Blair asked. "Two radio operators?"

Fresnais did not immediately reply. He had been pondering the variables. Anything and everything might go wrong. A ten-minute delay in Hitler's train departing, a change of itinerary, or, for reasons of security, even a deliberately misleading announcement of the departure time. Suppose Eisler was searched before being allowed to board the train?

". . . there are two of us because one of us, me, is excess baggage," Richard was saying. "They sent me to meet Karl. That's right, isn't it?" he asked Karl.

Karl, hesitating, looked at Fresnais. Fresnais said, "There are two of you so that if something happens to one, the other can back him up."

But Richard knew better. He had not taken his eyes from Karl, who finally said, "Does it make any difference? You're here, and there's a job to be done."

"Then at least I have a right to know what it's all about, and why."

Karl thought, And I said this boy was not like his father? He's a thousand times more stubborn. Karl glanced at his watch, and then at Fresnais. They read each other's mind. Time was running out. Mme. Lenoir might return at any moment from her daily search for coal or firewood. She had not been present when Karl arrived, and he wanted to be gone before she returned. For her to see him was an unacceptable risk.

There was no more time to waste. In two succinct sentences, Karl told Richard and Blair that the information he would telephone them was the departure time of a certain train. The RAF would do the rest. This was as much as he would tell them, which was already more than they should know.

Blair said, "All right, so we radio the message. What happens then? Is that the end of our assignment?"

"There will be plenty of work for you," Fresnais said. "More than you can handle, believe me. So let's get on with the job, shall we?"

"We'll do ours," Richard said. "But how you can be sure the RAF will do theirs?"

Fresnais searched for an intelligent reply. There was none. Very little the OSS or SOE did these days made sense. And this so-called Operation New Broom topped them all. A typically sloppy OSS-SOE project. No wonder the Germans were so successful in thwarting the Resistance. No wonder the longevity of agents was measured in weeks. He, Jean Fresnais, was an exception. He had been in the Resistance nearly a year, which meant that his time was rapidly being used up. They were probably closing in on him at this very moment.

He had discussed that possibility only this morning with his wife. Of course, Andrée had no idea of the momentous importance of the present project, and he intended that she never know, at least not until it was over. At that time, he would also tell her of Simon Conway's son having been in Paris.

Fresnais said to Richard, "I assure you that the RAF will do the job."

For a moment the room was so quiet that the garbled voices of people on the floor above were audible through the ceiling. Then Fresnais began talking. Karl paid no attention. He was watching Richard and Blair, who sat close to each other on the sagging divan, their hands clasped together, fingers entwined. They reminded Karl of frightened children. Well, they were children, he thought, and for an instant imagined that it was Si sitting on the couch, holding hands with this attractive young girl. Fathers and sons, he thought.

Fathers and sons. Karl wondered what Richard truly thought of him. But then what could anyone think of a man betraying his own country? Betrayal? No, not when you were attempting to save your country from a man who was leading it to destruction.

He said to Richard, "Do you understand what you are to do?"

"Yes sir, I'm sure I do," Richard said.

"And you?" Karl asked Blair.

"Yes."

"Then I shall be on my way." Karl buttoned his coat and put on his hat. He shook hands with Richard and Blair. "Good luck," he said. He nodded at Fresnais, and left.

"Good luck," Fresnais called after him, but then hurried to the door and stepped outside. "27 Rue d'Orléans," he said quietly. "If something goes wrong, go there: 27 Rue d'Orléans. In Ablon."

"If something goes wrong, I won't go anywhere," Karl said. "There will be nothing worth going anywhere for."

3.

Luckily, the Métro was running. Karl was back on the Champs-Élysées less than a half hour later. Arriving at his hotel, the Claridge, he walked past a well-dressed young man seated unobtrusively in the

lobby. As Karl entered the elevator, the man, a civilian, went downstairs to the lavatory where he obtained a telephone *jeton* from the
female attendant and stepped into the telephone booth, closed the
door, and dialed a number.

When his party answered, he said into the telephone in German,
"This is Gruber. He just arrived."

". . . . ."

"No, I don't know where he's been," the well-dressed young man,
Gruber, said. "He gave us the slip. He didn't use his car. He went off
by himself and took the Métro. That's where we lost him. For all I
know he might have gone back to that whorehouse."

". . . . ."

"Don't worry, from now on he won't be out of my sight."

Gruber's telephone call had been made to the Hotel Lutetia,
across the river on Boulevard Raspail, headquarters of the Paris detachment of the Abwehr, German army military intelligence. The
number he dialed connected him directly to a uniformed Wehrmacht
captain wearing the Iron Cross 2nd Class and a black wound badge.
When they completed the conversation, the Wehrmacht captain
walked across the hall to a small suite. There, in the parlor, a Luftwaffe
lieutenant colonel sat idly turning the pages of *Signal*, the Wehrmacht's bimonthly picture magazine, while a civilian barber cut his
hair.

The Wehrmacht captain said, "Eisler will be under twenty-four-
hour surveillance."

The lieutenant colonel said nothing. He continued to browse
through the magazine. The captain recognized this as a gesture of
dismissal and was glad to leave. He always felt uneasy with this officer,
whose scarred face reminded the captain of burn cases he had seen
in Russia, although this particular lieutenant colonel had never heard
a shot fired in anger. Reason enough for the captain's resentment,
and made worse because of his personal dislike for the lieutenant
colonel who, from the moment of his arrival in Paris last night, had
acted as though the Abwehr agents were his servants and the Lutetia
his private quarters. The presence of the barber graphically demonstrated that.

What the captain found most galling was his knowledge that the
lieutenant colonel sought help from the Abwehr only because the
Gestapo said they had more important things to do than follow Karl
Eisler around.

For his part, as long as someone followed Karl Eisler, the lieutenant colonel did not much care who did it. He made a mental note

to congratulate Eisler's assistant, Dieter Bauer, for his intuitive grasp of the situation. Karl Eisler would not have sent his wife to Sweden unless he planned to join her.

"Trim the sideburns a little closer, please," Anton Moerzer said to the barber.

20

From the bedroom Richard heard the telephone ring in the parlor. He sat up and looked at his watch. It was 3:35. He had been lying atop the unmade bed watching Blair at the dresser mirror combing her hair. They were both fully dressed, with sweaters over their clothes against the cold. They had been much warmer only a few minutes before, naked under the goose-down comforter, making love.

The phone stopped ringing. Through the thin walls they heard Mme. Lenoir speaking into the phone. A moment later there was a knock on the door and Mme. Lenoir entered the room. "It's for you," she said grumpily in French. "Either one of you."

"I'll take it," Richard said. He hurried into the parlor. As expected, it was Karl.

"Can we meet at Café Étoile at nine tomorrow morning?" Karl asked in French.

"Nine tomorrow will be fine," Richard said.

When he returned to the bedroom, Richard closed and locked the door and said to Blair, "The train leaves at nine tomorrow morning."

He slid the valise out from under the bed and began setting up the transmitter and receiver, while Blair removed the light bulb from the overhead fixture and replaced it with an adapter outlet. She plugged the portable transceiver unit's power cord into the outlet, and attached several feet of antenna wire.

"Okay," she said.

Richard waited for the tubes to warm up, then tightened the transmitter key and tapped out the London station's call letters in Morse code, AC5, and then his own call letters, WHT. AC5 from

WHT, AC5 from WHT. He hoped no lights were on in the building. Each time the transmitter was keyed all the bulbs dimmed.

Almost immediately, the high-pitched dots and dashes of WHT crackled in his earphones. He tapped out the numerals zero-nine-zero-zero-seventeen: 0900, on the 17th, the train's departure time. From WHT the operator repeated the numbers. Richard tapped the key twice to sign off and unplugged the power cord.

Now all that remained was to notify Jean Fresnais that the message had been sent. Fresnais would pick them up and drive them to the Gare de Lyon for the train to Ablon, to the safe house.

"Call Fresnais and tell him we're ready," he said to Blair. "Don't be nervous."

"I'm not nervous, I'm petrified!" She kissed him lightly on the lips. "And you're perspiring. It's freezing cold, and you're sweating." She pressed the palm of her hand to his forehead. "You're burning up. You have a fever!"

"Go make the call," he said.

Twenty-two miles to the south, at Villacoublay airdrome, Karl Eisler stood with a group of Luftwaffe officers watching a four-engined bomber, a specially modified Focke-Wulf FW-200C, touch down on the runway. The airplane's fuselage was armor-plated, with four 7.92mm machine guns mounted in two turrets, midship and aft. The cabin section had been replaced with eleven plush seats and a tastefully decorated private compartment containing an ingenious escape system. Even Hitler, who flew only when absolutely necessary, felt safe in this *Führermaschine*.

Karl had obtained the train departure information almost too easily. At Villacoublay, in the operations office of the 55th Bombardment Wing of Luftflotte 3, the first person he saw was Kurt Sigel, a young major he had known in Spain. Sigel was one of the first men to fly the KE-1 in combat. He admired the airplane, and its successor, the KE-2, even more.

When Karl casually mentioned that he would be accompanying Hitler on the train, Sigel unhesitatingly disclosed the departure time. And when Karl asked to use a telephone, the handsome young major offered Karl his own office for privacy. From there, Karl made the call to Richard.

Now, fifteen minutes later, with Sigel and the others, Karl waited for the *Führermaschine* to taxi to the tarmac.

". . . Oh-Oh wanted a military band here, and a red carpet, the whole bloody works," Sigel was saying, "but they told him the Führer wasn't in the mood for a show."

"Oh-Oh's looking for another oak leaf," Karl said. Oh-Oh was Lieutenant Colonel Otto Oberg, whom Karl knew Sigel despised. Oberg, Kampfgeschwader 55's adjutant, had engineered Sigel's involuntary transfer from fighters to bombers after being promoted to lieutenant colonel over Sigel's head.

"And he'll probably get the fucking medal, too," Sigel said glumly. He rubbed the flat of his hand over the lapel of Karl's double-breasted camel's-hair polo coat. "Very nice. Something new?"

"Hardly. I bought it back in '40, right here in Paris." Karl marveled at how glibly he invented that particular lie. The coat, which was brand-new, had been provided for him by Jean Fresnais and contained no manufacturer's label or other identifying marks.

Sigel plucked a single cigarette from a crumpled package in his tunic breast pocket and patted his uniform for matches. "Dr. Eisler, would you have a light?"

Karl pulled his silver lighter from his side trouser pocket. As he did so, some coins and a small metal key fell to the ground. Sigel immediately bent to pick them up. He returned the coins to Karl but fingered the key with curiosity. The key, two inches in length and unserrated, resembled those used to wind children's toys.

"What's this?" Sigel asked. "The key to someone's chastity belt?"

Karl strained to keep his voice steady. "Close," he said, and calmly took the key from Sigel's hand. "My safe-deposit box."

"I knew it opened some kind of box," Sigel said. "Hey, here's the airplane!" He slapped the lighter into Karl's hand and moved forward with the crowd as the *Führermaschine* wheeled around and stopped.

Karl dropped the lighter and the key back into his pocket. The tiny key, inserted into a receptacle on the top edge of a Munson electric timer, itself the size of a book of matches, wound a spring that activated the Munson's timing mechanism. The Munson, concealed under the top layer of cigarettes inside a flat José Genaro Cuban Cigarillos tin, fitted snugly against two miniature flashlight batteries. The entire bottom of the tin was filled with plastique explosive. The device, which according to Jean Fresnais was powerful enough to turn Hitler's private railway car into a box of toothpicks, lay heavily in the left-hand pocket of Karl's coat.

Hitler, trailed by his own aides and KG 55 staff officers, strode past. Suddenly, his eyes falling on Karl, he stopped. He appeared both surprised and annoyed. Karl cursed his own stupidity. As one of the few civilians in the crowd, and in that camel's-hair coat, he was as conspicuous as a strobe light.

Hitler crooked a finger toward Karl. Karl stepped forward. Hitler said, "Eisler, what in the world are you doing here?"

"I had hoped to see you, Führer."

Hitler sighed with exasperation. "About what? No, don't tell me, I know: this fixation of yours about the jet bomber. Will you kindly explain to me, Eisler, why you stubbornly insist on questioning my decision? We've been over this time and again."

"With all due respect, Führer, it is not a matter of your decision being questioned," Karl said. "It's—"

"—a matter of you knowing more than I do about it," Hitler said. "Well, of course you do. But I have to consider the problem in all of its aspects, the complete military and economic ramifications of this weapon, not merely what the manufacturer believes to be the most effective application. The subject is closed." He started away.

"May I accompany you on the train tomorrow, Führer?" Karl asked.

Hitler stopped again. He shook his head sadly. "You just never give up, do you, Eisler?"

"I mean no disrespect, sir, you know that."

Unexpectedly, Hitler smiled. He patted Karl's shoulder. "Yes, of course I know you intend no disrespect. If you want to come along, you're most welcome." He continued on toward the operations room. The crowd followed. Kurt Sigel rolled his eyes at Karl in an expression of awe. Not many people engaged the Führer in such intimate conversation. Karl nodded in acknowledgment. It was, after all, a kind of tribute.

That same evening, while Adolf Hitler dined with the commanding officers of the various fighter and bomber units stationed at Villacoublay—and Major Kurt Sigel entertained Karl Eisler at KG 55's officers' club—Richard Conway and Blair Moffet were on an SNCF commuter train en route to Ablon, a small town on the Seine south of Paris.

When the train pulled out of the Gare de Lyon they were alone in the second-class compartment, but a few minutes later the doors slid open and a woman entered. Her shoulder-length hair was a peroxide yellow and her face was a mask of layers of makeup and eye shadow. She wore a shabby fur jacket over a tight short skirt, black stockings, and high-heeled wedge shoes. The uniform of a *poule*, a streetwalker, one of the girls who patrolled the railway-station entrance at Boulevard Diderot.

Taking a seat opposite Blair and Richard, she said in French, "I am Nicole." It was a password, not an introduction. Jean Fresnais had told Blair and Richard to expect her.

Nicole, clearly no conversationalist, rummaged in her purse for a cigarette, lit it, and commenced reading a dogeared copy of a weekly newspaper, *Je Suis Partout,* whose headline read: PARIS SE DÉBARRASSE DE TOUS SES JUIFS!

" 'Paris gets rid of its Jews,' " Richard translated aloud.

"*All* of its Jews," Blair corrected, and in French said to Nicole, "My God, what sort of newspaper is that?"

"A very popular one, my dear," Nicole said, and resumed reading.

They walked from the Ablon train station, through the center of town—a few small shops and a café—and on to Rue d'Orléans, a quiet, tree-lined street on the riverbank. They passed several gated, high-walled villas and then came to number 27, a cottage that at one time had served as a carriage house for an adjacent villa. The cottage had no telephone, but there was electricity, running water, and indoor plumbing. The rear veranda overlooked the Seine.

After transmitting a brief coded message to London—confirmation that the operation was proceeding on schedule—Richard and Blair, bundled in scarves and coats, sat on the veranda and gazed at the silhouettes of houseboats anchored on the river.

Richard's whole jaw was swollen and inflamed from the broken tooth. Aspirin and cold compresses had helped slightly, enough to at least make the pain tolerable.

"After the war," he said, "I wouldn't mind coming back here to live."

"And how will you make a living?" Blair asked, teasing. "Pimp for that woman? Nicole, is that her name?"

"You're jealous," Richard said. The idea pleased him.

"Of her? Don't be ridiculous. She's old enough to be your mother. Answer me a question: have you ever been with a prostitute?"

"Why do you want to know?"

"I'm curious."

"Jealous," he said. "But to answer your first question, I don't know how I'll make a living. To answer your second, no, I've never slept with a prostitute. Not yet, anyway. By the way, where is she?"

"Inside, in the kitchen." The odor of cooking oil and garlic swirled fragrantly about the glassed-in veranda. "It smells wonderful."

"You mean she can cook, too?"

"I hope so. I'm starved." Blair wiggled out from under Richard's arm and got up. "I'll see what she's doing."

Richard leaned back against the divan seat cushion and tried to compose in his head a letter to his father. *Dear Dad: This time I know you'll be proud of me. I'm working on a plan to end the war. Karl Eisler is helping me . . .*

"Richard!" It was Blair, prodding him gently. "Darling, wake up."

He came awake with a start. Blair and Nicole hovered anxiously over him. "I fell asleep," he said.

"You were talking," Nicole said. "You were delirious."

"He needs a doctor," Blair said to Nicole.

Richard tried to smile. "I wonder if they give Purple Hearts for a toothache?"

"Tomorrow morning as soon as curfew is over, I'll go into the village and phone my contact in Paris for the name of a dentist," Nicole said. "In the meantime, dinner is almost ready."

Although the food was delicious, a rabbit fried with onions and peppers, Richard had no appetite. He fell into an uneasy sleep soon after dinner, tossing and turning, perspiring even in the cold damp room. Blair was awake most of the night bathing him with wet towels, trying to keep him comfortable. Early the next morning Nicole came into the bedroom.

"Excuse me," she whispered. In the harsh early-morning light her unmade face was gray and lined. "I'll go into the village now and try to arrange for him to see a dentist."

Richard stirred. He wrapped his arms around Blair and buried his head on her breasts. "Make me feel better again," he whispered. "Like you did last night."

Blair gasped with embarrassment. Nicole laughed quietly and started to leave. Richard continued to Blair, "I love you. Do you know how much I love you?"

"Yes, darling, I do," Blair said, her eyes fixed on Nicole, who had paused at the door. "I know how much you love me."

2.

Later that same morning, at Villacoublay, Karl Eisler waited outside KG 55's operations building for Hitler to emerge. The six-car convoy that would escort the Führer to the rail siding was parked at the edge of the winter-brown lawn in front of the operations building. Karl lit a fresh cigarette from the butt of the old one, his third in ten minutes. A thousand different pictures flooded his brain.

He would be searched before being allowed into the railway car.

After he placed the coat in the car and set the timer, someone would move the coat and discover the bomb.

Once on the car, he would not be permitted to leave.

If he was permitted to leave, some good Samaritan would notice him getting off without the coat and hand it back to him.

He did not know how long he stood in the cold, chain-smoking and pondering all these scenarios, but suddenly he found himself in the front seat of a staff colonel's automobile, the last vehicle in the column of six. Escorted by a dozen military policemen on siren-screaming motorcycles, the convoy drove out of the airfield, onto a narrow road, and to the rail siding a few miles away. The train was made up of three armored passenger cars and two open freight cars, one freight car behind the locomotive, one behind the last passenger car. Each freight car carried an antiaircraft gun and a squad of hel-meted infantrymen.

Karl, from the staff colonel's automobile, did not see Hitler get out of his limousine and start toward the train, then abruptly stop as an officer in the front seat of the car called to him. Nor did Karl see that the officer was talking excitedly into a field radio.

Karl followed some officers aboard the last car of the train. He went directly into the lavatory, locked the door, pulled down the window shade, and removed the cigarillo tin from his coat pocket. Carefully, separating the cigarettes as Jean Fresnais had demon-strated, he inserted the key into the Munson timer and rotated it one full turn to the left. It made a soft clicking sound as the tension on the spring increased. Then, with the spring fully wound, Karl rotated the key completely around in the opposite direction. This opened the relays and activated the battery. The device was now preset. In ninety minutes, the relays would close and detonate the bomb.

Karl slipped the tin back into his pocket, unlocked the W.C. door, and stepped into the railway car. He could hardly believe his luck. The car was empty. Everyone must have gone forward to Hitler's car. Karl walked down the aisle of the empty car to the coupling platform. The door to the center car, Hitler's, was open. Outside, on the siding below, two mess-jacketed soldiers, Hitler's personal orderlies, stood chatting with Hitler's valet, a trim, balding man in an unadorned army uniform.

Karl entered the car. He removed his overcoat and hung it cas-ually on a coat tree a few feet away from a large semicircular desk he assumed was Hitler's. Just then, outside, he heard the sound of agitated voices, and automobile engines. He whirled around to the window.

On the siding, at the parked automobiles, men were running back and forth, shouting at each other. Everyone appeared flustered and disorganized. Karl caught a glimpse of Hitler. His face was expres-sionless but his eyes were cold with rage. He climbed back into his limousine. The door slammed shut. Led by the motorcyclists and followed by the other automobiles, Hitler drove off.

Karl rushed out of the railway car and down to the siding, where a dozen or so Luftwaffe officers, clustered in small anxious groups, were engrossed in terse conversation. Towering over the others was the tall, militarily erect figure of KG 55's adjutant, Otto Oberg. Karl pulled Oberg aside.

"What the hell's happening?" Karl asked. "Where did the Führer go?"

"Back to the field," Oberg said. "He's canceled his trip to Calais and is returning to Berlin."

"What do you mean, 'returning to Berlin'?"

"They've just uncovered a plot to overthrow the government," Oberg said. "And to kill Hitler!"

"A plot?" Karl knew he had spoken the word but could not hear his own voice. He felt as though the breath had been knocked out of him. "A plot?"

"Ramsch was the ringleader. He's dead, the treacherous bastard!"

"Ramsch? Dead?"

"They came to arrest him and he shot himself."

Oberg continued talking, but Karl did not hear. Ramsch dead, he was thinking. The poor son of a bitch. But at the same time Karl was relieved. Ramsch could not talk, could not implicate anyone.

Karl wondered how the scheme had been discovered and how many other conspirators were arrested, how soon before his own involvement became known. Not long, of that he was sure. And what of the RAF raid? Why risk lives for nothing? They must cancel it.

He started back to the train. He had to retrieve the coat. He forced himself to walk slowly and steadily. Now he was at the train, at the center car. He gripped the handrail and started to pull himself up onto the vestibule. He felt a hand on his shoulder.

"Dr. Eisler . . ." A voice Karl had heard before. A face he had seen before. The voice, quiet and almost syrupy, and the face, blotched and scarred, belonged to Anton Moerzer.

"I heard you were in Paris," Moerzer said. His eyes were cold and hard. The scars on the left side of his face resembled pulsing red veins. "I thought we might have a little chat."

Karl knew that Moerzer's "little chat" did not concern the aborted plot. It was too early for anyone to have discovered Karl's role, but the man's very presence precluded any chance of Karl's running. Sooner or later it would be the Gestapo doing the interrogating. Karl knew he could not stand up to them. He would reveal everything, and everyone. On the other hand it was possible to save those other people, especially Richard Conway. He, Karl, owed that much to Si; more accurately, he owed it to himself.

"Certainly, colonel, it will be my pleasure." Karl was no longer nervous. It was as though he had flown out of a raging storm into bright, clear, smooth air. He knew precisely what he had to do, and how to do it. "Why don't we go into the car? We can talk in comfort."

Karl climbed onto the vestibule and entered the car. He strolled up the aisle to a parlor chair. Moerzer had followed him in but stood uncertainly.

"This is the Führer's car, isn't it?"

"It is, but he's gone back to Berlin. Shocking news, isn't it?" Karl twisted around to the coat tree and slid his hand into the left pocket of the coat. He removed the cigarillo tin and cradled it in the palm of his hand. "Come, sit down," Karl continued. "Tell me what's on your mind."

Moerzer hesitated, then sat in a parlor chair opposite Karl. "I'd like to know, Dr. Eisler, exactly what your business in Paris is."

"Would you care for a cigar, colonel?"

"I don't smoke."

"You won't mind if I do?" Karl opened the cigarillo tin. The lid obstructed Moerzer's view of the contents. Karl turned the key counter clockwise. Moerzer heard the soft whirring and clicking sound of the spring unwinding. He sensed instantly what it was and leaped from his chair toward Karl. It was too late. Karl had closed the relays. Karl's last thought was fear that it would be painful. It was not. He felt nothing and heard nothing. He saw only a glaring white flash. The whole world became white and then, in the same millisecond, black.

3.

Jean Fresnais heard the automobiles brake to a screeching stop. His office on the second floor of the factory building in Billancourt overlooked the front gate, but he did not bother going to the window. He knew that the vehicles blocked all exits and the men scrambling out of them were either agents of the French Gestapo, the Gestapides, or the Germans themselves.

He was not at all surprised that they had finally caught up with him, although it almost surely meant that Karl Eisler had failed in his mission. He wondered how they had connected Karl with him and what had gone wrong and what happened to Karl. All this ran through his mind as he sat at his desk and calmly dialed a number, his home.

Andrée answered. Fresnais spoke quickly and quietly. "Listen to me, darling, and don't say a word. Take the car and go out to the place in Ablon. A woman named Nicole is there with two Allied operatives. Andrée, one of them is Simon Conway's son." His voice took on a sudden urgency. "Tell Nicole that I've been arrested, and to get away from Ablon immediately! She'll know where to go. Do it now, darling. I love you!"

The phone went dead, but the words *Simon Conway's son* echoed in Andrée's ears. Within five minutes, she was in the subterranean garage of their apartment building, in the car, and driving away. She strained to keep her mind blank, to concentrate only on driving, and on the shortest route out of the city, and to not panic if a policeman should stop her. A woman driving a civilian car might arouse their curiosity. She would show them the vehicle permit and say she was on an errand for her husband.

No one stopped the dark-green Renault sedan as it raced south on the three-lane highway, N-19; no one paid it any attention. At a crossroads Andrée halted for a convoy of German flat-bedded tank carriers. A handsome young lieutenant in a small VW reconnaissance car saluted her smartly. She smiled back at him.

Hours earlier, at Ablon, Nicole had been instructed to take Richard to a dentist in Fontainebleau, Dr. Charles Valière. Richard and Nicole set off at ten that morning. Although Fontainebleau was only a forty-minute bus ride, the bus broke down and they did not arrive at the dentist's office until 1:30.

Dr. Valière extracted the remaining stump of Richard's broken tooth, packed the opening with a sponge soaked in peroxide, gave Richard a small canvas sack filled with ice, a supply of cotton swabs and peroxide, and a promise that he would live to be a hundred. He refused to accept any payment other than the patient's word that he would instantly and for all time forget the dentist's name and address.

On the street, walking to the bus station, Richard and Nicole passed dozens of German soldiers. The only ones who paid them any attention were two Wehrmacht supply sergeants and a *Blitzmädchen*, a female auxiliary. All three, immaculately uniformed, carried guide books. The *Blitzmädchen*, noting Richard holding an icepack to his swollen jaw, laughed and placed a hand to her own jaw in mock sympathy.

Nicole slipped her arm familiarly through Richard's. One of the sergeants winked at Richard and said, "Ooh la la!" The three Germans continued on their way. Richard breathed a sigh of relief and relaxed the fingers of his free hand, which were curled around the grip of the little Colt .32 in his coat pocket.

"Sightseers," Nicole said. She uttered the word as an epithet. "Visiting Versailles. They come here in droves, the swine!"

At the bus station, the line of waiting passengers reached halfway around the block. Richard and Nicole were unable to board the three-o'clock bus, and were lucky to find standing room in the aisle of the next bus that left at four.

Andrée drove into Ablon shortly before five. The sky was gray and gloomy, and a light dusting of snow whitened the ground. Only a few people were in the square, some women shopping and three children riding bicycles. Andrée continued through the town, across the narrow stone bridge, and onto the cramped, cracked asphalt strip of Rue d'Orléans.

A man and a woman were walking along the roadside. The woman, a blond, wore a short fur jacket and high-heeled wedged shoes. The man, in an overcoat that even from this distance Andrée saw was worn and shabby, appeared younger. Both, hearing the approaching automobile, turned.

Andrée could not believe her eyes. Although she had never seen Richard Conway, she instantly recognized him. He was the mirror image of his father. She drove up alongside the couple and rolled down her window.

"Get in!" she said. She reached behind her and opened the rear door. "I am Jean Fresnais's wife. Please, get in!"

Richard had started to pull the gun from his pocket. Nicole clamped her hand on his wrist and said to Andée, "Who is Jean Fresnais? I don't know anyone of that name—"

"—he's been arrested!" Andrée said. "For the love of God, will you get into this car!" She looked at Richard. "You are Simon Conway's son. Now, please, get in!"

There was a moment's hesitation, and then Nicole nodded at Richard, and both scrambled into the backseat. Before the door was closed, Andrée had started turning the car around.

"Where are you going?" Richard said. "We have to go back to the cottage!"

"The girl is there," Nicole said to Andrée. "We can't leave her!"

Andree backed into the road shoulder, swung the wheel hard, and headed toward the cottage again. As they drove, she told them of Fresnais's phone call. She might have been relaying a piece of gossip, she was that casual about it. Her calm amazed her, but then she realized she had been expecting this for a long time.

"Jean will be all right," she said, ashamed at the hollowness of her own words. "He'll be able to manage."

"Let's just get to the cottage," Richard said. He leaned forward, so that in the rearview mirror only his eyes and the bridge of his nose were visible to Andree. It was like looking into Simon's eyes. She wondered what the boy would say when she told him that she had known his father.

They drove past the ivy-covered walls of villas lining the riverbank, and then past an open stretch of trees and vacant land. Some fifty yards beyond this, the river and road curved sharply. The cottage, partially obscured by the bare branches of a large oak tree, was located on the bend.

"Oh, dear God!" Andrée cried. She braked to a lurching stop and pointed ahead through the tree branches. A black Mercedes sedan and two Citroëns were parked at the cottage gate. A half dozen black uniformed Milice, French special police, milled about. The left front and rear doors of the Mercedes were open, but no one was in the car.

Andrée threw the Renault into reverse and started backing up. It was too late. One of the Milice had seen them. Shouting and waving his hands, he and another policeman began running toward the Renault. Andrée continued backing the Renault through the narrow street, careening from one side to the other until she reached the road bend. She turned the wheel sharply to negotiate the corner. Now, briefly, the car was unseen by the policemen.

Andrée heard Richard shouting, words she could not understand. She knew only that she must get the car turned around and away from here. She must not be caught. They would put her into prison and torture her. Jean once told her of one of their friends to whom it had happened. Jean, she thought. They were probably torturing him at this very moment.

The car stalled. She punched the starter button and mashed her foot down on the accelerator. The motor ground raspily but did not catch. Again she tried, again it did not start. She tried once more, and this time the motor chugged into life. And then everything seemed remarkably obvious. There was only one thing to do.

"Get out of the car!" she cried to Richard and Nicole. "They don't know you're with me! They couldn't have seen you in the backseat! The trees! Hide in the trees!"

Nicole had already opened the door. She seized Richard's wrist and pulled him out with her. She slammed the car door and Andrée drove off, straight ahead again, toward the cottage. Flooring the accelerator, Andrée steered directly at the two policemen who stood in the middle of the road. They dove to safety as she sped past.

Nicole and Richard, crouched behind a large tree trunk, had a clear view of the cottage and Andrée's car as it raced past the policemen. One Milice fired a long burst from his machine pistol into the left side of the Renault. The sound of smashing window glass was louder than the gunfire. The Renault continued on, following the curve of the road beyond the cottage, and out of sight. A moment later came the sound of a metallic thud, more breaking glass, and the high-pitched wail of the car's horn blowing continually.

Richard knew that the Renault had plunged off the road and hit a telephone pole or a tree. Nicole tugged at his sleeve and indicated the cottage. A man was just emerging from the front door, a civilian wearing a black fedora and long leather coat. In his hands he clutched the valises containing the radio units.

"Gestapo!" Nicole whispered.

Two more men, also civilians and similarly garbed, had appeared in the cottage doorway. They were supporting Blair between them. Her clothes were torn, her head lolled inertly, her face was covered with blood. The men dragged her along the snow-covered walk. The toes of her shoes, scraping along the snow, formed two narrow black lines like the tracks of a sled.

The men pitched Blair into the backseat of the Mercedes and got in with her. The man with the valises slid behind the wheel. The car drove off. The Milice also drove away, but only a short distance. They stopped at Andrée's wrecked car. The Renault's front door, riddled with bullet holes, had popped open. Andrée slumped facedown against the steering wheel, her forehead pressed into the horn button. A policeman yanked her by the hair and pulled her away from the wheel. The horn stopped blowing.

All this was out of Richard's view, and he had completely forgotten her anyway. His thoughts were focused totally on Blair. In his mind, he had seen himself rushing forward, gun drawn, charging the Germans. Shooting them, killing them, rescuing Blair. But he knew he had done nothing. He had stayed here and watched it all happen.

He was vaguely aware of Nicole talking about a place they might hide. She took him somewhere—he thought it was a houseboat—but he did not remember how they got there or how long he stayed. His infection had flared up again; his temperature kept spiking and he slid in and out of consciousness. He did recall a conversation with Nicole shortly before he boarded the small airplane that flew him back to England, a conversation engraved indelibly in his memory.

"Blair is dead," Nicole had said. "She was taken to Vincennes and executed that same day. We were betrayed, Richard. Someone betrayed us."

Richard swore to hunt the betrayer down and kill him. But, as Brigadier Rowland informed him not long afterward in England, no one had betrayed them. In Karl's coat pocket the Germans had found the charred remnants of a five-franc note. On the back of the bill, Karl had scribbled the Rue d'Orléans address. It took the Gestapo all of five minutes to ascertain that it was an Ablon street number. The act of an amateur, Rowland sadly remarked. But then the whole damn operation was being conducted by amateurs. The whole damn war was.

The Germans had had Karl under surveillance and knew of his relationship with Fresnais. Within eight hours of Karl's death, Fresnais had been arrested and taken to 93 Rue Lauriston, the offices of the French Gestapo. He died following three days of interrogation at the hands of the Gestapides, who were even more enthusiastic about this work than their Gestapo masters.

For his role in New Broom and his subsequent work in establishing an AACS station under constant enemy fire on the Normandy beachhead, Richard received a battlefield commission as a second lieutenant. In September, two weeks after the liberation of Paris, he arrived at Orly Field with an AACS unit. Rowland, who was also in the city, invited Richard to accompany him to the apartment of Jean and Andrée Fresnais on Avenue Montaigne.

Although the premises had been thoroughly searched by the Germans and the Gestapides, Rowland wanted to see if something might have been overlooked. In the bedroom closet, in a jewelry box—whose valuable contents had long since disappeared—he found some photographs. Among them was a halftone, faded and creased, the photographer's name imprinted in elaborately scripted letters across the lower right: BELLEFOND, 58 RUE DULAMBRE, PARIS. And scrawled under this: *June, 1917.*

It was a photograph of Andrée Fresnais, much younger, gazing adoringly at an equally young man. Andrée's hair was bobbed. She wore a pleated white blouse and dark ankle-length skirt. The young man, staring sternly into the camera, was a French L'Armée de l'Air officer.

Simon Conway.

"Richard, come in here!" Rowland called.

Richard, who had been in another room, came to the doorway. "Find anything interesting?" he asked.

Rowland looked at him, and then at the photograph, and then at Richard again. Simon Conway's son felt guilty enough that Andrée Fresnais had sacrificed her life to save his. Why burden him with more? And it would be an unnecessarily cruel blow to his father.

"I thought I found something, but now I see they're just some old pictures." Rowland put the photograph into the jewelry box. He closed the lid and placed the box back in the closet. "Let's get the bloody hell out of here," he said.

PART FIVE

THE 1010

21

Si drove out of Conway Field, turned onto Jefferson Avenue, and jammed his foot down on the accelerator. The Buick surged smoothly forward. "Some power, eh?" he said.

"Glad you like it, Dad," Richard said wryly. He was slouched in the passenger seat, arms folded, staring broodily ahead through the windshield.

The car was Richard's, brand-new, a twenty-third-birthday gift from Si and Meg, one of the first '48s. A four-door Roadmaster convertible sedan, cream-white with black leather upholstery and a black top. Si wanted to "test-drive" it, especially its innovative aircraft-type hydraulic suspension system.

"Hey, shall we stop and put the top down?" he asked.

"It'll take too much time," Richard said. He tapped his finger on the clock in the center of the dashboard. "Ten after two. We're running late. We'll get hell from Mom as it is."

"Yeah, I guess it will take too much time," Si said. And talk about time, he thought, how about New York to London nonstop in an 880 in nine hours? Paris in ten hours.

The 305-mph four-engined Conair 880 was the company's first postwar transport and Pete Dagget's pride and joy. A truly magnificent airplane, its three vertical stabilizers riding high above the slipstream to provide almost feather-touch rudder control, the slender fuselage built in a gentle tapering curve to reduce drag, the nose tipped slightly downward to accommodate a shorter nose wheel.

Back in Si's office, hanging on the wall behind the sofa, was a framed four-color full-page ad that had appeared in last month's issue of *Fortune*, September 1947. The entire page consisted of a photograph of a Conair 880 in flight against a background of snow-peaked mountains. In a streamer across the bottom of the page were reproductions of the logos of the five U.S. airlines that had ordered the airplane. The only copy in the ad was the headline:

FIRST CHOICE OF THE WORLD'S CHOICEST AIRLINES!

The *Fortune* page had cost a cool $18,000, money Si considered well spent. Whenever he looked at it and thought of the 880's purchase price, $325,000, he was reminded of the 660's price, $65,000. It said something about either man's progress or his greed. Or both.

Now, just twenty-seven months after the end of the war, customers were pleading for seats on the new sixty-to-eighty-passenger airplanes capable of nonstop Atlantic crossings. Conair and Lockheed were backlogged two years on orders for 880s and Constellations. Douglas's DC-6, a stretched version of the DC-4, would soon be available. The airlines spoke of purchasing fleets of airplanes.

Fleets, Si thought, and said to Richard, "You look like you're in a trance."

Richard removed his glasses and rubbed his eyes. "I'm thinking, Dad." He put the glasses back on. "Thinking."

"About what?"

Richard said nothing a moment. What he had been thinking about was a letter he recently received from Paris, from his old army buddy Clarence Pribble, now a civilian. Pribble had been working as a flight radio operator for a one-airplane charter airline owned and operated by a former USAAF 8th Air Force pilot who had purchased a war-surplus 660. Fly anything, anywhere, anytime. It was interesting, but Pribble said he had gotten himself a bad case of the sweet-ass for an American lady, a former WAC, who gave him a choice of presenting her with a wedding ring or himself with a new girlfriend. So Pribble was quitting the airline and wondered if Richard might want to replace him. Richard was tempted.

"My sex life," Richard said. "I was thinking about my sex life."

Sex life, Si thought, remembering the old Dixie Clipper with its honeymoon suite. You wouldn't have time for "honeymoons" in a jet transport flying at 600 mph. It wasn't so far in the future: only last week an army major, Charles Yeager, had flown a rocket-powered experimental aircraft through the sound barrier.

Pete Dagget was developing three different jet airframe designs, and Don Jensen had promised a production model of a jet engine within two years. Don, Charlie's son, had stepped smoothly into Charlie's shoes after the old man's stroke last year. But Si wasn't holding his breath waiting for Don Jensen's engine. Si had a small ace up his sleeve, in the person of a brilliant young engineer who had designed the jet engine for Karl Eisler's KE-2.

Although the engineer was still in Germany, living in the Russian sector under an assumed name, Erika Eisler had been in contact with him and knew he was anxious to come to America. Getting him here was a little more complicated than buying a ticket, of course, but it could be done, and the man who could do it was U.S. Senator Morris Tannen. He had brought Erika to California shortly after Karl's death, and he could get the engineer out of Germany for Si. Si and Morris had much in common these days. They shared the same grandson.

Si said to Richard, "Did Karl ever talk about that fellow who designed the jet engines for him?"

"Dad, I saw Karl only that one time in Paris, and for less than an hour. He was killed a few days later."

Morris had told Si how Karl had died, and why, and of Richard's involvement, the barest details, which was all Morris really knew. It was enough for Si to feel very proud of Richard. Moreover, on June 10, 1944, as a newly commissioned second lieutenant, Richard had returned to France, landing on the Normandy beaches with an AACS mobile unit four days after D-Day. Si's new son-in-law, Morris's U.S. Marine son, Paul, was not the only hero in the family.

"Did you invite Enid Leonard to the party?" Si asked.

"Mother did."

"She's a nice girl. I like her."

"I'm sure she'll really enjoy a party for a two-year-old kid."

"That two-year-old kid is my grandson," Si said.

"And my nephew," said Richard. "Which doesn't make him any less of a pain in the ass."

"Wait till you see what I got him," Si said, pleased with himself for thinking of such a present, a gasoline-engined flying scale model of a Conair Hunter. Of course, as Meg remarked, only Simon Conway would give a two-year-old child so intricate a toy.

Si had always suspected Janet was pregnant three years before, when she and Paul Tannen returned from a Las Vegas weekend to announce they were married. The fact that David was born exactly nine months to the day after the marriage did not allay Si's suspicion. But then, as Meg said, what difference did it make? And since when did Simon Conway become such a paragon of virtue? Meg had his number. From the time he had started complaining about Janet and Paul "seeing too much of each other," Meg knew what Si's problem was.

"What are you afraid of, Si?" she had asked. "That Paul Tannen will be your son-in-law, or that Morris will be Janet's father-in-law?"

The irony of it now, three years later, was that David's very existence had forced a reconciliation, albeit a grudging one, between Si and Morris.

Si said to Richard now, "Why do you call him a pain in the ass? He's a good kid. Bright as hell."

Richard waited for Si to add, "Gonna make a great pilot," but Si did not say it this time. Actually, Richard was quite fond of David, who was a frequent visitor at the Conway's Corona del Mar Drive home. David's parents were living in a rented house in Santa Monica while Paul Tannen completed his final year of law at UCLA.

Richard said, "Gonna make a great pilot, too."

"You can say that again," Si said. "Wouldn't hurt you to think about marriage."

"Who do you have in mind for me? As if I didn't know."

"She's a nice girl," Si said.

"You already said that."

"You could do a lot worse."

The "nice girl" was Enid Leonard, Ross's daughter, whom Si had been pushing on Richard ever since he returned from the army. More of Si's dynastic aspirations, Richard knew, not to mention Ross's order for twenty 880s for his Intercontinental Air, with options on twenty more.

"I told you," Richard said, "I'm not ready to marry anyone yet. I'm not ready to settle down. As a matter of fact, Dad, I'm thinking of going back to Europe for a while. To France."

"France? What in the hell for? Did you leave something there?"

"A friend of mine offered me a job with a charter airline flying out of Paris," Richard said.

"Now what would you do in an airline? You only just got your private ticket, and we practically had to bribe the CAA inspector for that."

"I got it, didn't I?" Richard said. To Si's secret delight—and Richard's own sense of achievement—Richard had earned a private pilot's license.

Si said, "Yeah, you got it, and so now how about getting a commercial license?"

"I will," said Richard.

"You will," Si repeated acidly. "So until 'you will,' stop playing with yourself about jobs with charter airlines. Besides, you have a job right here with Conair."

"Dad, I didn't say I was going to work for the airline. I just might like to see what they're doing. And as far as my job here, I'm nothing but a glorified office boy. I'm Phil Granger's apprentice."

"You're learning the business," Si said.

"What I'm learning," said Richard, "is how to run a police state. Mr. Granger could have taught the Nazis a thing or two. He has spies everywhere. He also has dossiers on every executive in the company, including you, Mr. Chairman of the Board, I'll bet."

"Phil's like Mussolini. He makes the trains run on time. In this business it means he gets things done."

"Do I have to remind you what happened to Mussolini?"

"Mussolini was on the wrong side. And by the way, talking about Europe, I may go over there myself soon, to Germany. I want to talk to Karl's engineer. He's supposed to be a genius."

Richard was only half listening. He was remembering Si's wise-crack question "Did you leave anything there?" and thinking, Yes, I did leave something there. My self-respect. He had never told Si of that terrible day at Ablon when he watched, helplessly, as the Gestapo agents dragged Blair Moffet from the cottage.

". . . so forget France," Si was saying. "You're needed right here at the factory. It's a damned sight more important than some rinky-dink airline."

"Sure, Dad, you're grooming me to take over."

"Forget France, I said."

"Is that an order?"

"That's exactly what it is."

"Okay, I'll obey the order."

"Excuse me?"

"I said, I'll stay here. Isn't that what you want?"

Si eyed him skeptically. "Just like that?"

"It's called 'self-respect,' " said Richard. "I want to run this business someday. I'm serious about it, and I want to be taken seriously."

But even before he finished speaking, Richard knew "self-respect" was a misstatement. What he meant to say but did not, because even thinking about it made him feel like a small boy, was that he wanted to prove himself to Si. His wartime heroics and battlefield commission had partly succeeded in that, but he knew Si did not think much of him as an executive. For that matter, he did not believe Si thought much of him, as anything, ever. Maybe "self-respect" was correct after all.

The guest of honor, David Tannen, was too young to appreciate his lavish birthday party. The invited guests, some fifty adults, enjoyed themselves. There was a mariachi band, limitless bottles of Moët & Chandon '45, and food catered by Romanoff's of Beverly Hills, supervised by Mike Romanoff himself. When the sun went down and the afternoon grew chilly, everyone moved from the patio into the house. By then many guests had left, including the guest of honor and his parents. Si, Phil Granger, and Scott St. James went into Si's study for brandy and cigars.

Scott St. James's close-cropped gray hair and ramrod steel spine immediately betrayed his military background. A Class of 1923 West Point graduate and a highly decorated 8th Air Force fighter pilot, he had recently retired from the USAAF with the rank of major general. His final air force years had been served in Washington as deputy director of AAF Procurement. He knew everyone in the Pentagon. More important, everyone liked and respected him.

Granger had hired the forty-eight-year-old ex-general, at $35,000 a year, as a Conair public relations executive in the company's Washington office—"Public relations executive" being a euphemism for "lobbyist." In Scott St. James's case—because of his air force connections—it also meant sales representative. Si wanted to discuss General St. James's first Conair assignment, which involved a new airplane, a fighter.

". . . we call it the Firestreak," Si said. "Phil, be sure the general sees the mockup and the specs. It'll make Lockheed's P-80 look like a Spad. In wind-tunnel tests she does five-fifty in level flight. She'll do all of that with Jensen's new turbojet."

"I've heard that Jensen's having big problems with the engine," St. James said.

"I wouldn't exactly call them 'big' problems," Si said. "A lot of little bugs, maybe. We're straightening them out."

"The Firestreak will outperform any fighter in the air force's inventory," Granger said. "But we'll need development money. For that, we need your help."

"That's what you're paying me for," St. James said.

"That's right, general, that's what we're paying you for," said Si. Responding to a light tap on the door, he called out, "It's open!"

Erika Eisler came in to say good night and to thank Si for a lovely time. Si introduced her to St. James. They shook hands and mumbled "Nice meeting you" to each other, and Erika started to leave.

"Erika," Si called after her, "that young fellow who worked for Karl, the engineer? What was his name?"

"Dieter Bauer," said Erika.

"That's the one, Dieter Bauer," Si said, thinking that Erika had really aged in the past few years. Her hair was almost white. But then after what she'd been through, how could she help but show her age?

As soon as the door closed behind Erika, Si said to Granger, "I want to bring him over here and put him to work for us. Morris said he'd help get him out of there for me."

"Still dreaming about that jet transport, aren't you, Si?" Granger said.

Scott St. James cleared his throat. "Listen, I'd better get moving. I'm catching a midnight flight to Chicago. An Intercontinental 770." He grinned at Si. "I only travel on the best."

St. James shook hands with both men and left. Granger said, "What do you think?"

"I'll tell you after I see if he can deliver," Si said. "And for thirty-five grand a year, he damn well better deliver! I'm not crazy about getting back into the military business, don't forget. You're the one who talked me into the Firestreak. What was it you said? 'Conair has to diversify'? 'Diversify, or die.' "

"Absolutely," said Granger. "Especially if you're so determined to chase this dream of a jet transport."

"It's no dream, Phil."

"No," Granger agreed. "It's a nightmare. Have you stopped to consider what it'll cost?"

Si waved the question impatiently away. He said, "Before I forget: I still don't know exactly what Richard did in that scheme of Karl's to kill Hitler. He clams up every time I ask him. He says all he did was send a few radio messages, but they don't give battlefield commissions for tapping out some words in Morse code. Have one of those roving international PR guys of yours snoop around and see what he can find out."

"I thought you didn't approve of my private intelligence service."

"I think it stinks," Si said. "Now look, Phil, a jet transport is no dream. We know the British are developing one. They're years ahead of us."

"So is Boeing," Granger said.

"Believe me, Phil, even if Boeing came out tomorrow with a four-engined jet passenger airplane, the airlines would go broke in a week using it. Boeing's military jet engines are designed for performance, not efficiency. That's why, if this German kid can give us what we want—a jet engine the airlines won't lose money on—we'll clean Boeing's clock, and everybody else's. And please don't give me that song and dance about turboprops. What'd you call it? An 'intermediate step'?"

"Yes, Si, that's what I called it. An intermediate step, until a decent pure jet engine is ready. Pete says we can put turboprops on the 880—"

"—not without blowing a couple of years modifying the airplane," Si said. "No, Phil, I don't want any intermediate step. A turboprop still uses a propeller to pull the airplane. Sure, it's a turbine engine and there's no piston vibration, and that's great, but when we make the change it'll be straight to pure jets."

"I'll say it again, Si. We can't afford it."

"I'm not saying we'll go right out tomorrow and build a jet transport prototype. Look, this engineer of Karl's, what's his name, Bayer, Beer . . . ?"

"Bauer," Granger said.

"Bauer, yeah. Karl thought he was a genius, and the Germans wouldn't have used his jet engine if it wasn't economical. They couldn't afford to waste a damn drop of gasoline, or kerosene, or whatever it was they were using. So why can't we just get him started playing around with plans and ideas for our engine?"

It was a rhetorical question. Granger knew that Si had made up his mind. Granger said, "All right, Si, so when are you going to Germany to get him?"

2.

Wernher von Braun, two and one half years before, had told Dieter Bauer that the first man who walked on the moon would mistake it for Berlin. Dieter was in Leipzig with Analiese, visiting her relatives, when von Braun phoned from Berlin to say that the Russians were nearing the city and he intended to give himself up to the Americans. He urged Dieter to do the same. Dieter called him a traitor and coward and hung up on him.

But every day of that two and one half years, trapped in Leipzig, living in a cellar like a caged animal, dependent upon his wife's meager earnings as a seamstress, Dieter regretted not heeding von Braun's advice. Often, hungry and cold, he considered walking into the Soviet military governor's office and identifying himself. And he might have, if not for Analiese. She bolstered his courage and literally shamed him into not losing hope. She knew their prayers would someday be answered.

And they were.

It was like a spy novel. A woman for whom Analiese had altered an evening gown paid for the work with American money. Attached to the bills was a note with a telephone number and instructions to call the number at a certain time on a certain day. Analiese called. A man answered. His first words were "Good evening, Frau Bauer."

The man said he was an American agent and that arrangements had been made to smuggle Analiese and her husband out of the Russian sector. Obviously, he was who he claimed to be. If the Russians knew of Dieter's presence, they would simply have broken down the door and taken him away.

Now, three days later in Berlin, Dieter recalled the conversation with von Braun and thought that not even the moon could be so desolate as the Russian sector of that once beautiful, bustling, cosmopolitan city. However, in West Berlin, new buildings were under construction everywhere. Streetcars ran, and taxis, and the streets were clogged with private vehicles.

Happily, Dieter and Analiese were in the western sector. And later this very day, Dieter would meet the man responsible for ending their nightmare, Simon Conway. The same Simon Conway who, ironically, had once been a business associate of that archtraitor Karl Eisler.

And, more irony, it was through Karl's wife that Dieter's initial contacts with the Americans had been made. Clearly, the lady was unaware of Dieter's role in exposing her husband's treachery, an act for which Dieter had never felt the slightest remorse. The knowledge that he served his Führer and country loyally had helped sustain him through the bad years, and allowed him now in good conscience to offer his talents and expertise to his former enemies.

Dieter was thinking about all this as he sat uneasily in the lobby of Building A of the huge OMGUS complex in the Berlin suburb of Dahlem. OMGUS, an acronym for the U.S. Military Government Office, occupied a number of once-fashionable apartment buildings on Königin-Luisestrasse. Building A's lobby was cramped with the ladders of painters and masons. A bank of six open elevators moved constantly up and down, occupied mainly by American army officers and American and German civilian employees. Dieter could recognize the Germans immediately from their shabby clothes and drawn, pale faces.

". . . all right, so how you doing, Dr. Bauer?"

Dieter looked up at a U.S. Army major, a crew-cutted, broad-framed man in his late thirties whose name was Gilbert Wilson, better known to Georgia Tech football fans as Gibraltar Wilson. He was the Counter Intelligence Corps officer who met Dieter and Analiese after they had crossed into the American sector in a U.S. Army ambulance. The ambulance was allowed into the Russian zone ostensibly to return an ill Russian soldier. Dieter and Analiese were picked up at a deserted subway station entrance, given U.S. Army Medical Corps white smocks to wear, and blithely transported back to the checkpoint. The Russian sentries waved the ambulance through without even glancing at its occupants.

". . . you and the wife get settled in okay?" Wilson continued. He spoke in a lazy Southern drawl that Dieter found difficult to follow. "Get everything you need?"

Dieter, who had jumped to his feet, said, "Yes, yes, everything is fine, thank you. Where is Mr. Conway?"

"He's due in anytime now," Wilson said. "Look, I have to ask you some questions. Just routine, but let's get it over with and then you'll be clean as a whistle."

Dieter's stomach fell. He was certain the questions concerned his Nazi Party membership. He had heard of the denazification programs. The Allies had lists. "I'll be happy to answer any questions," he said. "Of course."

Wilson escorted him to the second floor of the building and into a small, sparsely furnished office. Two folding wooden bridge chairs were placed on either side of a battered rolltop desk that was piled high with papers and file folders. A field telephone lay buried under the papers.

"Okay, let's see what we got here," Wilson said. He untied the ribbon of a heavy black cardboard folder and removed a number of documents. A small photograph of Dieter was stapled to the top of one document: his ID photo for the Eisler Allgemeinmaschinenwerke factory at Stuttgart. Wilson ran a finger along the single-spaced type-written pages, reading to himself, his lips moving rapidly.

"Okay," Wilson said, still studying the folder. "What kind of work did you do for the Russians?"

Dieter was totally unprepared for the question. He had expected to be asked about dates of joining the Nazi Party. He would say he never wanted to join but was compelled to. Everyone was compelled to join. "The Russians?" he asked. "Did I work for them?"

Wilson's cold little smile made Dieter's heart beat even faster. "Didn't you?"

"No, certainly not! I never worked for them, and never would," Dieter said. "They did not know who I was!"

"Hey, take it easy," Wilson said. "I told you, these are routine questions. Of course, you'll be willing to swear that you never worked for them?"

"Of course!"

Wilson tapped his fountain pen on the bottom of the paper. "It says here you joined the Nazi Party in 1940."

"I had no choice," Dieter said. "It was join or lose everything. My job, my home, everything. You can't imagine how cruel they were."

"Who?" Wilson asked innocently.

"The Nazis," Dieter said.

"Yeah, I heard about some of the things they did. In fact, I saw some of their places with my own eyes. The Russians let us take a look at a place over in their sector, Auschwitz." He pronounced it Ostwhich. "You ever seen one of them camps, Dr. Bauer?"

"No, I never did. But I can tell you that the Nazis were criminals. They deserved what they got at Nuremberg."

"You bet," said Wilson. He slid his fountain pen into his shirt pocket and buttoned the pocket flap. "Well, that's it, Doc, thank you."

Dieter felt his whole body sag with relief. "Then everything is in order?"

"Can't see why not." Wilson closed the file folder, tied the ribbon, and placed it on the bottom of the pile on his desk. "Welcome to freedom, Dr. Bauer. Now let's go see where Mr. Conway is."

Mr. Conway was four miles west, in Russian airspace, standing behind the pilot's seat on the flight deck of a Military Air Transport Service C-54 that was riding the center line of the narrow aerial corridor from Frankfurt into Berlin.

". . . yes, sir," the young captain was shouting in Si's ear. "That's Berlin!"

Total desolation, block after block, mile after mile. Not a single building appeared habitable. It was as though someone had taken a hatchet to a doll's village and chopped open every structure. The streets were piled high with rubble. Miniature figures scurried about on the streets and in and out of the ruined buildings.

". . . biggest rockpile in the world!" the captain, who was the pilot of this MATS C-54, continued. "But look down there, Mr. Conway." He pointed out his left-side window at a large, open rectangular area surrounded on all sides by rubble. Stacked neatly in the midst of the clearing were concrete blocks, bricks, lumber, and other construction material. "They're getting ready to rebuild. Believe me, in a couple of years these people'll have a whole new city! I know them. I know what they can do! Listen, they damn near won the war!"

I know what they can do, too, Si thought. He had seen what they could do. Morris Tannen made sure of that. Morris, who arranged Si's trip to Germany, had instructed the U.S. Army to give Si a tour of the concentration camp at Dachau.

And Si agreed with the young captain: the Germans had come frighteningly close to winning the war. Hap Arnold himself told Si that, properly employed, the Luftwaffe's jets alone, the ME-262 and the KE-2, could have made the difference.

". . . excuse me, sir, time to go to work," the young captain said to Si, and continued into his microphone, "Tempelhof tower, MATS zero-five-seven. Request landing instructions, please."

The young captain, whose name was Terrance Deland and to whom Si had taken an immediate liking, listened to the landing instructions, acknowledged them, then spoke over his shoulder to Si. "For this time of year, the weather's not bad here. I've seen it when you have to feel your way around the apartment buildings on the airport perimeter."

Terry banked the big airplane around to begin his final descent. Si particularly liked the way Terry handled the airplane. He respected her. Although the C-54, like Si's own Conair 770, was an easy airplane to fly, she still demanded respect. The old axiom: Respect the airplane, she'll respect you.

"There's Tempelhof, sir," Terry shouted to Si. "Look familiar?"

No, Si thought, it does not look familiar. But then he had been here only once before, twenty-five years ago when he came to meet Karl and bring him back to America. And now history was repeating itself; he was bringing another man back to America, Karl's assistant.

Si hardly realized they had landed and were already parked, and that Terry Deland was grumbling about the crowded transient parking area. ". . . this place gets busier all the time. Whenever the Russians decide to slow up the food and fuel coming into Berlin, somebody in Frankfurt gets the bright idea to fly a few cans of beans in, or a ton of coal . . ."

Si was thinking about his last visit to Berlin twenty-five years ago, about Karl and the fiasco with Göring. But the *Reichsmarschall* had built an air force that damn near conquered the world. Give the devil his due. And even in the end he had his own way. The fat old fox swallowed a cyanide pill and beat the hangman.

". . . nice meeting you, Mr. Conway." Terry Deland had wiggled out of his seat and stood facing Si. He was a good-looking young man, tall, slender, with a choirboy's face and curly brown hair. Si judged him to be no more than twenty-four or twenty-five, Richard's age.

They shook hands and Si said, "You ever decide to fly civilian, come and see me."

"I might just do that, sir, sooner than you think."

A U.S. Army staff car, a four-door Ford sedan driven by a corporal with a SHAEF flash on his uniform shoulder, was waiting for Si. A teenage second lieutenant got out of the front passenger's seat. He opened the Ford's rear door and saluted Si smartly.

"Compliments of General Turner, sir. We're to take you into town."

They drove across the airport tarmac. Tempelhof was surprisingly undamaged. A row of large hangars, joined together as a single vast unit, extended in a semicircle around the airport terminal and control tower. The structures rose five stories above the ground and seven stories below, in underground factories where the Nazis had manufactured fighter planes. Si wondered if any of Karl's airplanes were built there.

At the airport gate a white-helmeted American MP scrutinized the car's occupants, saluted crisply, and stepped back. Another MP raised the barrier. As they left the field, Si leaned forward and said to the second lieutenant, "Would you believe, lieutenant? Twenty-five years ago I was in a taxi driving out of this same gate." He really did not know if it was the same gate but it sounded logical. "And would you also believe, the man I was with later on tried to kill Hitler?"

"That's very interesting, sir," the second lieutenant said politely. "Tried to kill Hitler, eh? Wow, that's really something!"

Si felt foolish. The next thing you'll do, he told himself, is tell this kid that your son was a second looey, too, working for OSS with the same man who had tried to kill Hitler. Thinking of Richard reminded Si of Richard's brief mention of a desire to return to France and Si's wisecrack question to him: "Did you leave anything there?"

I left something there, Si thought. He knew she was dead. The details, from Morris's U.S. intelligence sources, were vague. She had apparently been working for the Resistance and was killed by the Gestapo. He had tried to tell himself that their affair had been over for years, decades, a whole lifetime. It did not ease the sadness he felt.

". . . here we are, sir."

The car had pulled into a courtyard surrounded on three sides by large office buildings. High atop a flagpole in the center of the courtyard an American flag flapped in the wind. At the base of the flagpole, in a wire-fenced enclosure, whitewashed boulders formed the word OMGUS.

The second lieutenant opened Si's door, but Si did not immediately step out. The second lieutenant frowned with concern. "Mr. Conway . . . ? Are you all right, sir?"

"I'm fine." Si laughed lamely. "I was just trying to remember something." He got out of the car and followed the second lieutenant into the building. He had been trying to remember the name of Andrée's husband. It had slipped his mind entirely.

3.

It was pure coincidence that Captain Terry Deland, the army pilot who had flown Simon Conway from Frankfurt to Berlin in a MATS C-54, also flew Si, Dieter Bauer and his wife, and Major Wilson back to Frankfurt. It was no coincidence that on this return leg Si traveled on a Conair 770. Someone at AAF HQ in Wiesbaden got his ass chewed for not making a 770 available to the president of Conway Aviation Industries in the first place.

Si and the Bauers were to spend the night in a U.S. Army VIP billet near SHAEF HQ at the I. G. Farben building just outside Frankfurt. In the morning they would travel by train to Amsterdam and board an Intercontinental Air 880 for New York and Los Angeles.

Dinner was quite pleasant. Si found the Bauers charming and personable, although the wife, Analiese, seemed concerned that leaving her native land might be construed as an act of betrayal or desertion.

"It's true," she said. "I've heard them talk about Dieter's friends who have gone to work for the Americans. But it's all jealousy, you know. There isn't one who wouldn't jump at the chance, believe me."

"Can you blame them for being jealous?" Dieter asked. "How many chances does a person get to start a whole new life?"

Si was impressed with Dieter Bauer. The engineer knew his business, and when he said he could produce the jet engine Si needed within two years, Si knew it was no boast.

After Dieter and Analiese went to their room, Si remained in the lounge for one more brandy. He had decided to start Dieter at a salary of $1,500 per month on a two-year contract with a raise to be negotiated the second year. Granger would scream bloody murder. But if Granger could pay a lobbyist like Scott St. James $35,000 a year, then Dieter Bauer's $18,000 was peanuts.

". . . hey, there, Mr. Conway, how you doing?" Major Gilbert Wilson sat heavily down beside Si. The major looked a little drunk.

"The paperwork on Bauer go through okay?" Si asked.

"Like a dream. He's all yours," Wilson said. "'Course, having a U.S. senator grease the way didn't hurt."

"It helped, that's for sure."

"He's a Jew, isn't he? Senator Tannen, I mean?"

"Yeah, he's Jewish," Si said. He wondered what the major would say if he knew Morris Tannen's son was married to Si's daughter.

"I have to laugh when I think about it." Wilson's smooth round face wrinkled in a sly smile. "A Jewish senator getting your boy Bauer's name erased off a Justice Department watch list."

"What watch list?"

"You didn't know?"

"Major, what in the hell are you talking about?"

"Bauer's name was on the list of German scientists that aren't supposed to be admitted into the United States because of their Nazi background."

"They were all Nazis," Si said. "Tannen knows that."

"Sure, but there are Nazis and there are Nazis. And anyway, we don't want them working for the Russkies, do we?"

"This watch list," said Si. "What did they do to get on it?"

"What *didn't* they do? You name it. Listen, we got documented evidence that some of them people we cleared are known war criminals. They used slave laborers. One guy that did high-altitude experiments on concentration-camp prisoners is in the States, in Alabama, working on a top-secret rocket project."

Slave laborers, Si thought. On his visit to Dachau, the U.S. Military Government Office representative, a civilian, had explained that many of the prisoners were slave laborers. After being declared medically unfit for further factory work, they were shipped to Dachau and other camps for extermination.

". . . and Bauer, he was at Nordhausen almost right up to the end," Wilson was saying.

The Dachau guide had mentioned Nordhausen, now in the Russian sector, where V-1s and V-2s were manufactured. Many of those put to death at Dachau came from Nordhausen.

". . . old Doc Bauer, though," Wilson continued, "he was an honest-to-God Nazi hero. They gave him a commendation, if you please. Bauer don't know that I know it, but it's right there in his personnel jacket. Seems he helped expose a plot to knock off the Führer."

A dozen alarm bells went off in Si's head. "What plot?"

"The man Bauer worked for, some bigwig plane maker, tried to—"

Wilson was talking to himself. Si had bolted from the chair and was striding across the lounge to the stairway. Wilson called after him, "Hey, Mr. Conway! Where you going?"

Si ignored him. He ran up the stairs to the first floor and banged on the door of Dieter Bauer's room. "Bauer!" he shouted. "I want to talk to you!"

Dieter Bauer, in pajamas, opened the door. Si pushed past him into the room. The night-table lamp cast a dappled shadow over Analiese Bauer, sitting up in bed, the top of the heavy comforter clasped over her chest.

"What's wrong?" she asked in German.

"What kind of a medal did they give you for reporting Karl Eisler to the Gestapo?" Si asked Dieter.

Dieter stared at Si.

"Goddammit, did you turn him in?" Si asked. "Yes or no!"

Analiese Bauer said in German, "Dieter, what is he saying? What does he want?"

"I think he's drunk," Dieter said to her in German. To Si, he said, "Please, Mr. Conway, what is this all about?"

"Just answer my question, yes or no."

"How can you ask me a thing like that?" Dieter said. "I loved Karl!"

Si wanted to laugh in his face. "That's all I wanted to know," he said, and turned and left the room. He felt Dieter's eyes on him as he walked down the corridor. What amazed him was that he had held his temper.

Wilson waited in the lounge. Si said, "I'm withdrawing my sponsorship of Dieter Bauer." He raised his hand to silence any protest. "It's not open to debate, major. My mind's made up."

Si moved to leave. Wilson stepped around to face him. "Mr. Conway, we need men with Dieter Bauer's knowledge and experience."

"Nobody 'needs' scum like that, major. Smarten up."

"The Russians need him."

"Then let the Russians have him." Si moved to leave again, and again Wilson blocked him.

"All due respect, sir, it's not you that's sponsoring Dr. Bauer, it's the U.S. government. He'll come into the country with or without you, sir."

Si brushed past Wilson and started toward the stairway. At the foot of the stairs, he stopped. He turned. He walked back to Wilson.

"Major, as you said, there are Nazis and there are Nazis, and most of them are probably working for us—with our government's blessing—but I guarantee you that Dieter Bauer will not be one of them. Now you hear me good, mister. If that man steps foot in the United States, I'll have my PR people plant the story in every newspaper and magazine in the country, with *your* name in headlines! By the time I'm finished with you, you'll be lucky if your next assignment is with graves registration!"

Si wheeled around and went straight up the stairs to his room. He did not have to look back to know that Wilson stood staring after him, mouth open, fists clenched. He also knew that the major would see to it that Dieter Bauer never entered the United States. The major was not about to take on Simon Conway. He was not that dumb.

In the morning, Si felt like a drunk recalling with stomach-fluttering remorse the events of the previous evening. He had blown his chances for Conair to beat Douglas and Boeing with a jet transport. It wasn't the end of the world. Conair would survive, so would he.

The Conways were experts in survival, as Si learned several weeks after his return from Germany. Phil Granger phoned him at home one Saturday afternoon. David was at the house. Si had rigged up a miniature set of airplane controls, a stick and rudder pedals, and was trying to teach the boy the fundamentals.

Si took the call in his study. Granger spoke in the same toneless, matter-of-fact voice he used announcing the company's quarterly financial statements.

"You asked me to do some checking on Richard. My people located a woman he worked with on that hush-hush operation, the scheme to kill Hitler. When the Germans found out about it they moved in on the place where Richard and the others were hiding. Besides Richard and this woman, there were two other agents, another Frenchwoman and a young English girl. They were both caught and killed. If Richard had gotten to the place five minutes earlier, they'd have caught him, too."

Granger paused. It was a pause that Si recognized from long experience as a precursor of information that was either bad or sensational, or both.

"Si . . . ?"

"Go ahead, Phil."

"It seems that Richard and the English girl had a little more going than just a professional relationship. He was pretty broken up over it."

"No wonder the kid doesn't want to talk about it," Si said. He felt a sudden warmth for Richard, almost a new understanding. "Thanks for the information, Phil."

Granger, sitting in his office at the factory, reread the last paragraph of the report on Richard. In relaying the information to Si, he had omitted one critical item: although Richard saw the Germans taking the English girl away—he had witnessed the incident from a place of concealment—he made no attempt to save her.

Granger had withheld this from Si to spare him any needless embarrassment. The act was not altogether altruistic, for at the same time, by keeping it to himself, Granger possessed knowledge about Richard Conway that someday might prove useful.

He jotted a note on the desk calendar, a reminder to award a bonus to his people in Europe for their efficiency. He glanced at the altimeter-faced clock on the wall: 1:05. If he left now he could get to Wilshire Country Club for at least nine holes.

22

Terry Deland knew that the tall good-looking brunette everyone called Mrs. Tannen was Simon Conway's daughter, and that she had a six-year-old son. But no one bothered to inform Terry, who had been working at Conair only two months, that Mrs. Tannen was the widow of a U.S. Marine Corps major killed in Korea nearly a year before.

Terry's formal introduction to Mrs. Tannen, Janet, was at the Riviera Country Club, at a reception following Richard Conway's wedding to Enid Leonard. Terry had wandered out to the terrace overlooking the eighteenth green and was watching an exhausted foursome trudge toward the hole when he heard a familiar voice behind him.

"What do you say, kid?" It was Si, looking very uncomfortable in his black cutaway coat and striped morning trousers. "Having a good time?"

"Enjoying it very much, Mr. Conway. I appreciate your inviting me."

"You're full of crap," Si said good-naturedly. "Why don't you go back inside and mingle? Lot of good-looking girls here."

And a lot of boring people, Terry thought. Family friends or important aviation-industry figures, and a few big Hollywood names. The only ones Terry felt anything in common with were Richard and Richard's best man, an old army buddy from Kentucky named Pribble.

He said, "That's what Southern California's famous for, isn't it? Good-looking girls?"

"And weather," Si said. "When you get to my age, it's the weather that's interesting."

"Somehow, I kind of doubt that, Mr. Conway. By the way, let me congratulate you on Rich's marriage."

"Congratulate him," Si said, and began grumbling about being pleased enough with Richard's marriage but maybe not so pleased with Richard's new father-in-law, Ross Leonard, the president of Intercontinental Air. Ross had ordered sixty Conair 885s but wanted the airplane redesigned and fitted with the new GE turboprop engines.

". . . I think it's a dumb idea," Si went on. "And since you'll be flying the 885 prototype next week, I'd like to know what you think about it."

Terry felt trapped. It was a question he dreaded answering. Well, he thought, here goes nothing. "I don't think it's such a dumb idea," he said. "I mean, the 885's really only a 'Super 880,' isn't it? She's bigger than the 880. Sixty-seven seats, with a thirty-five-hundred-mile range and a pressurized cabin. You put turboprop engines on her and she's a whole different airplane, a really new one. And a hundred miles an hour faster than the 880."

"It'll take six months to a year to roll it out and get it certified," Si said. He sounded almost angry. "Another six months or more before the first one comes off the production line."

Jesus, what have I done? Terry asked himself. But he'd gone this far, he might as well go all the way. "It might be worth it," he said.

"Not with Douglas's new DC-6B coming off the lines even as we speak. We hold back a year—it'll be more like two years—we lose all our 885 sales. Don't forget, we built her to compete with Boeing's Stratocruiser, and at half the Stratocruiser's price. We'll never catch up, no matter how good a turboprop is."

Terry felt as though he had been pushed into a bottomless pit, but at that moment Janet appeared on the terrace. Si's dour expression seemed to amuse her. "Daddy, what's this man done to you?"

Terry said, "I'm afraid I told him something he didn't want to hear."

"Everybody seems to be doing that lately," Janet said. "Introduce me, Si."

Si did, explaining that he had waited four years for Terry to leave the air force and come to work for Conair. Si sounded good-humored again. Terry started to relax.

"You picked a good time to get out, Mr. Deland," Janet said. "In the middle of a war."

Terry bristled but forced himself to reply calmly and quietly. "It's like this, Mrs. Tannen: the air force invited me to get out. I was flying the Korean Airlift for MATS. A bus driver's job. They agreed with your father that I'd be a hundred times more useful testing new airplanes."

"We're converting 880s to tankers," Si explained to Janet. "Terry's in charge of the project, but I want him to fly the 885 as well," he said, and turned to Richard and his bride, who had come to say goodbye before leaving for their brief Mexican honeymoon.

Terry congratulated the newlyweds and discreetly moved on to the bar. He was annoyed with himself for having responded to Janet Tannen's smart-mouth, stooping to her level. He had no sooner sat down than Janet sank into a chair beside him. She signaled the bartender to pour two glasses of champagne.

"My father just read me the riot act," she said. "He said you flew thirty-five missions over Germany before you transferred to ATC. And then you flew the Berlin Airlift from start to finish. I acted like an ass. I'm sorry."

"Forget it," said Terry.

"Now will you have a drink with me?"

"How can I refuse?"

"Since I'm the boss's daughter, you can't."

She clicked her champagne glass against Terry's, and they drank. Close up, Terry thought she was even better-looking. He liked her face, strong like her father's, with wide-set green eyes framed by black hair that fell silkily past the shoulders of her white dress.

Terry said, "I saw your son the other day. Si had him in his office. Handsome little boy."

"David is a spoiled brat, thanks to Si," Janet said. "But then Si and my mother have practically brought him up. Look, why don't you and I slip away? I know a marvelous place up the coast. They make the best margaritas in town. Do you like margaritas?"

"I never had one."

"Come on, we'll break your cherry."

Terry felt himself blush. "Excuse me, but what about your husband?"

"He's dead."

"Christ, I'm sorry."

"Save the apologies," Janet said. "I'll tell you all about it on the way to Malibu."

They drove in her car, a yacht-sized white Cadillac El Dorado convertible. Janet told him she and David had moved into her parents' house when David's father, Paul Tannen, was called back into the service two days after the Korean War started. And how one sunny Sunday morning not long afterward, she received a visit from a navy chaplain and a marine colonel.

"They gave him the Navy Cross and a nice ceremony at Arlington," she said. "At Arlington, some moron complained about the Jewish star on Paul's gravestone. Paul was my second husband." Her voice grew flat. "The first one was killed in action, too. He was in the RAF. I'm a kind of jinx, wouldn't you say?"

They had several drinks at the Malibu roadhouse, Holiday House, a hotel-restaurant built into a cliff overlooking the ocean. They talked. Terry told her about himself. He was from St. Louis, an only child, his father a brewery foreman, his mother a schoolteacher. He had enlisted in the army at age eighteen, on the day he graduated high school. After a year of sweat and study, he qualified for flying cadets, and in late 1942 received his wings.

They talked for hours, about themselves, about aviation, about Janet's son, whom Simon Conway was already grooming to someday take over the empire, and even about President Truman's firing of General MacArthur, which Janet considered nothing more than a cheap political ploy. Before they knew it, it was dark outside. Janet excused herself to call home. She wanted to make sure David was giving Meg no trouble, and that he had had his supper and been put to bed. When she returned, she sat, leaned across the table and straightened Terry's tie, and said, "I booked us a room."

Terry thought she was joking. "Did you spell my name right?"

"I need to make love, and be made love to," she said. "Consider it a favor you're doing me. A service."

He was just drunk enough not to worry about the consequences. "Well, since you put it that way, how can I refuse?"

"I told you before, you can't. I'm the boss's daughter."

Two weeks later, ten thousand feet over Santa Monica Bay in the spacious, almost club-chair comfort of the left seat of Conair's 885 prototype, Terry remembered those words, but with foreboding. Standing on the flight deck directly behind him, greasy old fedora pushed back on his head, cigarette dangling from his lips, was the boss, Simon Conway.

For the past two weeks, Terry and Janet had seen each other nearly every night. Each night was more exciting than the last. By now he was wildly in love with her. This morning, when Simon Conway gruffly said he wanted to talk to him, Terry was sure it concerned Janet. But he had anticipated this scene ever since the relationship started. He was prepared.

I'm in love with your daughter, Mr. Conway. I'd like to marry her. Yes sir, I love her and want to take care of her. And I'll be a real father to the boy. Beautiful speech. Terry wondered what Janet would think about it. He had not yet mustered the courage to raise the subject.

Terry needn't have worried. If Si even suspected Janet and Terry were seeing each other, let alone sleeping together, he gave no indication. What Si wanted to talk about was the pressure Richard and Phil Granger were putting on him to introduce the 885 as a turboprop.

Si was adamantly opposed to such a redesign, especially if a Conair passenger jet was to compete with De Havilland's Comet, the world's first jet transport. Conair, said Si, would bring out a pure jet, the 1010, within three years, no later than 1954. But this might not be possible if the company's resources and production lines were committed to a turboprop. He therefore wanted Terry to keep an open mind.

There was no mistaking Si's definition of "open mind." He expected Terry to agree with him: no Conair turboprop. So now, sitting in the 885's left seat, with Si breathing down his neck, Terry tried to sort all this out. If he crossed Si, he might hurt himself with Janet. On the other hand, Si was too smart to be bullshitted. Terry knew Simon Conway well enough by now to know that with Si honesty was the best policy. And since when did a $2,000-per-month test pilot's opinion influence the policies of a multimillion-dollar company?

Besides, he thought, Janet Tannen was way out of his league anyway. He took a deep breath, half turned to face Si, and said, "She's a beautiful machine, this 885." He rubbed his hand caressingly over the control yoke. "But with turboprops on her, she'll be so far ahead of anything else in the air, you won't be able to keep up with the orders!"

Si said nothing. Again, Terry felt as though he had been pushed into that bottomless pit, only this time the walls were studded with poison-tipped iron spikes.

Terry said, "I realize it'll put you a couple of years behind with the pure jets, but you asked me and I have to tell you what I think."

Si remained silent.

Terry faced forward again. He fiddled with the engine controls, then called to the flight engineer to start pressurizing the cabin. The flight engineer's station, directly behind the copilot, was the airplane's nerve center, a huge panel of hundreds of gauges, toggles, and levers extending from the ceiling down to the floor.

". . . appreciate your frankness, son," Si was saying. He patted Terry fondly on the shoulder. "But I think you're wrong."

Good, Terry thought, now that we've got that over with, will you give me a reference for my next job? He said to Si, "I'm going to take her up to eighteen thousand, Mr. Conway—"

Si was not there. He had returned to the cabin, up front where two rows of three-abreast passenger seats had been installed. He sat in the first seat of the first row. He wanted to think. He had much to think about and, contrary to Terry Deland's belief, he had other, more important problems than the 885. One was Conair's jet fighter, the Firestreak. The other problem was a man named Bennet Anderson. Both issues, the Firestreak and Ben Anderson, were intertwined and each posed a grave threat to Conway Aviation Industries.

2.

A short, wiry, prematurely gray man, Ben Anderson looked more like a country doctor than a brilliant aircraft designer. He was forty-three years old, a U.S. Naval Academy graduate, Class of 1928, with an MIT doctorate in aeronautical engineering. In 1940, he formed Anderson Aircraft Manufacturing Company and produced a superb wartime fighter, the Sting Ray.

The Anderson Sting Ray was followed by the Tiger Shark, the first U.S. Navy jet fighter capable of landing and taking off from a carrier. By 1951, Anderson Aircraft was one of the nation's most important suppliers of military aircraft. And now Ben Anderson wanted a piece of the commercial market. But to produce his own transport would require years of development, a prohibitive investment, and the difficulty of competing with the established manufacturers. There was a simple solution: merge Anderson Aircraft with an established company.

The likeliest candidate was Conair, whose military business had been reduced to a single contract for tankers and only one substantial project, the Firestreak. The new fighter, still undergoing final testing before full production, was more expensive and more complicated and did not perform as well as Anderson's competing model, the Devilfish. And yet it was Conair's Firestreak, not Anderson's Devilfish, that had received a lucrative air force contract.

Ben Anderson knew precisely how, when, and by whom all this had come about. Conair's Washington representative, Scott St. James, had cajoled, coerced, and finally prevailed upon his old wartime buddies in the Pentagon to bypass Anderson in favor of Conair. It was a scandal waiting to happen.

At Richard Conway's wedding, Anderson asked Philip Granger to arrange a meeting with Simon Conway to discuss the possibility of a merger. Granger relayed the request to Si, whose response was predictable.

"Why the hell should I meet with that son of a bitch?"

Granger's reply was equally predictable. "To keep us out of the poorhouse!"

Ten days after Si's flight with Terry Deland in the 885 prototype, Ben Anderson flew into Los Angeles in his personal Devilfish. Instead of parking in Conway Field's transient area, he taxied the rakish little delta-winged jet fighter across the main runway to Conair's maintenance hangar and, deliberately, parked next to a Firestreak.

". . . kind of reminds you of a big fat ugly lady standing next to some luscious little blonde, doesn't it?" he wisecracked to the ramp man.

Ben Anderson's flying that jet into Conway Field was like spitting in Si's face. Si had flown jets—from the front seat of a T-33 trainer —but never a high-performance aircraft, and now, at fifty-six, was too old, too slow, and probably too fragile. He would have to settle for the left seat of his 1010, the Conair subsonic passenger jet, which was already off the drawing board and into mockup.

The meeting was held in Si's office. Phil Granger had wanted it in the conference room, but Si said that since only four of them would be present, himself, Granger, Richard, and Anderson, there was no sense wasting time on formalities.

Ben Anderson's first words were "Now I know how Wyatt Earp felt when he walked down the street toward the Clancy brothers." He smiled when he said it, which only annoyed Si more, but there was also the matter of civility, so Si offered the guest a drink. Anderson declined but did accept a cigar. Granger observed the proceedings irritably. He wanted to get on with the business.

"How was Acapulco?" Anderson asked Richard.

"Not bad if you like warm, clear, sunny days and beautiful, balmy nights," said Richard, who had returned from his honeymoon a few days before. "And great food, and marvelous swimming."

"Reminds me of my honeymoon. The first one. The other two weren't nearly as good," Anderson said, and without pausing continued to Si, "Phil told you why I wanted to see you?"

"He did, and I'm not interested."

Anderson said, "Then would you be interested to know that the air force is about to cancel the Firestreak contract?"

Si glanced quizzically at Granger, who said, "Ben thinks the GAO is about to open an investigation into the Firestreak contract."

"Ben doesn't 'think,' " said Anderson. "Ben 'knows.' "

"Why?" Richard asked. "Because we're late delivering?"

"Because of the way Conair won the bid," Anderson said.

"No, you mean because Conair won it, period," Si said. "Because you lost out."

"We submitted a price of four hundred and fifty thousand," Anderson said quietly. "Yours was six hundred and twenty-five thousand."

"Ours is more airplane," Richard said.

"Please, guys, let's cut the bullshit," Anderson said. "First, Scott St. James sweet-talked a civilian secretary in the Defense Department into showing him a look at the sealed bids. We know this for a fact. I have an affidavit from the lady. Then he called in some old markers from air force cronies. They put the pressure on the Pentagon—"

"—come on, Ben, there's nothing new about that," Si said. "They've been doing it since the Signal Corps gave Orville and Wilbur Wright their first contract."

"Sure, Si, but Orville and Wilbur's contract was for a huge twelve thousand five hundred dollars," Anderson said. "We're talking about a hundred million!" He leveled his cigar at Si. "I happen to know you dumped twenty million of your own money into developing the Firestreak. If there is an investigation, and if they cancel the contract, you won't have enough cash to pay the phone bill."

Si said nothing. Twenty million, he was thinking. And you could probably add another five if you included the money he had been siphoning from other projects into the 1010. Twenty-five million. Twenty-five with six zeros. It wasn't so long ago they were breaking into warehouses for fifty-five-dollar tires. He could still see Ruth Tannen, big with her child, distracting the Thompson Rubber Company watchman while Si and Morris stole the tires.

Big with her child, he thought, Paul.

Poor Paul, and poor Morris, too. He had never been the same since Paul's death and had already announced his intention not to run for another Senate term.

". . . merge Anderson Aircraft with Conair," Ben Anderson was saying. "Anderson will take over the Firestreak project and assume responsibility for the successful completion of the contract—"

"—hold on!" Si said. "There won't be any merger!"

Anderson's response was partially drowned out by the sound of engines directly overhead. The 885 had just taken off on its continuing series of test flights, Art Hamel in the left seat today. Art was getting burned out and shaky. You could almost see him trying to force the big airplane off the runway. Terry always got her off at the exact instant she wanted to fly. Si reminded himself to talk to Art about flying less, maybe taking a desk job.

The sound of the 885's engines receded. Si faced the men again. "I said, no merger."

"Si, let's not reject this out of hand," Granger said. "The stock of a merged Anderson-Conair company would be worth a fortune. But even better, Anderson will absorb all our current debt."

Richard said to Granger, "I don't understand you, Phil. We're sitting with an air force order to convert thirty 880s to K-88 tankers. We have firm orders for 885s from Intercontinental, TWA, and American. We might have a temporary cash problem, but we can manage."

"And in a few years we'll be flying the 1010," Si said. "The kid is right. No sale, Ben."

"Let's talk it over privately," Granger said to Si.

"Sure, Phil," Si said. "Whatever makes you happy."

Ben Anderson took a long, appreciative drag on the cigar, then placed it carefully in the oversize glass ashtray on the coffee table. "I'm staying in town tonight. I'll be at the Beverly Wilshire." He rose, shook hands with everyone, started out, and then came back to pick up the cigar. "Great cigar, too good to leave behind," he said to Si. "Upmann, isn't it?"

"Monte Cristo," Si said. "I'll send you a box."

"You're a sport," said Anderson. He left.

Si said, "Is that all he has to do? Fly twelve hundred miles for a five-minute meeting?"

No one replied. The windowpanes rattled as another airplane, an 880, rolled down the runway on its takeoff run. This was followed immediately by the banshee wail of a Firestreak's jet engine as the fighter taxied into takeoff position.

Si said to Granger, "How serious is this business about an investigation?"

"St. James says Anderson has two Texas congressmen in his pocket. He gives the word, they'll break the thing wide open."

"I think your boy Mr. Major General Scott St. James fucked up," Si said.

"He only did what we told him to," Granger said. "We said get us the contract. He got it."

"Fire him," Si said.

"We do that, Si—and if they investigate the Firestreak contract —Scott's sure to blow the whistle," Granger said. "He'll protect his own hide first."

"Fire him."

"No, Si," said Granger. "You want him fired, you do it."

"Somebody goddam well better fire him!" Si hurled his cigar into the ashtray and stalked into the bathroom. He slammed the door closed.

Richard said to Granger, "I'll do it. I'll fire St. James. I never liked the pompous bastard, anyway."

Granger said, "No, it has to come from a corporate officer."

"What am I?" Richard asked. "The gateman?"

"You're a junior executive," Granger said.

"Hey, for me that's a promotion," Richard said.

"Don't delude yourself. You've got a long way to go before you sit in that seat." Granger nodded at Si's desk.

Richard peered at Granger, enlightened. "That's the whole point, isn't it?" he said. "You're worried about the ascension. Anything happens to Si, all of a sudden I'm not a junior executive anymore. All of a sudden I'm somebody you have to contend with."

Granger said, "If your father keeps burning up money trying to bring out a four-engined jet ahead of Douglas or Boeing, there'll be nothing left for any of us to contend with. Look at the books, for the love of God! Read the numbers!"

"Merging with Anderson won't change that."

"Of course it will. It'll give us a solid cash basis we've never had, and a real lock on the military market. It's a marriage made in heaven." He smiled. "Like yours, Dick."

"I'll take that as a compliment."

"It was meant as one."

"Yeah, I just bet," Richard said. In the bathroom the toilet flushed. "You'll never convince my father about a merger."

"No, but maybe you can."

"Me? I couldn't even convince him to button his fly."

"You could try."

"For the common good, eh?" Richard said dryly. "And then, when Conair's a division of Anderson, you wouldn't have to worry about me taking over the company anymore, would you?"

Si emerged from the bathroom. He had caught the last few words of the conversation. "Who's taking over what company?" he asked.

Granger evaded the question. He said to Si, "I want us to seriously consider Anderson's offer."

"I did," said Si. "And I'm seriously turning it down." He picked up the cigar from the ashtray and walked to his desk and sat down. "Get the hell out of here, both of you." He made a point of studying some correspondence. After a moment, when he heard the door open and close and knew the room was empty, he said aloud, to himself, "Nice going, Phil. I always knew it would end up like this."

Had Granger written it out in gigantic letters on the wall, it could not have been any clearer to Si. Granger, who so obviously favored a merger, intended to offer Ben Anderson his 75,000 shares of Conair stock. Granger was of course obliged to offer it first to the company, which meant Si. The stock carried a value of at least $20 million, a sum Granger knew Si did not have and could not raise.

"Yeah, Phil," Si said aloud again. "Nice going." He puffed on the cigar. It was out. It left a cold bitter taste in his mouth.

3.

In a boxing match the referee would have mercifully called a halt. It reminded Si of newsreels of last year's Sugar Ray Robinson–Jake La Motta fight. The canvas floor of the ring and the referee's white shirt were splattered with La Motta's blood.

The ring for this contest was the Caucus Room of the U.S. Senate Building. The blood on the floor—figurative, of course—belonged to Conair's Washington representative, Scott St. James. The ex-general's tormentor was a thirty-five-year-old United States senator from New Hampshire, Ralph Wynant, chairman of the select committee hearing testimony on accusations of Defense Department waste and influence peddling.

The Wynant Committee hearings were held in late October 1951, the same week that Douglas Aircraft Corporation's experimental rocket-propelled aircraft the Skyrocket broke its own world's altitude and speed record: 72,000 feet, 1,000 mph. A gratifying week for Donald Douglas, a most distressing one for Simon Conway.

The Caucus Room was crowded with noisy spectators and abrasive newsmen. The lights of the newsreel and television cameras were blinding. Senator Ralph Wynant, who everyone said bore a remarkable resemblance to Abraham Lincoln, called the meeting to order. His first witness was Scott St. James.

The committee counsel, an aggressive young attorney, led St. James briefly through his distinguished military career. Wynant then took over. He wasted no time on pleasantries.

"You accepted a position with Conway Aviation Industries almost immediately following your retirement from the air force, is that correct, general?"

"That's correct, senator." St. James sat erect, hands folded tightly on his lap. His attorney sat beside him, a dapper silver-haired man with a perpetual frown.

"What was the nature of that employment?"

"My job was to represent the company here in Washington."

"By that I take it to mean you were looking after your employer's interests?"

"Yes, you might say that."

" 'Looking after its interests,' " Wynant said. "Exactly what interests did you look after, general?"

"Any and all, I suppose."

"Could you be a little more specific?"

"If you ask specific questions, senator."

"Oh, I will, general. Believe me, I will."

Si, seated with Phil Granger directly behind the witness table, remembered the last time he was in this room, eighteen years earlier. Nothing had changed. The committee chairman, then Hugo Black, had gripped the gavel with the same ferocity. And now, as then, they told you that you would receive a fair trial before the hanging.

". . . so the Defense Department issued a GOR—a General Operative Requirement—for a Mach One all-weather fighter," Wynant was saying. "This evolved into Air Force Project AP26Y dash six, more familiarly known as the Firestreak, which on March twelfth, 1949, was awarded to Conway Aviation Industries of Culver City, California. Is that correct, sir?"

"Yes, senator, that's correct," said St. James. He brushed some lint from the shoulders of his blue serge suit, a pretense of indifference. It seemed to amuse Wynant.

"Thank you," said Wynant. "The GOR called for two hundred and forty planes. What was the price per unit on the bid submitted by Conair?"

"I believe six hundred and twenty-five thousand dollars," St. James said.

"Yet a competing bid from Anderson Aircraft Corporation quoted a unit price of four hundred and seventy-five thousand dollars. How do you explain that?"

"The air force decided that the Firestreak was a better long-term investment."

"But at the time the contract was awarded, the Firestreak had flown only a total of eleven hours," Wynant said. "It was loaded with problems. 'Bugs,' I believe is how you refer to them."

"Well, general, all aircraft have bugs—"

"—and to this day, two years later, the same 'bugs' are still there. How do you explain that?"

"Those bugs are being—"

"—General St. James, are you friendly with Major General Frank Egan?"

"Yes, he's—"

"—a former subordinate, isn't he?" Wynant was consulting the open pages of a small loose-leaf notebook. "A combat pilot who served under you in the 619th Fighter Group, and who was promoted to squadron commander on your recommendation."

"A promotion he richly deserved, sir."

"I don't doubt it for a moment," said Wynant. "In point of fact, General Egan, a major at the time, is credited with nineteen enemy planes shot down. I believe General Egan owns a ski lodge in Aspen, Colorado?"

The question, so out of context, startled St. James. "Excuse me?"

"I asked you if General Egan owns a ski lodge."

"I believe he does."

"You 'believe' he does? That piece of property was purchased by you, and the title subsequently transferred to General Egan. Correct?"

St. James turned nervously to his attorney. The attorney nodded. St. James said to Wynant, "Correct, but it's not that simple."

"The purchase price of the property in question was twenty-seven thousand five hundred dollars, was it not?"

"Yes, but as I say, it is not that simple."

"I'm certain of that, general, and we'll discuss the 'simplicity' of it shortly. Now tell me, sir, at the time the Firestreak bid was submitted, General Egan commanded a fighter wing based in Germany, did he not?"

"Yes, I believe so—"

"—and would you say that General Egan's opinion carried considerable weight in the Defense Department?"

"Egan is a man of vast experience."

"Precisely," said Wynant. "So that when a Frank Egan recommends one plane over another—despite a substantial difference in price—such recommendation will certainly be taken seriously. Is that a proper assumption?"

"Yes."

Si, listening, vaguely recalled Granger's mentioning that St. James wanted the company to purchase some Aspen property as a gift for somebody or other. Si, preoccupied with a thousand other problems, had paid little attention. Talk about closing barn doors.

The interrogation continued. Wynant established that the $27,500 for Egan's purchase of the ski lodge had been advanced to him by St. James in the form of a long-term low-interest loan. Egan, testifying in an earlier deposition, had stated that in his opinion the Conair Firestreak was a potentially more promising weapon than the competing Anderson Devilfish, a fact that outweighed any cost differential.

Not to mention an Aspen ski lodge.

By the time Wynant dismissed St. James it was evident that heads would roll and careers be destroyed.

Si's turn at the witness table came a day later. ". . . I understand, Mr. Conway, that upon learning of this situation, you immediately fired General St. James?"

"I certainly did," said Si.

"Why did you hire him in the first place?"

"Why did I hire him?"

"Yes, Mr. Conway, why did you hire the general?"

"He appeared to be qualified for the job, senator."

"What are the qualifications for such a position?"

"A solid aviation background," Si said after a moment. "Experience."

"Experience," Wynant repeated flatly. "Is that spelled with a C?"

"I beg your pardon?"

"The word I want begins with a C, I think. Contacts. The qualifications for the job referred to are contacts. Contacts, and influence, Capital I. The influence former military officers might have with officers still on active duty, particularly if those officers are former comrades-in-arms who presently occupy positions of importance. I have no further questions for this witness."

Si remained at the table, answering questions from other senators. More of the same. He replied automatically, his mind swimming with the ramifications of all this. Cancellation of the Firestreak contract not only meant mass layoffs, but would inevitably snowball into a loss of industry confidence in Conair's commercial products. Airlines would begin canceling their 885 orders.

Throughout the proceedings Si could not help but note that Phil Granger seemed almost pleased. Si knew why. An Anderson merger now appeared to be Conair's only salvation. He raised the issue with Granger on the flight back to Los Angeles.

". . . don't even bother arguing about it," Si said. "We will not—repeat, not—merge with anyone. We've been in jams before, we've gotten out. We'll get out of this one."

"This is more than a jam, Si."

For an instant Si seemed unable to utter the words already on his lips. He felt himself enveloped in a great wave of fatigue. It was gone as quickly as it came.

"I knew you'd say that, Phil. That's all you know how to say."

"I can read a balance sheet, Si."

The stewardess had just brought drinks. Scotch for Si, a ginger ale for Granger. They were comfortably settled in the little club lounge at the very rear of the 880's cabin, with a small table in front of their plush leather seats. The stewardess was a leggy, willowy redhead. Intercontinental Air was famous for its good-looking stewardesses. Coffee, tea, or me.

When she left, Si said to Granger, "Conair is my company, Phil. My son's, and my grandson's. I mean for it to stay that way."

"It's also my company," Granger said. "I've put thirty years of my life into it. I simply will not stand by and let you flush it down the toilet."

"I'm sorry, Phil. The matter is closed." Si drank down half his scotch. It warmed him and, with the steady smooth drone of the engines, made him drowsy. "I'll tell you the same thing I told you when you blew your stack because I charged the Israelis five thousand dollars each for those fifteen surplus Conair Hunters: 'You don't like it, Phil, take it up with the board.' " He raised his glass at Granger in a mock toast. "I am the board."

Although he still felt drained of energy the next day—what the hell, at fifty-six you couldn't traipse from coast to coast, get the hell bashed out of you at a U.S. Senate hearing, then fly back and expect to feel like running the Boston Marathon—he felt strong enough to get into a CT-8 and fly down to San Diego.

He took David with him and let the boy handle the controls most of the way. Although David's feet could not reach the rudder pedals, a couple of seat cushions propped him high enough to see over the instrument panel. David, not quite seven, was a marvel. He reminded Si of Frank, with the same natural instinct for flying. But then, why not? It was in the genes, wasn't it?

"Honest to God," Si said when they landed, "in two years, three at most, I'll have you soloing."

"Make it two years, Gramps."

" 'Gramps'? Didn't I tell you to call me Si?"

"Okay, Si."

"Okay, yourself, Dave." Si drew the boy into his arms and held him tight. "Two years it'll be."

Morris was waiting for them at the little private airport at Poway. He looked gaunt and pale, still not recovered from Paul's death, a day Si would never forget. It had fallen to him, Si, to break the news to Morris and Ruth. They had been on a weekend cruise to Mexico. It was a Sunday morning, a classic Southern California November day, sunny, clear, warm. Earlier that morning a navy chaplain and a marine colonel had notified Janet. She asked Si to go down to San Pedro and meet Morris and Ruth. She could not face them. The moment Morris saw Si standing nervously on the pier, he knew.

Since then, whenever Si saw Morris—which, because of David, was fairly often now—he always recalled the unexpected feeling of warmth and empathy he had felt for Morris that terrible Sunday. Now they shared a tragic experience, the loss of a child, in Morris's case all the more devastating because Paul was his only child.

As they drove into La Jolla in Morris's big black Lincoln Town Car, Si related the events of the past week to Morris, most of which Morris already knew. Morris also knew Si, and knew that this visit was no casual drop-in, despite Si's claim that "since I was taking the kid out for a lesson, I thought maybe he'd like to say hello to his other grandfather."

Morris said, "Let me save you a lot of time and trouble, Si. There's nothing I can do. The Firestreak is a lost cause." He swung the Lincoln into the graveled driveway of the pleasant little beach house he and Ruth had moved into after selling their Del Mar home last year, not long after Paul's death. "My advice to you is follow Granger's advice," he continued. "Make the deal with Anderson."

"What do you mean, there's nothing you can do?" Si asked. "You still have plenty of clout in the Senate. You can do something about Wynant."

Morris did not immediately reply. Ruth had just rushed out to greet them, sweeping David up in a breathless bear hug. After exchanging a few words with Si, she herded David into the house. Si leaned against the Lincoln's fender, suddenly tired again. It was almost an effort to drag on his cigarette.

"Si, all the clout in the world wouldn't help," Morris said. "Ralph Wynant is probably the most ambitious man in Washington, and for sure the most calculating. He makes old Tail Gunner Joe McCarthy look like a Boy Scout. Ralph means to be the Republican Vice Presidential nominee. The Firestreak is his ticket."

Si said nothing. He dragged deeply on the cigarette. The smoke seemed to choke him. He threw the cigarette away. He knew Morris was right and felt like a fool for rushing down here to seek help when no help was possible.

It was after five and almost dark when Si taxied the CT-8 into the executive aircraft hangar at Conway Field, and nearly six by the time he and David arrived home. Meg gave him hell for being so late. Not only had Si ruined David's appetite with hot dogs and soda pop, but Richard and Enid were coming to the house for dinner.

"Can't you cancel?" Si asked. "I'm bushed."

"They're already on their way," Meg said. "Now please go and change. At least put on a clean shirt. David!" she called. "Go upstairs and get ready for bed!"

"Where's Janet?" Si asked.

"Out on a date."

"With who?"

"Your star pilot, Terry Deland."

Si knew Janet and Terry were seeing each other, and he couldn't be more pleased. Terry Deland was a fine young man, and a superb pilot. He also seemed to be able to handle Janet, no small task.

But if Janet did marry again, there was one serious drawback: she would move out of the house and take David with her. But Si thought he might have the answer for it. Offer the couple their own quarters in the house. Renovate the existing guest suite, enlarge it, create an entire new wing.

God, but he was tired! He went to say good night to David, spent a few extra minutes relating a Lafayette Escadrille dogfight story, tucked the boy into bed, then joined Meg and Richard and Enid in the dining room.

Although Meg was serving one of Si's favorites, roast leg of lamb and broiled potatoes, he only picked at the food. His throat felt raw. He thought he might be coming down with a cold. He managed to get through dinner, and even through most of the conversation. They were talking about General Eisenhower's turning down Harry Truman's offer to sponsor Ike as the Democratic nominee in the 1952 Presidential election. Si said that if Ike wanted to be President he could run on the Communist ticket and win.

After dinner Richard and Si brought their coffee into Si's study. Richard had some news, which came as no real surprise. As of 4:35 that afternoon, the Firestreak contract was officially canceled. The Defense Department had invoked the nonperformance clause.

"Who'd they notify?" Si asked. "Phil?"

"He got the call, yes."

"And I bet right away he started working on you about you working on me for the Anderson merger?"

"That's no bet, Dad. It's a sure thing."

"What'd you tell him?"

"I told him I'd discuss it with you."

"You, too, eh?"

"No, Dad, not 'me, too.' What I'm worried about is this thing costing us our other military contracts, especially the tanker conversions, the K-88s. If that happens, we have no income until the 885 is in full production. How in Christ's name do we pay our bills?"

"Listen, kid, take Enid and go home. We'll talk about it tomorrow. I'm tired as hell."

Something about the way Si said "tired as hell" surprised Richard.

It sounded like a statement of surrender. But Richard felt sure that after a good night's sleep Si would be himself again, racing around scheming up ways to beat the rap. And, if a way existed, finding it.

Richard finished his brandy and left. Si drained his own glass, then got up and poured another. He opened the humidor and started to extract a cigar, but decided on a cigarette. He lit the cigarette and inhaled.

He thought a ten-ton truck had smashed into his chest. He gasped for breath. The room began swaying. He felt nauseous. He gripped the cigarette in the fingers of one hand and with the other hand groped for the couch armrest. The room stopped swaying. He sat down and watched the smoke curl bluely up from the cigarette.

He touched his forehead. It felt clammy. He was sweating, and the ten-ton truck still rested on his chest. He took another drag on the cigarette. The truck was crushing him.

Somewhere, almost as an echo, he heard Meg's voice screaming. "Si . . . !" He could not seem to raise his head to look up at her. On the carpet, at Meg's feet, was a silver tray she had dropped, and a smashed coffee cup and saucer. The cup had been empty, which Si thought was lucky, or else the carpet might have been stained.

"Jesus, it hurts!" he said.

He knew he was dying, and he was very disappointed. Not that he was dying, but that this was not the way he wanted it to happen. He had often fantasized it. Leaving the doctor's office after having been diagnosed with some terminal illness, driving straight to the field, and getting into an airplane. Over Santa Monica Bay, he would simply push the stick forward and dive toward the water.

The waters of the bay rushed up at him now. He could make out each individual wave. But everything was so slow, so slow. The airplane's propeller spinner brushed the surface. The propeller tips, churning into the waves, sprayed water across the windscreen. The nose of the airplane struck the water. The pain in his chest stopped. Everything stopped.

23

David knew his grandfather would not die. His grandmother said so. He heard her talking to his mother about it the day after Si's heart attack. Meg had accompanied Si in the ambulance to St. John's Hospital and remained there all through that first night and most of the following day. Late in the afternoon of the second day, while Meg was trying to rest in the doctor's lounge, a nurse came in to say that Mr. Conway demanded to see his wife immediately.

Under the transparent plastic oxygen tent Si's face was white, his lips blue. Although heavily sedated, slipping in and out of consciousness, he beckoned Meg to him.

". . . tell Richard," he said, struggling for breath with each word, ". . . not trust Granger! Little bastard treacherous! Tell Richard . . . !"

Si closed his eyes and fell asleep. Meg remained with him a few minutes, then returned to the lounge, where Janet anxiously waited. For a heart-sinking instant, seeing her mother's calm, reflective expression, Janet thought that Si had died and that Meg was thankful his suffering was over.

Meg read Janet's mind. "He won't die," Meg said. "He knows exactly what's happened to him. He'll will himself to live. I know him, Janet. I know what I'm talking about."

Si's message about Granger's treachery was no great revelation to Richard, and he discovered it for himself anyway. Three days after the heart attack, when Si's survival was still in doubt, Granger summoned Richard to his office and informed him that the air force had reduced its K-88 tanker order by half.

"They're really sticking it to us," Granger said. "Between this and the Firestreak, we've lost close to one hundred and fifty million dollars in canceled orders! I sent Anderson a wire this morning telling him we're ready to reopen merger talks," Granger continued.

"You could have at least waited until after the funeral."

"Your father won't die," Granger said. "He doesn't want to make that many people happy. I've asked our lawyers to start drawing up the merger papers."

"I like your suit, Phil," Richard said. It was a double-breasted greenish-gray flannel. "It matches your face. I used to see guys on the Normandy beach with that same complexion."

"Cracking jokes won't change anything, Rich. This company is in real danger of going under. We're pink-slipping four thousand people this week. You can just imagine what hell the union'll raise."

"You can't negotiate with Anderson," Richard said. "Not without Simon Conway's consent."

"Si is incapacitated. You, as a company officer and next of kin, are legally entitled to act on his behalf."

"In that case, Phil, we'll just hold off on the merger until he's well enough to make a decision. In the meantime, we'll borrow whatever money we need. I spoke to a man at Goldman Sachs in New York this morning. He says that on a short-term basis they can raise as much as fifty million for us. At four and a half percent interest."

"Sure, and twenty-five percent—if not more—of the company if we default. Forget it."

"My father said no merger. That means no merger."

Granger rose and walked across the room to a glass-framed oil painting of a panorama of a busy nineteenth-century New England wharf. He touched the bottom corner of the frame, which swung entirely free to reveal a small wall safe. Granger dialed the combination, opened the safe, and removed a file folder. He tossed the folder onto Richard's lap.

"Read it and weep, sonny."

The file was a summary of an interview in Paris in 1948 with a woman named Nicole Guilbert, a member of a wartime Resistance Group. It was the woman's account of the 1944 incident at Ablon. Richard read it carefully. It was all fairly accurate, until the very last paragraph:

> . . . the Gestapo were inside the cottage, and we knew they had arrested the British agent. I wanted to do something to help her but I knew this would be impossible without Mr. Conway's assistance.

"... seems you weren't the hero that everyone thought," Granger was saying.

It was all unreal to Richard, a fragmented memory. Real, however, was the self-serving intimation in Nicole's statement that Richard had prevented her from trying to save Blair.

What surprised him was that he felt no anger, only sadness. "This is slightly out of context, Phil," he said.

"That's a matter of opinion," Granger said. "Why don't you take the whole thing home with you and study it? I have another copy."

"You've been seeing too many cheap movies."

"The newspapers might not think so. It'll make juicy reading: the wartime 'hero' who sat by and watched the Germans capture his girl-friend. The hero who didn't lift a finger to help her. You can say it's 'out of context' from now until next year, Richard"—Granger slapped the flat of his hand on the file—"but those are the sworn facts!"

"I never realized what a menace you really are," Richard said. "You'll stop at nothing."

"When it comes to saving this company, I won't," Granger said. "Now, Rich, please dictate a memo to me indicating your support of any action I take with Anderson."

Richard said nothing. He was thinking, You're running a bluff, Phil. The publicity will have an adverse affect on Conair's few remaining military contracts, and therefore not be to your personal benefit. It will depress the value of your own shares of Conair stock.

Granger said, "Dammit, boy, don't you understand? This company is about to go under!"

On the other hand, Richard thought, Granger might not be bluffing. He might be so anxious to get rid of Richard that he was willing to risk the damage to the company's image that could result from making the dossier public.

"If we don't merge, we die," Granger continued.

"Let me think about it," Richard said.

"There's nothing for you to think about."

The hell there isn't, Richard thought, especially when I have no intention whatever of approving a merger. There is plenty for me to think about. To start with, I have to consider how eager Goldman Sachs will be to lend fifty million dollars to a company whose acting chief executive officer is accused of wartime cowardice.

He was standing near the window that overlooked the main gate on Jefferson Avenue. A few days before, an automobile had smashed through the gate and into the brick wall in front of the administration building. Three Mexican workmen were quickly and efficiently repairing the wall.

"I'll think about it," Richard said. "I'll talk to you in the morning." He strode past Granger, out of the office, and out of the building. He walked around to the front and watched the bricklayers. They worked with mechanical precision, applying the mortar, positioning the brick, applying the mortar. It was relaxing to watch them.

Years before, as an LAPD motorcycle officer, Julian Garwood had stopped Philip Granger for an illegal U turn. A $10 bill not only failed to fix the matter but nearly landed Granger in jail for atempted bribery. The officer refused $20, and then $50. Such professionalism impressed Granger. When Julian Garwood retired from the LAPD, Granger offered him the position of Conair security chief.

Late in the evening of the same day that Granger had shown Richard the file, Julian Garwood received an urgent telephone call from the night watchman at the Conair administration building. Something very strange was going on. Mr. Garwood had best come down and see for himself.

Something strange was definitely going on. Three Mexican bricklayers were busily sealing up the door of Philip Granger's office. Observing them, looking very self-satisfied, was Richard Conway.

"Mr. Conway, what in the hell is all this about?" Julian Garwood asked.

"What in the hell does it look like?"

"Does Mr. Granger know about it?"

"Not yet," Richard said. He could not repress a smile at the prospect of Granger heading down the corridor to his office, walking confidently past it and then, realizing, whirling around to stare at a brick wall.

"Hey, you!" Garwood yelled to the workmen. "Stop it! Pull down those fucking bricks!"

"No, no," Richard said to the men in Spanish. "Just keep working. You work for me, I'm the boss! You, Garwood," he said in the same breath, "you *don't* work for me! You're fired! Now go run and tell Granger what happened!"

Which Garwood promptly did. By the time Granger arrived the Mexicans were gone, their job completed. There was no office door, only a brick wall. Richard, flanked by two uniformed Los Angeles deputy sheriffs, greeted Granger.

"Good evening, Phil. Gorgeous night, isn't it?"

Granger appeared more amused than angry. "Would you mind telling me the point of all this?"

"It should be obvious," Richard said. He looked down at Granger. He towered over the smaller man, which he knew made him uncomfortable. "After tonight, Phil, you won't be allowed onto these premises. You're fired."

"I'm a stockholder," said Granger. "I own part of this company. You can't fire me."

"I just did."

Granger's face tightened. It was as though he had suddenly realized this was no prank. "All right, Richard, that's enough. I want these bricks taken down."

"You're trespassing on private property, Phil. Please leave or I'll ask these officers to remove you forcibly."

"You're crazy, Richard. You're stark raving mad!"

"Goodbye, Phil."

"When your father hears about this, you'll be the one who's out on the street."

"I have news for you, Phil," Richard said. "When my father hears about this, he'll congratulate me."

A few days later, when Granger returned with a court order demanding the release of certain personal effects, Richard invited him to help himself. The files were gone, of course. Richard had broken into the safe, removed Granger's private personnel records, and burned them all, including both copies of Nicole Guilbert's version of the Ablon tragedy.

Richard's confrontation with Philip Granger earned him Granger's complete respect. Ever the astute businessman, Granger retained his Conair stock, for he saw in Richard a no-nonsense, pragmatic executive who could turn Conair around. If eventually Richard saw no other solution than to merge, he would merge. No matter which way it went, Granger would benefit.

While Granger's prediction of Richard turning the company around remained to be seen, no one could dispute his assessment of Richard's executive ability, not even Si. In Si's second month of recuperation, as Si prepared to commence a medically mandated vacation, Richard ordered 885 production halted. To compete with the Vickers Viscount and Lockheed's Electra, the 885 was to be redesigned as a turboprop.

2.

When Si's father practiced medicine the family doctor treated everybody and everything, children and adults, gallstones to gonorrhea. Nowadays all doctors were specialists. The cardiologist who treated Si's myocardial infarction was a thirty-six-year-old Yale Medical School graduate named Bernard Goldberg. Dr. Goldberg was bright, brash, and blunt.

"This is the way it stands, Mr. Conway," he said when he discharged Si from the hospital. "You either take it easy, or you'll die. Come and see me in a month." He folded his stethoscope into his jacket pocket and started out.

"Hey, kid, hold it!" Si called. Dr. Goldberg, with an impatient glance at his watch, stopped. Si said, "What does 'take it easy' mean in your language?"

"It means no work for at least six months. Preferably retirement. Shall I repeat that in Yiddish?"

"You're not about to let me forget my little slip of the tongue, are you?"

"I don't know which is more serious, Mr. Conway," Dr. Goldberg said. "Your cardiac problems, or your foot-in-mouth disease."

Foot-in-mouth, all right, Si glumly thought. Shortly after he began feeling better, he had good-naturedly asked Dr. Goldberg what in the hell a Jewish doctor was doing in a Catholic hospital. The doctor replied that he was on the staff here at St. John's because of his ability to handle big-mouthed millionaire industrialists, and because he was also the best cardiologist in the city.

". . . and I'll tell you another thing," Dr. Goldberg now continued. "If you want to remain my patient, you do exactly as I say. Otherwise, go and find yourself a nice respectable gentile doctor who'll let *you* prescribe to *him*!"

Dr. Goldberg flipped Si a lazy salute and left. Si lay back in bed. Retire, he thought. The son of a bitch was crazy. How the hell could he retire? With Phil Granger gone—and good riddance to him—the whole shebang was being run by a kid, Richard. Sure, there were hundreds of good men to help—Si had long since lost count of all the vice presidents and project directors and division managers—but it was the boss who still made the big decisions. And the boss was flat on his ass in a sickbed.

Although Si would not admit it, young Dr. Goldberg had given him the fright of his life. Stress, said the doctor, was what would kill Simon Conway, and Simon Conway was a textbook example of a man living constantly with stress. Si decided dying was not worth it. He'd turn the business over to others, mainly to Richard, and if it went down the drain, it went down.

Everyone was surprised, not to say suspicious, that Si caved in so easily when Richard informed him that he had arranged a $50 million line of credit to finance the 885's redesign. The decision would mean at least a year of inactivity at Conair, except for the remaining K-88 tanker contracts and an order for forty new CT-8 trainers.

It was a week after Si's return from the hospital, his first time downstairs with the family. They had finished dinner and were in Si's study. "All right," he said when Richard gave him the news. "We'll stagger through it."

"There's one other thing," Richard said.

"Richard, if it's business, it will have to wait," Meg said.

"Dammit, Meg, stop treating me like an invalid!" Si glowered at her. "I never felt stronger or healthier in my life. Okay, spill it," he said to Richard.

Richard's voice lost some of its confidence. "The 1010 program," he said. "I'm canceling it."

"Why?" Si asked calmly. "Because Juan Trippe ordered three Comets for Pan Am?"

"Because we can't afford to continue with it," Richard said.

"Okay," Si said.

Si's "okay" was so unexpected that Richard paid it no attention. "I told Terry about the 1010 this afternoon," he went on. "He's not too happy."

"I said it was okay," Si said.

Richard glanced quizzically at Meg as though wondering if she had heard the same words. The 1010, Conair's four-engined, 500-mph, 120-passenger pure jet, the airplane that would fly coast to coast in five hours, New York to Paris in seven hours, was Si's great dream.

Meg said, "Just like that, Si? No objection?"

"What the hell's to object?" Si said. "The kid's running the place now. Let him run it."

Janet laughed. "It's too easy, Daddy."

"Well, I've got a little announcement of my own," Si said. "Meg, you remember that place up in Santa Barbara we saw last year? The one we both liked?"

"It was in Montecito," Meg said.

"Santa Barbara, Montecito, same thing," Si said. "Two acres, up on a hill with a view of the ocean on one side, the mountains on the other. Oak trees and a stream running through the middle of it. Not a bad house, Spanish Rancho I think they call it." He waved his hand around the room. "We'll sell this house. I talked to a real estate agent today. He said we could get at least fifty thousand for it. The whole parcel in Santa Barbara is only twenty-five thousand." Si paused. Everyone was staring at him.

"I don't believe it," Meg said.

"Do you disapprove?" Si asked.

"My God, no!"

"Naturally, Janet and David will come up there with us," he said. "I've already checked. There are at least three good schools for him."

Janet said nothing. Si knew she was thinking about Terry Deland. "You planning to marry him?" he asked abruptly.

"Si . . ." Meg gently admonished.

"It's all right, Mother," Janet said, and to Si, "No, Daddy, I am not planning to marry him. I'm not planning to marry anybody. Terry and I are good friends, nothing more, nothing less."

"You could do a lot worse," Si said.

"Si, that's enough!" Meg said.

Si shrugged innocently. "I only wanted her to know that she had my blessing."

"Thank you, I'll keep it in mind," Janet said. "Since we're talking about Terry, what's going to happen to him?"

"I'll find something for him," Richard said.

Si said, "I already have something for him. I planned to get into this with you later," he continued to Richard, "but now's as good a time as any." He removed a folded sheet of white paper from his bathrobe pocket. It was St. John's Hospital stationery and contained a penciled sketch of a small twin-engined, low-winged monoplane. Across the bottom of the paper was scrawled *Sirocco*.

"I didn't spend all my time in that hospital staring at the ceiling or ogling the pretty nurses. I got to thinking about the big corporations that fly their executives around in old DC-3s or 660s. I bet they'd jump at a smaller, more economical, really modern airplane. I figure that for under two hundred and fifty thousand dollars we can build one. The Sirocco," Si said, dangling the sketch in front of Richard. "We'll fit her with those turboprops you're so crazy about, and put Terry in charge of development. In Atlanta," he added.

"Atlanta?" Richard asked, as Si knew he would. "Why Atlanta?"

"Because we have an empty plant there, and because in Atlanta nobody'll pay any attention to what we're doing."

Richard knew his father well enough to know that this was a quid pro quo. Si was willing to give over total control to Richard in return for the Sirocco. Not a bad trade.

"Okay," Richard said. He swirled the liquor around in his glass and inhaled the bouquet. "Great cognac, Dad."

"I talked to Pete Dagget the other day," Si said. "His consulting business is doing great. He says he has all these bright young guys working for him, who are all smarter than he ever thought of being. He says he's going crazy with boredom. He's willing to hire on with us as a free-lancer."

"To do what?" Richard asked.

"To head up the Sirocco's design team," Si said. "And by the way, that's not cognac. It's Armagnac."

3.

Meg thought it amazing that Si had remained "retired" more than a year now. Even more amazing was his resolve not to interfere with Richard. He held his silence even when Richard told him they had used $25 million of the $50 million credit line to complete development of the 995, as the Conair turboprop transport was now designated.

Although the 995 and 885 emanated from the same basic airframe, the 995 was an entirely new and different airplane. Bigger, wider, faster—it cruised at 390 mph—with an eighty-seven-passenger seating capacity, it was also, at $1,100,000, considerably more expensive than the 885.

So Si, hoping that Richard would not end up bankrupting the company, kept his distance—literally. From Santa Monica, Montecito was a two-hour drive on Route 1's newly asphalted three-lane highway. For Si, however, in his gleaming black Jaguar XK-120 roadster—a fifty-ninth-birthday gift from Meg—it never took more than an hour and a half, which included time consumed stopping to receive speeding tickets. Si made the trip at least once monthly. He would call Art Hamel or Mike Doyle or some other old crony and meet them in Hollywood at Musso-Frank's for some of Charlie Carissimi's incomparable broiled covina, or at Sal Martoni's for a plate of spaghetti *alla carbonara*, or in downtown L.A. at the Pacific Dining Car for a pair of the famous Saratoga lamb chops.

Other than these outings, Si was meticulous with his diet. No fried foods, dairy products, or desserts. He lost twelve pounds, began exercising regularly with brisk two-mile daily walks, stopped smoking, went to bed before midnight, and rose early. Even Dr. Goldberg, whom he saw every three months, was impressed. It was a remarkable recovery, with little or no residual effects, not even mild hypertension.

If Si found Montecito tolerable, Meg loved it. True, the house was half the size of their Pacific Palisades residence, but it possessed a charm all its own, and the village was quiet and clean. Santa Barbara was ten minutes away, a rustic little city with department stores and good markets.

For Si and Meg both, it was a new, tranquil life. Moreover, in the eleven months since they moved there, Meg believed she had seen more of Si than in all their thirty-two years of married life. But now, as he started his second year of retirement, Meg sensed signs of increasing restlessness. There were almost daily phone calls to Terry Deland in Atlanta. Si demanded continual Sirocco progress reports. And in the past three months he had flown to Atlanta twice, once remaining there nearly a week.

Richard occasionally questioned Si about the Sirocco. Si said it was coming along nicely. When Richard said he might like to take a look at it himself—it might be time to begin preparing a sales campaign—Si said he wanted the airplane to be a surprise to everyone, even Richard. And once, when Richard complained that the Sirocco's development costs appeared excessively high, Si reminded him that the 995's costs were twice their initial estimate. Richard could not argue with that.

"Listen, it keeps me out of your hair, doesn't it?" Si said. "Don't press your luck."

Richard could not argue with that, either.

Janet was a regular commuter to Atlanta. Yes, she told her mother, she thought she was in love with Terry Deland, and yes, they had discussed marriage. But Janet found the idea of a third husband unappealing. Meg read "unappealing" as "fear." Janet feared losing another husband.

Other than the Atlanta visits, Si devoted much of his time to David. He drove the boy back and forth from Wentworth Academy, a prestigious private school David attended as a day student. As a reward for keeping up a B grade average, Si had promised David flying lessons. To Meg it brought back memories of Frank. She pleaded with Si not to repeat that mistake. No, no, he assured her, I've learned. And the words were hardly out of his mouth when he packed David off to the little airport at Goleta, just north of Santa Barbara, for a ride in the sporty four-place Beechcraft Bonanza he had recently bought as a fifty-ninth-birthday gift to himself. To his credit, although his CAA medical certificate had been reissued, when David was aboard Si always hired another pilot to accompany them.

On December 12, 1953, the first production 995 rolled off the line. The turboprop airplane, bearing the red-and-white lightning-streak logo of Intercontinental Air, the first one of twenty-five ordered by the airline, set a new transcontinental speed record—Los Angeles to New York nonstop in six hours and twelve minutes, nearly an hour faster than Douglas's new DC-7.

By February of 1954, ten 995s were flying on Intercontinental Air's long-haul domestic routes. That same month Si and Meg went to Europe aboard the *Île de France*. In England, at the Farnborough Air Show, Si saw the Comet 2, a bigger, faster, and infinitely safer airplane than its ill-fated predecessor, the Comet 1, which had entered commercial service with BOAC nearly two years earlier. The airline had retired its entire fleet of Comet 1s after three had broken up in midair, killing all aboard. Comet 1's aluminum fuselage, machined down to a thinness of twenty-eight thousandths of an inch, was unable to withstand the sudden changes of pressure created by rapid changes of altitude.

That tragic mistake would not be repeated in Comet 2. As one of BOAC's directors told Si, "It was an expensive lesson, Simon, but you'll benefit from it. All you American manufacturers will."

"Conair won't, I'm sorry to say," Si had replied.

He was only confirming what was now common knowledge in the industry: there would be no Conair passenger jet in the foreseeable future. This, as late as March 1954, is what everyone believed. It was what Simon Conway wanted everyone to believe.

4.

Not without good reason was Intercontinental Air's Flight 9, daily nonstop service from Los Angeles to New York, known as the Star Shuttle. Flight 9's passenger manifest invariably included the name of at least one Hollywood celebrity.

Today, March 3, 1954, was no exception. In Intercontinental Air's new $500,000 Los Angeles terminal, eager newsmen and photographers surrounded Lois Wright, she of the flaming red hair and smoky voice that had earned no less than $60 million for her employer, Columbia Pictures. She had signed to play the lead in a Broadway revival of the musical *Bloomer Girl*, a not especially newsworthy item except for the fact that the leading man had been the second of Lois's five husbands.

Flight 9's captain was a ruggedly handsome Texan named Steven Sepesy, a man who had begun his career as a copilot on Ford Tri-motors and who, thirty years and twenty thousand hours later, considered the 995 the finest airplane he had ever flown. She was fast, cruising at 390 mph at eighteen thousand feet, high above the weather. She could fly on two engines if necessary, with the latest state-of-the-art instrumentation and communications. A radar unit in the nose scanned the sky miles ahead for turbulence. Her turboprop engines created so little vibration in the pressurized cabin you could balance a coin on a tray table. The spacious flight deck accommodated the three-man crew—pilot, copilot, and flight engineer—in near-luxurious comfort. Newspaper and magazine ads proclaimed her "Queen of the Skies." It was no exaggeration.

Ninety minutes into the flight, at twenty-two thousand feet, the stewardesses were serving breakfast. In the cockpit, Steve Sepesy's copilot switched on the cabin intercom to address the passengers. He was a moon-faced, pleasant young man named Tim Pelham, recently separated from the military, with two years and nearly two thousand hours left-seat time as a USAF MATS pilot. Before he punched the mike button he grinned at Sepesy.

"Hey, Steve, shall I say hello to that movie star? Lois what's-her-name?"

"She's too old for you, kid."

"Well, that's what she needs, then. Fresh young meat!"

"I'll put in a good word for you," Steve said.

"Yeah, and I bet that's not all you'd like to put in," Tim said, and spoke into the p.a. microphone, "Ladies and gentlemen, hello again from the front office. Just want to tell those of you on the left side, you'll have a nice view of the Grand Canyon—"

The airplane vibrated. It was as though it had struck a solid wall and bounced back. Immediately, it began falling off to the right.

"What the hell happened?" Tim shouted.

"Controls!" Steve said. The control yoke was wobbling violently back and forth in his hands. He looked like a man riding a bucking bronco. "Help me, for Christ's sake!"

But Tim Pelham was staring, astounded, out his side window at the right wing, or what remained of the right wing, which was little more than the root. More than half the wing, including both engines, was gone, and the remaining aluminum surface was peeling away like a sardine can being opened.

Vaguely, Tim was aware of a voice shouting into his ear. He recognized the voice as Hank Preslowski's, the flight engineer. He thought the words were "We're over! We're over!"

We're over, meaning the airplane was over on its back. Yes, he could feel the centrifugal force pressing his body forward against his seat belt and shoulder harness. No, they were not over. If they were over, the fuselage would have broken up. They were upright, but falling.

He heard more frantic shouting in the cockpit, and then, in his earphones, Sepesy's voice: ". . . Albuquerque Center, this is Intercontinental Nine. We have a Mayday situation. I say again, Intercontinental Nine. Mayday! Mayday!"

Tim Pelham did not hear Albuquerque Center's reply. He knew only that the horizon, through the windscreen, looked almost vertical. They were rolling, yawing back and forth. And falling. He knew he was dead. He and Steve Sepesy and Hank Preslowski and the fifty-seven passengers, and the four stewardesses. All dead. Not yet, but soon.

At 11:14 A.M., March 7, four days after the crash of Flight 9, Intercontinental Flight 12, a 995 flying nonstop from Chicago to San Francisco, reported its position to Omaha Center. It was at nineteen thousand feet, on course, fifty miles east of North Platte, Nebraska. Exactly five minutes later, Omaha Center heard a "Mayday" from Flight 12. At 11:45 that same morning the smoldering wreckage of Flight 12 was found in a cornfield twelve miles east of North Platte. Seventy passengers and seven crew had been aboard. There were no survivors.

One week later, at 2:30 P.M., Intercontinental Air Flight 10, a Conair 995 en route from Denver to Los Angeles, was cleared for takeoff. Flight 10, filled nearly to capacity with seventy-five passengers, rolled down the runway and flew into the air. She climbed out smoothly and began a procedure turn to the right. All at once her nose rose sharply. In an instant she went into a stall configuration so acute that she was nearly vertical. Then, like a kite on a string, she nosed over in a shallow dive and plunged straight down. She struck the ground three miles from the airport boundary. The tail section broke off intact, but the wings and forward section smashed into a parked furniture van, exploded, and plowed in a ball of flame into a row of houses.

In less than two weeks, 215 human beings had lost their lives in crashes of Conair 995s. The Civil Aeronautics Board ordered all 995s grounded. That same day a Conair spokesman, on behalf of the company's acting president and CEO, Richard Conway, announced an immediate halt to all 995 production.

Production would not resume until the cause of the tragedies was determined and remedied. American Airlines and Eastern Airlines, each of whom had ordered twelve 995s with options for an additional twelve, canceled their orders. A week later, Ross Leonard asked Richard to meet him for dinner at Matteo's, a small but elegant Italian restaurant on Westwood Boulevard in West Los Angeles.

Richard arrived at the restaurant early. He needed an extra drink or two to fortify himself. He knew what Ross wanted to discuss. He had talked it over on the phone with Si earlier.

"I decked the son of a bitch once," Si said. "I bet I could still do it."

"I bet you could, too, Dad," Richard said. "I'll let you know what happens."

But both were already well aware of what would happen. It was obvious. Ross wasted no words. "I'm canceling the remainder of my 995 orders, Rich. I'm going for the Viscount instead."

They were at the bar. Richard was on his third martini, and fifth cigarette. His stomach felt like a washing machine. It was no consolation that Ross looked as bad as Richard felt. But then, as Ross said, the events of the past two weeks had made an old man of him. They had also prevented more than 150 other men from reaching old age.

Richard thought of a dozen different responses to Ross's pronouncement, all of them inane. He wanted to say, Hey, Ross, you're my father-in-law, give me a break! That would have been silliest of all.

Instead, he said, "Ross, not only is the CAB running an intense investigation, we've got dozens of our own engineers on it. We'll find out what caused those accidents, and we'll fix it. It shouldn't take long, either."

"You call a year 'not long'?"

"It'll be a lot less than a year."

"I'm sorry, Rich, I really am."

"The Viscount isn't half the airplane the 995 is," Richard said, and instantly wanted the words back. Three Viscounts had not crashed in two weeks. No Viscounts had crashed.

"The Viscounts are flying, the 995s aren't," Ross said. "I've committed Intercontinental to turboprops. I'll have to lease DC-6s and 7s until I get delivery, which won't be for at least four months. My people project a net loss of more than three million dollars for this quarter alone. I have stockholders to answer to, Rich."

"Instead of DCs, why can't you put your 885s back into service?"

Ross's eyes turned cold. "Conair is not a popular name with the public these days."

Nor was the name popular inside the company itself. Within two months, two thousand more Conair employees were furloughed. The Culver City factory was confined to completing modifications on K-88 tankers and subcontracting wing assemblies for Anderson's new ground-support jet, the King Cobra.

Only a sizable U.S. Navy order for CT-8N advanced trainers kept the Atlanta plant open. Richard requested from Terry Deland a definite date for completion of the Sirocco prototype. Terry referred the question to Si. One year, said Si, not a day longer. Richard was too harassed and too preoccupied to demand more details.

In late May the CAB's Accident Investigation Division announced its preliminary findings on the March 3, March 7, and March 14 crashes. This last accident, at Denver, was attributed to a hydraulic-system failure, which was then compounded by pilot error. The cause of the first two crashes, however, was far more catastrophic.

Structural failure.

In the thin air of altitudes above seventeen thousand feet, at their cruising speed of 390 mph, the 995's engines had begun to vibrate so severely that the right outboard engine propeller shaft cracked. The propeller, running away, shook the engine loose from its mounting, and now, aerodynamically unstable, the wing itself began shaking so violently that it tore completely away.

The obvious solution was to reduce the 995's cruising speed. Conair's engineers went further. They corrected the basic design flaw. The result was the 995A Sky King, which cruised safely at 415 mph, faster than any piston-engined airplane and faster than the Viscount. The Sky King first flew in July of 1954 and was CAA-certified the following October. The date of the 995A's first flight, July 16, happened to be two days after the first flight of Boeing's new passenger jet, the 367-80, later redesignated the 707.

The Sky King was more expensive than the 995—$1,450,000 per unit—but a decidedly superior airplane. Unfortunately, by the time it appeared, the airlines had either committed to the Viscount or to Lockheed's Electra or, in Pan American's case, awaited delivery of their order for fifty 707s. And to make matters worse, United Airlines had ordered thirty DC-8s, Douglas's pure jet, which was still in design stage and had not yet flown.

By January 1955, Conair had received a total of nine firm Sky King orders, six of these from a Florida leasing company, the remaining three from Intercontinental Air.

"Nine," said Si. His voice on the phone sounded old. "You'd need at least fifty to justify starting production. Take you twice that many sales before you broke even. More, probably. And as far as Ross Leonard's generous, gigantic order for three, you should have told him to shove the three Sky Kings right up his ass, propellers first."

"You're pretty calm about it," Richard said.

"It won't do me any good not to be calm, will it?"

"I'm waiting for you to say 'I told you so.' "

"That won't do me any good, either," Si said.

"No, it won't," said Richard. "Listen, Dad, I want to come up there and talk to you."

"When?"

"Today."

"It'll have to be late afternoon," Si said. "I'm taking David into town to get him a leather jacket. I'm flying to Atlanta Monday, and he's going with me."

"Why are you taking David?"

"For one thing, his mother's there and she wants to see him. For another, he wants to get a look at the Sirocco. Terry says the airplane's almost ready to fly."

"All right, I'll be up there to see you sometime after five," Richard said.

Richard's conversation with Si was his third long-distance conversation of that morning. Earlier, he had received a call from New York, from Robert McCallum, a Goldman Sachs vice president, reminding him that Conair was late with the third- and fourth-quarter interest payments on its $25 million note. Under the circumstances, it would be impossible to advance the other $25 million. The line of credit was terminated.

The second long-distance call was placed by Richard, to St. Louis, to Ben Anderson. Talk about humble pie. But yes, said Anderson, the merger offer was still open. And, surprisingly, on the same terms: fifty-fifty, with Anderson absorbing all Conair's outstanding debt, which included the Goldman Sachs obligation. Then we have a deal, said Anderson. Talk about throwing a drowning man a life preserver.

"One stipulation, Rich," Anderson had said. "This must have your father's unconditional approval."

"Ben, I'm the CEO," Richard had said. "I have complete discretion."

"Just let me have it in writing, Rich, Si Conway's approval."

Richard, faced with the unappetizing prospect of presenting his father with the facts and figures, knew Si could present a few facts of his own. Namely, that by stubbornly insisting on going to turboprops, Richard had single-handedly brought down the company. On the other hand, it was a gamble that could have gone either way. Given another month of testing the 995 under actual operating conditions, Conair's own engineers would have recommended a reduction in cruising speed. The accidents never would have happened.

If my aunt had testicles, Richard thought, as he reached for the telephone again, this time to call Enid to inform her he was going to

Santa Barbara and not to expect him for dinner. The intercom buzzer sounded.

"Fred Smiley's out here, Richard," said Helen Walters, Si's former secretary, whom Richard had inherited and who was convinced that without her guidance Richard could not run the company. "I think you should see him."

Fred Smiley, a trim, white-haired man of fifty, was Conair's comptroller. After Richard invited him to sit down, Smiley said, "It's about the Sirocco. This morning Atlanta sent me a 'received' invoice for three DHC-2 turboprop engines, and an authorization to pay Jensen three hundred and seventy-five thousand six hundred dollars. The price of a DHC-2 is sixty-eight thousand per unit, so the total price should have been two hundred and four thousand dollars, not three-seventy-five, six."

"It was obviously a mistake," Richard said.

"Obviously. But it rang a bell in my head. I went back over the books for the last two years." Smiley noticed Richard's expression of impatience and spoke faster. "This so-called 'mistake' was made before. Three times before! So I checked with Jensen, and they told me that they've never, not once, delivered a turboprop engine to Atlanta. What they've been sending to Atlanta, and what they've been paid for, are J-62 CPX pure jet engines, at one hundred and twenty-five thousand two hundred dollars each."

"J-62s?" Richard said. "What the hell are they doing with 62s?" The J-62 was a 9,600-pound-thrust Jensen military jet engine designed for high-performance fighters.

". . . we're talking about a difference of more than one hundred and seventy thousand dollars," Smiley was saying. "Somebody's pocketing a substantial sum of money."

"All right, I'll look into it," Richard said. He knew who the "somebody" was, and that no money was being pocketed, and why the engines were pure jets and not turboprops. He felt like a fool. He had been taken for a fool.

After Smiley left, Richard told his secretary to notify Si that Richard had been called out of town and would be unable to come to Montecito. He also asked her to contact Ted Miller for him. Ted Miller, a man Richard's age, was a Conair test pilot with whom Richard had become friendly and knew he could trust. Richard asked Miller to arrange for a company airplane, a 660 modified for executive use, to fly him immediately to Atlanta.

Atlanta, where the Sirocco prototype was being manufactured. Simon Conway's personal project, something to keep him busy during his retirement. The Sirocco, Conair's twin-turboprop entry into the private plane market. The Sirocco, which Richard now realized was a phantom, an airplane that had never existed and never would.

What did exist, as was now sickeningly clear, was an airplane specifically designed for those J-62 pure jet engines, a large-passenger jet.

Simon Conway's 1010.

24

It was as though she were on a stage, a spotlight trained on her. She was parked in the center of the concrete floor of the darkened factory, her aluminum fuselage and swept-back wings gleaming metallically under a bank of flat white fluorescent ceiling lights. Her four jet engines were enclosed in streamlined pods slung below the wings. Her rudder, emblazoned with the blue Conair eagle, rose nearly halfway to the top of the eighty-foot-high factory ceiling.

Under the light, with her long graceful body solidly fixed on the ten wheels of her tricycle landing gear, she resembled a giant silver bird poised to fly. And she was a giant, capable of carrying 130 passengers at speeds approaching 600 mph. She weighed 160,000 pounds, with a wingspan of 125 feet and length of 120 feet, which happened to be the exact distance of the Wright Brothers' first flight fifty-two years before.

The Atlanta plant was spread over several acres on the eastern boundary of Dekalb Airport, northeast of the city in the town of Chamblee, and consisted of three enormous production buildings. One building contained the CT-8A assembly lines, a second was presently unused, and the third building was also unused except for a section in the middle partitioned by corrugated metal walls and accessible only to employees with special passes. This was where the 1010 had been assembled.

Three uniformed security guards greeted Richard at the gate, and more were inside the fence, including two men patrolling the perimeter in a jeep. The guards of course recognized Richard's name, and were properly apologetic when they said that without a pass they could not allow him to enter. It took a phone call to Terry Deland and a twenty-minute wait for Terry and Pete Dagget to arrive before Richard was admitted into the facility.

When he saw the 1010 he had to agree that it was a beautiful piece of machinery, a work of art, but his first impulse was to ask how they had managed to build an airplane as conspicuous as the 1010 in secrecy. It was like hiding an elephant in your living room. He never got around to asking the question because he was too busy trying to control his temper after Pete said they needed $450,000 for new engines.

"Eleven-thousand-pound-thrust GEs," Pete said. "She'll fly okay with the J-62s that are on her now, but nowhere near fast enough. We fit her with the GEs, I guarantee you at thirty-five thousand feet she'll cruise better than six hundred."

"How much has this cost so far?" Richard asked.

Terry and Pete exchanged uncomfortable glances. Pete said, "Seven million."

Seven million, Richard thought, almost precisely 25 percent of the company's total net worth. He wondered how, and by what book-keeping legerdemain, Si had managed to divert that large a sum from the phantom Sirocco project into the 1010. Bookkeeping legerde-main? Fiscal irresponsibility was more like it. Irresponsibility on the part of the chief executive officer, him, Richard Conway.

". . . she's the finest airplane I've ever seen," Pete was saying.

Sure, Richard was thinking, and now there would definitely be no Anderson merger. Ben Anderson was not crazy, at least not crazy enough to be saddled with a $7 million turkey. Anderson would cancel the merger, wait for Conair and its $200 million worth of assets to be taken over by its creditors, and then purchase it from them at a fire-sale price.

Richard said, "You're not getting any more money. I'm closing this project down."

"Closing it down?" Terry said. "Rich, are you out of your mind? We can't be more than a few months behind Boeing, and this is a much better airplane."

"Boeing's jet has already flown," Richard said.

"So has this," Terry said. "She's been flying for weeks. Yesterday I took her up for altitude attainment. She made forty thousand feet without even breathing hard. Next week she starts her final shake-down flights. Right now, today, I could take her across the country."

"Shut it down, I said," Richard said.

"No," Pete said. "No way. Not when we're this close."

"When we take her back to L.A., she'll make a new coast-to-coast speed record," Terry said. "How's five hours sound to you?"

It was then that Richard informed them of the impending merger with Anderson Aircraft, and how their little conspiracy had jeopardized not only their future, but the futures of nearly ten thousand other currently employed Conair employees.

". . . so if you don't close down," Richard concluded, "I'll slap you with a court order to do it."

Terry said, "Rich, this is your father's project. The only way I close it down is when he tells me to. And even then I'm not so sure I'd do it."

2.

Fourteen hours after departing Atlanta, Richard rang the bell of his father's Montecito home. David answered the door. "Hey, Uncle Rich, how was the trip?"

"What trip?"

"From Atlanta," David said. "Terry called Gramps last night and said you were there, and to expect you back here first thing in the morning."

"Why aren't you in school?"

"Today's Saturday," David said. "Gramps is out in the patio." He followed Richard through the house and into the kitchen toward the patio. Meg was at the kitchen sink drying dishes. Richard kissed her.

David said, "Uncle Rich got here faster than Gramps said he would."

"Go and do your homework," Meg said to the boy.

"I don't have any."

"Then go and pack your bags for the trip," Meg said. "Si's taking him to Atlanta Monday," she reminded Richard. "Janet's there, and the three of them will come back home together. Go and pack, I said," she said to David.

"I'm already packed."

"Then read a book," Meg said. "Now, please."

David knew enough not to argue with that tone of voice. As he ran off, Meg called after him, "And don't go out to the patio. Your grandfather and uncle want to talk."

"You knew about this all the time, didn't you?" Richard said to her. "You knew he was building that airplane."

"Yes, of course I did."

Richard felt a surge of resentment toward his mother. He forced it away; he knew it was childish. Through the kitchen picture window, he saw Si on the patio. Si, wearing an open-collared knit sports shirt and chino slacks, sat reading the *Los Angeles Times*. Richard could make out the headline: REPORT SUCCESSFUL TEST OF POLIO VACCINE.

"Has he any idea what he's done?" Richard said to Meg. "Doesn't he have even the faintest idea of what shape we're in?"

"Of course he does."

"Do you know that he's dumped seven million dollars into that project? He's damn near bankrupted us!"

"It's his company, Richard."

"No, Mother, it isn't 'his' company. It belongs to all of us, to you, me, David, Janet. It belongs to everybody who works for us and depends on us for their livelihood." Richard paused abruptly, feeling foolish; he sounded like a labor-union organizer.

"You haven't slept at all, have you?" Meg asked, and answered her own question. "No, of course not. You've been flying all night. Are you hungry?"

"I had a sandwich on the plane."

"I'll fix you some coffee."

Richard stood a moment at the window. Si, who was still reading the newspaper, seemed quite relaxed. It annoyed Richard, but no more so than Si's greeting a moment later.

". . . so what did you think of her?"

"What did I think of who?"

"The 1010!" Si said. "Come on, stop playing games."

"What I think," said Richard, "is that you should be ashamed of yourself. The money you've spent! The payroll alone for that army of guards out there—" He felt like a parent scolding an errant child.

"You'll change your tune," Si said mildly. "I guarantee you, once that airplane gets into the air, every airline in the country'll be banging on our doors."

"We won't have any doors," Richard said.

"We sure as hell won't if you go with Anderson," Si said. "The boys in Atlanta told me all about it. Forget it, Rich. No merger."

All during the long flight from the East Coast, Richard had rehearsed his presentation. He had promised himself to deliver his arguments clearly, concisely, and calmly. But now, tired and frustrated, he simply wanted to get it over with.

He said, "Either I run the company, or I don't."

Meg came out to the patio just then with a tray of iced coffee.

Richard knew she had been watching them from the kitchen window
and had chosen this exact moment to appear.

Si said to her, "He's just given me an ultimatum." He sounded
amused.

"Sit down," Richard said to Meg. "This concerns you, too." Meg
sat, but almost reluctantly, as though wishing that it did not concern
her. Richard went on, "The only way we can keep the company solvent
is through a merger, and now, after this seven-million-dollar fling of
Dad's, Anderson will never agree to a fifty-fifty arrangement. He'll
want more. He'll probably insist on making Conair an Anderson division."

"Richard, what the hell is wrong with you?" Si asked, and then
lost his temper. He smashed his fist on the table. The coffee glasses
and spoons rattled. "I said no merger! End of discussion."

"No, Dad, it's only the beginning of the discussion," Richard said.
"You're acting as though all we have to do is get a few orders to pull
us through. It won't happen, not this time, not when we're seven
million in the hole on top of our overdue notes."

"That seven million, boy, is exactly what'll save your company,"
Si said. "The 1010 will do for aviation in the fifties what the 660 and
the DC-3 did in the thirties. I'm telling you, once she's certified, we'll
be building them so fast we won't even have time to count the profits!"

I do not believe I am having this conversation, Richard thought.
I am talking to somebody who is totally out of reality. "Even after the
1010 is certified, you'll need at least a year of shakedown time," he
said. "The only way you'll get it is through Anderson. It's either that,
or Goldman Sachs forecloses. There's no other way. Can't you see
that, for Christ's sake?"

"Then we'll take the company public," Si said.

"There isn't an underwriter in the country who'd take us on, not
with the amount of money we owe Goldman," Richard said. "Unless
we merge, we lose the company."

Si banged the table again. "You don't have any balls! For a while
there, you had me fooled! I thought you'd grown up a little. I thought
maybe the war made a man out of you. I was wrong. You're the same
little scared kid who ran away screaming whenever he heard an airplane engine!"

Richard stared at him, frozen. For a split instant Richard was a
ten-year-old boy, hearing his father call him a sissy and jerk in the
presence of his younger brother. He saw the contempt on Si's face,
the disgust.

". . . won't waste any more time talking," Si was saying. He had
risen and started walking away. At the kitchen door he called to Meg.

"Tell David I'll take him down to the village for lunch. That hamburger place he likes."

Richard got up and followed Si into the kitchen. Si stopped at the Sparkletts cooler to pour a glass of water. Richard seized Si's arm and pulled him around so they faced each other.

"You taught me the rules of the game, and how to play," Richard said. "Now you'll see how well I've learned." He addressed Meg. "I'll bring a mismanagement suit. There's not a court in this country that wouldn't order him to step down once they've examined the company's books. Especially this last stunt: seven million dollars!"

"You might as well start suing, then," Si said. "The 1010 is a Conair product and will roll out of a Conway factory, not an Anderson-Conway factory or a Conway-Anderson factory or whatever the hell they'll call it. I will not—repeat, not—give Ben Anderson my airplane!"

Si pushed past Richard and started away. He stopped and turned to face him once more. "And by the way, you're fired!"

"We'll let the courts decide that," Richard said.

"Yeah, well, in the meantime just clean out your office and leave. I'll be back from Atlanta Wednesday. I want you gone. I won't seal up your office like you did Phil Granger's. I'll give you five whole days to pack." He nodded tightly. "Then I'll seal it up!"

Si walked away again and this time kept going. His heels echoed on the tiled floor of the foyer as he strode along the hallway to the master bedroom. He entered the bedroom and slammed the door behind him.

Richard touched the back of his neck. It was wet. His shirt was drenched with perspiration. He poured a glass of water into the same glass Si had used and drank some. "I feel sorry for him," he said to Meg.

"I feel sorry for both of you," she said. "For all of us."

"I suppose you think it's wrong of me to bring a mismanagement suit?"

"You'll probably win," Meg said.

"Mother, that's not what I asked."

"Yes, I think it's wrong," Meg said after a moment. "I think it's a rotten thing for you to do."

"I'm my father's son, all right."

"And that's a rotten thing to say."

"I'll give you credit for one thing, Mother. You're loyal."

"Which is more than I can say for you, Richard. There's no point in my giving you a lecture on how your father started the company and kept it going, and about all his pioneering, and how aviation progress would not have been possible without people like him. All I'll say, which you should know anyway, is that he believes in what he's doing."

"Is that your way of asking me to just walk quietly away? To do nothing?"

"I'm not asking you to do anything, Richard. You do whatever you think you have to."

"What I have to do is stop him from destroying the company," Richard said, and added dryly, "His own company."

"He thinks that what he's doing will save the company."

"Is that what you think, too?"

"What I think doesn't matter."

"Is that what you said when he asked your opinion?"

Meg's face softened in a brief, wry smile. "Since when did you know your father to ever ask anyone's opinion?"

"That's why we're in this mess now," Richard said.

Meg had not heard him. Her mind seemed momentarily else-where, her eyes clouded with nostalgia. Richard knew she was thinking of the past, which he also knew had not always been happy for her.

"He'll fight you, you know," she said. "He'll bring up this last thing, the 995, as an example of *your* poor management. He'll make it quite unpleasant."

Richard wanted to say, So what else is new? Instead, he said, "He'll still lose. You know it, and I know it."

Meg nodded slowly, sadly. She was standing at the window directly in the sun. Richard noticed the deep wrinkles around her eyes and mouth. She looked old. He had never thought of his mother as old.

3.

The big airplane's four jet engines whined smoothly and quietly as she taxied out to the head of the runway. She wheeled around into takeoff position, stopped, and held. Inside, from the flight deck, the runway resembled a flat endless white ribbon. The bright early-afternoon sun flashed off the concrete surface.

Taxiing from the ramp to the runway, the flight deck had bustled with activity as the crew executed their pages-long checklists: thrust levers at idle, flaps fifteen degrees, leading-edge slats out, fuel and electrical control panels checked, hydraulic pressures and quantity checked, cabin pressure checked, item after item.

Now, at the head of the runway, each of the four men in the

cockpit entertained thoughts similar to Simon Conway's. Never, but never, has there been an airplane the equal of this.

"Okay," Terry Deland said finally. "Shall we see if it flies?"

Terry, in the left seat, had addressed the question to Si, but as a kind of courtesy. Although he had been checked out on instruments and emergency procedures, Si was really only a passenger. He sat in a jump seat directly behind the control pedestal between the pilot's and copilot's chairs. Behind the copilot, young Roy Minot, Jack Kessler sat at his ceiling-to-floor instrument-packed flight engineer's panel. Kessler was the oldest of the three-man crew, although not older than Si. Nobody, Si was thinking, was older than Simon Conway.

Which brought up a good question. What in the hell was he doing here, on this first full shakedown flight of the 1010? But he knew the answer. He was here because nothing and no one could have kept him away. He felt a little silly wearing his grease-streaked old fedora and battered leather jacket, but knew it was expected of him. His trademark.

"Sure," said Si. "Let's see if she'll fly."

At Terry's nod, Roy Minot pressed the radio transmitter button on the control yoke and spoke into the small microphone attached to his headset. "Dekalb tower, Conair Ten. Ready to go."

The tower operator's voice boomed over the cockpit loudspeakers. "Conair Ten, cleared for takeoff. Altimeter two niner point nine-five, wind one-two-zero at five knots. Good luck, gentlemen."

"Okay," Terry said. "Here goes nothing."

No, kid, here goes everything, Si thought, as Terry eased the thrust levers forward. The airplane trundled slowly ahead, then began rolling faster. The gentle whine of the engines increased to a smooth, steady, ever-accelerating low-pitched whir.

"Set takeoff power," Terry called quietly to Kessler.

Kessler, whose hands were wrapped around a duplicate set of thrust levers on his console, now began advancing them on his own. The airplane sped down the runway, past the yellow 1,000-foot marker, the 1,500-foot marker, the 2,500-foot marker.

"Seventy knots!" Roy Minot called. "Now!"

Terry's eyes swept the engine instrument gauges. All rpm were pegged between 95 and 99 percent. Exhaust-gas temperatures were in the green. He could feel the airplane straining to lift off. "We're committed," he said. "I'll unstick at one-four-four knots."

At the 4,000-foot runway marker, Roy Minot said, "Jesus, Terry, she's about to fly herself off."

"Let's let her do it, then," Terry said, and he relaxed his pressure on the yoke ever so slightly. The airplane flew into the air. "Gear up!"

The 1010 soared upward through a wispy bank of low-hanging clouds, then into clear air. Terry called for flaps up, and then climb power. To Si it seemed that one instant they were racing down the runway and the next instant were at five thousand feet.

"Well, it flies," Terry said to Si.

It flies. Si remembered Charlie Jensen telling him that Morris Tannen had elatedly shouted those exact words the day the first 110 flew. It flies!

It flies, but you hardly realized you were flying. No pounding vibration, no racketing noise, just the soft, steady whir of the jet engines. A bloody miracle, he thought. No, a revolution. This airplane would revolutionize the industry. It would conquer the world. He leaned forward to read the airspeed indicator: 305.

Three hundred and five knots, 420 mph, *climbing*!

". . . we'll level her out at eighteen thousand," Terry was saying.

"Good," said Si, not sure if Terry was talking to him or to the others. Terry had seemed startled when Si remarked that he wouldn't mind riding along with them on this first full-out test. Of course it was a statement, not a request, allowing Terry little choice in the matter.

Si had arrived in Atlanta the previous evening with David on an Eastern Airlines Constellation. He knew that the conflict with Richard and the myriad of new problems this created would leave him little or no time for the boy, but David had eagerly looked forward to the trip. Si could not bring himself to disappoint him.

Now, a day later, David was on his way back to California with his mother. They had left earlier that morning, although not without considerable protest from David, who wanted to join Si in the 1010. Nothing would have pleased Si more but it was of course out of the question. You don't take your ten-year-old grandson for a ride on an experimental jet.

The 1010 performed flawlessly throughout the two-hour flight. Terry did not push her to maximum, not with the J-62s. "When she's fitted with the new eleven-thousand-pound-thrust GEs, then you'll really see something," he said.

"What the hell else can you show me?" Si said. "I feel like Columbus must have felt. No," he corrected himself, "like old Orville and Wilbur felt that day at Kitty Hawk. Like they'd just seen God!"

"Want to try her?" Terry asked. "So help me, flying this thing is better than sex!" Terry's face tightened in horror; it almost made Si laugh. Poor Terry. Saying a thing like that to the father of the woman he was screwing.

But Si put him at ease. "Almost better than sex," Si said. "As I remember it, that is."

He got into the right seat, which Roy Minot had vacated for him, and strapped in. He gripped the yoke and motioned Terry to disengage the autopilot. The airplane hardly reacted. She flew serenely on, actually flying herself. Now Si began flying her. A gentle left turn, then right, then wider turns, and then a couple of 180s. An eighty-ton airplane, at a ground speed of over 500 mph, handling with the ease and response of a light trainer. It was unbelievable.

Reluctantly, almost like a child parting with a marvelous new toy, Si surrendered the seat. No one had asked him to move, but they were returning to the airport and he did not want put Terry in the embarrassing position of having to ask him to leave. Terry certainly wanted an experienced copilot in the right seat for the landing.

Terry greased the big airplane onto the runway. Immediately, he and Roy commenced the after-landing checklist: dozens of items that to Si sounded like a foreign language. Yaw-damper switches, annunciator switches, speed brakes, outflow valves, body gear steering control ratio selector. He was glad he had not asked to land the airplane.

A crowd of newsmen, Conair employees, and spectators were gathered outside the hangar. Si saw Pete Dagget clambering aboard the ramp truck that had backed up to the cabin door. A few moments later Pete was in the airplane hurrying up the aisle toward the flight deck. He met Si and Terry in the middle of the cabin.

"You came up with a winner, kid—" Si started to say, then stopped. Pete's face was grave. "What's wrong?"

"Si, something's happened." Pete's voice was tight with anxiety. "The plane Janet and David are on, it's down in El Paso—"

"—what the hell do you mean, 'down'?" Terry shouted. He seized Pete's jacket lapels. "It crashed? Is that what you're saying, for Christ's sake?"

Si did not wait for Pete's reply. He brushed past him to the door and vaulted down the ramp stairs, pushing aside newsmen and photographers as he ran into the terminal. He knew only that he had to find a telephone. He heard nothing and saw nothing, only Terry's voice and the word "crashed" reverberating through his brain, and the vision of a crumpled airplane containing the mangled bodies of his daughter and grandson.

25

ational Airlines Flight 492, Dallas to Los Angeles nonstop, had taken off on schedule, 1:10 P.M., with fifty-eight passengers and seven crew members. Janet Tannen and her son, David, occupied seats 3A and 3B in the DC-7's first-class section. They had arrived in Dallas an hour earlier from Atlanta in a Delta Airlines DC-6.

One of the tourist-class passengers on NA492 was a twenty-four-year-old former all-star high school baseball player from Fort Worth named Victor Sheehan. In 1950, at age nineteen, knowing he would be drafted into the U.S. Army and probably sent to Korea, he had married his childhood sweetheart who was six months pregnant. This earned him both a military service deferment and a contract with the Philadelphia Phillies, who assigned him to their Canadian-American League farm in Rome, New York.

In 1951, his first full season with the Rome Colonels, Vic Sheehan batted .192. In August of the following year, the Colonels released him. Victor found a $48-per-week job as a shipping clerk in the main office of a Dallas grocery chain. Over the next two years he tried out with four different minor-league teams. None signed him. In the summer of 1954 his wife, Patti Lou, left him, taking their four-year-old son and returning to her parents' home in Fort Worth.

That night Victor Sheehan got drunk. He stole an automobile, which he promptly smashed into another car, a police cruiser. After serving thirty-two days of a ninety-day sentence, Victor went to work as a sales clerk in a Dallas hardware store. In the meantime Patti Lou had met a man, the proprietor of a trucking firm, who wanted to marry her.

On Christmas Day, 1954, Patti Lou served Victor with divorce papers. By nature not a violent person, Victor at first wanted to kill Patti Lou. Then he wanted to kill her boyfriend. And then, finally, he decided to kill himself, which made considerable sense when he recognized it as the way to provide for his son's future.

Four weeks later, in a Dallas pawnshop, Victor Sheehan traded a gold Hamilton wristwatch for a .22 caliber pistol and six cartridges. The watch, his proudest possession, had been presented to him as the 1951 East Texas High School Athlete of the Year. From the pawnshop he went to the bank to cash his bimonthly paycheck, and then to Love Field, where he bought a one-way ticket on National Airlines Flight 492. At the airport's Mutual of Omaha Insurance Company kiosk, for an additional $15, he purchased a $150,000 life insurance policy. He mailed the document to his son, Victor Sheehan, Jr., the policy's sole beneficiary.

Twenty minutes after Flight 492 reached its cruising altitude of eighteen thousand feet, Victor Sheehan left his seat and strolled up the aisle into the first-class section. The flight-deck door, partially open, obscured Victor's view of the cockpit. He did not know that a small boy, a first-class passenger, was visiting the crew. The boy was chatting with the captain, discussing the function of various DC-7 flight instruments. The captain was impressed with the boy's knowledge of aeronautics and airplanes, although not surprised. He would have expected nothing less from the grandson of Simon Conway.

None of the three men in the cockpit noticed Victor Sheehan walk through the open door or, over the noise of the engines, heard the door lock click shut. The flight engineer was jotting instrument readings into a log book, and the copilot was studying a book of approach plates. The captain was leaning forward to adjust the automatic pilot.

The captain, Harold Heffner, a forty-five-year-old veteran of twenty thousand flying hours, became aware of Victor Sheehan only when he noticed his guest, David Tannen, staring wide-eyed at the pistol in Victor's hand.

Heffner said, "Sir, only authorized crew members are allowed up here. Please get back to your seat."

"Shut up!" Victor said. He nudged the flight engineer. "Turn around!"

The flight engineer immediately raised his hands. The movement attracted the copilot's attention. He looked at Heffner for some kind of guidance. Heffner said to Victor, "What do you want?"

Victor said to David, "You, kid, you get over there with him." He pushed David toward the flight engineer. David backed up with his hands raised. "Put your hands down, for Christ's sake! You too," Victor said to the flight engineer.

Victor had never considered the possibility of more than one person in the cockpit. His plan was to shoot the pilot. The plane would crash, thereby bequeathing to Victor Sheehan, Jr., the proceeds of his father's $150,000 life insurance policy.

Now he knew he also had to shoot the other two men. He hadn't counted on that. And a kid. He had to kill the kid, too. Sure, after he shot the pilot everybody would be killed in the crash, including the kid, but that was not the same as looking straight at him as he killed him. My God, he had a kid himself, didn't he?

". . . if this is some kind of prank, it's not funny," Harold Heffner was saying.

"I said shut up!" Victor said.

"Okay, okay, just take it easy," Heffner said. "Put down the gun and let's talk this over."

"I don't think he's kidding, Hal," the copilot said.

"Don't move!" Victor waved the pistol at Heffner and stepped back against the bulkhead. Now he could keep an eye on all three while he thought up a new plan.

The flight engineer said, "You'll only be able to get one of us, you know. You'll—"

"—shut up!" Victor said. It reminded him of a movie. The situation was similar: one man holding others at gunpoint, and someone reminding the gunman that he'd be able to get in only one shot. Victor repeated the movie gunman's words. "That's right, I'll only get one of you. So which one's gonna be the hero?"

As the words spilled from his lips he felt a sense of power he had never known. Now, finally, he was the man in control.

". . . at least let the boy go back into the cabin," Heffner was saying.

"He stays," said Victor, who all at once knew what to do. "Land the plane."

"Land?" Heffner asked. "Land where?"

"The nearest place," Victor said. "Do it, goddammit! And do it now!"

"Where's the closest alternate?" Heffner asked the copilot.

"El Paso."

"How far away are we?"

"Fifty, sixty miles."

Heffner said to Victor, "We have to radio them for permission to land."

"Okay," said Victor. He felt good, better than in a long time. He knew exactly what to do and how to do it. After landing, he would order everyone off the plane except the pilot. Then they would take off again, just the two of them. Victor would shoot the man. They would crash.

The fact that he could not hear what the copilot was saying did not trouble Victor. All that mattered was the $150,000 to Victor Jr. The kid would be rich beyond his dreams. In the end, Victor Sheehan would have done something good for his family, something noble.

Twenty minutes later, Victor Sheehan realized that there would be no $150,000 payment if the insurance company knew the insured's death was suicide. He realized this when the DC-7 braked to a stop at the end of the runway at Biggs Field in El Paso, and the airplane was surrounded by dozens of police cars.

From the flight-deck windows Victor saw the passengers and the three stewardesses streaming out of the cabin. Good. At least he would not be responsible for their deaths. And they did not figure in the new plan he had formulated. Only the pilots and the boy were important to the new plan. With the boy in Victor's hands everyone would follow instructions.

The new plan was ingenious, based on another movie, starring Van Heflin as a man who embezzled a fortune and took the money to a foreign country that had no treaty with the United States to send criminals back. Listen, maybe they played baseball there. Victor Sheehan could be a superstar.

". . . all right," Harold Heffner was saying to him. "We're here. What happens now?"

"Brazil," Victor said.

2.

Exactly three hours and twelve minutes after Si, in Atlanta, had spoken with the National Airlines station manager in El Paso, the Conair 1010 touched down at Biggs Field. The airplane flew the 1,205 miles from Atlanta in two hours and twenty-nine minutes. A record-breaking flight, at an average ground speed of 525 miles per hour.

Speed records and publicity were the farthest thing from Si's mind. His only thought was to reach El Paso as fast as possible. He knew little beyond the sketchy details provided him by the National Airlines station manager. A gunman, demanding to be flown to Brazil, had commandeered Flight 492 and was holding David Tannen and the crew prisoner. Si ordered Terry to refuel the 1010. Ready or not, fully flight-tested or not, the 1010 was flying to El Paso.

The National Airlines station manager had described the scene at the airport as chaotic. A barricade of cars and airport vehicles had been set up around the DC-7. It was a situation that had never been anticipated, and no one knew how to handle it.

". . . established radio contact with him," the station manager had told Si on the telephone. "He's says that unless his demands are met he'll kill everybody on the flight deck."

"Tell him the DC-7 can't make it to Brazil," Si had said. "Tell him you're waiting for a different airplane. A new airplane. The fastest airplane in the world. Tell him it will get him to Brazil or wherever he wants to go."

Waiting for the 1010 to be refueled, Si made two more phone calls. One to Morris Tannen, who immediately began making calls of his own to people in various law enforcement agencies. Si's other call was to Washington, to J. Edgar Hoover at the FBI. Hoover was at lunch and could not be reached. Si spoke to a deputy director.

". . . it's an unusual situation, Mr. Conway," the deputy said. "It seems to be an intrastate crime, and as you know, that is not within our jurisdiction—"

"—look, young man, I don't give a good goddam whose jurisdiction it's in!" Si shouted. "You get somebody on it! Now!"

"I'll have to speak with the director—"

"—my grandson is being held against his will by a man who's taken over an airplane at gunpoint. In my book that's kidnapping. Kidnapping falls under FBI jurisdiction!" Si felt himself losing control. "Now, please, I want to talk to Hoover. I'll try to contact you again through my company radio."

"I'll do my best, sir."

"Just do it," Si said.

They took off a few minutes later. Record flight, ideal weather, magnificent airplane, none of this mattered. The two and one half hours en route to El Paso was the worst two and one half hours of Simon Conway's life. He spent much of the time on the radio, relaying and receiving messages via Conair dispatch centers within radio range of the 1010. He did receive word from J. Edgar Hoover. The FBI would enter the case.

They tuned the command radio in on commercial radio stations along the flight route. The news became increasingly ominous. The Air Pirate—the undeservedly colorful term bestowed by the media upon Victor Sheehan—agreed to wait one hour for the arrival of the promised faster plane to take him to Brazil. If the plane did not arrive by that time he would kill the prisoners, the young boy first.

The hour passed. The fast plane did not arrive, but the Air Pirate agreed to extend his ultimatum an additional hour for the DC-7 to be refueled. Then, thirty minutes later, he agreed to a third and final extension. If, by 3:30, the police refused to remove the barriers for the DC-7 to depart, Victor Sheehan would carry out his threat.

A Birmingham, Alabama, radio station reported that the Air Pirate had requested food, water, and two bottles of bourbon. The items were placed in a basket and hoisted up to the cockpit by rope. The same station also reported that the young passenger-hostage had been identified as David Tannen, grandson of famed aircraft manufacturer Simon Conway and former U.S. Senator Morris Tannen. The FBI had entered the case.

By the time the 1010 landed at Biggs Field, FBI Special Agent Lawrence White had assumed command. White, an aggressive, athletic-looking thirty-five-year-old man, accompanied Janet Tannen out to the airplane to greet her father and Terry Deland.

The conventional ramp stairway left a drop of at least ten feet from the 1010's door to the ramp's top step. Si and the crew had to exit the airplane by climbing down a fire truck's extension ladder.

Janet embraced Si and whispered, "David's all right, Daddy. That man in the plane let him talk to us on the radio. I'm so glad you're here! What are we going to do?"

Si unbuttoned his leather jacket and loosened his tie. His whole body was soaked with sweat. He had no answer to Janet's question. The only words that came to him were, Everything will work out, don't worry. He could not bring himself to say it.

Special Agent White had an answer. "The individual thinks your plane will take him to Brazil—"

"—I only said it to give him something to think about," Si said. "To stall for time."

"That's right, and it worked," said White.

"It 'worked'?" Si said. "Nothing's 'worked' that I can see! He's still aboard, isn't he?"

"We'll straighten it out, Mr. Conway. Believe me, we will."

"You'd damn well better," Si said. "Who the hell is he? Why'd he do it?"

"All we know at present is his name, or at least the name he used on the ticket. Our immediate problem is to get him off that plane. He knows he has to transfer from one plane to the other. Once he's out of the DC-7, into the open, our sharpshooters will take over."

White pointed far down the runway at men crouched behind the vehicles surrounding the parked DC-7. The men held rifles leveled at the airplane.

Si said, "That's too damned risky. He's sure to stay close to the kid!"

"Do you have a better idea how to do it, Mr. Conway?"

Si's legs felt rubbery, his temples throbbed, and he was hot and cold all at the same time. Parked on a taxiway a quarter mile from the DC-7 were several trucks with television cameramen on the roofs. It was a circus, he thought angrily. A fucking circus.

He said to White, "One thing I'd do is get all those cameras and reporters away from here. All that can do is panic the guy into doing something crazy!"

"I can't order them away," White said. "This is a big story."

"Big publicity, you mean," Si said. He wanted to tell White that if anything happened to David the FBI would get publicity it wished it never had. But he knew the FBI agent was right: this was a big story. Nothing like it had ever happened before, a gunman taking over an airplane in midflight.

Ten minutes later, Special Agent White informed Victor Sheehan that they were ready to transfer him from the DC-7 to the 1010. Victor had seen the beautiful silver jet arrive and was elated. But no tricks, he warned. He was prepared to kill them all, himself included. He had nothing much to lose now, remember.

Some fifty yards away, Janet and Terry observed the proceedings from behind a police line. Janet leaned close to Terry for support. Si, White, two other FBI agents, and a half-dozen policemen waited at the foot of the ramp stairway. A small bus parked nearby was supposed to transport Victor and his hostages to the 1010.

For a moment there was no movement from the DC-7. Then, slowly, the cabin door opened. A few inches, then wider, and then the heavy door swung all the way over to the fuselage. The sharp-shooters repositioned themselves.

The first person to emerge was the captain, Harold Heffner, arms raised. The copilot and flight engineer followed. One by one all three clambered quickly down the stairway and were escorted into a police car.

And then David Tannen appeared. The boy, pale and grim, stood framed forlornly in the cabin doorway. Behind him, stooped partially down, his body shielded by David's, was Victor Sheehan, the muzzle of his .22 pistol pressed tight against David's temple.

Si spoke tersely into White's ear. "Your sharpshooters can't fire without hitting the boy, too. Call them off."

"They won't fire if it's not safe," White said.

"Well, it's not, goddammit! Call them off."

"Believe me, Mr. Conway, they know what they're doing. Now just let us handle this—"

"—call them off, I said!" Si said.

"Those men are experts," White said. "They won't endanger your grandson."

Si whirled to face White. "You do as I say, or I'll have your ass! I'll hang you out to dry! Do you read me? I'll go straight to Eisenhower if I have to!"

Lawrence White was not stupid. "Tell them to hold their fire," he said to an associate. He turned to Si again. "All right, Mr. Conway, now what do you suggest?"

"Let me talk to the son of a bitch," Si said, and without waiting for a reply he strode to the foot of the ramp stairway and called up to Victor. "My name is Simon Conway. That boy is my grandson. Please don't hurt him. We'll take you over to the other airplane."

Victor Sheehan regarded Si interestedly. "Your grandson, huh?"

"Yes."

"I got a kid, too, you know."

"Then you know how I feel."

Victor thought about this a moment. "Okay, but only one pilot flies the plane."

Si suddenly realized they might actually have to fly the 1010. But the airplane needed fuel, kerosene, and they had already been informed none was available here at El Paso.

He said to Victor, "One pilot can't control an airplane that size. You need at least two."

"Okay," Victor said after another moment. "But no tricks."

No tricks, Si promised, and to guarantee it assigned himself as the second pilot. Terry Deland, who of course would fly the left seat, never once argued with Si's decision. In a spot like this he wanted Simon Conway along, sixty-one years old or not, bad heart and all.

For Si, the next half hour was a nightmarish jumble that only became real when he heard the smooth whine of jet engines and found himself in the 1010's right seat. Terry sat in the left seat. Standing behind them, alone, was Victor Sheehan.

They had entered the bus, Victor holding the gun to David's head, and ridden across the taxiway to the 1010. A stairway ramp for the 1010 had been improvised by rigging a hydraulic lift onto a large flatbed truck. Si and Terry had boarded the 1010 first. Then, as one, David and Victor Sheehan. In the doorway, suddenly and unexpect-

edly, Victor had shoved David back out onto the hydraulic lift platform and pulled the cabin door closed.

David was free.

Si vaguely recalled saying to Victor, "Thank you."

"I got a boy of my own," Victor had replied. "Now let's get this
show on the road!"

3.

The two F-86s, scrambled from an air force base at Del Rio, Texas,
materialized shortly after the 1010 had taken off from El Paso. They
climbed with the transport all the way to twenty-two thousand feet
and remained with her, one on either wing.

"Hey, you think maybe they're gonna shoot us down?" Victor
asked. He aimed the pistol through Si's window at the fighter on that
side. "Rat-tat-tat-tat-tat!" he yelled. "Take that, you lousy Commies!"

"Glad you're enjoying yourself," Terry said.

"You know it," said Victor. He uncapped a bottle of bourbon and
took a long drink. He had consumed more than half the bottle, the
first of the two delivered to him hours before on the DC-7.

"Where are we?" he asked, the fourth time in the past ten minutes
he had asked the question.

"South," Si said, pointing to the compass. "Where it says 'S,' that
means south. That's where you want to go, isn't it?"

"That's where Brazil is," said Victor.

"Brazil's a long way off," Terry said. He leaned forward to tap
his fingernail on the main fuel gauge. He was telling Si they were
running dangerously low, which Si knew anyway. "Yeah, Brazil's a
long way to go," Terry continued to Victor. "We really should radio
our position—"

"—no radio!" Victor said. "I told you before."

Si knew Terry wanted to inform the nearest control center of
their fuel status and receive directions to an airport with a runway
capable of accommodating the 1010. But Victor not only had demanded that the loudspeakers be turned off, he ordered the pilots
not to wear their headsets.

"Five to seven minutes," Terry said to Si. "Ten, if we're lucky."
It was the amount of time he estimated they could continue before
the tanks ran dry.

"Hey, shut up, huh?" Victor said. "Just fly."

"Sure, son, whatever you say," Si said. They had been in the air
some twelve minutes now and were well into Mexico. The F-86 chase

planes had obviously received permission to enter Mexican airspace. He idly wondered how long the F-86s could stay with them, and why they had been sent up in the first place.

What he and Terry should have done, Si realized now, was simply refuse to take off once David was safe. But he had feared then, as now, that Victor might kill them. Moreover, as Victor continued drinking the whiskey, an unspoken hope had arisen that he would drink himself into a stupor.

Wishful thinking, for the liquor seemed to have had no effect, not with all the adrenaline that had to be pumping through the man's body. The drinking not only bolstered his courage, it also seemed to preclude any conversation. Special Agent White had suggested Si try to talk to Victor Sheehan, try to connect, establish some kind of rapport.

The man did not want to talk. Si kept trying. Ironically, he was about to ask Victor if baseball interested him—Victor looked like an athlete—when a loud series of buzzes resounded through the cockpit. Lights flashed on the instrument panel.

"We've got both inboards, two and three, flaming out!" Terry shouted, and began punching buttons on the panel. The alarm buzzers stopped and the warning lights went out. Terry manipulated the trim controls and adjusted the engine settings. He sat back, relieved. "I shut them both down." He smiled tightly. "You'd never know we're flying on only two engines, would you?" He turned to Victor. "We're out of gas, buddy. What do you want to do now?"

Victor laughed nervously. "Cut the shit, huh?"

"It's true," Si said. "In another few minutes this'll be the heaviest glider in the world." The words were not yet out of his mouth when he was thinking, What in the hell is wrong with you, Conway? The finest airplane you have ever built is minutes, if not seconds, away from running out of fuel, and you are making wisecracks about it.

And after this, he continued to himself, there will be no more fine airplanes. This is the last one. Because it will be a pile of charred junk in the middle of a Mexican desert, and no one at Conair will try to build another. There will be no Conair.

". . . you trying to tell me we're gonna crash?" Victor was asking.

"Yes, you stupid son of a bitch, that's exactly what I'm trying to tell you!" Terry said. "Unless you let me use the radio to find out where there's an airport we can land, yes, we're going to crash!"

"I don't believe you," Victor said, but he knew Terry spoke the truth. "You need gas? Okay, then get some."

"We have to use the radio," Terry said.

"So use it," Victor said.

Terry slipped on his headset and gestured Si to do the same. Si reached up for the loudspeaker button, but Terry blocked him. Si understood: Terry hoped to converse privately over the intercom. Behind them, eyes fixed ahead through the windscreen and briefly lost in his own thoughts, Victor stood stoically.

Terry flipped on the intercom switch and spoke tersely into his microphone. "Si, I'm going back to El Paso. I think we have enough fuel to make it."

Even as he spoke, Terry was banking the airplane sharply around. The abrupt movement pushed Victor back against the flight engineer's panel. He waved the gun wildly. "Hey, what're you doing?"

"There's a Mexican air force field nearby," Terry said. "They'll let us land and refuel."

Victor frowned suspiciously at Terry. "How come you didn't fill up back in El Paso?"

Si answered for Terry. "This airplane uses a special fuel. They don't have any at El Paso."

"Yeah," Victor said absently, looking out the window at the chase planes. They had turned with the 1010 and were once again on either wingtip. "I think I read someplace about that. She don't take regular gas."

Si spoke into the microphone to Terry. "There should be a fire extinguisher in the head. I'll see if I can get it."

As he spoke, Si was thinking, I must be insane to even think about trying to subdue this guy with a fire extinguisher. But he heard himself saying to Victor, "Listen, son, I have to take a leak. And that's no trick. Okay?"

Victor found Si's remark humorous. He chuckled. "You're all right, mister," he said. "Yeah, sure, go ahead."

Si slid back his seat, unstrapped his belt and shoulder harness, and rose. He stepped carefully over the pedestal and squeezed past Victor, who was backed against the flight engineer's panel, gun pointed at Si's stomach. Si went into the little lavatory at the rear of the flight deck.

The fire extinguisher, which had been stanchioned to the wall above the sink beside the mirror, was not there. Si gazed at the empty wall brackets, then at himself in the mirror. An unshaven, unkempt, red-eyed old man stared crazily back at him. He turned quickly away and checked the cubicle for some other weapon. Nothing, only a few miniature bars of Ivory Soap. He returned to the cockpit, strapped in, and put on his headset. Victor, engrossed in the terrain below, paid him no attention. They were at ten thousand feet now, descending.

"I don't see no Mexican airbase," Victor said.

"It's just ahead," Terry said. Over the intercom he said to Si, "I told El Paso we're coming back in. We're cleared for a straight-in approach and landing. Did you find the . . . gizmo?"

"All I found was a roll of toilet paper," Si replied.

"Terrific," Terry said, and unable to repress a wry grin, added, "Shit!"

Si said nothing. Below, on the drab brown ground, the shadows of boulders, brush, and clouds seemed to form a face. His own face, not the face of the old man he saw in the mirror, but young and strong. No, it was not his face, it was Richard's. They could have been twins.

Richard, he thought. My son, my nemesis, who is probably close in age to this young man standing behind me with a gun aimed at my back, who is also my nemesis. By now Richard had to be aware that the jewel of Conair's inventory, their one true asset, the $7 million 1010, was in dire jeopardy. The world's heaviest glider. The joke suddenly was no joke.

". . . there it is." Terry was pointing ahead through the windscreen at Biggs Field.

"You bastards!" Victor Sheehan cried. He had recognized the El Paso skyline in the distance. He jammed the pistol muzzle into Terry's neck. "Turn this plane around!"

"We can't," Si said. "We don't have enough fuel. We'll crash for sure."

"Then crash, goddammit!" Victor said, and in the same breath said, "Wait a second. Wait." He waved the gun at the windscreen. "No, land. Land, and fill up with gas. We'll start out all over again. Sure."

"You bet," said Terry. He spoke into his microphone to Si. "Si, hold the gear until we're almost over the fence."

The gear, Si thought. The landing gear was the answer to every-thing. He glanced cautiously behind him. Victor was watching the approaching runway. Si spoke into the intercom to Terry.

"Listen, kid, if we land, and this nut finds out there's no jet fuel, he'll probably damn well shoot us."

Terry looked at him and shrugged. The message in Terry's eyes read, What choice do we have?

"We don't lower the gear," Si said. "We belly-land her."

Terry's eyes widened with comprehension. "It'll wreck the air-plane," he said quietly.

"Probably," said Si. "But it'll toss our friend all over the place. We're strapped in, he's not. We're sure to be able to jump him."

"Not if we get our brains knocked out in the crash."

"We won't if you do it right."

After a moment, Terry said, "Okay, Si, you're the boss. It's your airplane."

And, Si thought, it is also my company. Although after this, for sure, Conair would no longer be his company. Or anyone else's. Who the hell would want it? Mortgaged to the roof, and all its cash poured into the 1010. The marvelous new airplane, which no airline had yet seen, whose one and only prototype was about to be destroyed. Not even Ben Anderson would come forward to save Conair now.

Ahead was the long black-asphalted runway. Si turned off the command radio. He did not want to listen to the forced calm of the Biggs Field tower operator's voice advising Conair 1010 that its wheels were not lowered.

Terry rested his hand on the gear lever and said to Si, "Last chance, Si. Let me land it in one piece!"

Si pushed Terry's hand away. "Steer away from the runway, Terry. Put her down on the dirt."

Terry started to argue, then sighed resignedly. "When I call for it, pull the thrust levers all the way back to 'cut off.'" He tapped the palm of his hand on another set of levers. "And then, at my call, pull the fuel-control levers. And then the firewall shutoff valves." He pointed to a row of four push-pull knobs atop the instrument panel. "After we stop, if there's time, turn off the battery switch." He indicated a switch on the lower-right-hand corner of the instrument panel. "All right, Si, full flaps."

Si pushed the flap lever down to full as Terry swung the yoke right and lined up with the stretch of sand and scrub abutting the runway. Victor seemed oblivious of the change in direction. He was more interested in the fire trucks and police cars that had suddenly appeared on the runway.

The airplane, flying parallel to the runway, sped past the vehicles. Terry raised the nose slightly and eased back the thrust levers. The airplane, flaring out, dropped lower and lower. Si could see the faces of the men in the crash vehicles racing alongside.

"Thrust levers to cut off!" Terry shouted. "Fuel-control levers off!"

Si pulled the thrust levers full off, and then the fuel-control levers. Warning horns sounded throughout the cockpit. Instrument-panel lights began flashing. The airplane skimmed over the ground.

"Firewall shutoff valves off!" Terry shouted.

Si pulled the four knobs open. For another instant the airplane continued smoothly along. Then, almost imperceptibly, the bottom of the fuselage scraped the ground and the airplane momentarily soared upward. And then down. She slammed into the ground and skidded to the right. Terry gripped the yoke, which was vibrating violently. The control column began yawing back and forth in his hands like a jackhammer.

The airplane careened through the sand, slewing to the right, then left, up and down. Even over the ear-blasting din of warning horns and klaxons, Si heard the metallic ripping sound of the fuselage skin shredding itself to pieces. From the corner of his eye he saw the nacelle of an engine tumbling across the ground. A portion of the wing on which the engine had been attached, the right wing, tore off and fell away. Si was unable to see the left wing but thought it too might have been severed.

He caught a glimpse of Victor Sheehan being whipsawed from one side of the cockpit to the other, into the flight engineer's panel, then across the floor to the opposite wall and then, once, forward into the pedestal. An instant later, with yet another impact, Victor's body pitched backward.

The airplane, now an uncontrollable missile, was hurtling straight toward the front of the fire-station garage. There were three stalls in the garage, all empty. On the facade above the stalls large, black-painted numbers read, 1 2 3. The numbers loomed closer, closer. So close that Si could clearly see how the paint had flaked off the top section of the 2 in the center stall.

The airplane plunged into the garage. The left wing and what remained of the right wing smashed into the stall's dividing posts. The entire garage roof collapsed behind the fuselage, which continued on toward the adobe wall. Si knew they were going to hit the wall, but now everything had slowed up.

A thousand thoughts kaleidoscoped through his mind, with time enough for him to focus briefly on each single thought, but always returning to the most important one, which was that in a few seconds he would be dead. Finally, after numerous airplane crashes and other assorted accidents and illnesses, finally his number had come up. At the hands of a maniac. And it was funny—if you could take a joke, if you had a sense of humor—that it had happened in the airplane that could have changed everything for him, turned everything around, made everything work.

The wall was closer, white and dirt-streaked, with a door, and the metal tongue of a hasp on the door, and a small wooden toolbox on the floor at the threshold. The door was partially ajar. Through the opening Si saw the sky. And then he saw nothing.

He awoke, choking in a sea of dust and air heavy with the odor of kerosene. The nose of the airplane was completely ripped open. Sunlight streamed down from a gaping hole in the garage roof. Terry was slumped against the control yoke, his face turned away from Si. Si heard him moaning quietly.

Si's whole body felt numb and heavy. It felt as though he weighed a thousand pounds. In the distance, he heard sirens. He remembered the battery switch. He flipped it off and then groped for his seat buckle. Something metallic was in the way. The control column was jackknifed across his lap like an iron clamp. He tried to move it and gasped with pain. The whole right side of his chest felt as though it had been pierced by a hundred sharp knives. He fell back against the seat and turned his head slowly and carefully toward Terry. He froze. He was looking into Victor Sheehan's eyes.

Victor's back was propped against the flight-deck door. His hands were empty, the gun nowhere in sight. His arms, each bent unnaturally, dangled limply at his sides. His face was a blotch of bruises, and one side of his head was matted with blood that was trickling down his cheek onto his shirt collar. For all that, he looked calm and composed.

"That was some ride," he said. He spoke quietly, almost conversationally.

"Yeah, some ride," Si said.

"I think he's okay," Victor said, nodding at Terry, who had stirred and was trying to raise his head.

"I think so," Si said.

"I guess we didn't make it to Brazil."

"No," Si said. "Not this time."

"Maybe next time, huh?"

"Sure, next time," Si said.

"Sounds good." A small, bitter smile creased Victor's face. "Yeah, next time. Fuck you, Charlie," he said and fell forward, facedown into the pedestal. His open eyes stared lifelessly at Si.

26

From here, from the promontory, with the lights of the city glowing in the background, the airport was an illuminated island in the center of a vast black ocean. From one end of the island to the other, the lights on each side of the parallel runways sprang out of the dark like dots of red and white on a velvet carpet. Here and there blue-lighted taxiways and access strips intersected and crisscrossed the runways.

Four miles north of the airport, Los Angeles International Airport as it was now known, was Conway Field. There, as though suspended in midair, lighting up the whole sky around it, was the huge blue neon Conway eagle, clutching in its talons the white letter C.

"Hell of a sight, eh, kid?" Si said.

"You bet, Gramps," David replied.

They had been here in Si's car for the better part of an hour. Occasionally they chatted, but mostly they just sat gazing down at the airport. Si had to get out of the car now and then to move around. The adhesive tape around his chest, binding the two broken ribs, felt like an iron corset. The ribs, slowly healing, were still sore. As the doctor said, Let's face it: old bones are brittle.

Si had driven down from Montecito that day to sign a number of legal documents. Meg and David had come with him, and they were all staying at Richard's. Janet had gone off with Terry to Palm Springs for the weekend.

After dinner, Si had taken David to the promontory for a last good look at the Conair sign. He said he wanted David to remember it. Now, after getting out of the car and briefly strolling around, he stood at the open window on David's side and said, "This may be the last time we'll see the old eagle, any of us."

"You said it wasn't coming down for a while," David said.

"It'll be soon enough." Si felt a sudden craving for a cigarette. He hadn't smoked in more than two years, since the heart attack. The only other time he had felt the urge to smoke was when they had carried him from the wreck of the 1010 and he saw what remained of the airplane.

". . . will the new sign still have an eagle?" David was asking.

"I doubt it. Probably just be something with a couple of letters. 'A-C,' probably."

"For Anderson-Conway, right?"

"Right."

"Should be 'C-A,' for Conway-Anderson," David said. "That sounds a lot better to me."

"It all sounds bad to me," Si said.

But not all of it was bad. The good part was that there would be a 1010, although not a Conair 1010, an AC-10, its new designation. The same airplane, only better, fitted with those great new eleven-thousand-pound thrust GE engines. She'd cruise at damn near 600 mph. Excuse me, Si thought wryly, Mach .84. Mach, pronounced *mock*, the point at which the speed of sound was exceeded, part of a whole new jet-age language. Six hundred miles per hour was Mach .84, 84 percent of the speed of sound.

Richard had driven a hard bargain with Ben Anderson. Si had to hand it to the kid, he knew what he was doing. The morning after the crash, Richard had walked into Si's El Paso hospital room with an armful of newspapers. Blaring black headlines:

FIRST COMMERCIAL JET BREAKS SPEED RECORD

INDUSTRIAL TYCOON CONWAY FOILS AERIAL HIJACK

JET AIRLINER RACES TO DRAMATIC RESCUE

"Good publicity, I guess," Si had said.

"Too good," Richard had said. "The underwriters want a piece of us or they'll foreclose immediately."

"Tell them to fuck off."

"I can't. You fired me."

"I'm rehiring you."

"Only if you agree to merge with Anderson. 1010 or not, it's the only way we can keep the company."

"Do whatever you want, kid," Si had said. "You're the boss now."

If Anderson Aircraft wanted the 1010—which, after the airplane's El Paso performance, it most assuredly did—Richard insisted on the initial fifty-fifty offer. It cost Ben Anderson more than $30 million cash to close the deal. It paid off every dime of Conair's debt, plus giving Conair a 25 percent interest in all Anderson Aircraft holdings.

Of course, part of the deal was Simon Conway's resignation as an officer in the corporation. Ross Leonard had a hand in that. Ross placed a firm order for thirty-five AC-10s, contingent on Si permanently getting out. Goodbye and good luck.

But the last laugh was Si's. He had already decided it was time to go. His day was over. He had known it even before El Paso. The only figures Si Conway has a head for are the ones inside skirts, Morris Tannen had always said. True enough. To Si, money was only a tool to make airplanes. From $55 custom-designed tires for a Conair 110—when $55 paid a month's rent—to $125,000 engines for an AC-10. If you had it, you spent it. More accurately, in Si's case, you spent it even if you did not have it.

Fiscal irresponsibility, Philip Granger always called it. In the old days it had worked, but the old days were gone. Today an ordinary piston-engined airplane cost $1 million plus, a jet three times as much, and ten times that amount to develop. No more one-man decisions based on hunches or guts. You needed boards of directors and cost accounting down to the last nut and bolt. You had to answer to someone. So it was no longer Simon Conway's game, which wasn't the end of the world.

"Hey, David, when that guy was holding his gun to your head," Si said, "were you scared?"

Si did not hear David's reply. He had been watching an airplane take off from LAX, a turboprop, and the smooth whir of its engines reminded him of the 1010 and, with it, Karl Eisler. Si thought that should some genie grant him a single wish it would be for Karl to see the 1010. And this time not to get one up on Karl, not to beat him, but to share with him the triumph. After all, in truth, the 1010 was part of Karl's dream, too.

The turboprop flew into the air, and Si said to David, "So, what was it? Were you scared?"

"I just told you."

"Tell me again."

"I said, Gramps, that you've asked me that question before. A hundred times, I think."

"Well, were you?"

"No, Gramps, I wasn't. I knew you'd come and get me out of there."